LONG FLIGHT
HOME

S.E.NETHERY

*To all those who served in RAF Bomber
Command during World War Two
and
In memory of Father Michael Kennedy
&
Father Laurie Cruikshank*

*special thanks to
Father Anthony Lemon for his valuable assistance
&
Samantha Elley my editor*

Chapter 1

Thursday, September 20th 2018. St Patrick's Catholic Church Sutherland, Sydney

BEFORE COMMENCING HIS sermon, Bishop Vincent Mulcahy looked out from his lectern at the large congregation in front of him. They had come together for the Requiem Mass of the Parish Priest of Sutherland, Father Frank Casey. He could not help but contemplate the diverse range of people who had come to pay their respects to the man referred to as the "knock-about priest."

Seated in the middle of the church was an older man with grey hair. He was wearing a splendid brown suit with a German Tyrolean hat on his head and was looking very dapper. The majority of the congregation would have been oblivious to the significance of the grey - haired man's relationship with Father Casey, but it was seismic.

Gathered were people from various backgrounds, faiths and beliefs. Seated in the front pews were members of Father Casey's vast family. Congregated to pay their respects were local parishioners and those that Father Casey had administered the sacraments to as children. Local school children dressed in their neatly pressed uniforms sat beside each other like a well-drilled army, holding the little white Mass booklets indicating the order of service.

Standing in the doorways were a mixture of blue-collar workers, arms folded, dressed in their high visibility work clothes and white-collar workers who had come straight from the office. Alongside them were people from the streets and others who Father Frank's generosity had touched. The knock-about priest who had dedicated his life to those less fortunate had influenced many.

In contrast to the diverse array of those gathered within the congregation, the group of seven priests seated behind Bishop Mulcahy could not have looked any different from those in front. They were there to concelebrate Mass with the bishop. The beautiful stained glass window situated directly above the altar beamed rays of sunshine down upon the ensemble of priests. They looked resplendent and unvaried in their white soutanes with clerical stoles draped around their necks.

Before beginning his homily, Bishop Mulcahy adjusted his glasses, cleared his throat, and started on his story in his Irish brogue.

I want you to close your eyes and imagine the scene I am about to describe to you. It is 1.00 am on the 23rd of March 1943, and it's a full moon over Nazi-occupied France. Lancaster Bomber T for Tango of No.377 Squadron RAF (Royal Air Force) Elsham Wolds Lincolnshire is flying at 16,000 feet and is approaching the Peugeot Motor Works in the town of Sochaux near the Swiss border. The British Ministry of Economic Warfare has classified the factory as the 3rd most important industrial site in France. Soon after the fall of France in 1940, the Nazis took control of the factory. The Peugeot family still control it, but they do so in the service of the Nazi regime, turning out planes and tanks. In 1943, the Germans assigned skilled workers to a secret project to build the V1 missile. For the British, it is imperative that the factory be taken out of action.

The crew of seven of the Avro Lancaster heavy bomber are on edge even though the Germans lightly defend the factory. No more so than 22-year-old Flight Sergeant Frank Casey strapped securely into his rear gun turret. He knows from his previous operations over Germany and Holland the constant threat of Luftwaffe night fighters and anti-aircraft flak. He is also fully aware the rear gunner has the highest attrition rate of all the Lancaster crew.

Frank's hands grip the trigger of his four Browning .303 machines guns in case a night fighter should suddenly appear out of nowhere. It is Frank's thirtieth and final operation. At this stage of his life, becoming a priest is the furthest thing from his mind. Besides, he has a girlfriend, and his sole desire is to get back to England in one piece so he can see her.

Even though Frank has an electric heated flying suit, he is cold as they approach Sochaux. Earlier in his operational tour, he had discarded the two sheets of perspex canopy from the rear turret, which had given him greater visibility but had made him even colder. It is a relatively smooth run towards Sochaux with only occasional anti-aircraft flak, coming from German 88mm cannons used to fire at allied aircraft. There is no sign of Luftwaffe night fighters. Both the radio operator and navigator are glued to their instruments and constantly reporting direction, drift and distance to the target. As the Lancaster draws closer to the Peugeot Motor Works, the crew's anxiety increases.

The Lancaster's pilot is Squadron Leader Reg Chapman, a tough but likable Australian from Maitland in the Hunter Valley region of New South Wales. He is on edge as he flies the aircraft towards the target. Reg dodges flak and searchlights from below by turning the Lancaster from side to side. He is in deep concentration as he follows the flares dropped earlier by the Mosquito pathfinder squadrons to the target.

As the target gets nearer, he contacts his crew on the intercom.

"Bomb aimer?"

"Ready, skip."

"Mid upper gunner?"

"Righto, skipper."

"Rear gunner?"

"Ready, skipper."

"Beginning bomb run now," says Reg.

Lancaster T for Tango begins its straight, rumbling run towards the target.

Frank is anxious and mutters to himself, "Come on, drop those bloody bombs and let's get the hell out of here."

Finally, when the tension is at a crescendo, and Frank feels he can't take any more, he hears, "Bombs away" from the bomb aimer, Flight Sergeant Jack Kearney from Liverpool, England.

Free of their payload, the four Rolls Royce Merlin engines roar in unison until the skipper throttles back to maintain height. Suddenly, the night is ripped apart by hundreds of bombs laying waste to the area below. Around, the Lancaster flak explodes as searchlights focus on the lumbering aircraft. Reg Chapman tosses the Lancaster violently from side to side as he tries to avoid being coned by the searchlights. Miraculously, none of the anti-aircraft flak hit the Lancaster. Reg can't seem to lose the searchlights no matter how much he tries, so he throws the Lancaster into a corkscrew nose dive to the port side. In the rear turret, Frank is being tossed around like a garment in a washing machine, while he tries to maintain his hands on the trigger of his machine guns. The Rolls Royce Merlin engines are screaming, but Reg's evasive action eventually pays off and the searchlights trail off into the distance. At the same time, the Lancaster returns to a semblance of composure.

Free of the searchlights, their navigator, Flight Sergeant Trevor Kay from Te Puke in New Zealand, sets course for their base in Elsham Wolds.

It is 1.10 am, and they are only ten minutes into their return flight when two Messerschmitt Bf 109 night fighters come from out of the moonlit silvery clouds.

"Rear turret skip. Night fighters incoming behind and below," says Frank into the inter-com.

Frank lets loose with continuous machine-gun fire, followed by tracer from one of the night fighters, which hits the cockpit of the Lancaster, wounding Reg.

Although slightly wounded, Reg puts the Lancaster into a roll to the starboard side and Frank almost vomits as the aircraft's nose goes down and he goes up. Reg uses the superior speed of the Messerschmitt, and the German fighter plane overshoots the bomber. One of the Messerschmitt's peels off to chase another Lancaster.

"Mid upper turret. Incoming 109 above skip," says Flight Sergeant Ted Porter, a sprog (rookie) gunner from Warrington in England.

Once again, Reg puts the Lancaster into a spiralling twist, and once again, he manages to lose the night fighter. Reg eventually levels the Lancaster, and after he does, Frank peers into the sky behind him, looking for signs in the darkness of their nemesis. His hands are tight on the trigger when he spots the lone Messerschmitt behind and below. As it approaches the bomber, the night fighter resembles a hungry shark going in for the kill on a defenceless fish.

"Rear turret skip, Messerschmitt 109 behind," says Frank.

With that Reg again drops the bomber's nose and it goes into a spiralling dive. Frank's harness bites into his shoulders, and so violent is the drop in the aircraft's altitude that he lets goes of the guns and braces against the turret. When Reg levels the aircraft out, Frank fires his guns, but the travel on them won't depress that far, and he is powerless to reach the night fighter, who is approaching from below. Frank is still firing his machine guns with a demon-like fury when the Messerschmitt opens fire. In a chatter of white-hot tracer, he rakes the Lancaster from wingtip to wingtip with thundering machine gun fire before unleashing his two 20mm underwing cannons. The result is a ruptured right fuel tank in the Lancaster.

Reg puts the aircraft into a dive to extinguish the fire, but to no effect, as the fuel tank erupts into a fireball. Reg realises the fate of the aircraft is dire, so orders the crew to abandon it. Frank enters the aircraft through the two access doors of the turret to retrieve his parachute, where a wall of fire in the fuselage hits him. He tries to clip his parachute on but struggles as the flames are close by. Frank manages to clip his chute onto his harness after much effort. He then watches Ted Porter, who is on fire, make his way to the front, where he jumps from the front hatch only to have his parachute catch alight after he opens it. Flames surround Frank and the aircraft is disintegrating around him. Frank is petrified and his flying suit is smouldering. His brain is racing as a thousand thoughts cram his mind as to how he will free himself from his predicament. Frank does not know that although his situation is dire, the fate of the rest of his crew is doomed as the aircraft is on fire. Just when he thinks his situation couldn't get any worse, the rest of the aircraft explodes into an inferno. Frank has no other choice than to renter the rear turret, where he turns it to the side and falls backwards through the two doors into the night sky.

A blast of freezing air hits him and he wonders if he will meet the same fate as Ted Porter. He opens his chute, and he feels the jarring jolt as his parachute canopy billows out, to his relief. His face is burnt, but below him, he can see the fields of France, and after a short time, he hits the ground with a thud………

Bishop Mulcahy pulled a white handkerchief from under his vestments and gently wiped his brow.

One can only imagine Frank Casey's terror in the moments after his Lancaster had been hit. To see his whole crew perish before his eyes must have been devastating. Frank had seen nothing yet compared to what he was about to experience. What would transpire in the months ahead would have a profound effect on him and ultimately lead to his life's vocation.

Bishop Mulcahy gazed at the stained glass window above and then looked at the congregation before continuing.

The Frank Casey that floated down to terra firma in the fields of France more than 70 years ago was a far different man to Father Frank Casey. As St. Augustine said, "There is no saint without a past, and no sinner without a future."

The young Frank Casey was indeed a man of the world. When he parachuted into Nazi-occupied France, becoming a priest was not on his agenda. After he landed, it was his following experiences that ultimately shaped the rest of his life.

As a young boy, Frank was always a rebel and had received the nickname of 'The Wild Colonial Boy' from his father.

To understand Father Frank's personality, you need to understand his upbringing. Frank's father, Hugh, had returned from the First World War, badly affected. He had served at both Gallipoli and the Western Front. Hugh had returned to the family farm, Banyula, outside Bingara in the North West of New South Wales, haunted by what he had both seen and done during the war. It was his steadfast desire that no child of his would ever go to war and experience what he had been through. Hugh had sought solace in his Catholic faith and, more ominously, in the bottle.

Sober, he could be charming, witty, and a natural raconteur who would entertain his family and friends with both alluring stories and by playing his harmonica. When the black dog of depression set in, and the memories of the Great War would raise their ugly head, Hugh was a different proposition. He was known to rant for hours, and his children would scatter for the hills of their 2500 acre property, lest they be in the firing line of one of his verbal or physical barrages. When Hugh was in the middle of one of his rages, the prospect of somebody receiving a hiding from his razor strap was very real.

If not for his quiet and beautiful wife Margaret, then the whole house would have turned into complete disarray. Her Catholic faith was the rock on which she had built her life, and it was her calm disposition that allowed the household to keep some semblance of normality.

A modern-day sociologist would label the Casey brood as 'a dysfunctional family.' Frank was more direct when asked about his upbringing and would call it a 'bloody lunatic asylum.'

Through this marriage of Hugh and Margaret, Francis Joseph Casey was born the eldest of nine children, on 21st March, 1921. From top to bottom, the brood was Frank, Kevin, Bob, Brian, Veronica, Noel, Vincent, Joan and Frances. As the eldest in the family, the heaviest of Hugh's tirades was directed on Frank's shoulders.

From a very early age, Frank resented his father. Although

he loved the hills of Banyula, it was his earnest wish that when the opportunity arose, he would get out of there for the outback of Australia. Frank's character was a paradox. From his father, he inherited a strict, no-nonsense approach and could be stubborn and wilful. The treatment Frank received from his father as a boy was to toughen him and prepare him for the events that were to happen during the Second World War. Like Hugh, he developed a liking for liquor when he reached manhood. His mother was a woman of great spiritual capacity and it was from her he had a predisposition for things of an ethereal nature. Frank had a great love of nature which was only exacerbated by his rural surroundings, and the Catholic faith was the very bedrock of his family's existence. When Hugh was having one of his moments, Frank often sought solace among the hills and trees of Banyula. It was here he felt most comfortable and able to converse with God about what was on his mind. The great paradox of his life was that although he disliked his father, he loved Banyula.

It was appropriate that Frank had received his nickname of 'The Wild Colonial Boy' from his father, considering his background. Both Hugh and Margaret were from Irish Catholic convict stock. Hugh's great grandfather Richard Casey was from Bantry Bay in County Cork, Ireland and his death sentence for stealing a cow was commuted to transportation to New South Wales. An unruly prisoner, he was sent to Port Arthur in Tasmania as further punishment before being issued his Certificate of Freedom at the end of his sentence.

Margaret's maiden name was Cronin and her ancestors were also from County Cork. Her great grandfather Brendan Cronin was also granted his freedom after completing his seven-year sentence. He had stayed in the young colony as a free settler, eventually taking up land in the New England region.

In 1859 Hugh Casey's paternal grandfather Edward (Ned) ventured from the Hawkesbury district, where he was working as a farm labourer, to the northwest of New South Wales in search of gold. It had recently been discovered north of Tamworth, where a settlement was formed named Bingera Diggings but later renamed Upper Bingara.

In 1861, the Crown Lands Occupation Act was adopted, which allowed an individual to select and purchase a parcel of crown land between 40 and 320 acres.

During this period, Ned struck gold, and although not rich, he did secure enough money to select 320 acres at Upper Bingara. Ned named the block of land "Banyula", which is an Aboriginal word meaning "many trees".

It wasn't a bad effort for the son of a convict and epitomised the pioneering spirit of the early settlers to Australia. Ned built a slab hut, bred beef cattle, started a large brood and in time purchased more land. It was a hard slog in the early years, scratching out a living from nothing, but by the end of his life, Banyula had grown to 1000 acres.

Ned's eldest son, Daniel, took over the running of Banyula after his father's death. He built a homestead and made many improvements to the property, eventually bringing Banyula up to 2500 acres. In his early years, he was a drinker, but put the cork in the bottle when the drink started to interfere with his life. He was by no means a wowser, but looked harshly on anyone who allowed the drink to take control of them, especially in their business dealings.

Down through the ages, the Casey's from Banyula were known to be hardworking and honest and believed there was no better contract between a man than his handshake. They drove a hard bargain in business, but were always fair in all their dealings. At the core of their ethics was the Christian belief that one should "do unto others as you would have them do unto you."

Frank grew up with the same philosophy that had sustained his ancestors. Although Hugh could be a tyrant and a drunk, he could also charm an individual's pants off and this was no more apparent than in his business dealings. Hugh tried to adhere to this core principle, even though the booze would send him astray throughout his life.

It was to this ancestral background Frank Casey was born. As was the case with the early part of modern Australia, he experienced the great sectarian divide between Protestants and Catholics. It was a divide that influenced his spiritual leanings and his political ones. Although the Casey's were landholders of Irish Catholic background and convict stock, they identified as the downtrodden and underprivileged. The Protestants of British heritage had the most influence in the young country, which Irish Catholics had the most animosity towards. It was only natural that their political affiliation should lean towards the Australian Labor Party, (ALP), who's many foundation members had been of the same cultural and religious background.

Hugh's ambition had always been that Frank, as the eldest, should be the heir to the family farm. Frank had an adventurous spirit and he desired to see Australia. Although life on the land was the most logical destiny, instinct told him his future lay somewhere else. Frank had always had strong spiritual convictions and from an early age, he felt his future lay in helping others.

Frank's desire to become a priest surfaced after his return from the Second World War. It wasn't the first time the thought had crossed his mind.

Chapter 2

Easter Sunday, April 16th 1933. Banyula, Upper Bingara, New South Wales

BY 12, FRANK had found a friend in the parish priest of Bingara, Father Riordan. Father Riordan was a kind man who acted as a buffer from Frank's harsh treatment by his father. Father Riordan's friendship had swayed Frank's thinking, and he had become convinced the priesthood was where his future lay. He knew he needed to talk to somebody about it. Although Frank would have preferred to speak to his mother, he knew it was his father he must approach, as he was the head of the family.

Frank felt there was no better time to talk to Hugh about such a matter than one of the most sacred days of the year, namely Easter Sunday. With the Casey philosophy of being honest in all dealings firmly fixed in his mind, Frank waited till after lunch to approach his father.

Unfortunately, Hugh was still sporting a rather large hangover from the previous night after he had consumed a flagon of sherry. Although calm by the family's standards, they knew to tread lightly around him.

Hugh was sitting in his favourite spot on the back veranda smoking a pipe and soaking up the afternoon sun when Frank stepped up manfully and said after a deep breath loudly,

"Dad, when I finish school, I want to join the priesthood!"

Hugh looked at him, his eyes blinking and his mind travelling around in circles, confused and wondering if what he had heard was correct.

Frank stood there in trepidation, not knowing how his father would react and in what seemed like an eternity, Hugh bellowed,

"You want to become a priest?" He howled with laughter.

Hugh stamped his feet on the timber decking of the back veranda and coughed uncontrollably in between fits of mirth. He bent over, coughed and laughed some more before trying to regain his composure.

"A priest?" he repeated before again curling over in laughter.

Frank stood there, his heart sinking. He was totally crushed and felt like crawling into a small hole he had spied at the end of the veranda.

Eventually, Hugh regained his composure and, with a finger pointing at Frank, said in all seriousness, "Let me tell you something, boy! Only men become priests, not boys. Do you understand?"

Frank shook his head but could not say anything.

"You're not even a semblance of a man and with your wilful and headstrong ways; you will probably never have what it takes to take holy orders. Do you understand?"

Frank was shattered and his father's rebuke had knocked his pride for a six.

Although Hugh believed Frank would never have what it takes to become a priest, it was not the real motivation for criticising him. There was a long held belief within the Casey family that the eldest son should take over the property from their father after his death. Hugh had it fixed in his mind that Frank would eventually run Banyula and nothing would sway him from that belief.

Hugh continued to rant and gave Frank a lecture on the sanctity of the priesthood for the next ten minutes when finally, with a wave of his hand, he said, "Be off."

As Frank turned, Margaret appeared on the veranda and gave him a reassuring look. As he brushed past her, she gently stroked his head and it gave him an incredible feeling of solace, managing to take the edge off Hugh's stinging rebuke.

Frank walked through the loungeroom where the rest of the family were seated and said nothing. His siblings wore a look of trepidation as they knew from past experiences their father's outburst was usually a prelude to some fireworks.

Frank went to his room, which he shared with Kevin, Bob and Brian. He sat on the floor in the corner, devastated by his father's outburst. He stayed there till nightfall, missing dinner until, true to form; Hugh got on the 'scoot' and pontificated about the sanctity of the priesthood.

Hugh never hit anyone that night but put on a royal performance as he ranted for ages while consuming a flagon of port.

Then around bedtime, Hugh broke into his rendition of the ballad *The Wild Colonial Boy*. It was a version Frank despised. Hugh always did it in a magnificent Irish brogue and it was meant to both belittle and infuriate the boy. Frank would have none of it, so he snuck out of the house undetected, where he hid behind the woolshed. As Frank listened to his father singing from inside the homestead, his feelings went from devastation to revenge. Although he may have wanted to become a priest, his rebellious nature came to the fore and he decided he needed to settle a score with his father.

There was a Wild Colonial Boy, Frank Casey was his name
He was a fiery tempered lad, which was a total shame
He was his father's eldest son, his mother's pride and joy
And clearly, did his father think he was the Wild Colonial Boy.
One verse was enough for Frank to hear.

"I'll teach you a lesson, you old bastard. Wait and see what the Wild Colonial Boy has got up his sleeve," said Frank with a maniacal glee in his eyes.

Hugh had a crop of young oats growing not far from the woolshed, which he intended to cut for hay when it matured. A large mob of merino ewes was grazing next to the paddock of oats. Frank opened the gate that separated the two paddocks and in walked the ewes. The sheep must have thought all their Christmases had come at once, being let loose in the succulent pasture.

Frank quietly entered the house and went to bed, content he had accomplished his mission. Any fear he had for the repercussions he may receive from his father were nullified by the inebriation felt over his act of vengeance.

The following day, Hugh had risen early, albeit with one hell of a hangover, and gone to carry out some fencing in the back blocks of the property. All was quiet in the Casey household as Margaret prepared breakfast for the children before they set about with their daily activities on the farm. As was often the case, Margaret possessed the ability to return the household to an even keel after Hugh had blown up.

When Frank surfaced, he never said a word to anybody about his misadventure. As it was Easter Monday and a public holiday Frank had been permitted by his mother to visit a friend who lived on another property a couple of miles up the road. By the time Frank arrived home late that afternoon, Hugh was still fencing at the back of Banyula.

It was just before sunset when Hugh returned to the homestead and, before entering the house, he went down to inspect his ewes. The sight that greeted him took his breath away, as the 100 merino ewes had trampled through his crop of oats while grazing extensively. After further inspection, Hugh noticed the gate to the paddock was open and he quickly about-faced and marched towards the homestead.

"Who left the gate to the oats paddock open?" he bellowed.

Inside the homestead, fear set in as the family could hear Hugh's ramblings.

"If I catch the person who left the gate open, I'll tan their behind, by the living Harry," Hugh screamed as he got closer to the homestead.

The door flung open to the homestead and Hugh marched in. He lined his children up on the back veranda like they were on a military parade.

"I want to know who left the gate to the paddock of oats open," he demanded with his finger raised.

No one said a word. With that, Hugh spent the next fifteen minutes interrogating the family with a level of terror that a member of the Gestapo would be proud of. As is often the case, someone had to crack, and it was none other than six-year-old Noel.

"It was Frank. I saw him sneak out of the house towards the woolshed when you started to sing The Wild Colonial Boy." Noel blurted out in tears.

Hugh swung his head around, his steely gaze focusing on Frank. He walked up to his eldest son slowly and stood only inches from him.

"Well, I might have known. Mr Holy Orders has certainly shown his true colours," said Hugh sarcastically.

Frank knew what was coming and stood up to his father manfully, without saying anything.

"You like to sneak out to the woolshed during the night, do you, Frank?"

Frank swallowed hard.

"If you like the woolshed that much, then it's the woolshed you're going to. On the double, you spiteful little bugger." Hugh hissed.

Frank turned and made his way to the woolshed for his inevitable punishment.

It was fifteen minutes before Hugh appeared in the dark shed with his razer strap in hand. He always liked to apply an ample level of psychological terror before inflicting physical punishment on his children. He knew there was nothing better than to let an adversary 'stew in their juices' to soften them up. He had seen the benefits of this action while interrogating captured Germans while serving as a sergeant on the western front during World War 1. Hugh had seen too many of his mates killed at the hands of the "Krauts" and it was the least he could do to exact some revenge.

Hugh ordered Frank into the holding pen and proceeded to administer a thrashing of the likes that had never been seen before in the Casey household. Frank never said boo and it was testimony to his physical toughness. It was a characteristic that would come to his aid when he was held in captivity by the Germans in the years ahead.

When it was over and Hugh had left the woolshed, Frank inspected the welts left on his body by the razer strap. Although he was in physical pain, he took a deep breath and shrugged it off as only a temporary infliction, for he was proud of himself for not whimpering. Frank made two solemn pledges before leaving the woolshed to face the world. Firstly, he would never let anyone bully him ever again. Secondly and most importantly, he would never entertain such a ludicrous thought of becoming a Catholic priest as long as he lived.

There was calm within the Casey household in the days that followed Frank's punishment. Margaret, with her customary good nature, had managed to settle Hugh and, at the same time, give solace to her eldest son. The family knew it was only a temporary truce because, as sure as night follows day, Hugh would erupt sometime in the future.

Hugh had stayed sober in the week after the punishment for good reason. He had done some serious thinking about his eldest son and what to do with him. Even though Margaret had protested, he had concluded that the answer to Frank's wilful nature was to send him off to boarding school.

After the Sunday roast, Frank was summoned to the back verandah by Hugh, where he found his father surprisingly sober.

"You're going away, Frank," Hugh said, pointing his finger.

"Where are you sending me to?" Frank said warily.

"I decided to send you off to boarding school."

"Boarding school?" Frank said with a look of angst.

"You heard me correctly. After much consultation with relatives, I've found the perfect choice. I will send you to the highly esteemed Catholic boarding school, St Joseph's College at Hunters Hill, on the Lower North Shore of Sydney."

St Joseph's or 'Joeys' as it was colloquially referred to, was an independent secondary school for boys run by the Marist Brothers. As a Greater Public School (GPS), Joeys had a reputation for academic excellence and producing fine sportsmen, particularly in rugby. It was on 40 acres, overlooking the Lane Cove and Parramatta rivers in Sydney's Hunters Hill. Joeys, according to Hugh's way of thinking, was far enough away from Banyula to knock Frank into shape. Although Australia was in the middle of the Great Depression and money was tight, he believed it was worth paying to ensure Frank's development in becoming a man.

"But couldn't you have found a boarding school for me in the country, Dad?"

"No, I couldn't," Hugh snapped, "besides, your Uncle Tony went there and he went on to study pharmacy."

Frank swallowed hard before he said, "But I won't know anybody there."

"You'll meet plenty of friends there. Now that's final. Your mother will book a train ticket for you in time to start in early May. Now be off with you," Hugh said with a wave of his hand.

Frank was shocked into silence. Although he despised his father, the thought of leaving the beauty of Banyula and his many friends was too much for him to bear. He was a country boy at heart and to leave the bush and go live in the city filled him with trepidation.

Frank trudged around the home for the next week as though some great calamity had just befallen him. When the time came, it was with a heavy heart he said his goodbyes to his mother and family after the Sunday roast. Hugh preferred to sit on the back veranda and smoke his pipe than bid his eldest son farewell before he departed for Tamworth and then onto Sydney via the train. The one positive that gave Frank some small consolation was at least he would be away from his father.

Chapter 3

Monday, May 1st 1933. St Joseph's College, Hunters Hill, Sydney

ANY HOPE FRANK may have had for a fresh start away from his father was soon quashed as his introduction to Joeys was a torrid one. Frank's situation was difficult as he had come to his new school midterm and did not know a soul. Frank was desperately homesick and initially stuck to himself. He felt uncomfortable in his new school uniform, which consisted of long trousers, a blue shirt, a tie and a blue blazer with a cerise trimming.

Even though Joeys had a long history of educating boys from rural areas since its foundation in 1881, many of his classmates saw their fellow first form student as an outsider. Because of this, within days of arriving, he had been picked on by the bully of his year, Tony Frost.

Tony Frost was a thickset boy of medium height with brown hair who sported a permanent scowl on his face. His father, Ernie, owned a removalist business named Frost Removals at Lithgow in the Central Tablelands of New South Wales.

Ernie Frost had returned from the Great War and started his business with very little capital, but with a will to succeed. He had managed to build his business up considerably before the Great Depression hit in the late 1920s and, like most in society, had taken a huge financial blow. Although things were tight on the economic front, Ernie had managed to scratch enough together to send his eldest son Tony to Joeys. It was a sign of great prestige to send Tony to an esteemed school like Joeys considering the Frosts came from humble working-class origins. With that in mind, the Frosts felt they never quite measured up compared to some of the families whose boys had been educated at Joeys for generations. This was no more exemplified than in Tony, who compensated for his inferiority complex by becoming the class bully, and in Frank Casey, he saw the perfect target. The paradox was that of all the people at Joeys, Frank Casey's origins were even more humble than the Frosts considering he was of convict stock. Frank was to have a lifelong aversion to bullies and always stood up to them, including those who were to hold him captive after being shot down in France.

Frank had only been at Joeys for three days when Tony confronted him in the playground at lunchtime. The reason was that Tony took exception to Frank's extra baggy school trousers.

"Hey parachute pants, what are you doing in my part of the playground? Don't you know I'm the new Adolf Hitler of Joeys? " Tony said aggressively.

"Who's Adolf Hitler?" Frank said.

"Who's Adolf Hitler?" Tony mimicked, raising his eyebrows.

Frank shrugged his shoulders.

"Are you thick? Why, he's the newly appointed Chancellor of Germany," Tony said sarcastically.

"I've never heard of him."

"Never heard of him? Where have you been hiding? Don't you know he will rule all of Europe one day? He's a great man and he will kick the arses of anybody who gets in his way, just like I'm going to do to you, newcomer," said Tony as he walked closer to Frank.

"Listen, mate, why don't you mind your own business? I haven't done anything to you," said Frank.

"Let's get one thing straight, newcomer. You and I are not mates," Tony said, only inches from Frank's face.

Frank pushed Tony away, which only aggrieved him more. Tony saw the slightly built frame and medium height of Frank as an easy target, but considering what Frank had been through at the hands of his father in recent times, it was a poor choice. Frank was anything but a pushover and inside him beat the heart of a lion. Tony grabbed him by the shirt before smacking him in the head. Frank responded with a right hook followed by a straight left to the head of Tony, which made him stagger backwards before a full-blown fight erupted.

Both Tony and Frank were going toe to toe, with a mob of students forming a circle around the melee, when who should step in but the Master of Discipline, Brother Ethelred. It was a bad mistake to be caught by this particular brother because he took great delight in dishing out the cane. As a result of their skirmish, both Frank and Tony received six of the best. Brother Ethelred wasn't finished with the two boys, as he hauled them in front of the principal Brother Placidus.

"I won't have a bar of this ill-discipline in my school," Brother Placidus said before summarily giving both of them six cuts of the cane across their hands.

Tony Frost had met his match in the art of fisticuffs and he never challenged Frank to a fight ever again. Frank had stood up to a bully and it was an important lesson he did not forget. It was to serve him well into the future. Although Frank had stood up to the class bully, it did not make his life easier.

He led a loner's existence in the weeks that followed. The other students saw him as an enigma as he kept to himself. He appeared to be a closed book to them. Frank observed Tony Frost from a distance, with his warped view of Hitler as some saviour. Frank noticed how he picked on the weaker students and he despised him. Frank's altercation with Tony was the catalyst for him to seek more knowledge about Adolf Hitler, and from the beginning, he hated the German Chancellor and everything he represented.

Frank seemed to incur the wrath of his teachers as he was behind in his schoolwork due to starting school midterm. Frank was regularly paraded in front of the class to receive the cane and to his credit, he never whimpered.

The one consolation was the stream of letters he received from his mother, which was a great solace for the boy. Frank read the letters continuously and Margaret reassured him that everything would turn out for the better if he gave it time and just hung in there.

Frank couldn't see much hope for the future, and one day after another caning at the hands of Brother Ethelred, he'd had enough, so decided to run away from Joeys. His dad's younger brother Herb ran a shearing team from his home in Quirindi on the North West Slopes region of New South Wales, so Frank decided to head there. Herb didn't see eye to eye with Hugh, so Frank figured he would be sympathetic to his plight and allow him to work with his shearing team as a roustabout.

It was a Friday when Frank hatched a plan to escape from his "prison" as he had come to see Joeys. His modus operandi was to catch the Northern Mail train from Sydney to Quirindi late on Sunday night. He would hitch the 65 miles (104km) out to Tambar Springs and meet up with his uncle, who was shearing on a property. Frank was adamant he would leave Joeys and his plan of escape was set when fate stepped in and changed everything.

It was Saturday morning, and Frank had been at Joeys for one month. He was sitting on a seat by himself on the school grounds, soaking up some sun and enjoying it immensely. It was a small consolation for a life that seemed to be perpetually shrouded in misery. In a small way, it reminded him of the times he would spend in the back blocks of Banyula, enjoying the solace of his natural surrounds.

While he was there, Frank folded his arms and contemplated his predicament and his impending departure from the school. Then, out of the blue, a nuggety little individual of the same age came swaggering towards him. Frank had not seen the boy before and his first thought was that it was another 'smarty' come to have a crack at him.

He stood in front of Frank with his hands in the pockets of his trousers and looked him up and down with an eagle eye. Before he had a chance to say anything, Frank said, "Look mate, if you want a shot 'at the title', I'd be more than happy to accommodate you, but I don't want a fight out here in the open as I'm sick of getting the cuts. If you want a blue, then let's go down to the boat shed and we can sort it out there."

The boy shrugged his shoulders and said with a smile, "Sorry mate, but I haven't come here looking for a 'barney'. I've come here to introduce myself. You are Frank Casey, aren't you?"

"Yeah, that's right. What's it to you?" Frank said warily.

"The name's Jim Cruikshank but everybody calls me Jimmy,"

he said, extending his hand. Frank looked at Jimmy warily before finally clasping his hand and shaking it firmly. Besides his mother's letters, it was the first act of kindness Frank had been shown for some time. It was the start of a long friendship that was to run deep and be tested under the most trying of circumstances.

"I haven't seen you at school before? Frank said.

"I sprained my right arm playing a trial match in rugby. I could write bugger all, so the school sent me home to recuperate."

"Where's home," said Frank.

"Out at Breeza on the Liverpool Plains. I come off a 5000-acre wheat and sheep property."

"It's some of the best farming country in Australia out there," said Frank.

"Yep, it certainly is. The soil is rich and dark, which allows us to grow a good wheat crop."

"Where are you from?" Jimmy said.

"I'm off a property at Upper Bingara."

"So you're off the land also?" Jimmy said.

Frank smiled at Jimmy and it seemed like ages since he had done so.

"I've heard you've been getting a bit of a hard time since you arrived at Joeys," Jimmy said.

"It's a bastard of a place and I've had to deal with that ratbag Tony Frost."

"He's a piece of work that so and so. I sorted him out when I first arrived here. He doesn't come within cooee's distance of me these days. He is typical of all bullies, as weak as piss."

Frank shook his head before saying, "I had a blue with him within days of arriving. It cost me the cuts, but he hasn't crossed my path since."

They chatted for another ten minutes before Frank looked

around to make sure nobody was listening before focusing on Jimmy.

"You look like you're a pretty fair dinkum bloke. Can you keep a secret?"

"I sure can," said Jimmy as he edged closer to Frank.

"I've been thinking of hightailing it out of here, as I've had a gutful of the place."

"Don't do that. I know it's a bugger of a place at first, but you get used to it, and besides, there are some good things on offer here."

"Like what?" Frank said sarcastically.

"Well, that's what I came to see you about. I'm playing scrum half for our rugby side and I need a decent five-eight. A few of these ning nongs in our weight division saw you throwing a footy around the other day and told me you have a pretty good set of hands. Do you want to be my five- eight?"

"That sounds interesting, but I'm still getting my head around rugby as I have only ever played Rugby League."

"The fifteen man game is a bit different, but you'll get the hang of it. Besides, Brother Kieran, the First XV coach, has been helping out lately, as our footy coach is sick. He knows what he's talking about and he's a pretty good bloke also."

"Yeah, I'll give it a crack," said Frank.

"We have a trial game this arvo down at The Park, so you should come down and have a game."

"Yeah, I'll be in that."

"Good stuff. We've got a big match against our arch-rival Riverview in a month, so we want to be on top of our game."

Frank shrugged his shoulders.

"Oh, you're not aware of our competition with Riverview? St Ignatius College, Riverview and Joeys are the two Catholic schools in the GPS competition. The rivalry between the two schools goes back generations, particularly on the rugby field."

"So the two Tyke schools going at each other's throat. Sounds like a great day at the office," said Frank, smiling.

"You got it in one, Frank. See you this arvo."

When Frank arrived at the park that afternoon for the trial game against TAS (The Armidale School), he was met with a cool reception by most of the other players in the side.

Frank was standing around twiddling his thumbs when Jimmy and Brother Kieran walked up.

"So you're the new five-eight Jimmy was talking about?" Brother Kieran said in his Irish brogue.

"I am, Brother."

"And what's your name?"

"Frank Casey, Brother."

"So you're a Casey, hey? That's a good Cork name. Well, I'm Brother Kieran. I'll put you into five-eight beside young Cruikshank here and we'll see how you play."

"I'll do my best, Brother Kieran."

Frank didn't get off to a good start with his opening passage of play. The game had only been in progress for minutes when Joeys were positioned on their line. Jimmy threw Frank a beautiful spiralling pass from the scrum base, which landed on his chest, but he took his eyes off the ball momentarily and it popped out and hit the ground. TAS's lightning- quick open side breakaway pounced on the ball and scuttled across the line for a try. After the conversion, the score was 5- 0.

"Brilliant Casey, just bloody brilliant," said Joeys hooker and captain Ed O'Shaughnessy.

Frank felt lower than a spider hiding under a rock. The situation was only compounded by the look of contempt shown towards him by his teammates, while they were standing under the goal posts waiting for the conversion.

"Don't worry about that little mishap, Frank. Get up on your horse and have another crack at these blokes," said Jimmy while he tapped Frank on the shoulder.

Frank took a deep breath and trudged back to the half-way line.

The match progressed, and just before halftime there was a scrum set down on TAS's 25- yard line. With a lightning-quick strike from Ed, they won the scrum against their own tight head. Jimmy picked the ball up from the scrum base and scooted around the blindside, darting, weaving and sidestepping through the opposition defence to score a try under the black dot of the goal posts. After the conversion, the scores were locked in at 5-5.

The second half was a tense struggle, with either side not conceding an inch. It was late in the second half with only five minutes to play and the score was still 5-5. There was a lineout on Joeys 25 yard line when the small crowd gathered on the sideline saw what Frank Casey was capable of for the first time.

With Joeys parked deep in their territory, one would have expected Frank to punt the ball and find the touch line to secure a safe position for his side. Frank knew that time was of the essence and if Joeys were to win the game, he would have to keep the ball in hand.

Rather than kicking the ball for touch, Frank kept the footy and took a chance. After Joeys had won the lineout, Frank secured the pass from Jimmy with silky smooth hands. He then sidestepped the opposition's open side breakaway, who was aggressively bearing down on him with a deft set of heels. He proceeded to sidestep, weave, dart and dodge his way through the TAS defence with a masterful display of attacking rugby that suggested his skills were beyond his tender age of 12. Frank was out in the open and approaching the TAS 25- yard line with only the opposition fullback to beat, when he put up a neat chip kick that sailed over the TAS fullback's head. After a difficult bounce, Frank regained the ball with one hand and ran like his life depended on it towards the try line and placed the footy down under the black dot. The Joeys supporters on the sideline were ecstatic and the try was converted to make the score 10- 5 in Joeys favour.

As the Joeys side was walking back to the halfway line for the kick off from TAS, Ed looked across at Frank and with a slight grin, said, "Well done Casey, that was a great effort."

Frank gathered the ball from the kickoff and punted it out over the sideline before the referee blew his whistle for full time. Joeys had won!

As the Joeys side walked from the field, Frank was met with warm congratulations from both his team mates and the Joeys spectators.

Frank was flushed with pride and he felt as though a great weight had been lifted off his shoulders. That day at The Park was the beginning of a great partnership between Jimmy and Frank and as their schooling at Joeys progressed, so did their reputation as one of the best scrum half/five-eight combinations in the GPS competition.

The win against TAS that day was to be the catalyst for new-found respect from Frank's team mates and his fellow students. Initially, it was the admiration of just his classmates, but in time it was to spread throughout the entire school as Frank and Jimmy's reputation grew as very gifted rugby players.

As much as Frank's rugby skills ascended throughout his years at Joeys, the same could not be said about his academic achievements. Frank wasn't stupid, but his disruptive home life and as a result his inability to concentrate in the classroom, saw him fall behind in his academic achievements. Also, it was the fact that sports held his interest while he was at school. Whether it was rugby, cricket, athletics, rowing, swimming or boxing, Frank excelled. If he wanted to, he probably could have reached the upper echelon of any number of sports. It was rugby that he loved, and the fact that he had an equally skilful player at scrum half in Jimmy Cruikshank only enhanced his passion for the game.

As much as his reputation grew while he was at Joeys, Frank always kept his feet firmly on the ground and never viewed himself as any grander than his fellow students. The ethos of Catholic education during that period of Australian history was to belt both religion and academia into students. Fear and discipline were the tools used to instil it and the Penny Catechism was the foundation of Catholic doctrine. There was no room for liberal thinking as the parameters were clearly defined. Frank was no exception to the rule and regularly received the cuts from the brothers, mainly due to his lack of academic achievement. Although he was far from pleased with his share of corporal punishment, he accepted it as par for the course and never complained.

Frank stumbled along with his studies, with one exception to the rule. He was able to study wool classing, which was something he loved. Studying wool classing was to provide for him a connection to the land. As a kid growing up at Banyula, Frank enjoyed shearing time. He loved both the laconic shearers he rubbed shoulders with and the feel and smell of the lanolin laced wool while working as a roustabout. As much as Hugh Casey desired for his eldest son to work on Banyula when he left Joeys, Frank had already made up his mind and was determined to leave home and work as a wool classer while he saw the country.

Frank's introduction to Joeys was in stark contrast to how he viewed the school by the end of his first year. Because of his sporting achievements and the fact he was a decent bloke, the initial disdain shown to him by many of his fellow students had dissipated and he had become popular among his peers. Tony Frost had also been expelled for his insubordination towards the brothers. Jimmy and he had become great mates, and he had grown to love the 'esprit de corps' of the school, particularly in the sporting arena.

Frank's lack of credibility in the classroom was offset by his relationship with the First XV rugby coach Brother Kieran. He had noticed Frank's rugby ability and understood the difficulties he was experiencing on the home front, so had taken him under his wing. Brother Kiernan was in his early thirties and had compassion for the underdog. Before entering the Marist Brothers, he had been an exceptional rugby player and imparted his knowledge to Frank, which the young lad lapped up. Frank had come to see this Irish brother with his pithy sense of humour as a father figure and it was an essential component in his development into adolescence.

During the Christmas break of 1933/34, Frank spent a week with the Cruikshanks on their property at Breeza, named Wilgara. It was not without protestations from Hugh, who insisted that Frank put his fair share of work in at Banyula and was opposed to his "swanning around out at Breeza". Only after Margaret intervened on Frank's behalf could she smooth things over with Hugh and secure a week's leave on the Cruikshank farm.

Clem and Anne Cruikshank had seven children, with Jimmy being the second eldest. Clem Cruikshank was the total opposite of Frank's father and had an easy-going nature that Frank liked. A WW 1 veteran who had served in an artillery unit in France and been injured, Clem was the total opposite of Hugh's personality.

In the week Frank spent with the Cruikshanks, he not only helped on the farm but rode horses and visited several other families who lived on nearby properties. Frank experienced what a stable family life looked like for the first time and it only heightened his awareness of how unstable things were on his home front. For Frank, it was to be the start of regular visits to the Cruikshank property during school holidays, and he would treat them as his second family, feeling comfortable in their company.

After a week, Frank felt refreshed spending time in a positive atmosphere, only to be plunged back into darkness when arriving back at Banyula. As much as Frank wanted to reciprocate the Cruikshanks hospitality and invite Jimmy to Banyula for a stay, he dared not inflict on his best mate the lunacy from his father, which he knew would surely come to the fore at some stage.

As much as Frank enjoyed the break from Joeys over Christmas, he was ready to get back to school in the New Year and involve himself in sport. The oncoming rugby season was important, including the rivalry between him and his opposite number from St Ignatius College, Dick Wilkinson.

It wasn't long after Joeys' narrow defeat to St Ignatius in 1933 that people soon realised both schools had a quality scrum half/five-eight combination. Opposing Joeys combination of Casey and Cruikshank were St Ignatius' scrum half Gerard Rogers and five-eight Dick Wilkinson.

As the years went on, their rivalry intensified as both combinations honed their skills and tried to outplay each other. Despite their age, it wasn't uncommon for older Joeys boys in the First XV to venture down to The Park on a Saturday morning to watch the Casey/Cruikshank combination. Their attack and defence skills were exceptional and a solid talking point throughout the GPS fraternity. Because of their mastery on the rugby field, the whispers begun to circulate the corridors of Joeys that on display were the future Wallaby scrum-half /five-eight pairing.

Despite Frank and Jimmy's talent, the combination of Gerard and Dick was as equally talented. Like Jimmy and Frank, the two Riverview boys, who happened to be first cousins, were also off the land. Gerard's family were graziers from Crookwell in the Southern Tablelands of New South Wales, where they bred fine wool merino sheep.

The Wilkinson's were an old established grazing family whose property, Windermere, was between Gunning and Yass, also in the Southern Tablelands. Windermere was a fine wool merino stud and had been in the Wilkinson family since the 1850s.

Gerard and Dick thought they were a cut above the rest, but no more than on the rugby field. In the three years from 1933 to 1935, Riverview held the advantage over Joeys by winning two games to one and the two Riverview boys loved to remind their rivals of that fact. Frank and Jimmy did not let that worry them, as both knew they were just starting to hit their straps on the rugby field.

By 1935, Frank had turned 14 and was in 3rd form, or Year 9 as it is known today. At the end of the year, he sat for his Intermediate Certificate, which he just managed to pass. After sitting the Intermediate Certificate, a student was able to leave school. If they wanted to go to university, they had to complete two more years of schooling and then sit for their Leaving Certificate.

Frank had no intention of going to university, so he planned to leave school once he sat for his Intermediate Certificate and work on Banyula. Besides, his parents couldn't afford the fees to put him through university. The Great Depression was in full force and the prospect of finding outside employment was minimal. Frank realised the only logical thing to do was to go home and work on the farm. That was until Brother Kieran stepped in and convinced Frank to complete two more years of schooling. He reasoned that Frank would be eligible to play in the First XV rugby side by doing so. After a lot of thought, Frank accepted Brother Kieran's advice and decided to stay on at Joeys for another two years. Unbeknownst to Frank, it was a decision to serve him well in the future.

Through 1936 and 1937, Frank laboured through his studies to sit and hopefully pass his Leaving Certificate. He was never far from the end of the cane from the Brothers, mainly due to his lack of academic ability and, at times, his outspoken nature.

Although his results in the classroom were down, there was one subject Frank took a keen interest in and that was history. It wasn't the history that was taught in the classroom during that period, which consisted in large part of memorising important dates. Instead, it was a general knowledge of important historical events and the major players. Frank was an avid reader, and he lapped up as much as he could about history, whether through books or newspapers. He was particularly interested in the rise of Adolf Hitler and his intentions.

Frank's knowledge of Nazi Germany was remarkable for somebody who was not academic. When Frank was interested in a subject, he would study it morning, noon and night, and the rise of the Nazi Party in Germany was a perfect example. He shared his views with many of his classmates. Many of them dismissed his fears of the Nazis as just plain ridiculous. They believed there was no way Europe would ever again be plunged into a conflict similar to the likes of the Great War. It was a testimony to Frank's covert intellect that he could see the danger Adolf Hitler and the Nazis held to the peace of Europe.

By 1937, Frank had turned sixteen and was in his final year at Joeys. He had shown particular interest in Germany as it held the summer Olympics Games in Berlin in August of the previous year. In particular, he had been suitably impressed by the efforts of the American athlete Jesse Owens winning four gold medals and Hitler's reaction to it.

Frank had more pressing issues on the home front though, for both Jimmy and he had gained selection in Joeys First XV rugby side. It was a very prestigious position, considering rugby's reverence at Joeys. It was held in such high esteem that Brother Kiernan would often say to his players that rugby and religion are the two most important things in life. And in that order!

The 1937 GPS rugby season had been a tight one. Both Joeys and Riverview were tied at the top of the table, with the last game of the season to be the decider between the two arch- rivals.

Frank and Jimmy had been in delightful form, carving up the opposition with their silky skills. Equally as impressive were Gerard and Dick, who had steered Riverview to the top of the table with their exceptional panache on the park.

In the week leading up to the decider, all of Riverview were banking on their talented halves duo to deliver the first ever GPS First XV rugby premiership for the school since its inception in 1892.

Those who were lucky enough to witness that memorable game at The Park that Saturday afternoon would talk about it for years to come as one of the greatest games of rugby they had ever seen.

There was a buzz around the ground before the kickoff, where thousands were crammed in to watch the game. As they waited for the start of the game, the Joeys and Riverview supporters were decked out in their cerise and blue and royal blue and white colours, respectively.

The match was a grinding affair, with neither side giving an inch from the start. Both sides missed opportunities, but at halftime, the scores were locked at 5 -5, with both teams scoring a converted try.

Fifteen minutes into the second half, Dick received a lighting quick ball from Gerard from the scrum base just inside Joeys' territory. Dick scurried down the blindside, where he showed incredible skills to sidestep around the two Joeys centres to score a try under the posts. He converted his try to make the score 10- 5 to Riverview. Joeys were parked on Riverview's line with fifteen minutes to go when Joeys captain and hooker Ed O'Shaughnessy darted around the back of the ruck with the ball to score a try to the right of the goal posts. Frank converted the try to tie the scores up at 10-10.

With five minutes to go, Joeys tight head prop took the ball in an offside position right in front of his own goal posts. Riverview was granted a penalty, which Dick slotted over with ease. The visitors were leading 13- 10 and after the kickoff, Dick punted the ball deep down into Joeys territory, where the ball found touch on the 25 yard mark. Riverview stole the ball from the ensuing lineout and over the next few minutes a tremendous battle took place, with neither forward pack giving an inch.

With a minute to go, the crowd was at fever pitch with the Riverview supporters willing their side home. They sensed that victory was in sight. The Joeys supporters yelled themselves hoarse with equal ferocity, urging their side to victory.

With only a minute to go, Dick received the ball from Gerard from a ruck and was positioned in front of the goalposts, ready to kick a drop goal over to secure a victory for Riverview. Just when all seemed lost for Joeys, the ever tenacious Ed O'Shaughnessy came bounding out of the other side of the ruck and hammered Dick with a damaging tackle around the waist that knocked the stuffing out of him. The result was that Dick spilt the footy on the ground just as he was about to pot the goal over. Like a blue heeler about to nip the heels of a stray steer, Jimmy picked the ball up and made a dash around the open side, with Frank on his outside. Drawing Gerard, who had scurried around the open side to cover his opposite number, Jimmy passed the ball to Frank, who could see an opening between the two centres. Frank sensed the occasion and, with lightning-quick speed, side-stepped through the centre pairing, leaving them flat-footed and in a state of disarray.

Frank was on open ground, but could see Riverview's open side breakaway coming across the ground in cover defence. The breakaway was almost on top of Frank when, once again, he side-stepped him and left him floundering in his wake. Frank was approaching the halfway line with only the fullback to beat when he put up a little chip kick which sailed over the Riverview fullback's head and bounced only yards in front of him. Frank scooped the ball up with one hand, pinned his ears back and sprinted towards the line.

The Riverview fullback was on the ground, but he got up and ran for Frank. He was swift, and as he approached Frank's left side, he made a beeline for the right- hand corner post. Frank could hear the heavy breathing of the fullback as he set his sights on the black and white banding of the post. Frank dived with only yards to the try line as the fullback tackled him around his boot laces. Frank slid across the grass and planted the ball inside the try line, and beside the corner post, the impact of hitting the ground knocking the wind out of him. Frank lay motionless on the ground before the rest of his side came sprinting down the field in celebration. Ed was first on the scene and, seeing Frank was winded, proceeded to pump his legs to revive him. Frank eventually came to and, while still lying on his back, viewed the scoreboard in the distance, which read St Joseph's College 13- St Ignatius College 13.

With Frank still sprawled on the deck, the referee approached Ed and informed him he would blow the full-time whistle if somebody didn't attempt the conversion within the next minute.

Ed knew Frank was the only player on his side that could kick a conversion from the sideline. With a look of desperation, he said to his five-eight, "Are you okay to convert your try, Frank?"

Frank got up on one knee, took a deep breath, looked at Ed and said, "Yep, I'll have a crack at it." Frank picked up the football and, while breathing heavily, approached the side line from where he would attempt the conversion. The ball boy passed him a bucket of sand, and after sprinkling a small amount on the ground, Frank placed the ball upright on the mound.

Frank walked back ten paces. He looked at the goalposts, then at the ball, then back at the goalposts. He drew a deep breath. He ran in and kicked the ball sweetly off the toe of his right boot. The crowd went silent as the ball sailed through the air. At first, it looked as though the ball would sail out to the left, but then it curved around to the right. As it approached the left- hand post it swiped it and then fell through. At first, no one was sure if the ball had found its mark. Frank gave an agonising look towards the two touch judges, who were poised under the black dot of the goalposts. They looked at each other for an eternity before they simultaneously raised their flags. Frank had converted his try and Joeys had won the premiership 15 – 13.

There was a sense of euphoria around the ground as the Joeys supporters roared with delight. Jimmy led the team as they hoisted Frank on their shoulders and carried him off the field through a crowd of Joeys spectators, who had rushed onto the field to support their hero.

Slouched on the ground with their heads in their hands were the Riverview players, devastated by their loss. Frank was perched high on the shoulders of his team mates, beaming with delight when he spotted the forlorn figure of his opposite number, Dick Wilkinson, standing by himself with his head down and his hands on his hips. Being the sportsman he was, Frank directed his team mates towards Dick, and as they approached the dejected figure, he lifted his head with a look of anguish. The two rivals looked each other in the eyes.

"You played a great game, Dick. You're a true champion. Don't let this loss set you back because there are great days ahead for you."

Dick looked at Frank and smiled. "Your gracious words testify to the giant of a man you are, Frank."

Frank waved at Dick before the ensemble carried him from the field through the cheers and applause of the spectators.

Frank's prophetic words were not only a measure of the man he was, but also of the fact Dick Wilkinson would indeed climb to the top of the rugby ladder in the future.

After the euphoria of the victory over Riverview, reality set in for Frank. A more significant hurdle was just up the track and that was for him to pass his Leaving Certificate.

Over the next few months, Frank endeavoured to cram as much information into his head. With the help of Ed O'Shaughnessy, who was not only a great rugby player, but a fine intellect and who would go on to study medicine, Frank managed to retain enough information in his skull.

When Frank eventually sat for his Leaving Certificate at the end of 1937, he had so much information crammed into his head he thought it would burst. When he had completed his exams, he honestly thought he had failed and was a dejected figure for some time afterwards.

Regardless of how he felt about his exams, at year's end, when he said his goodbyes to Joeys, he was overcome with a great sense of pride. He had achieved so much, considering the rough start he initially received, and left a lasting impression on both the teachers and his fellow students. Such was his reputation that the Joeys yearbook of 1937 said he was probably one of the most prominent sportsmen in the school's history. His feelings of exaltation were short- lived, for he realised he was going home to the family farm and the prospect of working with Hugh did not enthral him.

It was Friday, January 14th, 1938 and Frank was waiting at the mailbox at the top of the driveway at Banyula in nervous anticipation. This was the day Frank was to receive his results for the

Leaving Certificate. While he sat on a log next to the mailbox, his mind wandered and he thought back to what had taken place over the last two months.

Frank had arrived home from Joeys after completing his Leaving Certificate in late 1937 with a dark cloud hanging over his head. He was going home to work on the farm with Hugh and he was not happy at all.

The sound of a horse cantering broke Frank from his reverie.

"How are you going today Frank?" said Stan Walker, the postman, while sitting in his saddle.

"I'm pretty nervous, to be honest with you, Mr Walker."

"I realise this is the big day when you get your results for the Leaving Certificate. Don't worry; everything works out in the long run as long as you keep your chin up."

After chatting for a bit longer, Stan handed the mail to Frank, including a copy of *The Sydney Morning Herald,* which contained the Leaving Certificate results.

"Cheerio, Frank," Stan said before planting his heels into the side of his horse and trotting off.

Frank placed the mail inside a saddlebag, mounted his bay gelding Brandy and rode the one mile up the gravel road to the homestead. On reaching the front veranda steps, Frank was met by his mother and with a smile, she exclaimed, "So the moment has finally arrived, Frank."

Frank took a deep breath and said to Margaret, "Lucky, the old man is down the paddock working because I wouldn't want him around when he finds out I've failed my Leaving Certificate."

With that, Frank sat down beside his mother on the back veranda and opened the newspaper to the results section. Perusing down the page, he found the heading marked:

St Joseph's College, Hunters Hill.

He ran down the page with his finger where the names were listed in alphabetical order until he found his.

Casey F.J. 1. B (English. Second class pass) 2. L (French. First class pass) 7. L (General Mathematics. A pass at the lower standard) 10. A (Modern History. First class pass) 28. A (Woolclassing. First class pass)

Frank sat back in his chair and rested the newspaper on his lap before a broad smile came over his face.

"You did it?" Margaret exclaimed.

"I can't believe it, Mum. I passed."

With that, Frank handed the newspaper to his mother and, after reading the results, she also broke out into a smile.

"I knew you would do it, Frank, and to think you attained three first class passes in French, modern history, and wool classing is an absolute credit it to you. Congratulations," she said before embracing him.

Frank had passed his Leaving Certificate, but life on Banyula was now his reality and he wasn't sure if he could last the distance.

Chapter 4

Friday, November 8th 1940. Banyula, Upper Bingara, New South Wales.

IN THE THREE years Frank had been home at Banyula, he had filled out to be a strapping 19-year-old lad standing 5 feet and 8 inches tall with broad shoulders and a superb physique. Although he still attended a regular Sunday Mass, any childhood ambitions he may have had to become a priest were well and truly forgotten as he thought of himself as a man of the world.

With the start of World War II in September 1939, triggered by Germany's invasion of Poland, Frank thought long and hard about his involvement. He concluded he would not hesitate to play his part and decided that when his time came, he would volunteer.

Frank had grown sick and tired of Hugh in the three years he had been home working on Banyula. With hostilities increasing in the North African campaign against the Axis powers, Frank saw this as his opportunity to join the army and see the world.

As he lay in bed, he contemplated the state of the world and the momentous decision he was about to make; to join the 2nd

Australian Imperial Force or AIF. It had been on the 3rd September, 1939 that Frank heard Australian Prime Minister, Robert Menzies, declare war on Germany.

Sitting around a Bakelite radio in the loungeroom with his family, Frank listened to the Australian statesman in his low, dignified voice declare those famous words:

"Fellow Australians, it is my melancholy duty to inform you officially that, in consequence of the persistence of Germany of her invasion of Poland, Great Britain has declared war on her, and that, as a result, Australia is also at war.........."

Frank had followed the alarming rise of Hitler and knew that war was inevitable. As a Commonwealth country, he realised Australia would also be involved and his conscience told him that when war came, he would do his bit and enlist.

Here he was snuggled up in the safety of his bed, contemplating the enormous decision he was about to take. Frank was going to fight overseas.

Frank and Jimmy Cruikshank decided to enlist together and the plan was to rendezvous in a pub at Werris Creek on the Saturday.

As the family sat around the table for lunch on Saturday, nobody was any wiser about Frank's intentions. Early that day, he had covertly packed his bag and stashed it away in a wardrobe in his bedroom, ready for a speedy departure. Frank had no intentions of spending more time at Banyula than required, although he knew his departure would break his mother's heart.

After a quick check of his bag to ensure he had not forgotten anything, Frank made his way to the dining table where the family was gathered. His mother was seated beside him, where she instructed Frank's 9-year-old sister Joan to say grace. Nothing in Frank's demeanour suggested that anything was different from what the family was expecting from him. Frank was about to lay down a bombshell at their feet, the likes of which had never been seen in the Casey household before.

When lunch was finished, Frank rose from the dinner table and announced to his entire family his intentions to join the army with his mate, Jimmy Cruikshank, and that he would be leaving today.

Hugh glared at his eldest son and, with clenched teeth, said, "You listen to me, Frank. I don't need you playing games with me. Now you sit yourself down and behave."

Kevin, Frank's second eldest brother, was seated on the opposite side of the dining table and gave him an anxious look while he fidgeted in his chair.

"I am not playing games at all, Dad. I am serious. I am going to join the army," Frank said earnestly.

Suddenly, Hugh rose from where he was seated at the head of the table and, with his face flushed red and pointing his finger at Frank, said, "Now, you look here, Frank, let's get one thing straight. I'm not in the mood for copping any garbage off you. You have an obligation to work at Banyula with me. Now I suggest that you get rid of any hare-brained ideas about going off to war."

"I am no longer a boy; I am a man and I expect to be treated that way." Frank said with piercing eyes.

"You fought in the Great War and I'm going to do my bit and fight the 'Krauts'."

By this stage, Frank was breathing heavily and his heart was pounding, but he kept his presence of mind.

"You stop this nonsense straight away, Frank, or by the living Harry, I'll tan your behind."

"Easy does it, dad. Let Frank have his say," said Kevin.

"You zip up, Kevin or I'll tan your behind, also," Hugh said, waving his hand towards his younger son.

"You won't be tanning my behind as I have just said I'm off to join the 2nd AIF and fight in the Middle East."

The very mention of the word Middle East sent Hugh into a rage.

"No son of mine will go and fight in a stinking war."

Hugh attempted to grab Frank by the shirt front, but Frank raised his hand and caught his father's arm.

"Now, you listen to me real carefully, old man. I've had a lifetime of putting up with your abuse and it stops here. I've made up my mind and I'm going to join the army and fight the Germans. Is that clear?" Frank said with a raised voice while pointing his finger.

"Would you please lower your voice, Frank? It's disturbing the children," Margaret said.

"I am sorry, mum but this needs to be said. I am a grown adult and I have decided to go to war."

Hugh looked at Frank with a look of anger, but said nothing.

By this stage, Kevin's eyes were as wide as saucers and the rest of the family sat in shocked silence at the argument they were witnessing.

"You're the eldest boy in the family now, Kevin. You look after yourself and your mother and siblings and don't you take any nonsense off the old man," said Frank.

Kevin shook his head in agreement while Hugh continued to glare at Frank.

"Don't you listen to him, Kevin? Frank's a fool and he will get himself killed?" Hugh growled.

Margaret sobbed and with tears streaming down her face,

she grabbed Frank by the hand and echoed Hugh's words, "Oh Frank, don't be so foolish. You'll get yourself killed."

"I'm sorry, mum. I've already made up my mind. I'm going to do my bit and fight the Germans."

"Oh, Frank," Margaret said, continuing to cry, "I lost my brother in the Great War and to lose you would be devastating."

Frank held his mother in his arms and said, "What am I to do, mum? Go and let this little piece of filth Hitler destroy the world. Not on your life. I sure hope I return home in one piece, but there is no way I'm going to stand back idle and do nothing while this little creep casts his ugly shadow over the world."

After wiping away her tears with a handkerchief, Margaret composed herself. "I understand that Frank, but the Great War devastated our generation and I would hate for that to happen to you. Please look after yourself and I will be praying day and night until you come home."

"Thanks, mum I appreciate that," he said before hugging her.

"Ah, to buggery with you, Frank! You have always been a rebellious one and I hope it doesn't result in you getting killed!" Hugh said before exiting the table and walking to the back veranda to sit in his favourite seat and smoke his pipe.

Frank's siblings gathered around, where they extended their love and best wishes toward their eldest brother.

With that, Frank went to his bedroom and got his bag, then returned to announce, "I must go as I have planned to meet Jimmy Cruikshank in the Railway Hotel at Werris Creek. We are going to both do battle with Hitler!"

Frank waved everybody goodbye, and as he was walking out the door, he turned to his brother Bob and said, "You look after Brandy for me while I'm away, Bob. I don't know how long this little circus will last for, but he's yours until I return."

"I will, Frank. So long and take care," Bob said.

Frank then walked to the back veranda where Hugh was smoking his pipe and in one last act of defiance to his father, he broke out into song in an Irish brogue.

"*There was a wild colonial boy, Frank Casey was his name. He decided to go off to fight the war. Thank you all the same.........*"

Hugh looked at his eldest son long and hard, the reality of Frank's decision hitting home before he turned to him and spoke in a conciliatory tone.

"Frank, I've got something I want you to have," he said. "I know I've been a tough old man, but take this watch with you. My father presented it to me before I went off to the Great War and I want you to have it."

Hugh took off his wristwatch and gave it to Frank.

"You're a grown man now, Frank, and you are old enough to make your own decisions. I was the same when I was your age, so look after yourself and I hope you return home in one piece."

Frank looked at the watch before placing it in his shirt pocket.

"Thanks, dad. I appreciate that."

With that, the two men shook hands firmly before Hugh said, "God speed and be off with you."

With that, Frank picked up his bag, flung it over his shoulder, and trudged up the gravel driveway to the entrance of Banyula. Stopping, he paused and looked down the driveway towards the homestead. He was filled with mixed emotions, but the thought that predominated was that he had stood up to his father and prevailed. It was the type of courage Frank was to be called upon to show in the years ahead. Frank looked at Banyula and said, "so long, old home, I don't know if I'll ever see you again."

Frank turned and walked down the gravel road and hitched a ride towards Werris Creek. Little did he know that three of his younger brothers, Kevin, Bob and Brian, were to all defy their father and follow him into the services.

Frank was filled with mixed emotions as he walked south down the gravel road towards Barraba. On the one hand, he was pleased that he stood up to his father but also satisfied he had been able to shake hands with him before his departure.

As he trudged along the road in the mid-afternoon sun, half an hour passed before a vehicle finally approached. On closer inspection, Frank could see it was a red 1938 Chevrolet Maple Leaf truck, and after it pulled up, it left a cloud of dust lingering around. Behind the wheel was old Jock Armstrong, who owned a farm ten miles up the road from Banyula towards Bingara. Jock wore a black patch over his left eye, courtesy of being shot while serving in the Boer War.

"Frank Casey, what the blazes are you doing out here?"

"G'day Jock, I'm heading over to Werris Creek to catch up with a mate. Are you heading towards Barraba by any chance?"

"You're in luck, as I'm heading over there to pick up some fencing wire from my brother's place."

Frank slung his bag into the back of the truck, opened the passenger side door and took a seat.

Jock roared down the gravel road, leaving a cloud of dust behind him.

They had driven a short distance before Jock tilted his hat back on his head and said.

"So tell me Frank, you look you might be having a long stay at you mates place with that bag slung over your shoulder?"

"If the truth be known we are catching the mail train down to Sydney to join up and go and fight the Germans," Frank said seriously.

"Well, I'll be buggered. I hope you know what you are flaming well getting yourself into, young Frank, because I was in the Boer War and I copped it," he said, pointing to the black patch over his eye.

"I knew you were in the Boer War, but I have never heard you talk about it."

"It's not something one talks about. After all, I saw some pretty nasty things in South Africa."

Jock was silent for some time before he spoke again.

"I was in the New South Wales Mounted Rifles, and flaming hell, I copped some shrapnel while fighting at The Battle of Palmietfontein in the Orange Free State."

"Crikey Jock, that is serious."

Jock paused before saying, "what's Hugh saying about you going away to the war?"

"He wasn't too happy about the idea at first, but after we argued, he finally realised I can make my own decisions."

Jock looked up into the surrounding trees, deep in thought, before looking at Frank and saying,

"Hugh hates war, Frank, as he saw some nasty stuff at Gallipoli and the Western Front."

"I realise that, but I've made up my mind." Frank said defiantly.

Jock looked Frank up and down.

"Mmm, I can see that, Frank."

As they drove on, Jock told Frank stories about his experiences of fighting in the Boer War. He told him what happened when he copped the shrapnel in the eye, before they arrived in Barraba forty- five minutes later.

"You look after yourself, Frank," said Jock while he extended his hand.

"I'll do my best, Jock."

Frank grabbed his bag from the back of the truck and, with a wave, continued hitching towards Werris Creek.

Frank arrived just before 4.00 pm where he made his way over to the Railway Hotel, where he was greeted by Jimmy, who ordered two schooners of beer.

"Did Hugh give you a leave pass?" Jimmy gave Frank a wry smile.

"Not before we had a bit of a Donnybrook old mate. Don't worry, we sorted out our differences before I left and shook hands. "

"Well, that's good news,"

They sat down at a table and Frank took a sip from his icy cold beer.

"Ahhhh, that is good." Frank savoured the bitter taste.

The trip over to Werris Creek had left Frank dry and the beer tasted great.

"Too bloody right!" Jimmy said, raising his glass before taking a sip.

After sitting down at a small round table, Frank arrived back from the bar and proceeded to tell Jimmy about his altercation with Hugh. They had been drinking for about half an hour when two neatly dressed Royal Australian Air Force (RAAF) officers walked into the hotel. At first, Frank and Jimmy took scant notice of them until one of the officers, aged in his mid-twenties, approached the two of them.

"Excuse me for interrupting fellas, but aren't you Frank Casey and Jimmy Cruikshank who went to Joeys?"

Frank swung his head around with a beer in hand and exclaimed in a laconic drawl, "Yeah, who's asking?"

"My name is Ray Connelly and I was four years ahead of you at Joeys. I was there the day the two of you played for the school in the First XV rugby game against Riverview." He extended his hand to Frank.

"How do you do, Ray?" Frank said, shaking the hand offered to him.

"Bloody hell, what a cracker of a game that was. I'll never forget the try you scored to win the game for Joeys. And to think you dragged yourself off the ground after being winded to kick the conversion from the sideline. Crikey, that was terrific," Ray said.

A huge grin came over Frank's face and after he extended his hand to Ray and his fellow officer to take a seat, he exclaimed, "You blokes look like you're as dry as the bottom of a cocky's cage. My shout for an icy cold one, hey?"

"Too right, Frank. My fellow officer John Carruthers and I," Ray said, pointing to his colleague, "are absolutely parched. A cold beer would be just the ticket." The four of them laughed and after Ray introduced John to the young lads, Frank went to the bar and ordered four beers.

He walked back to the table, clutching the beers in both hands, with the icy cold froth running down the sides of the glasses.

"Ahhhh bloody hell, that's good," John said as he took a sip.

"What brings you two blokes to this neck of the woods?" Jimmy asked.

"We are recruitment officers for the RAAF and we are trying to find suitable candidates to join up," said John.

Frank and Jimmy looked at each and simultaneously let out a gasp of laughter.

"What's the joke?" Ray said with a wry smile.

Frank and Jimmy were grinning like a pair of Cheshire cats before Frank exclaimed, "if the truth be known, we are catching the Northern Mail down to Sydney tonight, where we are going to sign up for the army."

The two officers looked at each other with eyebrows raised before Ray said, "have you two fine upstanding gentlemen given any thought about joining the airforce?"

"Not really," Jimmy exclaimed, "why should we?" He was grinning with his glass up to his lips.

"It might interest the both of you to know there is a good chance you would be stationed in England. Being the exceptionally talented rugby players you both are, those talents may be used playing rugger on a regular basis."

"Is that so?" said Jimmy with a quizzical look.

"Absolutely! You would get a chance to see the old country and play some rugger in between operations. Not to mention some great girls waiting to meet some rugged Aussies. Why go and fight in the Middle East when you can experience all the history that the Old Dart offers?"

Both Frank and Jimmy had been starved of rugby since leaving school. They had both been working on their family properties and neither was close to a rugby club. Any aspirations they had of playing top level rugby seemed out of their reach with their current circumstances. The two officers had cast out the burley, and with a steady flow of the amber fluid flowing, both Frank and Jimmy had taken the bait.

A boisterous night of drinking followed, where the publican shut the doors after 6.00 pm and allowed the patrons to keep on drinking while the two officers plied their trade. What followed was not only Frank and Jimmy agreeing to sign up, but so did seven other men who had joined the shout. Included in the seven was a railway shunter who had slipped into the pub for a sneaky beer before 6.00 pm closing, only to be dragged into the shout and a new career with the RAAF.

Frank and Jimmy staggered out of the Railway Hotel close to 10.30 pm, just in time to catch the departing mail train to Sydney. They had been in hysterics at the sight of the two officers slumped over the bar in such a dishevelled state.

Chapter 5

Tuesday, November 12th 1940. No 2. Initial Training School (ITS) Bradfield Park, New South Wales

THE TWO BOYS had slept off their hangovers by Monday morning and made their way to RAAF Headquarters in Rushcutters Bay. After presenting themselves to the relevant personnel, and going through their medical examination, they signed up and were admitted into the RAAF by day's end.

In Frank and Jimmy's exuberance to join the RAAF, they assumed they would be trained as either fighter or, at the least, bomber pilots. Coupled with the fact they had drunk considerable amounts of booze with the two recruitment officers, their vision of where they might end up in the RAAF was seriously distorted.

The Empire Air Training Scheme (EATS) had been designed by the RAAF to train aircrew so they could be eventually transferred to the Royal Air Force (RAF) in preparation for the war developing in Europe. RAAF schools were being established across Australia to support EATS. This included Elementary Flying Training, Air Navigation, and Wireless Air Gunnery.

After being posted to No 2 Initial Flying School (ITS) at Bradfield Park, now Lindfield, New South Wales, it soon became apparent to the two boys they would not be trained as pilots. After initial examinations proved mathematics was not their fortè, they slipped down the ladder from observers to wireless air gunners (WAG) to just plain air gunners (AG). And that's where both Frank and Jimmy found themselves for their eight weeks of initial training.

ITS Bradfield Park consisted of miles and miles of parade grounds, and on more than one occasion, the two boys removed their white 'trainee' flash from their caps to appear as ground crew. They would then crawl through a hole in the fence and make their way up Lady Game Drive to Chatswood, where they would make their way to a nearby pub. One night, after returning from one of their excursions to the local, they crossed paths with an officer walking across the parade ground. Some quick talking from Jimmy, where he convinced the officer they were ground crew, diverted a potential disaster and being hauled in front of the brass for some severe punishment.

Evans Head, in the Northern Rivers of New South Wales, was where Frank and Jimmy were posted after they finished their initial training. It was here they learnt some of the rudimentary aspects of gunnery and flew in an old Avro Anson and Fairey Battle light bomber and fired a Vickers machine gun.

Being off the land, Frank and Jimmy were well-versed in handling a rifle, but many of the "green" gunners had never held a weapon in their lives. This got up the nose of one of the drill instructors nicknamed Cerberus, after the three-headed dog from Greek mythology. Cerberus stood over 6 feet tall, had three folds under his chin, a jaw as solid as the rock of Gibraltar and was one of the meanest bastards you would ever wish to cross paths with.

In the second week, Frank earned the ire of Cerberus and was hauled before the CO Buchan. One of the recruits was Jack Walsh, who was off a big station at Julia Creek in northwest Queensland. Jack had a fiery nature and liked to lead from the front, and Frank, being of the same temperament, took exception to the laconic Queenslander ordering him around one day. When Jack wouldn't back off, Frank invited him to sort it out after lights out that night in the dormitory. Jack was more than willing to accommodate Frank. With Jimmy running a book and taking bets on the fight, the two amateur pugilists ventured to the far end of the dormitory, where they proceeded to knock the living daylights out of each other. Unfortunately, in their enthusiasm to barrack for the fight, many of the recruits became very noisy, resulting in Cerberus marching into the middle of the gathering and breaking up the fight.

As a result, both Frank and Jack were hauled before Buchan and told they were skating on thin ice in no uncertain terms. The CO reminded them they were being trained so they could bash the living tripe out of the Krauts and not themselves. Furthermore, he told them, that stunts like the one they had just pulled off would not be tolerated. Buchan also punished Jimmy after it was found out he was taking bets on the fight.

Frank and Jack's stoush had a very positive effect on the two men as it unleashed built-up tension and consequently, they became great mates. As the two men got to know each other, Frank confided in Jack about his difficult relationship with his father and his reluctance to return to the family farm. As a result, Jack offered Frank a job in his shearing team back home at the war's end, which Frank gladly accepted.

Their training at Evans Head was rudimentary and hardly prepared them for the rigours ahead. On completion of their training, Frank and Jimmy were sent to Canada in mid-March 1941 to continue their gunnery training.

In early September 1941, the troopship *Narayan* steamed out of Halifax Harbour in Nova Scotia, Canada, bound for Liverpool, England with Frank and Jimmy on board. On arriving in Liverpool, Frank and Jimmy were sent to a gunnery school near Cardiff in Wales for more training. Once they had completed their training in Cardiff in late November 1941, the lads arrived in London, ready to be posted to an operational squadron.

Chapter 6

Friday, November 28th 1941.RAF Marham Norfolk, East Anglia, England

IT WAS EARLY morning and a biting wind was blowing from the North Sea when Frank and Jimmy arrived at RAF Marham Norfolk in East Anglia. Although it was late autumn, as far as the two boys were concerned, it may as well have been the middle of winter, as they were both freezing.

Many of the crew they had trained with at the gunnery schools in Evans Head, Canada and Wales had joined them, including Jack Walsh.

Among the new aircrew was Les Nicholson, a tough nuggetty bricklayer from Enmore in Sydney, aged in his early twenties. Frank and Jimmy first met Les in a pub in Liverpool in England. Days after arriving in Liverpool, they were surveying the devastation from a German bombing raid the night before. They were walking down the street when they heard the familiar strain of an Aussie accent coming from a corner pub close by. Once entering the pub, they noticed a bloke with sandy hair arguing hammer and tongs with the barman.

"Listen here, you Pommy bastard. I haven't travelled all the way from Australia to be served up a flat beer. Now get ya arse into gear and put a head on it, will ya?" he said, before sliding the pot of beer back towards the irate barman, the contents spilling all over the bar.

"Listen here, you upstart *Orstralian*. I've never served up a flat beer in this pub, so if you don't like it, I suggest you get the bleedin' hell out of my pub."

"I'm going to and you can shove your flat beer fair up yer arse?"

The banter between them highly amused Frank and Jimmy and they sidled up to the fuming Aussie and offered to buy him a beer in another pub.

"I'm up for that, fellas. Anything's better than drinking this cat's piss."

After Frank and Jimmy introduced themselves to Les, or Nicko as he liked to be called, they adjourned to another pub. They got the surprise of their lives when they found the beer was just as flat as the first place and it was only then they learned that English beer has no head on it.

Contrary to their introduction to English beer, the boys were suitably impressed by the warm welcome the Liverpudlian's extended to them. On top of this, they showed great admiration for the business-as-usual attitude and humour the locals possessed as they cleaned up from the aerial devastation.

On arriving in London in late November 1941, Frank and Jimmy were posted to No.377 Squadron RAF at Marham in the county of Norfolk. The motto of the squadron was *ad defendere libartatem (*to defend liberty).

The boys were dog-tired after travelling from London all night and were in need of some sleep on arriving at Marham.

Instead, they were paraded before a pompous English squadron leader in his late twenties with a pencil-thin moustache named Burnham. He spoke in a condescending tone and gave the new arrivals a long-winded brief about the illustrious history of No. 377 Squadron. He stressed it was up to them to uphold the fine traditions that dated back to the Great War.

"Crikey, who needs to listen to this crap? A good feed of bacon and eggs and a decent kip is all I need," said Jimmy under his breath.

Jimmy's offhand remark, which he thought was directed only to Frank standing next to him, caught the attention of the pretentious officer. He strode up to Jimmy and stood only inches from his face while delivering to the boy from Breeza a blistering sermon. Although he spoke to Jimmy, it was an attack directed towards the rest of the new arrivals.

"You colonials have a reputation for being nothing but crude, rude and ill disciplined and I want to make it absolutely clear that it is our business at Marham to knock you into shape. We expect you to adhere to the high standards set down by your predecessors'. Besides, most of you gunners are just shit and won't complete your thirty operations. The last we see of you will be when you're blasted out of your turrets with a hose."

With that, he turned on his heels and continued with his grandiloquent spiel, after which Frank quipped to Jimmy, "Crikey, hasn't this pompous Pommy bastard got an overcooked crumpet shoved up his arse."

It wasn't a great start for the latest arrivals to the squadron and only served to confirm their suspicions about the pompous manner of their superiors.

After this, the new arrivals were given breakfast and then taken to an igloo where they slept like logs, impervious to the sound of aircraft outside.

The next morning, Frank and Jimmy hitched a ride down to the hangars to inspect the aircraft they were to fly. The Vickers Wellington Bomber (Wimpy) was a twin engine long range medium bomber. It consisted of two Bristol Pegasus radial engines of 1050 HP each. There were two Browning .303 guns in the forward turret and two in the rear turret. It had a crew of six, including the pilot, co- pilot/observer, wireless operator (WAG), navigator, front gunner/bomb aimer and rear gunner. They were a formidable aircraft, and their black–fuselage made them an imposing sight. After inspecting the aircraft for some time, they made their way back to their igloo huts, satisfied with what they had seen.

That afternoon, they were marched into a classroom where they were met by the gunnery leader, a gruff English Flight Lieutenant by the name of Page. He reinforced the comments made by Squadron Leader Burnham the day before.

"Let me clarify that you colonials are just crap and I won't tolerate you're unruly behaviour. You have been posted to Marham to fly Wellington Bombers and you will do what you are told. Is that clear?" he barked.

"Hang on a minute. Who are you calling crap?" Nicko snapped.

Nicko was backed up by the rest of the boys, which only earned the Flight Lieutenant's ire.

"Keep this up and I'll have you all up on a charge of insubordination!"

"You do what you want, but I haven't come from the other side of the world to be spoken to like a piece of shit," said Frank.

"That's right. We're not going to cop this garbage from you," Jimmy said.

"How about you get off your high horse and come back down to earth," added Jack Walsh.

"That's it," said the officer, smashing his hand on the corner of the desk, "you, you, you and you," he said, pointing at Nicko, Frank, Jimmy and Jack, "I'm having you pieces of shit hauled up in front of the Wingco (Wing Commander)on charges of insubordination. Now get out of here on the double."

That afternoon, the four of them were paraded in front of Wing Commander Atkinson. The Wingco was a middle-aged Englishman, a little plump with short dark hair. They were expecting to be ripped into by him, so they decided they would stick together as there was strength in numbers. They figured if they were going to go down, they would go down together.

With sweaty palms, the four of them were addressed by Atkinson. Contrary to what the boys expected, he addressed them sternly but civilly.

"I believe you men have been ruffling a few feathers with your superiors?"

"Sir, we don't take kindly to being addressed to as crap," said Jimmy.

"Ahem, I don't believe it," Atkinson spluttered.

"It's true, sir," said Frank.

"Who said this?" the Wingco demanded.

"Flight Lieutenant Page said this, sir," said Nicko.

"Ahem, I don't believe you should be getting upset with language like that. Besides, that's common jargon in the RAF."

"We didn't come over here to England to be referred to as that. Besides, if need be, we will take our complaint to our Australian superiors in London, sir," said Jimmy, looking steely-eyed at the Wingco.

Jimmy had Atkinson leg before wicket (LBW), and the Wingco almost choked when he realised the last thing he wanted was Australian headquarters bringing the heat down on him.

He couldn't believe the boldness of these men from Australia. The average English aircrew would never have the audacity to address a commanding officer the way they had. They were content to take orders without complaining, but the Aussies, Kiwis and Canadians liked a scrap and took nothing lying down. After ruffling a few papers on his desk, Atkinson cleared his throat before addressing the men.

"My father was an officer who fought alongside the Australians at Peronne during the Great War. Never a finer bunch of soldiers did he ever encounter. What they did at Mont Saint-Quentin was one of the greatest feats of the war, he would often say to me. If you men are half the men they were, then I'm sure you will make fine aircrew," he said.

After a lecture on discipline and dress, the men were dismissed. As a result of their meeting with Atkinson, no charges were laid and more importantly, never again were air gunners referred to as faeces.

The next day after lunch, an order came through from headquarters. The men were told to meet in the hangar, where they would sort themselves out into crews. Frank and Jimmy were milling around among the crowd of other airmen, wondering what to do next, when they were approached by an Australian pilot by the name of Reg Chapman.

"I've heard on the grapevine that you two blokes are from the bush and are pretty handy on the trigger," Chapman said to the two boys.

"Ah yeah, we're pretty decent shots," said Jimmy laconically with his hands in his pockets.

"That's good, because I need both front and rear gunners as part of my aircrew. How about you join me?"

The two boys looked at each other for a while and nodded before Frank said, "Yeah, we'll join your show, skip."

Chapman was pleased and spoke to the boys a bit longer. It was decided that Frank would be given the rear gunner position while Jimmy became the crew's front gunner/bomb aimer. Reg held the rank of flying officer and was a surveyor from Maitland in the Hunter Valley of New South Wales before joining the RAAF. A tall man with ginger-coloured hair, he was twenty-four years of age. Reg was tough and emanated an air of confidence. He was a likeable bloke, and from the start, Frank and Jimmy felt comfortable with him. This was especially poignant after what they had recently experienced with the brass at Marham.

Reg then introduced Frank and Jimmy to the co-pilot, a Welshman from Pontypool named Bryn Jones, standing a short distance away. As a school teacher and pilot, Flying Officer Jones' approach to the two boys was rather austere. His initial feeling for the two Australians from the bush was one of disdain. As an officer, he thought he was a cut above them and there were some awkward moments when there wasn't much said between them. Reg managed to plug the gaps by explaining to them the reason they had joined the crew, because the pilot and front and rear gunners had been seriously wounded after their last operation over Holland. Jimmy was oblivious to the seriousness of Reg's remarks when he piped in and said, "Being Welsh, you must like your rugby, Bryn?"

"Like rugby? You're kidding, aren't you? I'm Welsh, so I love the game!" His answer came back as quick as a pass from the scrum base.

"That's good because both Jimmy and I played at school and we love the game also," said Frank.

"Well, we'll get on like a house on fire," Jones said in his high pitched Welsh accent. The ice had been broken and Reg invited Frank and Jimmy over to the other side of the hangar to meet the rest of the crew.

The rest of the crew were standing around their Wellington. It was still being repaired after their last operation over Holland. Frank could see the bullet holes in the aircraft after a German night fighter had hit it on the return flight and it was a sobering reminder of the dangers that awaited him.

Reg explained to both Frank and Jimmy their aircraft was named A for Apple, as all the aircraft in the squadron were given letters of the alphabet that coincided with a name. There was C for Charlie, F for Freddie and S for Sugar, etc. After explaining this, he introduced the two boys to the rest of the crew.

The navigator was a tall New Zealander named Trevor Kay, colloquially referred to as Kiwi. Like Frank and Jimmy, Kiwi held the rank of Flight Sergeant. He was off a farm that grew Chinese gooseberries, later named kiwifruit in the 1950s, which his family ran in a small town called Te Puke in the Bay of Plenty area on the North Island. A likeable character, he was training to be a civil engineer. The wireless operator/gunner was Flight Sergeant Freddie Hill from Bethnal Green in the East End of London. He operated a fixed fruit and vegetable stall before the war and was a quick-witted Cockney. Although Freddie possessed a great charm, he hated the Germans with a passion, as his family home had been destroyed in the first night of the Blitz in September 1940, resulting in his eldest brother Charlie being killed. Both Frank and Jimmy hit it off with Trevor and Freddie and from the start, the crew formed a tight bond.

Reg and Trevor had flown no operations, but Jones and Freddie had a scattering between them. It was a usual practice to send a sprog or new crew for a relatively safe operation for their initial run. It usually consisted of dropping propaganda pamphlets into France so the crew could get accustomed to a full-on op. Nothing could have been further from the truth for A for Apple, as their first operation was to Germany.

Chapter 7

Sunday, December 7th 1941. RAF Marham, Norfolk, East Anglia, England

IT WAS 6.30 AM and Frank was woken by the sound of bombers returning from their operations. He had a knot in his stomach as his crew had been informed they were to fly their first operation that night.

As he lay there, he was paralysed with fear as the moment of reckoning had arrived. His head felt like a can of worms as a thousand thoughts raced through his mind and he was gripped with terror.

"Hopefully, they will send us for a simple pamphlet run over France. Surely they wouldn't send a crew with our lack of experience for an operation over Germany," he thought to himself.

At the front of his mind was the belief that the crew didn't have enough operational experience. He thought that putting a bunch of sprog airmen in an aircraft and expecting them to bomb Germany was pure folly. It was Frank's earnest wish that he would get through this 'show' unscathed and here he was at the beginning, doubting his ability to perform.

He turned over to his right and Jimmy was lying in his bed, snoring away with his feet hanging out from the end of his blankets. He looked like he was home at Breeza without a care. "Lucky bastard!" Frank murmured.

Kiwi was out of bed first and was peering through the window, looking out on the dark skies.

"I reckon they'll bring the hammer down on any ops tonight, the way this weather is setting in," he said.

Kiwi had a keen interest in the weather and soon became the crew's unofficial meteorologist.

On hearing Kiwi's forecast, Frank immediately snapped out of his melancholy state.

"You mean we won't be flying tonight, Kiwi?" said Frank with excitement.

"Nah, this lot looks like it's set in. I reckon you can relax, Frank."

A tinge of excitement ran through Frank's veins. Kiwi's prediction was spot on and by lunchtime, the rain had set in, grounding all crews for that night's operation.

Frank felt like a pressure relief valve had been released and the tension slowly dissipated from him.

With operations being cancelled that night, some of the crew ventured down to the local pub named the Fox and Hounds in Marham, where they all had a skin full. For Frank, it was a surreal atmosphere to be in a smoke filled pub feeling the effects of numerous pints of beer and enjoying the company of his fellow aircrew after being in such an anxious state earlier in the day. It was a paradox Frank was to ponder in the future. They were the two extremes of operational flying or the cosy confines of the local pub. As Frank sipped on his ale that night, he felt content that all was safe for the time being.

By Tuesday December 9th, the weather had cleared and the crew expected they would fly that night.

By 3.00 pm, the Tannoy public address system spoke; informing all crews they were to report to the operations room at 4.00 pm. Frank felt the same apprehension from the previous Sunday morning as he headed for the ops room.

When Reg's crew arrived, the other crews were already seated. The long narrow room was packed with close to one hundred airforce personnel. Group Captain (Groupy) Young addressed them. He was English, aged in his early fifties, tall in stature, solid build, with brown hair and sporting a moustache.

"Righto chaps, I suppose you're all eagerly wondering what the target is tonight?" he said in a casual manner that suggested he may as well have been heading to a cricket match at Lords.

The Groupy pulled on two drawstrings and the curtains parted, revealing a massive map of Europe. Frank had never seen such a big map and he examined the many different cities and towns from one side of the continent to the other. On further inspection, he noticed a piece of red tape stretched from RAF Marham across the North Sea and into Germany, ending at the city of Duisburg.

"Okay chaps, the city of Duisburg in the Ruhr Valley will be the target tonight," the Groupy said.

There was a buzz of conversation within the room until the Groupy put up his hand for silence.

"I know it's a tough one and many of the crews feel as though they are a bit green. Let me remind you that this is a terrific opportunity to hit at the heart of Nazi Germany tonight and give old 'Harry the Hun' a good old British-style thrashing. Duisburg is situated in the Ruhr Valley, which is the industrial heart of Germany. There are a number of chemical and steel manufacturing plants that need to be taken out, so chaps, I urge you to bring your best game out there tonight and go and hit 'Gerry' the old tinker for six."

Frank looked at Reg with his mouth wide open.

"They have to be kidding, skip. Fancy sending a sprog crew like ours into the heart of Germany for our first operation. It's total madness if you want my opinion," whispered Frank.

"It's a tough one, I know Frank, but they're the cards we've been dealt with," said Reg.

The briefing continued and all the crews were informed of specifics such as the meteorological situation, navigational obstacles and wireless jamming techniques the Germans were using.

As a final parting gesture, the gunnery leader Flight Lieutenant Page made it clear in no uncertain terms that they were to be on the ball and not to nod off before being dismissed.

Before boarding the bus to take the crew to their aircraft, Frank vomited to which Jimmy gave him a reassuring pat on the back.

"Come on, Frank, we'll treat this operational like a hard game of rugger and we'll dish it out to the Krauts," Jimmy said.

Frank gave him a forced smile.

The moon was bright as Frank's crew arrived at A for Apple. They were the last crew out that night and there was silence and an air of apprehension as the crew boarded their Wimpy. In the bus, Frank overheard Reg and Kiwi discussing the problem of reaching the proposed flying altitude of seventeen thousand feet. Reg doubted if they would be able to reach that altitude with the weight of bombs they were carrying. Listening to their comments, Frank felt a lead weight in his stomach and his hands were sweaty.

Once entering the aircraft, Frank made his way down the catwalk where he hung his 'chute before entering the darkened rear turret. Once closing the doors behind him, he was over-come with a feeling of loneliness. It was a feeling he was to never completely come to terms with, even though he was only a short distance from the rest of the crew. Once strapping himself in and the crew had checked in with the skipper, he inspected the travel on his guns to make sure they were working by swinging them in an arc. No sooner had he done this, then the motors of the Wimpy roared to life and the aircraft shook as the smell of fumes filled his nostrils.

As A for Apple taxied out onto the runway, Frank stared out into the darkness behind him, not knowing what fate awaited him. Within no time, they were up in the air, and as Reg banked the aircraft over to the starboard side, Frank could see the station lights. He wondered if he would ever see them again. He was unsure what was expected of him and he was to learn later, neither did Jimmy.

All conversation on the trip over was shared between the pilot and navigator. Frank sat in his turret in silence, looking out into the abyss. His morbid mental state was broken when Kiwi reported they were crossing the enemy coast and Frank's heart missed a beat.

They flew until such time Frank could see red blotches way down below. He was unsure whether they were bombs going off or flak coming up from below and, in a quandary, reported to the skipper there was flak on the starboard side. At the very mention of the word flak, Reg took the Wimpy into a sharp nosedive to the port side before eventually levelling the aircraft out.

"I didn't see any flak, rear gunner. What are you on about?" Reg said angrily.

Frank was embarrassed and was stunned into silence. He did not say another thing for fear of being thought a fool.

"That flak was too far away to cause us any harm, tailey!" Kiwi said tersely. "There's enough pressure on us up here for you to be making crackpot calls like that. Now sharpen up, will you?"

It was a stinging rebuke from the usually calm navigator, but as Frank was to learn, when the pressure was on, Kiwi wasn't one to mince his words. Frank was to soon learn that A for Apple had both a first class pilot and navigator that were to be the difference in the operations that lay ahead. Frank was mortified he had made such an elementary mistake and sat there in silence in a muddled state of mind, wondering what he should do next.

As Frank sat in the rear turret feeling like a tourist along for the ride, he could hear both Reg and Kiwi discussing the problems with trying to achieve the correct altitude.

"We are flying at just over fifteen thousand feet, skip. Briefing stipulated that we have to be at seventeen thousand feet when we are over the target area," said Kiwi.

"I'm pushing this old girl as hard as I can, navigator, but with the weight of these bombs on board, it will be hard work to get up to the desired altitude," Reg said.

"Keep pushing it, skip because we are fifteen minutes to TOT (Time On Target)," Kiwi said.

They flew until they hit the defence perimeter and the sky lit up into an inferno. Flashes of red light raced across the horizon, and from a distance, the crew could see an aircraft falling from the sky as a streak of light followed it downward.

"Crikey, this is like cracker night back home. Does the brass expect us to fly into that mess?" Jimmy quipped.

They flew to the target with the aircraft being tossed back and forth as flak exploded around them. Jimmy moved from the front gun to the bomb aiming position as they got closer to the target.

Jimmy's voice came through on the intercom.

"Tracking in on target. Steady. Hold it. Right steady. Left, left, now hold it. Steady. Okay bombs away!"

The aircraft released its four thousand pound load and the Wimpy lurched upwards as it was finally free of its overbearing weight. Reg kept the aircraft on a straight course for twenty seconds so the camera could take photographs of the target. Then he banked sharply to the starboard side, making an about turn, and headed for home. Below, Frank observed an inferno and pondered how anyone could survive such a maelstrom. To Frank's untrained eye, it looked as though the entire city of Duisburg was alight. He was momentarily lost in thought as to the fate of the occupants down below, but soon snapped out of it when he thought of what Hitler had unleashed on the allies.

"Bugger 'em. They brought this on themselves," he thought.

Once free of Duisburg, the flak died down and Kiwi set a course for home.

"No dozing off back there. Night fighters rarely operate in the flak areas, so be on the lookout," Reg said.

As they flew further from the city, Frank's eyes were still peeled on the inferno below, affecting his night vision. Occasionally, he could see bright horizontal streaks race across the sky, which climaxed with an orange flash.

Eventually, the inferno receded and Frank settled into a cosy position, which was only exacerbated by the gentle rocking of his turret. As they flew, Frank thought about what he had just witnessed when he heard Kiwi say through his earphones, "Crossing enemy coast."

Shortly after, they encountered some spasmodic and erratic flak which was of no harm to their aircraft and once clear, Reg came over the intercom.

"Keep on your toes, you blokes. I've been told that night fighters have been known to chase unsuspecting bombers back over the channel. So don't fall asleep."

As A for Apple flew over the stretch of water between Holland and England, heading for home safety, Frank contemplated how Bomber Command had never sent a more inexperienced crew to take on the might of the Third Reich. Although they were still a distance from Marham, he instinctively knew they were through the worst of their first operation.

Dawn was breaking and Frank was finding it hard to keep his eyes open, when he felt a thud underneath him and looking out, he saw they had landed.

"Well done, crew. You've done just fine." Reg said.

Frank still felt sheepish about his careless observation earlier in the flight, but that seemed to be forgotten as Kiwi slapped him on the back and congratulated him once disembarking the aircraft.

Back at the base, Frank was introduced to an RAF custom and handed a glass of rum. This was a welcome relief after the tension of eight hours of flying. The rum helped so returning crews could loosen their tongues and divulge what they saw of enemy defence establishments and general information. With a few rums under their belts, the crews become a lot more talkative and embellished the stories of what they had been through the previous night.

After the crew disembarked from the Wimpy, Jimmy caught up with Nicko, who had already landed in his aircraft S for Sugar. Jimmy looked around sheepishly so as none of his own crew was listening and said to Nicko, "I had a crack at least two night fighters."

"I reckon I shot at three," Nicko said as quick as a flash.

"What were they?" Jimmy said sceptically.

"Definitely Messerschmitt 109s,"Nicko retorted.

Jimmy gave Nicko a look of cynicism. The crews' boasting was quickly thwarted when the Wingco announced four of the crews had not returned from the previous night's operation and another two aircraft were badly damaged. Included in the four was F for Freddie.

"Crikey Jimmy, that's Al Rogerson's kite," said Frank.

Al Rogerson was a likeable bloke who came off a dairy farm at Dunoon, north of Lismore in the Northern Rivers of New South Wales. Since initial training, he had been with the boys and his disappearance and subsequent death were a sore loss to the squadron.

A feeling of depression hung over all the crews as the reality of operational flying hit home. They waited at the flight centre in hopeful anticipation the missing crews might return, but soon realised their fate was sealed. The crews caught the bus back to the mess where a reward was given of two eggs each at breakfast.

Before going to bed, Jimmy tossed Frank a mail parcel.

"Forgot to tell you, Frank, but the mail came in yesterday and there's a bunch of it for you."

As Frank lay back in bed with his hands wrapped around his mail, he felt tremendous relief he had come through unscathed from his first operation. Although there were dark days ahead for him and the thought of getting through thirty operations was never far from his mind, nothing was as tough as that first flight over Germany. He dozed off, satisfied he had passed his initiation of fire.

It was midday when Frank was woken by the Tannoy informing all pilots and navigators they had an early lunch. Frank rolled out of bed and looked out the window and noticed the sky was clear and the sun was shining.

"Could be on again tonight," said Jimmy busily putting his shoes on.

"You'd have to be kidding," Frank said.

"I don't think so. That's why Reg and Kiwi have got an early lunch appointment. It looks like the brass will take advantage of this good weather and send us back out tonight."

"Well, I'll be buggered. After losing four aircraft and another two damaged, you'd think they would give us a spell," Frank said.

Just then, Jack Walsh walked out of the bathroom and, while still wiping his face from shaving, exclaimed, "I'll guarantee it, Frank, it will be on again tonight. It's a certainty with these clear skies."

Jack's comments were reinforced by Kiwi, who, after entering the hut, informed the rest of the crew he was off to an early lunch before heading to the ops room for a mid-afternoon briefing. Before leaving the hut, he threw a pillow at Freddie, who was still sound asleep and laughed, "Wake up, you cockney bastard; otherwise, you'll miss the best part of the day."

Freddie groaned and rolled back over to sleep.

Frank slumped back on his bed and opened up the large pile of mail sent to him from home. A smile came over his face as he read the first letter from his ten-year-old sister, Joan, about all that had been happening back home on Banyula. Over the next half hour, he perused through a number of letters and parcels and he was enveloped by a feeling of warmth by the good wishes extended to him from his family.

Frank's feelings of nostalgia were interrupted by the call to lunch. Afterwards, when the crew were back in the hut, Kiwi confirmed what they all suspected: that the 'show' was on again that night.

There was total silence in the ops room when Group Captain Young pulled back the strings of the curtains, revealing exactly the same flight path from the night before. He informed the gathered crews the photographs of the previous night indicated only a small percentage of the targets were hit and that it was vitally important they be destroyed. This was met with several expletives, which he hushed with a raised hand.

As was to become the custom, the gunnery leader looked at the gunners with disdain before stating they were to stay alert and not fall asleep, then adding with contempt, "and do try to come home alive!"

As Frank prepared for his second operation over Duisburg in as many nights, his level of anxiety was tempered by the letters he had received from home.

It was as if the Germans were waiting for them that night, as the flak was heavier than the previous evening. There was certainly luck on their side, but Kiwi's navigational skills were a significant factor in them avoiding being hit. Several aircraft plummeted to earth with sprog navigators on board, their inability to plot a course around the heaviest of the flak contributing to their demise. That night A for Apple managed to fly to the target, drop its bombs and set a course for home. They were lucky not to encounter any heavy flak or night fighters on the flight back home and, after an eight- hour operation, landed back at Marham in the early morning light. Although Frank's nerves had settled somewhat from his first operation, he was still on edge for the entire flight.

Chapter 8

Wednesday, March 18th 1942. RAF Marham Norfolk, East Anglia, England.

THREE MONTHS HAD passed since the crew's first flight over Duisburg and they had notched up eight operations. As well as six to Germany, they had flown two to the Netherlands, including bombing the Soesterberg Airfield in Utrecht and, in February 1942, the Philips Radio Works in Eindhoven. It was no coincidence Reg Chapman had been promoted to Flight Lieutenant during this period, as his skill as a pilot had gotten his crew out of a number of dangerous situations.

Frank had grown accustomed to his role and although he still got nervous before a flight, he had become a valued member of the crew for the skill in which he carried out his duties. There was an air of confidence about the crew now and their communication on the intercom was clear and concise.

They were to bomb the Krupp Armaments Works in Essen, Germany, for the first time. Essen in the Ruhr Valley was one of the major industrial towns and the armaments factory was a primary target. Krupp's steel works supplied material to produce tanks, artillery and munitions for the German war machine.

Frank nearly didn't make the flight though, after he had gotten himself into some strife the previous night. A for Apple was supposed to have flown to Essen the Wednesday night, but bad weather set in and all aircrews were grounded. The crew needed little encouragement to frequent the Fox and Hounds pub.

The air was filled with festivity when some of the squadron entered Marham's local. Frank, Jimmy, Kiwi, Jack, Nicko and Freddie were included in the group. Cigarette smoke hung thick in the air and the din made it difficult to hear what was being said.

The boys had just ordered their first round of beers when Freddie spotted a ukulele hanging up on the wall beside the bar and said to the others, "*Cor* blimey, this place aint *alf goen* off tonight. I *fink* we'll 'ave some fun lads."

Turning to the ukulele, Freddie approached the bar and said to the barmaid, Gladys.

"Mind if I play a song ,Glady?"

"Go for your life, *luv*," she replied.

With that, Freddie grabbed the ukulele.

"Can I 'ave everybody's attention?" With that, the din of the pub receded before Freddie continued. "*Fankyou.* Right, you lot, it's time for a song or two."

A collective cheer went up.

Freddie strummed a couple of chords and broke out into his rendition of *'Imagine Me on the Maginot Line.'*

> *You should see me out in France wearing my tin hat*
> *With shot and shell, it's worse – well, it's even worse than that*
> *Now imagine me on the Maginot Line*
> *Sitting on a mine in the Maginot Line*

Now it's turned out nice again
The army life is fine
French girls make a fuss of me
I'm not French, as you can see
But I know what they mean when they say 'oui oui.'
Down on the Maginot Line................

Over the next hour, Freddie entertained the patrons while he played both ukulele and the piano, which was positioned in the corner of the pub. Among the set he played were *Let's All Go Down the Strand*, Around *the Corner, Cleaning Windows* and some risqué versions of well- known songs, which had the pub singing along with great gusto and laughter.

Freddie Hill was a born entertainer and with his Cockney wit, he was to endear himself to the men of his squadron. Many a night was to be spent singing around the piano in the local pub and it was to take the sharp edge off the brutal reality that these airmen faced every time they took to the night skies.

Freddie was well into his set when Nicko spotted three WAAF (Women's Auxiliary Air Force) girls standing on their own.

"Crikey, get a load of those three sheilas. Not bad types, hey?" Nicko said.

"Not bloody wrong, Nicko. They look a bit lonely. We better go and have a yarn to them," said Jimmy.

Kiwi and Jack were at the bar ordering drinks when Frank, Jimmy and Nicko approached the three service women and introduced themselves. They were all English, aged in their early twenties and attractive. One was blonde, the other auburn, but the one who captured Frank's attention was the striking- looking brunette with shoulder-length hair, blue eyes and a gorgeous smile. With a grin, he said,

"How do you do? Frank's the name."

"Oh hi, my name is Geraldine," she said in an English accent. Frank's eyes met hers and he was smitten.

"Where do you come from?" Frank enquired.

Geraldine hesitated, but after he flashed a toothy grin at her she said, "I'm from Fairford in The Cotswolds in Gloucestershire."

She then lowered her eyes and asked, "What part of Australia are you from?"

"A little town named Bingara in the North West of New South Wales. I come off a wheat, sheep and cattle property."

"I've always wanted to meet an Australian from the outback."

"You wouldn't call where I come from the outback, but it's the fair dinkum Australian bush."

Geraldine flashed a smile and said, "My family are also woolgrowers in Fairford."

"How long have they been woolgrowers?" Frank asked.

"Oh, for generations."

As the rain fell on the pub's roof, Frank and Geraldine were both engrossed by each other's stories. Frank bought Geraldine a drink and the conversation moved along smoothly over the next half hour. The two were so absorbed in each other's company, they failed to notice a tall officer pushing his way through the throng of patrons. As he approached, Frank looked up and saw it was none other than Squadron Leader Burnham. Frank hadn't forgotten the dressing down he had given some of the boys on their arrival at Marham. Frank was green when arriving at Marham and was adamant he wouldn't let an officer talk to him like that again.

He gave Frank a steely gaze and said in a refined English accent, "Don't you colonials know how to salute an officer?"

"You'd have to be kidding, mate. We're in an operational

squadron and no one worries about that sort of crap around here," said Frank.

"What?" Burnham bellowed.

With Burnham's outburst, Freddie stopped playing the piano and the pub suddenly fell silent. He stepped closer to Frank and with his face only inches from his, barked.

"I'll have you arrested for insubordination," Burnham yelled.

"Go to hell, you drongo. Crikey, you really have got tickets on yourself. Didn't somebody tell you there's a war on and we don't carry on with that sort of pompous bullshit around here?" said Frank sarcastically.

"With your breathtaking impertinence to the side, what is a little scrapper like you doing with my girlfriend?" Burnham shouted.

By this stage, the entire pub was focused on the confrontation between the officer and Frank. Well and truly inebriated, Frank had a heavy dose of Dutch courage on board, so he didn't hold back. He took a gulp from his beer, looked around and said in a laconic drawl.

"I didn't ask her to marry me. Yet! Besides, we were having a right little sing-a long and Geraldine's having a ball."

A huge belly laugh went out from the patrons. They were genuinely delighted to see an Australian gunner sticking it up this toffee–nosed English officer, even though it could have him up in front of the "brass" on some serious charges.

"Right, that's the final straw. You haven't heard the end of this!"

With that, he grabbed Geraldine by the hand and marched her to the other side of the pub, where he made a call on the telephone.

The din slowly resumed and despite Frank's witty remarks

to the officer, it wasn't the charge of insubordination hanging over his head that worried him. It was more to do with the fact that he had the grass cut from underneath him and had lost the English beauty.

"Don't you worry about that Pommy upstart, Frank? We aren't going to let him destroy our night of festivities. Isn't that right, Nicko?" Jimmy said.

Nicko agreed, but was stunned by the bawling out Frank had received. Freddie resumed his position on the piano and the pub was in full voice once again, when within fifteen minutes, three guards entered the pub and marched up to Frank.

"You're under arrest for insubordination, Flight," one of the sergeants said.

"You would have to be bloody kidding?" Frank said.

"I'm afraid so, Flight. I know you're aircrew, but I have my orders," the sergeant said reluctantly.

The two of them grabbed Frank by the arm and marched him out of the pub before Burnham stopped them.

"You uncouth colonials think you can say anything, don't you? Let me remind you, you're not out in the back of beyond now. Think about that when you're cooling your heels in a cell."

The Fox and Hounds exploded into jeers as the two sergeants continued to march Frank out of the pub. Frank was stunned into silence and it wasn't until he was back at RAF Marham and locked up in a cell that he exploded.

"Get me Flight Lieutenant Chapman," he screamed while his hands were clenched on the bars of the cell door.

The sergeant who had locked up Frank was most apologetic.

"Sorry, Flight, but Burnham's a squadron leader, so I didn't have a leg to stand on."

Jimmy, Kiwi, Jack, Nicko and Freddie followed Frank

back to the lock- up and were in hysterics when they saw his predicament.

"Stop you're laughing, you blokes, and go and get the skipper will ya?" Frank barked.

Within half an hour, Reg Chapman appeared at Frank's cell, wiping the sleep from his eyes. On seeing his predicament, he gave Frank look of angst.

"What the bloody hell have you got yourself into, Frank?"

"I refused to salute Burnham and gave him a bit of lip for good measure."

"What?" Reg said incredulously.

"It's fair dinkum, skip."

"Doesn't he know we're in an operational squadron and we don't carry on with that nonsense, especially in the pub?" Reg said while running his fingers through his hair.

"You try telling that pompous bastard that," Frank yelled.

Seeing that Frank was becoming increasingly heated, he held his hand up.

"Leave it with me, Frank. I'll go and sort this thing out. In the meantime, you get some-shut eye and I'll see you in the morning."

With that, Reg and the others left Frank. The sergeant who had locked Frank up responded to his request for a couple more blankets. After handing them to him, Frank settled in for a cold night in the cell.

By mid-morning of the next day, Group Captain Young had received the charge sheet, which Burnham had both prepared and signed, and he was bemused by its contents. Shortly after, Reg managed to secure an appointment with the Groupy. On reading the charge, shrieks of laughter could be heard from his office as the Groupy and Reg discussed Burnham's complaint. The Groupy was on the telephone and had Frank released immediately. A trial was set down in his office within an hour and Reg appeared beside Frank's side.

Burnham appeared at the trial with contempt, confident he had nailed his man. He stood there looking smug as the Groupy read out the charge.

"What in heaven's name are you charging this man for?" the Groupy barked at Burnham.

With that, Burnham went as red as a beetroot.

"Don't you realise we dispense with such formalities as saluting in an operational squadron?"

"But sir, the Flight Sergeant showed a blatant disregard for protocol."

"Protocol? What a load of nonsense. You were in the pub for god's sake."

"But sir…"

The Groupy raised his hand for silence.

Burnham stood to attention with sweat pouring off his brow.

"On top of that, Flight Sergeant Casey has flown eight operations with his squadron and isn't some sprog gunner who has recently arrived at Marham. This is utterly ridiculous and I have decided this charge should be dismissed."

Frank stood there, trying his hardest not to smile.

"Everyone is dismissed except Squadron Leader Burnham."

Once out of the office, both Frank and Reg were closer enough to overhear the conversation between the Groupy and Burnham.

"Pack your bags, officer. You're being transferred out of the squadron."

"Transferred out of the squadron, sir?"

"Yes, you heard me correctly," he said tersely. "You're being transferred to RAF Waddington in Lincolnshire to be trained on the new Avro Lancaster bomber. Your new posting starts in three days' time."

Standing on the other side of the door, Reg and Frank both broke out into a huge, big grin and had to do their level best to contain themselves from breaking out into laughter.

Chapter 9

Monday, April 13ᵗʰ 1942. Krupp Armament Works, Essen, Germany

BY EARLY APRIL 1942, the crew had developed into a tight unit, completing nine operations. Although they had received their fair share of flak and had a number of close shaves with night fighters, they believed their success had been due to their professional approach to operations and a large dose of luck. Their operation to Essen in the Ruhr Valley in Germany on Monday 13th of April 1942 was to test the very limit of their skills. Nothing they had experienced before compared to what unfolded that night as they flew into the industrial heartland of the enemy.

Although the weather had closed in on Sunday night and grounded all aircrews, by lunchtime on Monday, it had cleared and the Meteorological Officer had given the all clear to fly that night.

There was a small amount of cloud around when they departed Marham at 9.30 pm but by the time they were approaching the Dutch coast, the cloud had set in, reducing visibility. The enemy pounded them with flak and the searchlights were relentless. Shortly after crossing the coast, an almighty big whoomph from below forced the aircraft upwards and it began to vibrate. Frank thought the aircraft was going to fall out of the sky and looked around frantically with his finger on the trigger for any marauding night fighters.

As Reg tried to gain altitude, the aircraft was labouring and it was apparent that something was seriously wrong.

"The starboard motor has copped a bad hit. I reckon she's pretty well buggered," Reg said.

"Is she going to make it to the target?" Kiwi asked.

Reg looked at his instrument panel several times. "It will be touch and go as the pressure is down."

"If there is anyone who can get *vis* bird to the target and back, it's you skip," Freddie said.

On they flew while Reg corkscrewed the aircraft, trying to avoid the searchlights and the flak that came with it. Frank could see a number of aircraft being hit by flak and watched them as they exploded into a mushroom of smoke, then spiralled downwards in a burning mass.

"Poor buggers," he said to himself.

They were still short of the German border when the pressure fell rapidly while the starboard motor was barely firing. Reg consulted his co-pilot Jones, and a decision was made to abort the flight. This was not made lightly as both Reg and Jones knew what the ramifications of this would be. They would have to face an enquiry. Shortly after turning the aircraft back, they copped more flak. Reg was able to avoid the worst of it by turning the aircraft to the left and avoiding the cones of light which were searching for them, but there was still damage done to the tip of the port wing. By this stage, the aircraft was only flying on one engine and to make matters worse; they were attacked by a night fighter, which both Frank and Jimmy were able to fight off before it disappeared into the darkness. Once they were flying over the channel, they dropped their bombs to avoid an explosion on landing.

As if things couldn't get much worse, as they came back over the English coast, they encountered a convoy of Lancasters heading out over the North Sea. The gunners in the Lancs decided the only aircraft heading towards home so early must have been an enemy one. Consequently, the Lancaster gunners peppered them, despite Jimmy firing the colours of the day (200 rounds of coloured red tracer mixed in with the ammunition).

Once again, Reg's skill behind the controls avoided a catastrophe, although they did incur some damage to the wings. As they were approaching home, Freddie reported to Reg that Marham was out of action due to heavy fog. They were diverted to RAF Downham Market in Norfolk. On landing, A for Apple was a sorry sight, with bullet holes and damage by flak rendering the aircraft inoperable.

After midnight, the crew tramped into the mess dressed in their flying apparel, which was met with looks of displeasure as the base was not an operational one. The crew's unsightly appearance was only exacerbated when it was made clear they wanted a drink. A balding, plump steward told them the bar and dining room was closed. This caused a real stir, and no prodding by the skipper could get him to change his mind. A row developed, which saw the intervention of a Warrant Officer.

"Don't you realise we are part of an operational squadron? We had to abort a flight to Essen tonight because of mechanical failure and we've had the shit shot out of our aircraft. Now get that bloody bar open quick smart, or there'll be some flaming trouble," Reg shouted to the ashen-faced W/O.

"I'll see what I can do," he said.

"You bloody well better, or there'll be hell to pay!" Reg shouted.

After a few minutes, he returned.

"I am sorry but I can't open the bar, but I can open the dining room so you can have some supper," he said nervously.

Reg stood there with a snarl on his face and, after what seemed like an eternity, said, "Okay, but they better serve up something decent in there!"

After fumbling with a bunch of keys, the W/O opened the door to the dining room. The crew were taken aback by the sheer opulence of the dining room where it was decked out with table cloths, crockery, cutlery and all the fineries one could imagine.

"This is a cut above what we are used to at Marham," said Kiwi.

"We won't be slumming it here tonight, boys," Jimmy said.

After a considerable amount of time, a beautifully prepared selection of sandwiches and pots of hot tea were served. Shortly after supper, Reg and Jones indicated they were ready for bed and were shown to the officers' quarters by an orderly.

It was late when an orderly ushered Frank, Jimmy, Kiwi and Freddie to their plush rooms compared to their ones at Marham. On entering the room, the orderly peered around to ensure no one was looking and produced a bottle of Johnnie Walker scotch whiskey.

"I am sorry about all the trouble here tonight and I appreciate what you lads are doing. My brother is a gunner in a Wimpy. This drink's on me," he said with a smile.

"Crikey, you're an absolute champion mate," Frank said, slapping him on the shoulder.

"Make sure you don't make too much noise though lads, because the W/O will have my balls for breakfast if he finds out I've knocked off that bottle of whiskey."

"Don't you worry if that W/O should come skulking around, we'll make sure to hide the *pimple and blotch*," whispered Freddie.

The four boys settled in for a nice session and more than a few drams of whisky were consumed as they contemplated how close they had come to not getting back to England. It was a satisfactory end to what had been a perilous night.

As A for Apple was unfit to fly the next day, the crew was transported by road back to Marham. As the bus drove them back to their base, both Reg and Jones contemplated on the outcome of their aborted operation and hoped they wouldn't be hauled over the coals. Meanwhile, Frank, Jimmy, Kiwi and Freddie were unusually quiet on the trip back as they were all nursing sore heads.

After lunch, they arrived back at Marham and Reg and Jones were ordered to see Wing Commander Atkinson immediately.

"This doesn't look good," Reg said to Jones as they walked to his office.

The Wingco wasted no time and bawled them out for not continuing to their target and dropping their payload. Reg protested and highlighted that the aircraft was only flying on one engine and had been badly shot up.

"Rubbish. The mechanics had the starboard motor running in next to no time. Besides, they said you could have easily flown the aircraft to Essen on one engine."

Reg raised his eyeballs to the ceiling, which only increased the fury of the Wingco.

"Watch your step, Flight Lieutenant, or I'll have both of you charged with LMF."

A shudder went up the spine of both Reg and Jones for the mere mention of those words. Lack of moral fibre covered all forms of despair, defeatism and cowardice and no airman wanted that label bestowed upon them by the RAF. Although the two officers didn't know it at the time, only non–commissioned officers could be charged with LMF, but officers couldn't. Regardless, it left a bitter taste in both of their mouths.

When Reg arrived at the dining room, he didn't mention what had been said, although he was fuming to have his ability and, in particular, his courage questioned. He believed he should have been commended for getting his crew home safely in an aircraft that could have dropped out of the sky.

That night in the mess, there was a sombre mood among the crew, as six aircraft from the previous night's operation had not returned home. Several men they had trained with at the Bombing and Gunnery school at Evans Head were among the missing. At first, it was a kick in the guts to see so many aircrews lost on operations and to sit in the mess and see empty seats at the dining table. In time, they got used to it and many of the men, including Frank, blocked out their emotions, as it was the only way they could deal with the trauma of losing so many mates. It was always difficult to watch the Committee of Adjustment come through a hut and place all the belonging of a deceased airman on the bed before packing them away. It was so final, and for Frank, it only reinforced how close they came to an end every time they took to the skies. He contemplated that yesterday he could be laughing and joking with a fellow aircrew, only to see his belongings packed away for good the next day. Frank constantly wondered if his number was up next.

On the bright side, Geraldine entered the mess and informed the crew they were to get a new aircraft to fly. Because she worked in the Sector Control Room as a plotter, she had overheard the Groupy telling the Wingco they were to receive another aircraft. She swore everybody to secrecy as she would be in trouble if news got back to headquarters about what she had told them. It was a welcome relief for the crew as they all believed that even before their flight to Essen, A for Apple was past its use by date. Before leaving the table where the crew was having supper, she flashed a big smile at Frank. Frank and Geraldine had become an item after Burnham had been transferred from Marham. Compounding their breakup was Geraldine finding Burnham's actions repugnant after having Frank arrested for insubordination. Like so many relationships with aircrew, there's was intense, for they both knew Frank could soon be gone.

Chapter 10

Friday, May 1ˢᵗ 1942. Raid over Cologne, Germany.

AFTER THE OPERATION over Essen, the crew had been allocated another Wimpy. C for Charlie was a later model Wellington and a much more superior aircraft to fly.

Fresh in Reg's mind was the stinging rebuke that both Jones and he had received from the Wingco for aborting the mission to the Krupp Armaments Works. What grated Reg even more was that the high command at Marham had decommissioned A for Apple, as it was too severely damaged. There was no apology forthcoming from them that Reg had made the correct decision that night, and it was only his skill and blind luck that saved the whole crew from perishing.

On Friday, 1st of May 1942, the crew's tenth operation was to Cologne, Germany. The first sign the crew knew something different was on was at the briefing when not only the Groupy and Wingco were present, but the Group Air Vice-Marshall. He was a tall Englishman with short, dark hair and a moustache. Aged in his mid-fifties, he wasted no time in getting down to business.

"Righto chaps, I suppose you're all wondering what I am doing here. Well, the fact is that tonight we are going to throw the lot at Gerry. We are going to hit the enemy with 410 aircraft.

The Wingco drew the curtains back and a red tape went from Marham right across Germany to Cologne. There were rumblings among the gathered airmen before the Wingco continued. He informed them that tonight Bomber Command was going to strike at the heart of Germany.

"So we are to be guinea pigs, are we, sir?" Frank said.

There was laughter met with a contemptuous look from the Wingco in Frank's direction.

When the frivolity had died down, he informed everybody they were to put on their best show and to remind Gerry who was going to win this war. The squadron was to go in at eighteen thousand feet and the raid was to be carried out in ninety minutes, starting at 1.30 am and finishing at 3.00 am.

"This will be interesting," Kiwi said, turning to the rest of the crew.

The Wingco then handed it back to the Air Vice – Marshall, where he spent the next half hour giving further details about the operation, including the fact they would be carrying an increased bomb load.

The one consolation for the crew was at least they had a new aircraft to fly in what could prove to be a tricky operation. This operation would prove to be a tricky one indeed.

As C for Charlie climbed into the night sky, the engines strained and the aircraft shuddered under the weight of the increased bomb load.

They had been flying for some time and Frank was peering out into the darkness, deep in thought about the impending operation, when Kiwi reported they were approaching the enemy coast. They crossed the Dutch coast when suddenly flak rose up to meet them. Reg, conscious of being over the target on time, chose to climb rather than take a nosedive to avoid the interruptions.

They continued to fly, trying to avoid the flak as the aircraft laboured under its huge load of bombs. All the while, Kiwi was monitoring C for Charlie and it was clear to him the aircraft was not gaining the appropriate height and lacking in speed.

"You'll have to get this kite moving skip, or we'll never make the target in time," said Kiwi.

"I'm doing my best, navigator, but with this increased bomb load, this girl isn't responding."

"Well, you'll have to hurry on; otherwise, we are going to be late to the target."

"I'm doing my bloody well best to get this aircraft to the correct height and speed, so give me a break," Reg snapped.

There was a long pause before Kiwi responded.

"Sorry, skip. I know you're doing your best, but we must get there on time, as we have a lot of aircraft around us."

As C for Charlie lumbered towards the target, sprog pilots, confused, flew off course and into the merciless flak from below. Frank could see aircraft being hit and exploding into flames as their own aircraft rocked back and forth with flak narrowly missing them.

They were expecting a barrage of flak as they approached Cologne, but to their surprise, the enemies' hate was directed towards the 'heavies', flying a few thousand feet above them.

"Shit, if those heavies let their payload go before we reach the target, we'll be stuffed," said Frank.

"Too bloody right. I don't want to be around when they let

go of their load," Jimmy said, before moving back to the bomb aimer's position.

On they flew, all the while being rocked back and forth by flak while cones of light rose from below, desperately trying to latch onto them. They were fifteen minutes late to the target and flying two thousand feet too low as C for Charlie lumbered towards its appointment.

"Come on, drop the bloody bombs," Frank said to himself.

Reg stayed true to his course while Kiwi directed him to the target as the tension mounted among the crew.

"Steady skip, left a touch, keep steady, right a little, okay hold that line…okay bombs away," Jimmy said finally.

There was collective relief from the crew when Jimmy said those words. Reg kept the aircraft on a steady course for twenty seconds so the target could be photographed and just as he was about to turn, the heavies from above dropped their incendiaries. Miraculously, none of their payload hit the aircraft, but Frank could see others being smashed. As Reg turned for home, the flak seemed to increase, and as it did, their aircraft was rocked back and forth, but fortunately, none hit them. Some of the heavies were not so fortunate, and a number of them, after being hit by flak, came tumbling downwards, one in particular narrowly missing the starboard wing of C for Charlie.

Frank had a bird's-eye view of the havoc wreaked by the bombers and Cologne was an inferno as bombs, incendiaries and flaming aircraft added to the fiery maelstrom below. In the distance, he could see the twin spires of Cologne Cathedral as all around the historical landmark burned.

"This is madness to destroy such a beautiful structure." Frank thought to himself. Although it received damage, the cathedral managed to survive the war.

Then, out of the night sky, the Luftwaffe night fighters came to exact their revenge. Both Frank and Jimmy fired at them incessantly, managing to thwart the attack by the German flyers. As they flew towards home, aircraft were being hit by both flak and gunfire by the night fighters, but the crew was blessed as they avoided any serious damage to their aircraft.

They were a couple of hundred miles from Cologne and the flak and night fighters had abated somewhat. The crew had time to gather their composure and assess any damage to the aircraft and themselves when a fanatic came out of the night sky. This pilot must have been touched on the forehead by Hitler himself, for he was determined to get himself a kill this night. Jonesy had his head in the astrodome, inspecting the damage done to the aircraft and did not see the fighter when a stream of horizontal tracer came straight for him. One consolation is he wouldn't have known what hit him, for it was a direct hit. None of the crew was aware of what had happened to their co-pilot as they were too occupied with the Nazi trying to blow them out of the sky. He came from every direction and both Frank and Jimmy fired like men possessed. The Messerschmitt Bf 110 had just turned and was heading dead astern when Frank screeched into the intercom.

"Skip starboard, quick!"

Reg reacted and sharply turned the aircraft to the left with lightning-quick reflexes, not before Frank and the German directed gunfire towards each other. The result being that Frank's gunfire ripped off the tip of the port wing of the 110, but the German's bullets ripped a hole through the bottom of his rear turret and Frank received shrapnel to his right foot.

"Shit, I've been hit in the bloody foot and it's burning like hell!" Frank screamed into the intercom. The rest of the crew were oblivious to Frank's expletive as they were focused on the fanatic heading directly for them.

Although damaged and overshooting his mark, the German was not deterred and he turned, and out of the night he came, this time heading straight for the nose of C for Charlie.

By this stage, Jimmy was back in the front gunner's position.

"Turn port now!" Jimmy screamed.

Reg turned the aircraft viciously, and on came the night fighter. Jimmy waited until he was within firing range. When he was close enough, he swung the turret around to starboard and let loose with a burst of gunfire that smashed the windscreen of the Messerschmitt. The 110 careered out of control, narrowly missing C for Charlie before it spiralled downwards in what seemed an eternity, eventually hitting the ground and exploding into a fireball.

"Great work, Jimmy. You got the bastard with a direct hit." Reg said in exaltation.

"Thanks, skip. Either I hit him or we would have worn him."

The crew were so preoccupied with Jimmy's kill, and the chatter was constant on the intercom that they forgot about Jonesy.

"There seems to be a lot of wind and noise coming from the astrodome. You better get up there Freddie and see how Jonesy is?" Reg said.

"Righto skip," said Freddie.

Freddie made his way to the astrodome behind where he was seated. What he saw made him scream in horror. Jonesy's head had been shot up, and after vomiting, Freddie staggered back in fright at the dreadful sight. He groped his way forward to his position and relayed what had happened to the rest of the crew.

"Jonesy's dead. He's an absolute mess," he sobbed.

The crew was stunned into silence and a cold shiver went up

Frank's spine. He forgot about his foot, which was throbbing in pain. There was a long silence when Reg took charge.

"There's nothing we can do for Jonesy, so be on alert for any more night fighters," Reg said.

They flew back to Marham with no further engagements with the enemy and were given the all clear to land immediately. Frank staggered from the rear turret, his foot throbbing with pain. He looked at the bloody and mutilated body of Jonesy, who was lying on the floor, all shot to pieces. Frank shook at the horrific sight. As Jonesy was blocking his path, he had to manhandle him before stepping over him. As a result, Frank's hands were covered in blood and he stared in disbelief at what remained of the rugby- mad Welshman. The sight of his mangled body would be etched in Frank's memory for the rest of his life.

Frank was soon driven away in an ambulance to the sick headquarters. On seeing the seriousness of Frank's injury, he was taken to a nearby RAF hospital. No sooner had the crew departed than the erks (RAF ground crew) were on the scene and busily cleaned up the remains of Jonesy, hosing out the aircraft and scrubbing the area with brushes.

As Frank rode in the back of the ambulance, he breathed a huge sigh of relief.

It was a sad feeling in the mess that night as the crew ate their supper. Jonesy was killed, but two aircraft from their squadron were missing as were countless from the operation. Many of the men missing were great mates with the crew, but they were all grateful they had survived one hell of a show.

In silence, they sat until Jimmy said, "We've been through so many ops together. Duisburg, Essen and now Cologne, to mention a few. Now, to lose Jonesy and have Frank injured is a big blow."

Freddie was sitting in silence and picking at his food, which was unusual for him, as he usually ate like a horse. At the mention of Jonesy's name and the sight that had greeted him in the aircraft, he started to rock back and forth before throwing his head in his hands and sobbing uncontrollably.

"Poor Jonesy, what a way to cop it!" Freddie cried.

"You okay Freddie?" said Kiwi, placing his hand on his shoulder.

Freddie was inconsolable and sat at the meal table, continuing to cry.

Freddie was far from okay and the strain of what he had witnessed coupled with his house being destroyed and his brother killed in the London blitz, had pushed him over the edge.

Jimmy and Kiwi managed to get Freddie down to the sickbay, where he was attended to by a young English medico who spoke with a plum in his mouth. Jimmy explained what he had just witnessed and how he had cracked under the pressure.

After an initial inspection, which included giving Freddie a couple of slaps on the face, he concluded by saying. "Cracked up? A likely story! This man is a shirker, and if he isn't careful, I will have him charged with LMF!"

"A shirker? Why, I've got a mind to kick your arse in," Jimmy growled.

Jimmy and Kiwi continued to glare at the doctor and their body language suggested he was about to get decked. He quickly summoned two orderlies to the door, where Freddie was quickly whisked away. That day, the crew lost both Jonesy and Freddie. Freddie became another statistic of the war, largely never discussed, and he was never to return to the squadron.

As Jimmy and Kiwi watched Freddie being led away, Kiwi handed his front gunner a cigarette.

"Ya blood's worth bottling, old mate," Jimmy said while placing a Woodbine in his mouth. Small pleasures like this were a highlight in a very bleak world.

By the time Frank arrived at the hospital, he was physically incapacitated, and mentally at an all-time low. It wasn't only the macabre sight of Jonesy shot to pieces, but losing such an integral part of the crew. Frank and Jonesy had formed a close bond and their mutual love of rugby had cemented their friendship. The last thing he wanted to do was fly in an operational crew again. As far as he was concerned, he would have been just as happy to be classified unfit for operations.

Frank had been at the hospital for a day when he was operated on to remove shrapnel from his foot. A few days later, he was lying in bed in a state of depression when he received a visit from Geraldine.

The mere sight of her cheered him immensely and he felt his spirits lift. Geraldine spent the best of an hour with Frank, and when she left, his depression had lifted.

A couple of days later, Frank felt like an inspection of the wards was what he needed. After securing a set of crutches, what he saw left him in disbelief. Here was the best of Bomber Command's young men, shattered and broken. As Frank hobbled through the wards, gathered around him were men with numerous injuries. There were men missing limbs, eye injuries to head wounds and belly lacerations, to name a few. As Frank surveyed the flower of his generation, he felt his afflictions were superficial compared to many of those who were at the hospital. He sat down and spoke too many of the aircrews who had received their wounds from all over the battlefields of the occupied territories. His spirits were buoyed by the humour and character of many men he spoke to, regardless of their injuries.

A few days later, Frank was hobbling around the beautiful gardens which surrounded the hospital when he came across a rickety old timber gate with *Do Not Enter* written on it. Curious, he entered anyway. He wandered around for a while, scratching his head, trying to make out what this place was, when he heard an Australian voice behind a hedge.

"Hey mate, we're over here," he said to Frank.

Frank walked over and noticed four men seated around a table having a game of cards. From a distance, Frank guessed something was not quite right with them. As he walked closer, he could see they were all burns victims. They were missing ears, noses, or eyebrows and their faces were grotesquely mutilated. Frank stopped in his tracks and was lost for words at such a sight. The man who had addressed him had no ears and took the lead, seeing Frank's discomfort, "Don't be alarmed, mate. We won't bite you."

"It's just that you're so ..." Frank said, fumbling with his words.

"It's okay, mate. I know you feel embarrassed, but we'd like to have a yarn with you," said the Aussie.

After composing himself, Frank said to him, "You're an Aussie?"

"Yep, I certainly am. So are the other three blokes and I can hear from your accent, so are you. The name's Norm Newcombe," he said, extending his hand.

After Norm introduced the other three, Frank sat down and spoke to them. He felt incredibly embarrassed and could not look at them, so he dropped his eyes to the ground.

"Don't feel embarrassed about our appearance. I know it's a shock, but regardless of the way we look, we're still human beings," said one of the other men.

"Crikey fellas, if you don't mind me saying, but my problems pale into insignificance compared to yours," Frank said.

Norm shrugged his shoulders. "They keep us hidden over here as our injuries are too disturbing for the average Joe blow to cop."

Frank chatted with them for the next half hour and although he never felt comfortable in their company when he left, he felt grateful his injuries were only minor compared to theirs. When he departed, he had no intention of returning.

The next day he felt compelled to revisit the burns patients once again. This time, the mood was more relaxed and there was a lot of laughter as they swapped yarns. For Frank, it only reinforced the compassion he always felt for the underdog and those less fortunate than him. He believed we were all the same, regardless of our appearance. Frank was to visit the burns patients regularly during his stay in hospital and each time he did, he felt his own problems diminish.

Frank had got to know the young English medico, Dr Housego, who had been looking after him. He was a decent man with a lot of compassion for the airmen who had been injured as well as Frank, and as a result, had developed a good rapport with him. He informed Frank, because of his injury and ten operations under his belt, he could have him classified unfit for active duty. Dr Housego informed Frank he could have him transferred to a training school. Frank had not been keen on operational flying after arriving at the hospital, but after meeting many of the patients who were a lot worse off than him, he felt as though he should still do his bit when he had recovered from his injuries. Frank's commitment to staying in operational flying was secured after he asked the doctor if he would be labelled LMF. Dr Housego said there was a possibility in which Frank bellowed, "Be buggered if they're going to put a label like that on me, Doc. I don't want to be known as a coward. I'll return to ops, thank you very much." Frank tapped his fingers on the office desk and continued, "besides, my best mate Jimmy is still flying and I don't want to leave him up there all by himself."

From that moment, Frank took on a hard-nosed approach to flying and was determined that no matter what happened, he would survive his operational tour at all costs. It was an approach that ultimately saved his life.

At the beginning of week three, Frank was sitting in a chair in a sun room when he was paid a visit by Jimmy, Nicko, Walshy and Kiwi, which lifted his spirits. With the death of Jonesy, Freddie being discharged medically unfit and Frank injured, the crew had been given some well-earned leave. On closer inspection, Frank could see Jimmy was sporting the ribbon of the DFM (Distinguished Flying Medal) on his tunic.

"Well, I'll be buggered. Old Cruikshank has gone and got himself a gong," Frank said with a grin.

"Reg recommended Jimmy for the award immediately after our return from Cologne. He reckons we would have been a goner if that night fighter had got to us first," Kiwi said, leaning against the door.

"If the truth be known, Frank, half of this belongs to you because you had a crack at the Nazi fanatic first and managed to blow off the tip of his wing."

"You won it fair and square, Jimmy, as you blew the bastard out of the sky," Frank said.

They sat and had a long yarn where Jimmy informed Frank the news had come through that 377 Squadron was to be converting from the Wellington bombers to the four-engine Avro Lancaster bombers. He said the first of them was to be delivered to their new base at RAF Elsham Wolds, Lincolnshire. Frank was enthusiastic about the opportunity to fly the heavy bomber as he had heard good reports about them flying at a higher altitude. Frank informed the boys he had another three weeks to spend in the hospital before returning to the squadron.

Chapter 11

Sunday, May 31st 1942. RAF Elsham Wolds, Lincolnshire

FRANK ARRIVED AT his new base at Elsham Wolds, Lincolnshire, to be met with a warm welcome from many of his mates from 377 Squadron. There were unfamiliar faces on the base, as many of the aircrew were KIA or MIA.

Frank had been at Elsham Wolds only a few days when he argued with a Flight Sergeant from another squadron. It was further proof of the tough-nosed approach he had embraced since his accident.

Frank and a sprog pilot from 377 Squadron were out walking on the perimeter track of Elsham Wolds one afternoon when they came across a Flight Sergeant idly sitting on his push bike smoking a cigarette. Noticing the sprog pilot, the Flight Sergeant made it clear what he thought his chances were of surviving.

"You won't last a week of operations!" said the cocky Englishman.

Without hesitating, Frank stepped in and gave him a mouthful.

"Don't you come here with your negative crap, you smart-arse," he said with his finger raised.

"This bloke may be a sprog, but he's got a heap of guts and will last the distance. Is that clear?" Frank said, only inches from the Flight Sergeant's face.

He stared at Frank wide eyed.

"Now piss off!" Frank barked.

Frank turned to the sprog pilot and said, "Let's get one thing straight if you are to survive. No LMF, no negativity, no self-pity. Survival at all costs. Is that clear?"

He nodded in agreement to Frank.

As well as being acquainted with a new base, Frank met three new crew members. With a crew of seven on the Lancaster, it included a flight engineer who sat to the right of Reg. His job was to control the aircraft's mechanical, hydraulic, electrical and fuel systems. This position was taken by twenty-four-year-old Flight Lieutenant Arthur Harvey DFC (Distinguished Flying Cross) from Norwich, England. Arthur was training to be a doctor before the war and with eighteen operations under his belt in both Wellingtons and four engine Halifaxes, he was an experienced airman. Arthur was a very measured individual and a gentleman and was a welcome addition to the crew. He had earned his DFC after the stricken Wellington he was a co-pilot in, was severely damaged after an operation to the German industrial town Bremen. With his pilot seriously wounded, Arthur took over the controls of the damaged Wellington and managed to land it on one engine. In place of Freddie Hill as the wireless operator was Roland (Rolly) Curtis, a Canadian from Battleford, Saskatchewan. Rolly Curtis was a twenty-three-year-old truck driver with ten operations on Wellingtons behind him. A no-nonsense character, Rolly had a dry sense of humour probably forged from the –20 degree Celsius temperatures often encountered in Battleford during the winter months.

Graham Farquhar, a railway signalman from Aberfoyle in Scotland, was the bomb aimer. Graham was a wily Scotsman with a total of eight operations on Halifaxes. He had a penchant for making a quick buck with many of his ingenious schemes and his quick wit endeared himself to the crew. He had a favourite line, which he would often quote:

"You're a long time died, so lighten up; you've got plenty of time to be a misery after you die."

The navigator was Kiwi, and Jimmy took over the position of mid- upper gunner, while Frank remained the rear gunner.

When 377 Squadron watched the first of the Avro Lancasters swoop down to Elsham like a flock of majestic birds, a collective cheer went up to those gathered at the base. After the heavy losses Bomber Command had incurred, the Lancaster was seen as a saviour.

The Avro Lancaster was a heavy bomber powered by four V12 Rolls Royce Merlin Engines. It was designed by Roy Chadwick and could carry a fuel and bomb load equivalent to the aircraft's weight. Its length was over 69 feet, a wingspan of 102 feet and a height of 20 feet 6 inches. The Lancaster could operate at a higher altitude of up to 23,500 feet and could comfortably fly a greater distance than was needed for bombing missions. It had a maximum speed of 232 mph (373 kph) while its cruising speed was 200 mph (322 kph) and it had a range of 2530 miles (4073km). The Lancaster could carry 4000, 8000, and 12000lb bombs plus small incendiaries. The front and mid- upper guns had twin Browning .303 machine guns, while the rear turret had four Browning .303 machine guns. It was the superior bomber of its time and seen as the one aircraft that could take the war to the heart of Nazi Germany, and by doing so, became an icon of World War Two.

The conversion from the Wimpy to the Lancaster was an eight- week non-operational training course. As an experienced crew, they were given a new Lancaster to fly as opposed to some of the old worn out crates that some sprog crews were given in the Heavy Conversion Units.

It wasn't without its challenges in learning how to fly, and one afternoon after returning home to Elsham from a training flight, a mishap took place that, if somewhat funny, could have been dire.

Squadron Leader, Ian Meads DFC, was a decorated New Zealand pilot who had completed one operational tour. He was the crew's instructor and a bit condescending towards his Australian understudy Reg Chapman. He was, nevertheless, an excellent pilot.

Towards the end of their conversion period, the mishap occurred while returning to Elsham one afternoon. Ian was at the controls and was taxing down the runway. He was deep in conversation with Reg, instructing him on some of the finer points of flying the Lancaster. He failed to notice a fuel truck travelling up a side track that was running parallel to the aircraft. The truck driver, who was nonchalantly going about his business, got the shock of his life when the shadow of the Lancaster loomed over the top of his truck. With no ability to outrun the fast- moving aircraft, the driver bailed out of the cabin, only to see the prop of the Lancaster carve a swathe of destruction through the cabin of the stricken tanker. Red-faced, Ian was hauled over the coals for his mistake and his attitude towards Reg and the rest of the crew changed considerably.

The changeover period wasn't without its fun though, such

as the time Reg was returning to Elsham, not long before the end of their conversion training.

Reg was flying the aircraft without Ian and came across a wheat field. Bringing the Lancaster down perilously close to the ground, he cut a swath through the field with the four props, cutting the heads off the wheat stalks. As a result, the crew was hysterical at Reg's flying skills. The irate farmer complained to the RAF, but the perpetrator was never found and it remained the crew's secret.

The first operation for the new crew of Lancaster F for Freddie was to Dortmund in the Ruhr Valley. The raid consisted of 590 aircraft made up of Mosquitoes, Lancasters, Halifaxes, Wellingtons, and Stirlings.

The crew thought it was more than coincidental that their aircraft should be named Freddie, for close to their thoughts was the loss of both Freddie Hill and Bryn Jones. The countless airmen who the crew had known and lost had hit them hard, but none more so than Freddie and Jones. Their loss only reinforced how fragile their existence was.

There was an unwritten rule in the RAF that when a mate was lost you drank to his memory once and never mentioned his name again. For this reason, Freddie and Jones were never spoken about openly.

Not all problems on an operation concerned the enemy, as Frank found out, coming back from the raid over Dortmund. They had dropped their bombs and were twenty minutes into their return flight when Frank contacted Reg on the radio and requested to leave the turret.

"What for Tailie?" Reg asked.

"I've been passing wind, skip, and well ah….well."

"Come on, what is it, Tailie?" Reg said impatiently.

"Well, to be perfectly honest with you, skip, I think I've come on a bit strong and made a bit of a mess of myself back here," Frank said.

There was silence on the intercom before Reg responded.

"I am sorry, flight, but there are hundreds of night fighters out there wanting to blow us out of the sky, so you will have to stay put in the turret," said Reg.

A few hours later, they were over the North Sea when Reg remembered Frank's predicament. He contacted Frank and told him he could leave the turret and clean himself up. There was a long pause before Frank responded.

"I don't think I'll bother now, skip, as it seems to have baked hard!"

Over the next three months, between early August and late-October 1942, they flew eight more operations bringing Frank's total to 18. These operations included Essen twice, Duisburg, Mannheim, Dortmund and Baltrum in the North Sea, where the crew went gardening, 'planting vegetables' (mines).

On Frank's 18th op to Frankfurt, in early November, the flight went off without any trouble. They found their target, bombed it and were heading home. The ever reliable Kiwi got into some strife with his navigation after Reg diverted the air-craft while trying to avoid both flak and night fighters.

After crossing the Dutch coast, Frank called out flak while Jimmy alerted Reg to a couple of marauding night fighters in the distance. Kiwi had taken an astro fix from a star shot, but it showed F for Freddie was 50 miles out from where they should have been. Kiwi wanted to take another shot from the astro dome, but Rolly was busily trying to repair a fault in his radio set under the cover of his black curtain.

"I need you to turn that light out, Rolly, so I can take a star shot from the dome," Kiwi said hastily.

"I've got a fault in this set I need to fix," said the cantankerous Canadian in his nasally drawl.

"It'll have to wait until I take this shot, because I can't get an accurate fix with your light on," snapped Kiwi.

"Oh, be damned, buddy, do what you have to do then," Rolly growled.

With Reg eager for Kiwi to fix their position, the pressure was on for the normally unflappable navigator to set their course. Suddenly, Kiwi was overcome with fear as he realised the crew's fate was in his hands. With high - level cloud setting in, it was hard for Kiwi to take an accurate shot, but Reg flew on, trying to make radio contact with the base.

"Hello, Rising Dawn! Hello, Rising Dawn! Hello, Rising Dawn! This is Olive H Hog! This is Olive H Hog! Are you receiving me?' Are you receiving me?" Reg said anxiously.

But there was no reply.

"Where the blazes are we, navigator? I need some astro to get us out of this mess." Reg barked.

"I'm doing my best, skip."

"Well, make it snappy, will you?" Reg growled.

With that, Kiwi jumped up into the dome and shortly after, hoping he was correct, relayed their position to Reg.

On they flew into the ever- increasing cloud cover while Reg tried desperately to make radio contact with Elsham, but to no avail. Then finally there was a crackle on the radio, and a beautiful, modulated English female voice came over.

"Hello Olive H Hog! Hello Olive H Hog! Hello Olive H Hog! This is Peaky Mountain bluff replying! I repeat, this is Peaky Mountain bluff replying."

For the crew, hearing that beautiful English female voice was like an angel sent from heaven. It was like somebody opening the door to a home with a warm fireplace after standing outside in the snow for hours.

Then, out of nowhere, they saw the searchlights of the coastal town Mablethorpe in Lincolnshire and Reg let out a huge sigh while Kiwi wiped the sweat from his brow.

"Phew, that was close," Kiwi muttered.

Even though they were 50 miles south of Elsham, they were in England and never had such a feeling of relief come over the crew. It was more evidence that proved even an experienced navigator like Kiwi could get confused in the heat of battle, let alone a sprog airman.

On returning to Elsham, Frank received a pleasant surprise when Geraldine met him. She had applied for a transfer from Marham to Elsham, and it had just come through.

On Tuesday 29th of December 1942, F for Freddie, along with another 700 aircraft from other squadrons and bases, were given the job of bombing Berlin. It was Frank's 22nd operation in what was a long and dangerous flight deep into the heart of Germany.

They reached their target, managing to avoid the worst of the flak, and were well into their long trek home when a lone night fighter attacked them. As a result, the hydraulics was severely damaged and the rear turret was rendered useless, so Frank was merely a passenger for the flight back home. On top of that, a fire broke out in the fuselage, which he managed to put out. Reg showed considerable skill to keep his crew cool while he outmanoeuvred the night fighter, eventually shaking him off. F for Freddie was able to safely return to Elsham, albeit with some serious damage to the aircraft.

For his outstanding skill, Reg was awarded the Distinguished Flying Cross.

After the operation to Berlin, Reg was promoted to Squadron Leader and the crew was given two weeks' leave. The operation was also Arthur Harvey's 30th and final op. A mad party was held with the ground crew at Elsham the night after they returned from Berlin, which happened to be New Year's Eve. The crew was worse for wear, and Frank had a bad hangover, but in these early days of his drinking, he was able to recover in a short time.

Frank and Jimmy hightailed it out of Elsham and took a train down to London on New Year's Day. On arriving in London, they headed to The Boomerang Club. The Boomerang Club cared for Australian personnel from all three services. Frank and Jimmy felt a world away from where they had just come. While they were there, they enjoyed hot showers, played billiards, had a haircut and took in several shows at the West End.

Graham Farquhar had been on leave some months before and had recommended they pay a visit to a restaurant named Dirty Dicks, situated just off Fleet Street. He informed them the steaks were great and they would kick themselves if they didn't pay the place a visit. Being country boys and starved of some home-grown beef, Frank and Jimmy made a beeline for the establishment after consuming their share of pints at a local pub.

Dirty Dicks was dark and dingy with Victorian-style upholstery on the seating. It resembled a scene out of a Charles Dickens novel. Frank and Jimmy had taken a seat and were settling in when Dick himself approached the table to take their order. Dick was a short, fat, shady looking character with a dark complexion sporting a five o'clock shadow. He had a front tooth missing and looked like he would have been more at home in a fortune teller booth than running a restaurant.

"Hello, gentlemens. I'm Dick. How can I help you?" he said in a Middle Eastern accent.

"G'day mate, I'm Frank and this here is me mate, Jimmy."

"Please to meet your acquaintance, Mr Frank and Mr *Shimmy*," he said with a big grin.

"We'll both have the juiciest steak you have to offer. Thanks, Dick." Jimmy beamed while he smacked his hands together.

"Certainly sir, and how would you gentlemen like your steaks done?"

"Nice and burnt on the outside," Frank said with a laconic grin.

"Absolutely. And for you, sir?" Dick said to Jimmy.

"Take a blow torch to mine, also old mate," Jimmy said, grinning from ear to ear.

"Can I have mine served with vegetables and gravy, thanks mate?" Frank said.

"Certainly, sir."

"The same for me also, mate," said Jimmy.

"It will be my pleasure, gentlemens," Dick said before about-facing and making his way to the kitchen.

After ten minutes, Dick exited the kitchen, holding two steaming plates. Jimmy got a whiff of the contents and said to Frank, "Crikey, that smells good. I'm that hungry I could eat the arse out of a flaming rocking horse." To which Frank replied. "Too bloody right, mate."

"Enjoy gentlemens!" Dick said with his customary grin.

No sooner had Dick left than the boys wasted no time tucking into their meals.

"Crikey, this is a good feed,"

"You're not wrong, Jimmy, though this steak has a rather unusual taste!"

"It tastes all right to me," Jimmy said while munching on his piece of meat.

"It's not that there is anything wrong with it. It's just got a peculiar taste, that's all," Frank said, prodding at the meat with his knife.

When they had finished, they both sat back, satisfied with their feed. Frank was looking at the menu, deciding if he should order some dessert, when he noticed something written in fine print at the bottom of the page. Frank's eyes were wide open and glued to the bottom of the menu when Jimmy said,

"Crikey Frank, you look like you've just discovered Tutankhamen's Tomb!"

"Tutankhamen's Tomb be buggered, Jimmy," Frank said, before looking around. "Do you know what we've been eating?"

"What?"

"It says here that under health regulations, this restaurant has permission to sell horse meat," Frank said in a whisper.

"Bloody horse meat! Why the little filthy Gypo," Jimmy screeched.

"Shhh, keep it down, will ya?" Frank whispered.

"Keep it down, be buggered, Frank. Fancy serving up that crap to us."

Just then, Dick appeared at the door to the kitchen.

"Everything okay, gentlemens?"

"Yeah, everything is just beaut over hear, thanks Dick," said Frank.

"Be buggered; its beaut Dicko. What's this crap you've been serving up instead of steak?"

Dick approached the table and, with hands outstretched,

said, "Please, kind sirs, the war is on and meat is hard to come by. We have permission to sell horse meat. Did you not like what you ate?"

Jimmy looked at Frank for what seemed like an eternity and said,

"Yeah, it was pretty good, but I never imagined eating a horse. We both come off farms in Australia and the thought of eating one of our prized horses is abhorrent to us."

"If you are not satisfied, I will not charge you for your meals."

Frank looked at Jimmy and said, "It's okay, Dick. We actually enjoyed the meal. It's just that it surprised the living daylights out of us when we realised we had been eating horse meat."

Frank and Jimmy were to eat at Dirty Dicks several times over the next week and were served up chicken, but they were sure it was a crow or seagull they actually consumed.

After the first week, Frank and Jimmy went their separate ways as Geraldine had been granted a week's leave, where she made her way to London. Over the next week, Frank and Geraldine enjoyed the sights of London, including a show at the West End and visiting some of the sights.

Regardless of what Frank had been served in London, his stay had been an enjoyable one and when he and Geraldine returned to Elsham, he felt refreshed.

Chapter 12

Friday, January 15ᵗʰ 1943. Elsham Wolds, Lincolnshire

THE NIGHT AFTER Frank arrived back at Elsham, Jimmy and he were at The Dying Gladiator pub at Brigg, not far from Elsham. The boys were talking to a lad named George, an air framer in the ground crew. Like most ground crew, George was dedicated to maintaining the aircraft and was devastated when an aircrew member did not make it home.

George Marsden was a country boy from Yorkshire who was only nineteen years of age. He was a short man with sandy hair, fair skin and dry wit. George had two great loves in life, rugby football league, as he called it, and shooting game. It was his liking of game that led him to take an interest in the local estate of the Earl of Edmundsbury. Sundry Park was a well-established equestrian establishment that had been in the family of the Earl for generations. It was nestled on 100 acres and consisted of a ten- bedroom house with three training yards and 47 boxes. The earl bred racehorses but kept the back portion of the estate, consisting of approximately 50 acres, with fallow deer. This part of the estate was heavily wooded and provided ideal grounds for hunting the elusive prized deer.

The earl was a huge, cantankerous man in his early sixties who had threatened to shoot anybody seen poaching on his estate. The threat of being shot wasn't enough to deter George from venturing onto the estate for some poaching. Fresh in the minds of Frank and Jimmy was their culinary experience in London and they didn't need much encouragement to join George in his hunting expedition. The thought of tucking into some cooked venison made their mouths water, so George secured several double- barrel shotguns.

They joined George in a hunting trip on the Earl's residence the following evening. Surreptitiously, they entered the grounds under the cover of darkness. They noticed two hares dart from the field on a slight rise towards some thick bush. Jimmy didn't hesitate and fired. The result being the kick on the shotgun sent him hurtling backwards while a puff of dust came up, narrowly missing the hare.

"These here shotguns kick like a mule," said George in his thick Yorkshire accent.

"Ya not bloody wrong," exclaimed Jimmy lying on his back.

It was well into the evening before the three arrived back at Elsham empty- handed.

A couple of nights later, they were down at the pub at Scunthorpe and Frank asked George who would cook the fallow deer if, by chance, they were lucky enough to shoot one.

"Don't you worry about that, Mr Frank. I got the head cook, Maxi, on the take. He's a Yorkshire man and a rugby football league enthusiast, to boot," said George.

Over the next two weeks, the three of them went out onto

the estate in the evening four more times but could not manage to shoot a deer, although, on two occasions, they spotted one.

They noticed one of the staff in the distance on the second trip, but darted back into the woods before they came to his attention. On another occasion, they failed to spot even a hare, so got stuck into a bottle of sherry George had secured from the kitchen and, as a result, arrived back at the base rolling drunk.

Then, on the fifth trip, they were walking through some thick bush when, 50 yards in front of them, they spotted a magnificent buck grazing not far from a cluster of trees. Frank motioned the other two to stop.

"You're right on the limit of your range, Mr Frank," whispered George.

"Stay still, you two. I've got this bugger," said Frank coolly.

With that, he raised his shotgun, and after carefully aiming, he pulled the trigger. Bang! The deafening sound of a 12-gauge shotgun being discharged echoed through the darkness. Frank had killed the massive beast with a clean headshot, instantly dropping the deer to the ground.

"We better butcher this animal quick smart lest we have someone from the estate investigate where that noise came from," said George, looking around warily.

They dragged the carcass into the woods, where George produced an old hessian sack. After unravelling it, he produced an array of butchers' knives.

"Crikey George, you've come prepared," said Jimmy.

"I told you, Mr Jimmy, I had Maxi the head cook at Elsham on the take, and he supplied me with these here knives."

It took them the best part of half an hour to butcher the deer and place the choice cuts into several hessian sacks.

They had placed the final portion in the bags and were walking out of the woods when some 200 yards away in the darkness of the field, they saw two men riding on horseback towards them. A shotgun sounded from the men and then another before a voice bellowed, "Stop, you scoundrels!"

One of the figures on horseback was a huge man who the boys figured must have weighed at least eighteen stone.

"That's the earl for sure," said George, before the three of them darted back into the woods. Weighed down by their venison, they hauled the sacks onto their shoulders and ran for their lives. The slain animal's blood dripped from the sacks down onto their civilian clothes. Shotgun blasts roared out and voices could be heard demanding them to stop as the two men had now dismounted and were on foot. The three poachers scrambled through the dense bush in the pitch black. Eventually, they saw a clearing, and upon entering the field, they ran for their lives. They soon came across a dry canal, and after they trudged through the mud and out the other side, they quickly evaded their captors.

When they eventually arrived back at the base, they were covered in a mixture of blood and mud, and the three of them resembled the wreck of the Hesperus. George woke Maxi and his appearance took the cook so much by surprise that he screamed in fright.

On gathering his composure, Maxi was met by the other two, waiting outside where they made their way to the kitchen. The prized venison was hidden in the freezer room.

By the following day, the earl came marching onto Elsham, frothing at the mouth, looking for the culprits. At that stage, only George, Frank, Jimmy and Maxi knew what had happened and were tight-lipped about the whole affair.

Around lunchtime, Frank and Jimmy approached George, working on an aircraft in the hangar.

"What are we going to do about all that venison?" Frank said, looking around cautiously.

"Don't worry lads, Maxi will keep it hidden in the freezer room until it's ready to be consumed," said George.

"If the Wingco finds out about this, he'll have our balls for breakfast," Jimmy said.

"Don't you worry about a thing, lads. Tonight the mess will be dinning on venison, and by Christ, if anybody spills the beans, there will be hell to pay."

That night, the entire mess dined on a sumptuous dish of roast venison and vegetables. The word had gone around prior, that nobody was to let on where it had come from, although it was common knowledge who the poachers were.

In the meantime, the earl put pressure on the top brass at Elsham to find out who had committed the heinous act. Wing Commander Jackson pretended to appease the earl, but gave scant regard to his request as he had more pressing issues on his mind, namely taking the war to the Germans.

Then one morning, two weeks after the event, Frank was summoned to the Wingco's office.

"Ah crikey, I knew some bastard would eventually spill the beans. We're in for it now, Jimmy," said Frank shortly before departing for the Wingco's office.

Jimmy looked at Frank, stunned into silence, before saying, "We'll end up inside for this little stunt, Frank."

Looking smart in his neatly pressed uniform, Frank walked up to the Wingco's office in a state of anxiety, expecting to be charged.

Frank waited for ten minutes before being led into his office. He didn't acknowledge Frank, as he was totally consumed with his head buried in paperwork. Frank stood there nervously, like he was awaiting the executioner's block.

Eventually, the Wingco addressed him and said without lifting his head, "I've thought long and hard about what I should do with you. I've come to the conclusion that you deserve what's coming to you."

"Sir, you have to understand…"said Frank.

"Understand what, Flight Sergeant?" the Wingco said abruptly.

"Ah well, it's like this…." Frank blurted out.

The Wingco stared at Frank for a considerable time before he said, "What in heaven's name are you on about Flight Sergeant? If it's about Cruikshank and yourself being implicated in the lighting of that incendiary device in the officer's dining room a month ago, forget about it. I have a more serious matter to discuss with you two."

"Sir, we had nothing to do with that," Frank protested.

The Wingco raised his hand.

"I know we have already found the culprits. Don't you realise that Squadron Leader Chapman has recommended you for a Distinguished Flying Medal after the raid to Cologne in May last year?"

"The DFM?" Frank said incredulously.

"That's correct, Flight Sergeant."

"I had no idea sir," said Frank.

"Squadron Leader Chapman felt your actions warranted the award after you shot the wing tip off the 110 and you were subsequently shot in the foot."

Frank was stunned into silence.

"It has taken some time for the award to come through, but I think your exemplary actions have warranted this decoration on several occasions, Flight Sergeant Casey!" the Wingco said.

They talked for some time before the Wingco dismissed Frank and, as he was halfway out the office door, he called him back.

"One last thing, Flight Sergeant?"

"What is that, sir?" Frank said, walking back warily into the Wingco's office.

"Have you ever tasted venison, Flight Sergeant?"

Frank looked at the Wingco ashen- faced.

"They tell me it is delicious," said the Wingco.

"I think I may have had it once some time ago, sir."

A slight grin came over the Wingco's face before he gave Frank a wink.

"That will be all, Flight Sergeant."

No one at Elsham ever leaked who the culprits were who shot the earl's deer. It was common knowledge the Wingco knew who they were, but although he was a man of rank, he was also a good sport and he never investigated the matter any further. Eventually, the whole incident died a slow death as the Wingco couldn't care less if a deer had been shot and consumed by the men.

Chapter 13

Wednesday, February 3rd 1943. RAF Elsham Wolds, Lincolnshire

AFTER ARTHUR HARVEY had completed his thirty operations, he was transferred to a training squadron for Lancasters at Brighton. His replacement as flight engineer was 23-year-old Flying Officer, Kenneth, better known as Ken Dodsworth from Shrewsbury in Shropshire, England. Ken had 20 operations under his belt flying Halifaxes and Lancasters, and had been studying law prior to the war.

It was Frank and Jimmy's 25th operation, and their crew were part of 500 aircraft that were to bomb Hanover in Germany. Hanover was the fifth largest industrial centre in the Third Reich, producing tyres and other rubber parts for military vehicles and aircraft.

It was 10.00 pm, and the crew were going through their customary ritual of pissing on the front wheel of the Lanc. Jimmy was standing beside Frank and there was silence. Suddenly Jimmy turned to Frank and said, "Crikey, we've had some bloody great times together."

Frank was taken back by Jimmy's melancholic statement. It seemed out of place for the normally routine approach Jimmy took prior to an operation, and Frank gave him a puzzled look.

"That final we played against Riverview was a cracker of a game. It will live with me for the rest of my life."

"So much has happened between now and then. It seems like another lifetime," Frank said, turning to Jimmy.

Jimmy smiled at Frank before he climbed aboard the aircraft with a look of serenity on his face. It was an unusual reaction from Jimmy, for the crew were usually silent as there was always an air of apprehension when embarking on an operation.

As Frank strapped himself into his turret and put his gloves on, he pondered Jimmy's statement as the aircraft taxied down the runway.

On the way to the target, the weather closed in and the thunder and lightning tossed the Lancaster around violently. It was so dark, Reg was afraid they would run into another aircraft and his fears came to fruition when approaching the target.

"A Lancaster approaching us from the starboard side," Frank said. Reg dipped his port wing and the other aircraft narrowly missed colliding with them.

After they dropped their bombs on the target and set course for home, they were met with another threatening situation. They flew into dangerous cumulonimbus clouds and the aircraft was caught in a mixture of violent up and down draughts. The result saw Reg, one minute applying full throttle to get them out of a nosedive, then taking it off as they were caught in an updraught. At one stage, Reg got caught in such a bad nosedive that even with both hands pulling back on the controls; he could not straighten out the aircraft. He told the crew to prepare to jump before Ken stood behind Reg and, with the both of them pulling back on the controls; they were able to pull the aircraft out of the nosedive.

Then they were met with another frightening situation. As they cleared the cumulonimbus cloud, lightning erupted around them. As a result, static electricity caused tiny blue lights to jump around the wings and propellers, which lit the aircraft up like a blue star and made them a sitting target for night fighters. Fortunately, they flew out of the lightning shortly after, and the blue lights disappeared.

Reg told the crew to be on their toes for flak and night fighters as they crossed the Dutch coast. Frank felt unusually uneasy about this operation, which was reinforced by something he witnessed in the distance. He could see a Lancaster being coned before exploding into an orange flame. He swallowed hard before taking a deep breath and checking the travel on his guns was working.

After seeing the Lancaster explode, he noticed the tracer from the wings of a night fighter coming for them. Before he knew it, the tracer from the 109 raked the fuselage of F for Freddie before Frank fired off a return round of tracer, narrowly missing the night fighter.

Jimmy called, "Incoming night fighters are approaching from starboard, skip."

Frank heard the words from Jimmy, and they were words that would haunt him for the rest of his life. What followed was an almighty explosion that shook the aircraft violently.

"We've been hit severely!" Reg said.

Reg then put the aircraft into a downward spiral in an effort to lose the night fighters, but when he eventually levelled out, he was met with three Messerschmitt 109s. Reg dived under the 109s and as he did, Frank let rip with a burst of fire, managing to hit one of the night fighters before it exploded.

"I got him," Frank said.

"Well done, Tailie," said Reg.

Frank was expecting congratulations from Jimmy, but he heard nothing from him.

He was worried Jimmy had not responded, and he frantically looked around for the marauding 109s, but they had pulled out of the attack.

Shortly after, two Lancasters lumbered up beside them before Frank spotted the propeller of a 109. He thought it was going to come in from below and target their aircraft. Instead, it concentrated its firepower on the Lancaster above, and shortly after, the wing tanks of the bomber exploded, showering debris throughout the sky. Frank then heard the wing tanks of the other Lancaster beside him explode. Frank swung his guns around, but the travel would not reach as the Messerschmitt was too far below. Then the 109 flew up to their starboard side, preparing to attack. Frank said, "corkscrew port, skip." With that, Reg switchbladed the aircraft and the left wing went down. Frank then shredded the 109s canopy and engine with machine gun fire.

Frank watched the 109 fall in a flaming spiral towards the ground. Above them, shredded and burning bits of Lancaster were falling from the sky. Silhouettes of parachutes from the airmen of the bombers could be seen descending around them.

They flew on until they were well over the safety of the North Sea when Ken approached Frank's turret with a beaker of coffee and some dark chocolate. He handed Frank the coffee and chocolate and said without a hint of emotion, "I'm sorry, Frank, but Jimmy got the chop."

"What?" Frank said in shock.

"I'm afraid so, Frank. He copped a burst of machine-gun fire and he's in a hell of a mess."

There was no sentimentality or emotion between the aircrew. They spoke to the point and they didn't mince their words. Frank was stunned into silence and could barely comprehend what he had just heard.

Jimmy was dead!

The Lancaster limped on, when eventually Frank glimpsed the first rays of dawn as the English coast and its fields appeared. Before he knew it, there was a bump and they were down and safe, but Frank's life would be forever changed.

The rest of the crew shielded Frank from the sight of his best mate's mutilated corpse. Jimmy's body was removed and placed on a stretcher and taken from the aircraft. Shortly after, Frank unstrapped himself from the turret and as he walked up the fuselage, he could see the mid- upper gunner's turret and the blood- stained and broken perspex. He was in shock at the extent of the damage. Once they were out of the aircraft, Reg took Frank to the side and spoke to him.

"I am sorry, Frank, but Jimmy got the chop and there's nothing we could do."

"I understand, skip," Frank said without emotion.

"We'll make sure we give Jimmy a good send- off in the pub, Frank," said Reg.

"Thanks, skip. I appreciate that."

That night in the Dying Gladiator Pub, as was the custom after losing a crewmate, they toasted Jimmy Cruikshank. It was a toast that went long into the night, and alongside the crew of F for Freddie, many of the ground crew and locals were there to drink to the popular gunner.

After that night, as was the custom, the crew never mentioned Jimmy again. Frank was to bury his emotions about Jimmy deep inside and not release them until many years later.

In the aftermath of Jimmy's death, including his funeral, Frank grieved in silence. He felt as though his right arm had been cut off, such was the bond that had existed between them.

He remained stoic as there was aircrew dying and his crew might think him weak. Silently, he contemplated all that they had been through. From the time Jimmy had strolled up to him all those years ago at Joeys, and he had felt so lonely and ostracised by his peers. Jimmy had offered Frank his hand in friendship and it had been a deep one. Jimmy was a bloke he could share his innermost secrets with and now he felt like he did all those years ago at in his early days at Joeys.

A couple of days after their op to Hanover, the weather closed in and the squadron were stood down. That evening, The Dying Gladiator was full of patrons and Frank drank his fair share of booze to blot out his emotions. Frank could handle the booze and the signs that were to lead him into a spiralling downward slide had yet to appear. What did appear were the first signs of Frank losing a grip on his faith. Frank wouldn't have said it at the time, but subconsciously he was bitter at losing Jimmy and blamed God for his death.

The one bright spot was that Geraldine was able to give him solace in his darkest hour. Although he could not adequately express the deep level of loss in losing Jimmy to her, she proved to be a tower of strength to Frank in his time of need.

Within days of the op to Hanover, the crew were sent a new mid-upper gunner named Ted Porter from Warrington in England. Ted was only 19 years-of-age, a sprog gunner, and before he had signed up, he had worked in the steel industry. He was a nice enough bloke, but he was green and he found it very hard to fill the shoes of such an experienced gunner like Jimmy. Nevertheless,

Frank took him under his wing and taught him the ropes, but nothing beats the anvil of experience and it was to show.

Two weeks after Ted joined the crew, they were back on operations. After the damage incurred by F for Freddie, the crew was given another Lancaster to fly. T for Tango was an older Lancaster that had copped its fair share of punishment on operational sorties. The crew felt T for Tango was cursed, for it was beset by mechanical problems from the onset.

Reg complained to the Wingco about why an experienced crew like his was forced to fly such a clapped out banger, but it fell on deaf ears. Reg complained further to the Wingco when he was told that in mid-February 1943, they would be sent to bomb Berlin.

"Why send us out to bomb deep into the heart of Germany, especially when we have a sprog gunner on board?" Reg said to the Wingco forcibly.

"You'll be right," said the Wingco.

"If we get the chop, I'll haunt you for the rest of your life, sir!"

"See you when you get back to Elsham," the Wingco said with a wry smile.

Reg's crew were part of a 750 force of aircraft sent to Berlin.

They released 10 of their 1000-pound incendiary bombs on reaching Berlin, but the giant 8000-pound cookie would not dislodge from the bomb bay. Reg did all he could to make the bomb dislodge by throwing the aircraft from side to side, but to no avail. On reaching the North Sea, Reg instructed Graham Farquhar to grab the fire axe. After he chopped through the cable which held the cookie in place, the bomb fell into the ocean and exploded. Everybody let out a huge sigh of relief when they returned to Elsham unscathed.

Over the next three weeks, the weather was clear and the crew flew a further three operations bringing Frank's total of operational sorties to 29.He could see the finish line so tantalisingly close and allowed himself to dream that he may be able to finish his operational tour. But then they were sent to bomb a target in France, and everything changed.

Chapter 14

Monday, March 22nd 1943. Elsham Wolds, Lincolnshire

BY FRANK'S 22ND birthday on 21st March, 1943, he had flown 29 operations. With only one more to go, he had allowed himself to dream that he might be able to complete his tour. It was nothing short of a miracle that Reg, Kiwi and himself had completed 29 operational sorties when so many aircrews had been killed before reaching 30 on their first tour.

On their 30th operation on 22/23rd March, their luck was to run out. They had lost one of their port motors from flak on returning from Nuremburg in their previous operation. Frank felt Jimmy's death had cursed the crew. They thought their final operation was to a relatively soft target in France. Frank thought differently, though. By the afternoon of Monday, March 22nd 1943, they were told they were to bomb the Peugeot Motor Works in Sochaux. Frank had an uneasy feeling as it was the first time they had been on an operation to France.

The night before the operation, Geraldine took Frank to a floor show at the Oswald Hotel in Scunthorpe, some 15 miles from Elsham, for his birthday. They had a great night and on arriving back at Elsham, Geraldine kissed Frank before handing him a photo of the two of them.

Frank placed the photo in the pocket of his jacket prior to embarking on the aircraft.

On Monday, 22nd March, Bomber Command sent 90 Lancasters and 65 Halifaxes to bomb the Peugeot Motor Works. The Nazis had taken over the factory in 1940 and were producing tank turrets and Focke–Wulf fighter plane parts. The Germans were also engaged in a secret project to produce the V1 missile. For the British Government, the factory needed to be taken out.

There was a full moon and the night was clear when the Mosquito pathfinder squadron dropped their flares 500 yards beyond the factory. The bombers subsequently dropped their payload on the outskirts of a nearby village. A few residents were killed and injured while a number of houses were destroyed and damaged. Very little damage was done to the factory and production was up and running straight away.

The crew of T for Tango had dropped their bombs, thinking they had done a satisfactory job when searchlights coned them. Reg tossed the Lancaster from side to side before putting the aircraft into a spiralling nosedive, his actions managing to lose the searchlights. Kiwi set a course for Elsham. Ten minutes into their return flight, two Messerschmitt Bf 109 night fighters were hiding in the clouds. One of them sprayed the cockpit of the Lancaster with machine- gun fire, wounding Reg, before peeling off to chase another bomber. Although wounded, Reg managed to keep flying, putting the aircraft into a series of spiralling turns to try and avoid the other night fighter. The 109 came in for the kill and let loose with both machine gun and cannon fire, resulting in the Lancaster's right fuel tank exploding. Hungry to finish the job off, the 109 came from behind. Frank was ready on the trigger and sprayed the cockpit with machine- gun fire and the night fighter tumbled away before spiralling downwards, where it eventually hit the ground in a huge fireball.

The Lancaster was in dire trouble by this stage, so Reg put the aircraft into a nosedive to extinguish the flames, but the fuel tank exploded into a fireball. Realising the Lancaster was doomed; in a strained voice, Reg told the crew to abandon the aircraft. Frank crawled out of his rear turret and put on his parachute before noticing Ted Porter jump from the front hatch only to have his chute catch alight and spiral downwards like a 'candle in the wind'. Frank had no time to comprehend the fate of his mid- upper gunner and the rest of the crew as flames engulf the fuselage. He climbed back into the rear turret before turning it to one side and falling backwards through the two rear doors into the night sky. Miraculously, his parachute did not catch alight and as he floated down to terra firma in the cool night air, he saw T for Tango hit the ground and explode into a fireball. Instinct told Frank he was the only one of his crew who had survived.

Frank hit the ground awkwardly, twisting his right ankle. That was the least of his problems, as the most important thing was not to be captured by German soldiers who may be in the vicinity. On further inspection, he could see his clothes were burnt and he had received some minor burns up near his hairline, but he had come through his ordeal unscathed. He quickly gathered his parachute and surveyed the wreckage of his Lancaster from a distance. He dared not go near it for fear of running into Germans. Frank felt sick at the thought that all his crew had perished, but he had no time to mourn, as his major concern was to bury his parachute.

He found a branch and dug a shallow hole where he placed his chute and covered it with dirt and rocks. Frank could see in the distance that another bomber had come down. He decided to walk towards the aircraft with stealth to see if anybody had survived. Frank was unsure where he was, but in the distance, he could see a town as it was a full moon. He knew the town was not Sochaux, as they had flown a considerable distance from the village after they bombed the factory. Frank walked towards the bomber, looking for Germans and preparing to hide. He was 300 yards from it, where he hid in some thick bushes and surveyed the scene. He cautiously approached the burning aircraft. He looked inside the wreck and could see four deceased bodies, but there didn't appear to be anybody alive. After a while, he cautiously walked on towards the town, silently hoping he may encounter some members of the French Resistance.

Frank had been walking for fifteen minutes when he was startled by the rustle of branches in some nearby bushes. He stopped in his tracks and froze in terror, as he was expecting to be met by gun- wielding German soldiers. Instead, a well- modulated English voice from within the bushes said, "Psst over here!"

"Who is it?" Frank whispered.

"I am an English pilot," he whispered back.

Frank cautiously walked towards the bushes before he was met with the sight of a man with blood streaming from a gash on his forehead.

"Where did you fly from?" Frank said.

"RAF Wickenby," he said. "What about yourself?"

"Elsham Wolds," Frank replied. "Are you on your own?"

"Yes, I am, but I believe two more of my chaps got out, but I have not seen them."

"I believe all my crew are dead. I am the rear gunner and I've managed to get out alive, although I have burns to my face and twisted my ankle."

"I have this nasty gash on my head, but other than that, I am okay."

Frank looked at the officer, and he suddenly realised he knew him. He was Geraldine's old boyfriend.

"I know you," Frank said.

"I'm Squadron Leader Burnham."

Frank looked at the Englishman, dumfounded.

"I thought it was you. You tried to have me charged for insubordination for not saluting you," Frank said.

Burnham looked at Frank carefully before saying in a condescending tone, "Oh, it's you."

"Yes, it's me, sir, and with the greatest respect, I'd think it would be best if we put the past behind us and get the hell out of here before we get captured."

"I'll give the orders around here thank you very much, Flight Sergeant," he said to Frank. Burnham then gave Frank a look of disdain before motioning with his right hand to start walking.

They had been walking for five minutes when they spotted a group of four standing in a field in the distance. They both dropped to the ground, then slid on their stomachs. From there, they observed the group from behind the safety of a rock. They noticed they were not Germans but French civilians, so they approached them. In his rudimentary French, Burnham told them they were downed airmen and if they could help. They showed no interest in helping them, but a boy in his mid-teens said in broken English they might find some help in a farmhouse only a short distance away.

"Merci beaucoup," Burnham said before they exchanged a few pleasantries and kept walking.

They had been walking for five minutes and reached the crest of a small hill when they heard shouting coming from where they had left the French civilians. They looked around and saw a group of six German soldiers with two German shepherd dogs being held on a leash.

"Halt, Halt!" one of the German soldiers screamed.

He then let out a burst of machine- gun fire, which reverberated around the surrounding countryside.

With that, they ran for their lives. All the while, they could hear the dogs barking while the Germans screamed for them to stop.

"Halt halt!" the Germans bellowed.

Frank was hobbling. The Germans were slowly gaining on the two airmen, screaming for them to halt while the dogs barked incessantly. The two of them were panting heavily, and Frank's ankle was throbbing, but they kept on running. After one burst of machine- gun fire, which landed very close to them, Burnham grabbed Frank by the arm and said.

"It's no use, Flight Sergeant. We will never outrun them. They are gaining on us. I suggest we surrender."

Frank had an uneasy feeling about the situation and turned to Burnham and said, "Surrender to them? You'd have to be kidding. I can imagine what those bastards will do to us if they capture us."

"Look here, Flight Sergeant, this is a direct order from an officer. We are going to surrender to the Germans. As POWs we are protected by the laws of the Geneva Convention."

Frank looked at Burnham and was torn between an order from an officer and his instinct to flee. Once again, Frank's rebellious streak came to the fore.

"There is no way I will let those kraut bastards take me into captivity. They will probably shoot us first," said Frank.

"As downed airmen, they must take us in as POWs. It's in the Geneva Convention."

"You can shove the Geneva Convention up your arse, Burnham. I'm not sticking around to find out what happens if they capture us."

"For the final time, Flight Sergeant, I order you to surrender. Otherwise I'll have you charged."

"Have me charged? Get a grip of yourself, man," Frank growled.

"This is my final order!"

"You can do what you want, Squadron Leader, but I am off." Frank looked around and noticed they were close to a large tree-covered hill.

"I am heading up there," Frank said, pointing. "Are you going to join me?"

Burnham shook his head and said, "You'll pay for this Flight Sergeant."

"You've got that wrong, Burnham. You're the one who is going to pay once those arseholes capture you."

With that, Frank ran. He ran like there was no tomorrow. He ran until the pain in his ankle was excruciating, but he dared not stop. He was expecting to receive a bullet in his back at any moment, but still he kept running. He could hear the Germans barking orders in English to stop, but nothing would stop him until he was in the safety of the thick blanket of trees on the hill. Finally, he made it and he clambered up the slope of the hill until he was able to hide behind the safety of some trees. He peered out and could see in the distance that the Germans had caught up to Burnham and were beating him mercilessly while the dogs were snapping at his heels. They were shouting and they kept up their assault for the next few minutes.

"Who is *za ozer terror flieger?*" *terror flyer?* The German soldier screamed at Burnham.

"I don't know him. I've never met him before," Burnham kept repeating.

"You are a liar, *terror flieger*," they said as they repeatedly beat him. To his credit, Burnham did not divulge Frank's name and after another five minutes of this treatment, one of the German soldiers shot Burnham with his machine gun, killing him.

Frank stood there in horror at what he had just witnessed. He was so shocked he could not move. That was until he heard one of the Germans scream, "Surrender *terror flieger* before you suffer *za* same fate as your friend."

With that, Frank scrambled up the hill through the trees, all the while stumbling on rocks and fallen branches. Then the Germans fired and bullets sprayed close by, but luckily nothing hit him. Frank was struggling, but he kept running. They were gaining on him when one of them yelled out,

"*Schnell, schnell fang ihn ein.*" *Quick, quick, capture him.*

Frank kept running and they fired at him, but he managed to avoid being hit. The soldiers were screaming orders and the German Shepherds were barking madly. Frank was petrified and thought it was only a matter of time before he received a bullet in the back, but he dared not stop.

"Stop *terror flieger* or we *vill* shoot you dead," a German officer brandishing a Luger pistol screamed at him.

Frank was almost out of puff and ready to collapse when from deep inside the cover of the woods came an almighty roar of machine gun fire. He hit the ground and landed on his face, managing to bloody his nose. From where he lay, he could see flashes of orange light up the darkness while the noise of machine- gun fire thundered through the surrounding countryside. The Germans were taken by surprised and didn't know what had hit them. They had little time to respond as they were mowed down by continuous machine gun fire. It was over in minutes and Frank lifted his head off the ground and surveyed the carnage. In front of him were five dead German soldiers dressed in camouflage uniforms and their two dogs. The officer carrying the pistol was critically wounded and he struggled in the dark to fire his Luger but it would not respond. Frank was lying on the ground trying to figure out who had fired at the Germans when out of the darkness of the woods walked three French civilians, all brandishing machine guns and wearing the Cross of Lorraine on their armbands. There were two men. One was middle- aged, carrying a German MP 40 machine gun and the other was in his early twenties brandishing a Sten gun. What took Frank by surprise was the other person, a woman in her early twenties with striking shoulder-length red hair. On her head was a black beret with a red scarf around her neck, while she wore light brown trousers and a black leather jacket. In her hands was a Bren gun with the muzzle covered with a wet rag.

The mortally wounded German officer propped himself up on one arm and pulled the trigger on his pistol, but it did not fire. He tried repeatedly, but the pistol would not fire, so he threw his pistol down in disgust.

"*Heil Hitler*," he screamed defiantly to the French woman.

She strolled over towards him, pointing her Bren gun at him.

" *'Eil 'Itler, vous dites? C'est le dernier 'Eil 'Itler que tu prononceras, espèce de porc allemande,*"

Heil Hitler, you say? That's the last Heil Hitler you will ever utter, you German pig, she said before zipping him across his midriff with a burst of fire that nearly cut him in half. He slumped over, dead in a pool of blood.

"The wet rag '*elps* the gun to make a lot more noise. It gives the impression that a bigger force is facing the enemy," she said in good English.

Frank nodded in agreement while his eyes were wide open.

"Better dead than alive," she said with venom. "They were filthy Waffen–SS."

Frank lay there stunned by what he had just witnessed, while the younger French man approached him.

"The Waffen-SS are the scum of the earth, *Monsieur*. They should *err…* all be buried into the ground *oui,*" he said in broken English before spitting on the dead officer.

"They were the SS?" Frank said to him.

"Yes, *Monsieur,* they were err…part of the 40th Waffen Grenadier Division of the SS. The stinking *err….*pigs have been sent to this part of France to err….fight the Resistance," he said, before spitting on the dead officer once again.

Then the older Frenchman approached Frank and, with a hand on his shoulder, said to him, *"Vous etes bless*é *Monsieur?" You are injured, Mister.*

Frank's rudimentary school boy French came to the fore, and he could just pick up what he had said.

"Cheville tordue et saignement de nez," Twisted ankle and nosebleed. Frank managed to struggle out.

The French woman approached Frank and produced a handkerchief from her trouser pants and, with the love and devotion of a mother, held it up to his nose and wiped the blood away.

"Merci, Madame."

She smiled at Frank.

"Your face is also burnt, *Monsieur?"*

"Yes."

"We will attend to that."

"Thank you, Madame."

"You need not worry about struggling with your French, *Monsieur,* as my English is *goot.* My father was French, but my mother was Scottish. They met during the Great War when she was a nurse stationed in France and she tended to '*im* after '*e* had been injured fighting on the front line."

"You are very kind, Madame. I don't know how to repay you after saving my life."

"You are Australian *Monsieur, oui*?"

"Yes, I am."

"It is to you we owe a great debt. My late father often spoke about the bravery of the Australians during the Great War. And now you are trying to save our country. We say thank you *Monsieur.*"

Frank smiled.

With that, the younger Frenchman approached Frank and said, "We must move quickly, *err…* before there are more, *err….* Germans looking for you."

"Raphael is right, *Monsieur.* We must move quickly and '*ide* up in the hill of Planoise for tonight. Tomorrow we move you somewhere a lot safer," said the woman.

They walked in silence until they were near the top of the hill of Planoise, which was heavily wooded and overlooked the city of Besancon. As Frank lay back on some branches and rested, he contemplated what he had been through. The previous night he had been spending a pleasant evening with Geraldine and had been blasted from the sky the next day. Frank had no time to contemplate what had happened to his crew, for survival instinct had kicked in, and for the time being, that's all that mattered.

He eventually dozed off, not knowing who these people were, but grateful they had saved his life.

On awakening the next morning, the red-haired woman introduced herself as Marguerite Balloux, the older man as Philippe Pichot and the younger man as Raphael Legrand. She told him they were members of the Maquis or French Resistance. Frank then introduced himself.

Marguerite explained the Maquis had been formed after the Nazi occupation of France. Young working- class men were conscripted into the * Vichy government's Compulsory Work Service or STO to be forced labour for Germany. (*The government of France under the leadership of Marshal Philippe Petain, who collaborated with Germany during World War Two. They set up their capital in Vichy in the unoccupied part of southern France.)

To avoid capture and deportation to Germany, many had become increasingly organised into resistance groups. These groups also helped downed allied airmen escape as well as Jews and any others who the Milice, a paramilitary force of the Vichy government, or Germans were harassing.

She explained that they would take him to the Jura Mountains on the Swiss border, where their band of Maquis operated from. From the protection of the mountains, he would be able to recover from his injuries and then they would help him escape back to England through the Comet Line. This was a resistance organisation that helped allied airmen escape through Brussels, France, neutral Spain and onto British controlled Gibraltar.

Marguerite told Frank it was pure luck they had been hiding on the hill of Planoise when he had been trying to escape from the SS. They had come down from the Jura Mountains to settle a score with some members of the Milice. They had been betraying members of the Maquis to the Germans, who had summarily been executed in the 17th-century Citadel at Besancon. She said the French civilians he and Burnham had initially contacted were members of the Milice and it was them that had informed the Waffen –SS of their whereabouts.

Marguerite then drew her finger across her throat and said to Frank, "It is them that we have come to deal with, *Monsieur*."

"I will be forever in your debt, Madame."

Marguerite nodded and smiled at Frank.

"We were going to deal with them last night, but your arrival changed everything," she said with a wry smile. "Tonight, Raphael will stay 'ere with you while Philippe and I 'ead down the 'ill and take care of business."

Raphael then gave Frank some of the meagre amount of food he had with him, which he was most appreciative of, before they all rested for the remainder of the day within the cover of the woods. It was late in the afternoon when they noticed a small patrol of Waffen–SS walking up the track from deep inside the woods. The Germans searched the area for fifteen minutes but did not detect them as they were so deeply nestled in their hiding place. As soon as the SS left, Marguerite decided they should move to the nearby hill named Montboucon as their encounter with the Germans had been too close for comfort.

It was approaching 10.00 pm when Marguerite and Philippe left the safety of the hill of Montboucon. Marguerite informed Frank when they returned, they would leave immediately for the Jura Mountains as it was too risky to stay where they were any longer.

Once they had left, Raphael sat down beside Frank and explained to him how important it was for Marguerite to deal with the Milice who had betrayed him to the SS.

"*Monsieur Franc* ....it is important *err*.... you understand why Marguerite *'as* gone to seek revenge on the dirty Milice, *oui,*" Raphael said in halting English.

"Tell me Raphael?"

"It is because..... *err 'ow* do you say in English? *Err...* The filthy bastard Milice betrayed Marguerite's father *'Enri,* ....*oui.* He was a member of the Maquis in *Besançon err...* and they betrayed him to the rotten Waffen-SS, *oui.*"

"Is that so?" Frank said.

"This is true *Monsieur Franc err.......'Enri* was *'iding* how do you say ... er Jews in his *'ouse* and the Milice gave *'im* up, *oui.*"

"When did this take place, Raphael?"

"*Err* ...... about twelve months ago," Raphael leant across and grabbed Frank by the elbow and, while looking him in the eyes, said earnestly, "Marguerite is not one *err*..... to be messed with *Monsieur Franc... oui.* She is dangerous with *'er* Bren gun and won't *'esitate* to kill. Those filthy Milice traitors that *err....* she and Philippe *'ave* gone to find are as *goot* as dead."

Frank looked at Raphael intently and he knew he was right by what he had seen Marguerite do to the Germans. They talked for a little longer before Frank lay back, and his thoughts turned to his crew and then Geraldine. He soon fell asleep, and it was only a few hours later that he was awoken by Marguerite tugging on his elbow.

"Wake up, *Monsieur Franc.*"

"What time is it?"

"It is the early *'ours* of the morning. We *'ave* to leave now as there is a *'ouse* in a local village where we will *'ide* you until a truck will take you to the Jura Mountains."

With great stealth, the three Maquis led Frank down the hill of Montboucon, where they walked in a southeast direction 9 miles (15km) to the small commune of Mamirolle, situated on the first plateau of the Jura Mountains.

They walked in silence, always on the lookout for danger. Frank's ankle was still swollen, and painful, but he put up with it and the effects of the burns on his face. After a couple of hours, they stopped briefly for some water within the cover of a wooded area.

"Did you sort out your business, Marguerite?" Frank asked.

She gave Frank a wry smile and said, "Those Milice traitor bastards are ……'*ow* do you say? … *err* 'pushing up daisies', *Monsieur Franc.*"

It was before dawn when they arrived at a small farmhouse just outside Mamirolle, where they were met by André Fabron and his wife Sophie, who were members of the Maquis. Soon after arriving, Sophie produced some civilian clothes, which Frank put on and she burnt his battledress in a fire in the backyard. Frank presented himself to the Resistance members and to the unsuspecting outsider he passed admirably for a French farm worker. Sophie was also able to apply jelly to Frank's burns, which provided some relief. Soon after, he retired to a warm bed and managed to fall asleep despite the trauma he had experienced. It was just after midday when Frank woke and he was introduced to two other local members of the Maquis, Gabriel Boucher and Leon Gagne, a local farmer. Gabriel and Leon spoke no English, but after they provided Frank with some *Gauloise* French cigarettes, it reinforced the trust between them.

They had also come to inform the others the Germans were in a rage after the deaths of the six Waffen – SS soldiers and were exacting revenge on anybody who they thought may have been responsible. Leon informed them they would have to be very diligent when travelling to the Jura Mountains.

Sophie had prepared some lunch, which consisted of some joints of meat which Gabriel had provided and boiled potatoes and carrots, which Leon had brought. The lunch was washed down with a few bottles of homemade red wine and Frank appreciated their generosity.

It was early the next morning when Leon arrived in his truck to transport Frank and Raphael the 44 miles (71km) to the Jura Mountains. Marguerite and Philippe were to take another vehicle to the Jura Mountains later in the day.

Leon had lifted the boards from the truck's tray to provide a compartment to hide the weapons while Raphael and Frank were to ride in the cabin with him. He then placed a stock crate on the back, where he put three pigs and some hay. Before they left, Marguerite gave Frank some papers with his proof of identity, including a pseudonym name, Raul Dupont. She also instructed him to say as little as possible if the Germans or Milice should stop them.

They set out without any problems, but when they arrived at the commune of Valdahon, which was 18 miles (29km) southeast of Besançon, they struck trouble. Set up were elements of the 40th Waffen Grenadier Division of the SS. A Waffen-SS soldier brandishing a Bergmann MP 35 sub-machine gun stopped the truck before an SS officer approached them and demanded to know where they were going. Leon explained they were taking the pigs to his brother's place, who lived 15 miles (24km) down the road. Frank pulled his beret down to hide the burn on his hairline. The officer then demanded to see their papers and, after inspecting them, screamed they were lying. He then ordered them to get out of the truck. Once out, the Germans thoroughly inspected the vehicle and began to ask them questions. Frank's heart was beating at a furious pace as the SS officer approached him and asked him who he was. Frank's mind went blank in the heat of the moment and he couldn't remember his pseudonym. The officer was only inches from Frank's face when Leon spoke up and said to the officer that the man was stupid and had been that way since birth.

"*Tu es un menteur*," *You are a liar*, the officer screamed at Frank in French.

The officer produced a pistol and held it at his side when Raphael stepped and said, "*Non, il est stupide*," *No, he is stupid.*

The officer barked at Raphael to step aside.

Just when the situation appeared to be dire, Frank turned to the officer and blurted out in a most convincing French accent, "*Raul Dupont.*"

The officer's head snapped back, and he glared at Frank and said,

"*Que faites- vos ici?*" *What are you doing here?*

Frank looked at the officer, threw his hands in the air with a big smile, and exclaimed, "*Je vends mes cochons!*" *I sell my pigs!*

Leon once again tried to explain to the officer that Raul was stupid and the only thing he lived for was his pigs. He said after breeding them, he was going to sell the pigs to his brother.

The officer asked Frank why he was limping, and he responded by saying that he had twisted his ankle while rounding up the pigs.

The officer glared at Leon and continued to ask him questions for the next few minutes before barking in German, "*Gehen!*" *Go!*

Leon and Raphael stood dumfounded, not understanding what he had said before the officer screamed at them in French. "*Aller*!" *Go*! He then pointed for them to go and screamed in German. "*Schnell!*"

Leon motioned for the others to get into the truck quickly and with haste; he took off, leaving the Germans in a cloud of dust.

Leon drove to the base of the mountains, where Raphael then escorted Frank deep into the cover of the terrain. It was early spring, and the temperature was still cool, so Raphael provided Frank with an overcoat. On reaching the main camp, Frank was introduced to the leader of the Maquis, Raphael's elder brother named Raynard, who was aged in his mid-thirties.

Their group consisted of 1000 Maquis scattered in small groups throughout a network of camps in the dense forests. Their operations included harassing the German occupying forces and the Milice. They had also been aiding the SOE (Special Operations Executive) with the destruction of infrastructure, including railway tracks, trains and German equipment.

The SOE had been formed by Prime Minister Winston Churchill in 1940 to 'set Europe ablaze' by helping local resistance movements and conducting espionage and sabotage in enemy- held territories. The SOE had dropped radio sets into occupied France so members of the Resistance could receive messages from London. They were also responsible for dropping weapons and explosives to aid resistance fighters.

It was evening when Marguerite and Philippe arrived at their base in the Jura Mountains. On arrival, Frank realised the important position Marguerite held within this group of *Maquisards*. She was the leader of a group of 50 who came under her direct command. It was rare for a woman to be in such a powerful position, but she had a fierce reputation as a fighter and was a born leader. The Maquis knew Marguerite wasn't afraid to use a weapon and she took no prisoners.

Frank lived in a tiny one-room hut deep inside the forest cover, and as the days wore on, he slowly recovered from his injuries. Only then could he fully comprehend what had happened to his crew.

He was pragmatic about their fate and he knew his escape was paramount. Nonetheless, he mourned for the men he had forged an unbreakable bond with.

He was not directly involved in any of the activities of the Maquis and he observed small groups heading out regularly to perform their clandestine operations.

Frank had been in the hut for a week when he experienced a reprisal by the Germans on the Maquis. Twelve Maquis had ventured down from the mountains to pick up weapons, explosives and a radio set dropped by the SOE. During the night, they were flashing a signal to the RAF aircraft, dropping the supplies when they encountered a unit of Waffen-SS soldiers. The result was the Germans killed six Maquis. In revenge, Marguerite led a group of ten to destroy the Waffen – SS's valuable military equipment with explosives the SOE had dropped. Their raid left an incredible amount of damage and seriously disrupted the Germans' operations. They also killed several foreign soldiers who were Byelorussian and Ukrainian, of which the Waffen – SS unit largely consisted.

While hidden in the mountains, Frank came to understand not only the operations of the Resistance movement but also the complex nature of their organisation. Before meeting the Maquis, Frank was under the opinion the French Resistance fought under one unified banner. Nothing could have been further from the truth. There were those members of the Resistance who were communists and had actively mobilised after Operation Barbarossa, the German invasion of the Soviet Union on the 22nd of June 1941. Within those communist groups, there were factions who were aligned with Marx, Lenin, Trotsky or Stalin, and they bitterly opposed each other.

There were the socialists who hated the communists. Then, those like the Maquis, who aligned themselves with Charles de Gaulle, the leader of the Free French and exiled in London. They hated the communists and, if the opportunity arose, would steal weapons and explosives from them. Within the de Gaullists, small factional leaders loathed each other. Then there were double agents collaborating with Germans who had infiltrated resistance groups and the Comet Line. There was also the constant threat of the Milice, who actively dealt with members of the Resistance by reporting them to the Germans.

After the D-Day landings, when the Germans had been removed from particular areas of France, there were often reprisals against those who had collaborated with them. Sometimes, there was scant evidence that somebody had collaborated, other than a petty grievance against an individual and many were executed without a trial.

The SOE operatives were uniformed and armed combatants and were on the ground in France, organising the resistance groups. They had a tough job trying to unify all these groups. They had to try to align all these different factions into one fighting force so they could defeat the common enemy, namely the Germans and their allies.

It was in this environment Frank found himself. Although he was safe with Marguerite and her group of Maquis, it was going to be difficult once he left the cover of the mountains and attempted to make his way out of France and back to England.

By mid-April 1943, Frank had healed from his wounds, and although he was sad to leave the Maquis, it was time to try and make his escape out of France.

The Maquis had been in contact with the Resistance in Besançon, where they were going to take him so members of the Comet Line could arrange his escape. It was here Frank would meet the man who would help alter the course of his life.

Chapter 15

Mid April, 1943. *Cathedrale Saint – Jean de Besançon.*
Cathedral of St John of Besançon.

RAYNARD DECIDED FRANK should be taken to the *Cathedrale Saint – Jean de Besançon*. A young Catholic priest who was a member of the resistance was *vicaire or* curate in English-speaking countries there.

Father Jean Baptiste Fournier worked under Cardinal Pierre Cerruti, the Catholic Archbishop of Besançon.

Father Fournier was 28 years of age and had only been at Besançon for five months. A slim man, athletic, of medium height with dark hair, he possessed a big smile that went with his likeable personality. He loved outdoor activities, including rugby, but particularly skiing in no small part because he was brought up in the small French village of Argentiere, where his parents owned a local café and he learnt his other great love, cooking. Argentiere was part of the commune of Chamonix – Mont Blanc. Mont Blanc is the highest mountain in the Alps and a premier ski resort. As a young man, Father Fournier fell in love with the slopes and, in particular snow-skiing, which he excelled at.

He could have been any young woman's catch, but he had a higher calling at eighteen and decided to study for the priesthood at the Catholic seminary at *Seminaire Saint – Irenee* in Lyon.

After being ordained, Father Fournier was sent to a parish in Lyon in 1940 as the *vicaire*. After the German invasion and the subsequent fall of France in June 1940, he joined the French Resistance. Initially, his role was handing out clandestine press material, but in time, it included aiding Jews and allied airmen to safety.

The Catholic Church in France was traditionally associated with the right and it was true that some clergy members supported the Vichy French. They liked Marshal Petain's message of repenting sins, restoring authority, discipline and returning to the land and family. They were attracted to the Vichy motto of work, family and country.

However, following the roundups of Jews carried out in the French Free Zone in the summer of 1942, there was a crucial change in the attitudes of Catholics and their spiritual leaders. Several bishops had proclamations read out in churches and quietly distributed them in parishes despite all the efforts of the Vichy police to intercept them. The result is that thousands of priests, monks, nuns and lay persons performed acts of charity toward the persecuted Jews. These acts were seen as defiance toward the Petain government.

Father Fournier's conscience had been awoken long before the proclamations were broadcast, as were many Catholic clergy members in France. They saw clearly the poison of Nazi ideology and rejected it, assisting the Jews as much as possible.

As Father Fournier's activities within the Resistance grew, so did the attention of the Gestapo (secret police of Nazi Germany) in Lyon. The Gestapo questioned him concerning his association with the Resistance on several occasions. Still, they could not prove he belonged to it, let alone that he had aided Jews or airmen. Nevertheless, Father Fournier came under the radar of the Gestapo and the Catholic hierarchy thought it prudent he should be transferred out of Lyon for his safety.

This was something he objected to openly with the hierarchy. Still, all his protestations were to no avail as he was transferred to what seemed like a somewhat benign location, namely Besançon. Although Besançon was not a hotbed of resistance activity, it was still a place to tread carefully as the 17th- century citadel in the town was controlled by the Germans. In mid October 1942, Father Fournier arrived in Besançon, where the intellectual Cardinal Pierre Cerruti was his superior.

Cardinal Cerruti was one of those Catholic clergy who had originally been attracted to the Vichy regime. Although soon finding their actions abhorrent, he nevertheless remained silent. It was a criticism directed at the Catholic Church in France after the war. The Vatican and, in particular, Pope Pius XII came under fire over inaction regarding the fate of the Jews. Although he was well aware of Father Fournier's clandestine activities, the cardinal turned a blind eye to them.

It was approaching 8.00 pm when Frank was led to the cathedral by Marguerite and Raphael. They were only about a mile from the cathedral when four drunken Wehrmacht soldiers approached them. They were in such an inebriated state they had their arms around each other to stop themselves from falling to the ground. They were an untidy mess and frequently fell to the roadway, laughing hysterically before one of them tried to pick his comrade up.

On seeing Frank, Marguerite and Raphael approach, the

most senior German soldier, who held the rank of *Unterfeld-webel, Sergeant* immediately ordered the three of them to stop, where he demanded to see their papers. On producing them, he screamed at the threesome in broken French, demanding to know what they were doing walking around at that time of night.

Marguerite explained they were walking home after visiting a friend before she was abruptly interrupted by the *Unterfeldwebel.*

"*Tais – toi salope Francaise,*" *Shut- up, you French slut*, he screamed, smacking her across the face with his open hand before staggering backwards.

Blood trickled from Marguerite's nose and she glared at him with the look of death in her eyes. Inside her coat was the Luger pistol she had taken from the Waffen - SS officer she had shot. Thoughts of revenge circled Marguerite's mind and she most desperately wanted to pull the pistol out and shoot the German pig in the head. Discretion got the better of her, for she knew they were close to the citadel and if she shot him dead, they would have Germans crawling all over the place.

"*Qu'est-ceque tu regardes, putain?*" *What are you glaring at, whore?* He barked at her.

While Frank and Raphael were shocked into silence, Marguerite took a deep breath; composed herself and realised her priority was to get Frank to the safety of the cathedral. She replied,

"*Nous serons en route Monsieur,*" *We will be on our way Monsieur.*

With that, Marguerite signalled the other two to get going. They walked past the Germans, not knowing if they were armed and if they would be shot from behind. As they did, the Germans screamed at them to stop. They dared not stop; instead kept walking down the street, all the while hearing the screams of the Germans. They eventually came across a side street where they abruptly did a right- hand turn before making a hasty advance towards the cathedral.

When they reached the rear of the presbytery located a short distance from the cathedral, Marguerite pulled a handkerchief from her trousers and wiped the blood from her nose.

"I '*ad* to use all of my willpower… *oui,* not to shoot the German pig," she said to the others.

An organ could be heard playing within the cathedral, which drowned out the noise of Raphael knocking on the door of the presbytery.

Frank turned to Marguerite and Raphael as they stood in the darkness and said, "Thank you so much. I will never be able to repay you for all you have done for me."

"It is our pleasure *Monsieur Franc,*" said Marguerite, still wiping her nose.

"I will be forever in your debt."

"We will be ever in your debt *Monsieur Franc* for all you '*ave* done in trying to defeat these Nazi pigs."

With that, Frank embraced Marguerite. He held her tight before he shook Raphael's hand.

The door opened to the rear of the presbytery, and Frank was met by Father Fournier, who was dressed in a black cassock. He looked around warily, ensuring they were not noticed before shaking Frank's hand.

"*Goot* evening, I am Father Jean Baptiste Fournier. You must be *Franc*?" he whispered in good English.

"That I am Father."

"We will leave *Monsieur Franc* in your care, *Pere Fournier,*" said Marguerite.

Father Fournier noticed Marguerite's bleeding nose and

asked what happened. After she explained their altercation with the Germans, he insisted she come in and clean up. Marguerite declined his invitation and told him they must be going and Frank was now in his care.

"*Oui, il sera en securité avec moi,*" *Yes, he will be safe with me*, said Father Fournier.

They turned and walked away into the darkness before Frank whispered, "Give my best wishes to Philippe, also," They waved and continued to walk.

"Quick, we must '*ide* you, *Franc*," said Father Fournier before ushering him inside.

Frank nodded, and while looking around warily, Father Fournier turned to him and said with a smile, "That is Cardinal Cerruti playing the organ. '*E* is a very accomplished pianist. '*E* often plays at this time of the night. It '*elps* him to take his mind off the terrible state our country finds itself in with the occupation by these Nazi devils."

Father Fournier led Frank to the back of the presbytery, where a set of stairs led down to a small room underneath the building. He opened the door with a key and lit a gas lantern just inside the door. The room was kept as a storage area with a number of bookshelves, beds and miscellaneous items. They walked past some stored items where they came across a set of cupboards similar to those under a kitchen sink. To the right of the cupboards was a broom closet. Father Fournier opened the door of the closet and shone the gas lantern in. Frank stared in amazement as he could see a set of stairs leading down to a room.

"It looks like a dungeon, Father," Frank said in amazement.

The priest laughed before he turned to Frank.

"It '*as*… been used as a wine cellar in the past but today it is used to… '*ide* downed airmen and Jews. We call it the Caverne."

"Well, I've got to give you points for ingenuity, Father."

Father Fournier smiled before he said, "Come, I will show you your new 'ome."

Father Fournier led the way down the creaking timber stairwell until they reached the bottom. Inside the small room were three single beds and a wardrobe. There was a very rudimentary bathroom, which consisted of a toilet and a very tiny washbasin in the corner. There was also a small timber table with three chairs around it.

They sat down on a couple of the wooden chairs, the flickering light of the lantern illuminating the room's contents.

"This is your new 'ome, Franc. It is, 'ow do you say? ...... no Buckingham Palace, but it will keep you safe."

"It is more than adequate, Father. I can't express how grateful I am for you looking after me."

"You will be safe 'ere until we can organise for the Comet Line to get you out of France and 'ome again. It might take a while before we can move you from 'ere because the Germans are very active at the moment and we do not want to risk you being seen. Rest assured, we will get you on your way when the time is right. I must go now, but I will return to bring you some food. I will leave you with this lantern and there is a box of matches in the drawer of the table next to the bed."

"Thank you, Father."

"Oh, and on no account are you to leave this room without me. The citadel is close by, and many German soldiers are around."

"I understand."

After Father Fournier left, Frank took off his shoes and lay back on the bed. It felt comfortable, and as he rested his head on the pillow, he was overcome with a great sense of serenity. He felt like a child tucked up in the safety of their own home.

As he rested, his thoughts turned to all that had happened since his Lancaster had been shot down. He thought about his crew, his family and what they were doing on the farm. He remembered all of his mates who had been killed in Bomber Command, especially Jimmy. It all seemed like a distant memory with what he was now faced with, and his thoughts drifted to Geraldine. Frank realised both his family and Geraldine would think he had been killed and a feeling of melancholy came over him.

He was deep in contemplation about his predicament when he heard the door to the Caverne open. Father Fournier walked down the staircase, holding the lantern in one hand and a cane basket in the other. The cane basket was covered with a towel, and Frank could smell the aroma of freshly baked bread.

" '*Ere* is some food that will satisfy your appetite *Franc.*"

With that, Father Fournier removed the towel and Frank was met with the sight of a freshly baked baguette. Accompanying it was a chicken dish that gave out a delicious aroma.

"I 'ave also brought you a French dish. It is *coq au vin…* which is how do you say *er…* will make your mouth water. It is braised chicken with wine, mushrooms, salty pork, onions, garlic and brandy."

He had also brought a bottle of red burgundy to go with the meal.

"Gee, who did you rob to make this meal? I certainly wasn't expecting something as appealing as this."

Father Fournier laughed.

"*Bon appétit Monsieur Franc.*"

He gave Frank a big smile and left him to enjoy his meal.

As Frank tucked into his sumptuous repast, he was overcome with gratitude for Father Fournier to have prepared such a beautiful dish when so many around him were going without. After finishing off the bottle of burgundy, Frank went to bed, where he slept like a man without a care in the world. The wine had been the icing on the cake for a delicious meal.

Frank stayed in the room for the next three days, not venturing out once. Father Fournier brought him food and supplied him with a couple of books on the French language. He had many conversations with Frank in the ensuing days and was very interested in his background. They soon struck up a close rapport and Father Fournier realised that Frank could be trusted.

After midnight on the fourth day, Frank was in bed when Father Fournier entered the room with another man.

"*Franc,* this is Cicero. *'E* is English and he *'as* come to stay with you here at the Caverne. Rest assured we are doing our best to get you out of here. I ask you to be patient. I will leave you two gentlemen to get acquainted."

"Thank you, Father," said Cicero.

With that, Father Fournier exited the Caverne as quickly as he arrived.

Cicero, whose real name was Stan Reid, was in his early thirties and was of a thin build and dark hair. He was handsome and spoke with a dignified accent.

"Frank Casey's the name," said Frank, extending his hand.

"Cicero is my name."

"Cicero? What type of a name is that?"

"It's my code name. I'm a member of the SOE."

"What brings you here?" Frank enquired.

Cicero looked at Frank cautiously.

"Father Fournier told me you are a downed airman and assures me you can be trusted."

"I give you my solemn promise that anything you say to me will go no further than this room," said Frank.

"Thank you," said Cicero.

Cicero looked Frank long and hard in the eyes before he continued.

"I was hiding in the home of a Resistance member in Besançon when a *Feldgendarmerie* group got wind that I was there and pounced on the place. I just escaped in the nick of time," he said, wiping his brow with a handkerchief.

"The *Feldgendarmerie,* who are they?"

"They are the German military police. They're a bad lot. They come under the control of the Wehrmacht, but they work in close unison with the SS." Cicero leaned forward and looked Frank in the eye. "There is a traitor in our midst. He has given up several SOE operatives in this area. We aren't sure who it is, but let me assure it will be lights out when we find out who they are," Cicero said, drawing his finger across his throat.

"Let's hope so!" Frank said.

Cicero folded his arms and said, "So, what happened to your aircraft?"

"I was a rear gunner in a Lancaster that bombed the Peugeot factory at Sochaux, but a night fighter got stuck into us. Unfortunately, they blew up our aircraft and I was the only one who survived. I am waiting for the Comet Line to help me escape to Spain and then to England," Frank said.

Cicero raised his eyebrows.

"You seem surprised," Frank enquired.

"I know all about you chaps."

"You do?"

"I certainly do. You probably don't realise it, but the bombing raid you did over the Peugeot factory was a complete disaster."

"It was?" Frank said, surprised.

"Your lot largely missed the factory and smashed the outskirts of a village a short distance away. As a result, a number of people were killed and wounded."

Frank looked at Cicero, dumbfounded.

"I thought it was a successful operation."

Cicero shook his head.

"Nothing could be further from the truth. The locals aren't real happy about Bomber Command's raid on the factory and that's why I am here."

"What are you going to do?"

"SOE has managed to convince Bomber Command not to raid the factory anymore, provided they send in operatives to sabotage the plant. With some help from members of the Maquis and workers inside the plant, I will lead a group into the Peugeot factory and sabotage it."

"Go on!" Frank said, clasping his hands in front of him.

"I don't know if you realise, but as well as making tanks, the Germans have been manufacturing parts in the Peugeot factory for their top- secret V-1 flying bomb."

"What's that?"

"It's a new rocket armed with a warhead that the Germans are in the stages of developing. They plan a terror bombing campaign of England and causing as much destruction as possible."

"What a bunch of bastards," said Frank, leaning back in his chair.

"You're spot on there, old boy. The British government has prioritised that the factory is to be taken out."

"When are you going to sabotage the factory?"

"Our plans have been way laid a trifle since I was moved out of the house in Besançon, but if everything goes to plan, we will hit the factory in two night's time. We have everything in place to severely disrupt the manufacturing of the V-1 bomb. We will save many lives by Bomber Command not raiding the factory."

Before retiring that night, Cicero made it clear to Frank he was not to mention to anybody the upcoming sabotage of the Peugeot factory.

Frank reiterated his solemn promise that he would not say a word about the impending operation.

"I can see you're a good man, Frank, and I know you can be trusted. Believe me, I have seen my fair share of rouges and I know you're not one of them. I'll be off early in the morning and back in the evening," Cicero said.

Frank nodded in agreement before Cicero tucked himself into bed and went to sleep.

On awaking the next morning, Frank noticed Cicero had departed the Caverne without leaving a trace of evidence he had been there. His bed was made and he had taken the small bag he brought with him.

Shortly after, Father Fournier delivered Frank his breakfast, consisting of parmesan croissants and coffee.

"Cicero *'ad* to leave very early as he *'ad* urgent business to attend to." Father Fournier said.

When Frank finished his breakfast, he settled in and read his book on the French language. He felt confident about how well he was brushing up on his French and wanted to test the waters with a stranger. He didn't have to wait long. He sat on his bed reading for about half an hour when Father Fournier entered the Caverne, followed by a man and a woman in their early thirties.

"*Franc,* this is Jacques and Marion Deneuve. They are… *er* 'usband and ...er wife and are members of the Comet Line. They are here to 'elp you escape," he said in a whisper.

After a cordial introduction, the conversation took a nose-dive when Frank decided to try his French out on them and got it muddled up, resulting in a sizzling rebuke from Marion.

"*Je suis trés heureux de rencontrer votre connaissance.*" *I am very pleased to meet your acquaintance*, Frank said with a smile.

"*De méme Franc. Pere Fournier nous a parlé de vous. Il a dit que vous étiez un homme merveilleux,*" Likewise, Franc. Father Fournier *spoke to us about you. He said you were a wonderful man,* said Jacques.

What Frank meant to say in response was, "*Merci Jacques. Je suis súr que vous étes un homme merveilleux, et Madame Marion est une femme charmante.*" *Thankyou Jacques. I am sure you are also a wonderful man, and Madame Marion is a lovely woman.*

Somewhere in between Frank using his rudimentary French, he mistakenly called Marion a beautiful slut. Silence fell on the room as Frank wondered what he had said.

Marion glared at Frank, comprehending that what she had just heard was correct.

Suddenly, she exploded.

"*Vous honteux porc!*" *You shameful pig!* Marion bellowed at Frank before she stepped forward and slapped him across his face with her open hand. She stormed out of the room, ranting obscenities in French.

"What did I say wrong?" Frank said, holding the side of his face.

"You called my wife a...er... slut, you ignorant buffoon," Jacques bellowed at Frank, only inches from his face. "I 'ave a *goot* mind to '*it,* you," he screamed at Frank with his fist raised.

"Oh, I am so sorry, Jacques, I got my French muddled up. I meant to say that she is a *femme charmante.*"

Meanwhile, Father Fournier was standing in the background with his hand over his mouth, trying to hold back muffled laughter. Eventually, he composed himself and stepped forward to address the situation.

"Jacques, I am certain *Franc* meant no… *er ´arm*. He is *er*… still trying to *er*… polish up on *'is* French. It was a simple mistake, that's all."

"Please forgive me, *Jacques*. I apologise most profusely and sincerely. I simply got my French muddled up," Frank pleaded with him.

Jacques looked at Frank for an eternity and then at Father Fournier.

"It is a simple mistake that anyone can make," he said before breaking out into muffled laughter. "No *'arm er*… done, *Franc,*" he said, covering his mouth with his hand, trying to drown out the sound of his laughter. "Now comes the *'ard* part, trying to convince Marion," he said, raising his eyebrows before heading up the stairs and out the door.

From inside the Caverne, Father Fournier and Frank could hear an animated conversation taking place in French between Jacques and Marion. Eventually, Father Fournier turned to Frank and said,

"I think everything is all smoothed out now, *Franc.*"

After a few minutes, the couple re- entered the Caverne, with Marion looking rather coy.

"*Franc,* Marion *'as* told me that … *er* all is forgiven," said Jacques.

"Fine, I am glad she has accepted my apology." Frank said.

The conversation resumed as if nothing had happened and Jacques and Marion informed Frank he was in the final stages of his escape and he would be on his way to England. They explained in detail that through a network of people; he was to be taken from Besançon to Bordeaux, Bayonne over the Pyrenees into neutral Spain and then to San Sebastian, Bilbao, Madrid, and then onto British controlled Gibraltar. From there, he would be flown back to England. Frank felt enormous relief when he heard this, but none more so when they informed him he would soon receive a visit by the man who was organising the escape. The man's name was Thiery Bonaparte and he too worked for the Comet Line.

It was just after lunch when Thiery visited Frank. As was the custom, he was led into the Caverne by Father Fournier and after a brief introduction; he was left alone with Frank.

Thiery was an overweight Frenchmen short in stature with sandy hair and a pasty complexion. On first impression, Frank didn't think he was the type of person who could run a couple of laps around a football oval, let alone lead an escape party. It was only after he introduced himself to Frank in both fluent English and French and confidently explained the escape plan's modus operandus, he relaxed.

"I believe Jacques and Marion Deneuve paid you a visit today, *Franc*?"

"They did indeed."

"They are fine people and a great asset to the Comet Line," Thiery said with a mischievous grin.

"I found them very helpful," Frank said.

Frank's hopes were further boosted when Thiery explained the five journeys he had made taking downed airmen to Spain via the Comet Line. Thiery spoke passionately about the good fight the allies were taking up to the Nazis and his earnest wish was that Frank make it back to England so he could resume flying.

As much as his plans accentuated Frank's hopes, his instinct told him he should still exercise a certain amount of caution in what he said to Thiery.

The two of them talked for about fifteen minutes when Thiery offered Frank a cigarette, which he accepted. He lit Frank's cigarette, then crossed his legs before drawing back and exhaling. He looked around the room inquisitively, which Frank noticed, before turning to him and saying.

"'As anyone else been staying *'ere* or visited you *'ere, Franc?"* he said with narrowed eyes.

"Other than Father Fournier and Jacques and Marion, nobody else has visited."

Thiery looked Frank straight in the eyes before drawing on his cigarette.

"Are you certain of that, *Franc?"*

Frank looked at Thiery poker- faced and said,

"Come to think of it, I did have a visitor last night," Frank said, drawing back on his cigarette.

"Who was that?" Thiery said, edging forward in his seat.

"I saw a big fat rat scurry into that crack between the ceiling and the wall," he said, pointing to the spot.

Thiery looked at Frank seriously before leaning back in his seat and laughing loudly.

"I appreciate a sense of humour in a man, *Franc!"*

"Brevity is the soul of all wit," Frank said with a grin.

"Indeed, it is,*"* Thiery said before clearing his throat and saying.

"Still, we *'ave* to be very careful, as we believe there is a trai-tor among us."

"Is that so?" Frank said, expressionless.

"Yes, indeed, and if you do 'ave a visit from anybody, make sure you inform me."

Frank nodded in agreement.

Thiery then asked Frank for all the names of those who had helped him since his Lancaster had been shot down. Frank became suspicious, to which Thiery explained it was customary to reward those who had helped downed airmen escape, with 100 francs each. Frank acknowledged his generosity and gave him the names of all those who had assisted him. He thanked Frank and said his escape would occur the following night. They talked for another half hour, and as a parting gift, he left Frank with a pouch of tobacco, which he appreciated.

It was just after 7.00 pm when Cicero arrived back at the Caverne with a bottle of Merlot hidden under his coat that Father Fournier had given him.

Cicero placed the bottle of red wine on the table and smacked his hands together.

"Well, it's on, old boy," he said enthusiastically.

"What night will the big bang take place?" Frank said with a grin.

"Tomorrow night."

"Excellent, let's drink to that," Frank said.

With that, Cicero opened the bottle of Merlot and poured a generous amount into two cups and handed one to Frank.

"Cheers, old boy," Cicero said, before raising a cup.

"Cheers to your operation Cicero and my impending escape, which will be tomorrow night also."

"Oh?" Cicero said, raising his eyebrows.

"I had a visit from a number of members of the Comet

Line today and they outlined a detailed plan of my escape route into Spain."

"What members visited you?"

"A married couple named Jacques and Marion Deneuve, and after lunch, a man named Thiery Bonaparte."

"Oh! What did he look like?"

"He was a fat little bugger with sandy hair and a pasty complexion."

"Mmm, I've never heard of him," Cicero said with suspicion.

"Come to think of it, he didn't look like he could knock a fly off a chop, let alone lead an escape party," said Frank.

"You didn't mention I had been staying here?"

"No, not at all, although he did ask if anybody had been staying here with me."

"Mmm, I would be very cautious of what you say, Frank, as he sounds suspicious."

"I was cautious of telling him too much."

"That would be very wise."

Frank and Cicero had been talking for the best part of an hour and had finished most of the bottle of Merlot when there was a knock on the door. Father Fournier appeared at the top of the stairwell, holding a lantern and a food basket. He slowly walked down the stairs.

"Gentlemen, I 'ave prepared something extraordinary for the both of you for supper."

With that, he removed the cloth from the top of the basket to reveal a sumptuous dish.

"This is one of my favourites and my mother Antoinette's signature dish. It is called *Blanquette de Veau,* or 'ow do you say in English … *er* veal stew. It is *tres, tres bien," very, very good gentlemen.*

"There is no doubt about you, Father Fournier. You are quite simply a *cordon bleu* chef. It smells delicious," Frank said, taking a big whiff.

"Please, *Monsieur Franc,* you embarrass me. I *'ave* my parents, Maurice and Antoinette, to thank for my love of cooking, which I learnt from them when I was a young boy," he said, holding his hands close to his chest.

"Father Fournier, I will remember your generosity for the rest of my life," said Cicero.

"Ahhhh, you are too kind, *Monsieur* Cicero." Father Fournier said with a big smile, "after all, we are *'ere* on earth to serve one another, not to destroy each other like these Nazi devils are doing."

With that, Father Fournier produced a bottle of Cabernet Sauvignon from underneath his black cassock.

"I think this bottle of wine should complement your meal, gentlemen," he said.

"You are too kind, Father," said Frank.

"It is the least I can do to *'elp* you gentleman," he said. "Now, I will leave you to enjoy your supper."

As they ate, Cicero turned to Frank.

"I think I will make this my last supper with you, Frank. I feel a bit edgy about this Thiery character. Tomorrow morning I will be off."

"I have no other option but to rely on Thiery to help me get back to England," said Frank.

"That may be the case, but be careful, Frank!" Cicero said.

After their meal, Frank and Cicero finished both the Cabernet Sauvignon and Merlot while they talked before they retired for the night. Frank was in such a well- oiled state that the risks associated with his impending escape were furthest from his mind.

It was early evening of the next day and as Frank waited in the Caverne for Thiery, he contemplated Cicero's departure in the pre-dawn earlier that day.

"I'll be off, old boy. The best of British luck to you and I hope everything goes to plan," he said.

"Likewise, Cicero and I hope you blast the living daylights out of the Peugeot factory."

"With a little luck, we hope to give Jerry the old tinker, the best Guy Fawkes display he has ever seen," he said with a grin.

Cicero grabbed his bag and made his way for the Caverne door before giving Frank a final wave. With that, he disappeared into the darkness.

A knock on the door broke Frank from his reverie. Frank opened the door to Father Fournier and a smiling Thiery, dressed in a black beret with coat and trousers.

"Are you ready to leave, *Franc*?" Thiery said.

"I am."

After they walked up the stairs, Father Fournier embraced Frank and said, "All the best to you *Monsieur Franc,* it '*as* been a pleasure meeting you and I '*ope* our paths will cross again one day."

"Likewise, Father Fournier and I will carry your memory with me for the rest of my life."

They were prophetic words, for little did Frank realise how much influence the French priest would have on his life.

Thiery led Frank out into the night and down the street, where there was a black Peugeot waiting in a dark alley with the motor running. Sitting inside the car were two men, one in the driver's seat and one in the back seat. Aged in their early thirties, the one in the front had a scar that ran down the left- hand side of his face, while the other was unshaven.

"Take a seat, *Franc*," Thiery said, pointing to the front passenger seat.

"Aren't you coming also, Thiery?"Frank said nervously.

"I will join you a little later. In the meantime, these two gentlemen will take you to Jacques and Marion Deneuve's '*ouse*."

Frank got in, albeit anxiously, and as the car drove off, he watched as Thiery about turned and walked away into the night. It was the last he would ever see of him.

"All is well, *Monsieur!* " the driver said to Frank in a thick French accent.

"Yes, *Monsieur,* all is well," the man in the back seat said while resting a hand on Frank's right shoulder.

He also spoke with a heavy French accent and as the car drove along, he reassured Frank everything was fine and they would soon arrive at their destination.

But things were anything but fine from where Frank sat, as he could see the towering figure of the Citadel of Besançon come into view. Frank became anxious before it became apparent they were driving straight towards the citadel.

Little did Frank know, Father Fournier had inadvertently introduced him to the notorious multi–lingual double agent Gaspard Petit, who was using the alias of Thiery Bonaparte. Posing as a member of the Comet Line, Gaspard was, in fact, a double agent for the *Geheime Feldpolizei Secret Field Police* (GFP). He specialised in tracking down the so- called 'internal enemies' like the French Resistance and members of the Comet Line. Gaspard had been successfully infiltrated into the Comet Line and claimed to have taken several downed airmen to neutral Spain. He had been responsible for the betrayal of numerous allied airmen, French Resistance and Jews, whom he then handed them over to the GFP.

The GFP had received classified information that there was an SOE operative in the Besançon area. They had passed that information onto Gaspard, hoping he could find out who it was, and more importantly, what they were planning.

"I thought we were going to Jacques and Marion's house? This looks anything but their house to me!" Frank said with a raised voice.

"Please, *Monsieur,* I will '*ave* to ask you to keep your voice down," said the man driving.

"Keep my voice down? I'll be buggered, you prick," screamed Frank. "This isn't Jacques and Marion's house. That Thiery, the treacherous bastard, wait till I catch up with him! I am getting out of here," he yelled before opening the door.

Frank had the car door open and was about to jump onto the roadway when the man in the back seat smashed him on the back of the head with the butt of his pistol. He then pulled him back into the car with Frank in a dazed state.

"I suggest you calm down, *Monsieur,* before you end up in real trouble," said the man in the back seat.

He held the pistol to Frank's head while the driver sped along. In his dazed state, Frank vaguely recognised the moat of the citadel.

Chapter 16

Mid April, 1943. Citadel of Besançon

FRANK WAS STILL shaky when two SS soldiers dressed in grey dragged him out of the car at the Citadel of Besançon.

"I '*ope* you enjoy your new safe '*ouse Monsieur Franc*?" said the driver with a sinister laugh.

Frank gave him a look of contempt before he said, "You're a couple of treacherous bastards. All of France will condemn you for what you have done!"

"So long, airman!" the driver said before the two Frenchmen disappeared out of sight.

"*Schnell, schnell aufstehen!*" *Quick, quick, get up*, one of the soldiers screamed before smashing Frank over the back of the head with his fist.

Frank was dragged inside the Citadel, where he was taken to a room with no windows and a lone chair positioned in the middle of the floor. His hands were tied together behind his back.

Ten minutes elapsed before an SS soldier dressed in grey and carrying a bucket of water entered the room. The soldier was a brute of a man standing well over six feet tall with closely shaven hair and a scar above his top lip. The soldier threw the bucket of water over Frank's head. "*Wach auf Schwein*!" *Wake up, pig!* The soldier screamed at Frank.

Frank shook his head from side to side before giving the soldier a look of disdain.

"*Wisch dir diesen Blick aus dem Gesicht,*" *Wipe that look off your face*, he said before smashing Frank over the face with his open hand.

Minutes later, an SS officer holding the rank of *Hauptsturmfuhrer, Captain* dressed in an immaculately pressed black uniform, walked into the room. He was the symbol of Aryan arrogance, with blonde hair and blue eyes. In his early thirties, a slim build of medium height and sharp features.

"*Ve vould* have had you arrested days ago, *terrorflieger,* but *ve vere* trying to find out who *za* SOE operative was, staying with you at *za* Cathedral," the officer said in fluent English.

Frank gave the officer his name, rank and serial number and denied anyone was staying with him. This resulted in him being hit over the head, followed by a blow to the shins by the jack boot wearing soldier. Frank reeled in pain.

"*Ve* know somebody was staying in *za* room with you *terrorflieger. Vhat* was his name and *vhere* is he and *ve vill* spare your life?" screamed the officer.

"Nobody was staying in the room with me," Frank said.

Frank was hit again and again, but would not reveal the name of Cicero to the officer.

The brutal interrogation went on for what Frank felt was an eternity. They didn't realise what a tough individual he was and they became increasingly frustrated that he would not divulge any information. After an hour of this treatment and angry he would not give them a name, they left the room.

It was in the early morning hours and Frank was in a dazed state, when he could hear the moaning of a man in the room next to him. Suddenly, he realised it was Father Fournier.

"Comment s'appelle l'homme qui sejourne a la Cathedrale?" *What is the name of the man staying at the Cathedral?* the officer screamed at Father Fournier.

Father Fournier would not divulge Cicero's name to the Nazis and as a result, they administered a brutal beating to him till the dawn. Father Fournier informed the officer that Frank was a downed airman and he didn't know of any man hiding in the Cathedral and that he should be treated as a POW. He also told them Cardinal Cerruti had no knowledge that Frank was staying at the Cathedral. Father Fournier was more concerned for Frank's welfare than his own, and although badly beaten, he argued incessantly with the SS officer that Frank should be treated as a POW. As Father Fournier sat severely beaten, he prayed the rosary, which gave him comfort and strength.

Meanwhile, in the early morning hours, the SS officer with his brutal subordinate re- entered Frank's room for another session of integration. Frank was badly beaten and bruised from tip to toe, but what the Nazis hadn't counted on was his incredible resilience. It was resilience forged on the anvil of experience as a young man at the hands of his father. Frank's strong spirit was as tough as a blue-heeler cattle dog. Still, Frank would not speak except to remind his brutal oppressors he was a downed airman and should be afforded all the rights that a POW should receive.

"You are a filthy *terrorflieger* and you *vill* be treated accordingly, *Herr* Casey," the officer barked at him.

"I am a POW and must be treated as one."

"*Ve* have just received information in *za* last hour *zat za* Peugeot Motor Works at Sochaux has been sabotaged. The damage is extensive and it *vill* be out of operation indefinitely. *Ve* know you have information concerning who was involved *wiz zis* attack," said the officer.

"I don't know what you are talking about," said Frank.

Frank's response incurred another beating, this time knocking him out. As a result of their treatment, both Frank and Father Fournier had been rendered unconscious. Unbeknownst to them, the SS had rounded up Gabriel Boucher and Leon Gagne, the two members of the Maquis who had helped Frank escape to the Jura Mountains. They were also taken to the Citadel and badly beaten before Gabriel, at breaking point, divulged Cicero's name, and those who were assisting him, to the SS officer.

While Frank and Father Fournier were being tortured, Cicero had slipped into the Peugeot Motor Works just after midnight, disguised as a factory worker. Stocks of incendiary devices and limpet mines had been parachuted into France a couple of weeks before and hidden inside the factory. Cicero and his team spent an hour planting the bombs, and after shaking hands with them, he slipped out of the factory unnoticed.

It was around 1.15 am the first of the explosives went off, with steel doors flung a hundred feet into the air. Fire swept through the factory, leaving only a blackened ruin.

After the sabotage, Cicero rendezvoused with Jacques and Marion Deneuve in Besançon, where he stayed at their place for the night. Marguerite, who was still in Besançon, had made her way to their place and informed them Gabriel and Leon had been arrested by the Gestapo. With that knowledge, the three of them felt it was prudent they leave as soon as possible. They left before dawn the next day, avoiding being captured by the

Gestapo by less than half an hour. They made a hasty retreat to the Jura Mountains, avoiding German patrols who were scouring the countryside for them. As for Father Fournier, his fate had already been sealed, and retribution by the SS was swift and brutal.

It was late the next day when three SS soldiers, led by the *Hauptsturmfuhrer,* came to Father Fournier's room. They took him to an area close by with an open roof, but surrounded by sandstone walls on all sides and a cobblestone floor. They lined him up on the wall with his hands tied behind his back and stood to attention with rifles by their sides, waiting for the command from the officer to fire.

Father Fournier understood his fate and with blood dripping from his nose, he prayed openly as he was taken to his place of execution. He continued to defend Frank as a downed airman who should be treated as a POW. Father Fournier was brave and looked his executioners in the eye as he spoke passionately about the cause he belonged to. He gave the SS officer an impassioned speech in English so Frank could hear.

"In condemning me, you condemn all of France and our freedom you 'ave taken from us. You condemn all the members of the clergy, both past and present."

"*Maintenant tu m'ecoutes pretre!*" *Now you listen to me, priest!* The officer screamed at Father Fournier.

"*Non! Tu m'ecoutes!*" *No! You listen to me!* Father Fournier roared while looking directly at the officer. "You 'ave made enemies with most of the civilised world and the actions of your regime will not be forgotten. You and the brutal band of thugs you represent will be accountable for your despicable deeds. I 'ave lived my life as best as I can to Christ's teachings and I am not afraid to die, for I am on the right side of my maker. Like me, you will also be accountable to God one day. *Vive la France!*"

The officer looked at Father Fournier and swallowed hard before turning to the firing squad. After some time, he said,

"*Zielfeuer bereit.*" *Ready, aim, fire.* The bullets struck Father Fournier in the heart and his body slumped to the ground. A short time later, a trickle of blood ran down his lifeless body and onto the cobblestones.

Gabriel and Leon were soon marched from their rooms to their place of execution. Gabriel screamed and professed his innocence while pleading for them to spare his life as he had a family. As Gabriel cried unashamedly, Leon stayed silent throughout the entire ordeal. The sound of bullets could be heard shortly after and they also lay dead on the cobblestones.

By this stage, Frank's heart was racing and he believed his number was up and that he too, would be executed. He waited in trepidation for what he thought was his end, but to his surprise, they did not come for him.

Frank spent a frightful night wide awake. When the morning came, instead of facing a firing squad, he was given a breakfast of cold porridge, the antithesis of anything Father Fournier had served up.

Soon after, he was placed into the back of a secured truck and driven through the countryside. At first, Frank thought the Germans might haul him out into the country somewhere to finish him off, but when the vehicle did not stop for over an hour, he realised they had something else planned for him.

Although the drive was bumpy, Frank eventually fell asleep. He had been in the truck for four and a half hours when he was awoken by the blast of the truck's horn. He lifted his head and looked out the rear window, which had bars on it, to be greeted by the sight of the Arc de Triomphe in Paris.

Chapter 17

Mid April, 1943. *Prison de Fresnes, Paris* **(Fresnes Prison Paris)**

ON SEEING THE *Arc de Triomphe*, Frank realised he was in Paris. He was perplexed as to why he had been taken from Besançon to France's capital.

As the truck roared through the streets, Frank reflected on the juxtaposition he was in. He was a prisoner, but at the same time being given a guided tour of Paris. Although he had been given a severe beating by his German captures and witness to Father Fournier's execution, he shook his head at the diabolical situation he found himself in.

"Even if the krauts finish me off, at least I can say I've seen the sights of Paris," he said to himself, succumbing to a bout of black humour.

Frank had always managed to handle the big situations where the small ones could bring him undone. It was because of this he had kept his head.

The truck drove south of Paris, eventually turning off onto a cobbled road lined with poplar trees. The truck stopped at the main gate and the driver spoke in German to the guard. Frank could see twin statues of the Sisters of Mercy at the gates and at first thought, he must be in a convent. Nothing could have been further from the truth, for Frank had arrived at Fresnes Prison 12 miles (19km) south of Paris.

No sooner had he arrived then Frank was bundled out of the truck and taken inside. Here, he viewed for the first time the prison that housed mainly French prisoners jailed for crimes such as insurrection and insurgence.

Frank was given a small cell surrounded by stone walls and covered with crumbling plaster. There was no lighting in the cell and a straw mattress was provided for his bed. There was a toilet, washbasin, tap and a small wooden shelf. There was a tiny peep hole where a guard could shine a torch through the small inspection slit. Frank stayed in that cell in isolation for seven days, where he was fed very inadequate food and irregularly. His isolation allowed him to recover from his injuries and to regather his thoughts, although unbeknownst to him, the Gestapo were softening him up so they could interrogate him.

On the eighth day, he was bundled into the back of a prison truck and taken to Gestapo Headquarters in the centre of Paris. He was again subjected to a brutal interrogation for the best part of an hour, where he was stripped and searched. He demanded to be treated as a POW, but this fell on deaf ears with the Gestapo. They labelled him a police prisoner as they saw him as a *terrorflieger*. Any sign of resistance was met with quick and brutal retribution, including a kick to the shins or a blow to the head. The Gestapo was a law unto itself and had no respect for the rules of the Geneva Convention or the appropriate protocol for treating POWs. They asked him about his knowledge of any SOE operatives in the Besançon area, but he said nothing. Once again, Frank was unsure if he was to get out of this alive, but after divulging nothing more than his name, rank and serial number, he was bundled back into the prison truck and driven back to Fresnes Prison.

Frank returned to his dark prison cell, where he stayed in isolation for two weeks. Twice, he was sent back to Gestapo HQ for more questioning, but would not divulge any information about the French Resistance or SOE operatives. He could hear the groans of other prisoners being tortured from his cell and shots rang out periodically. This sent a shiver up his spine as he concluded he would be next.

One day, Frank had an altercation with a prison guard after he had demanded to see an officer about his predicament. The guard roared at Frank in German to stay back, and Frank, having had enough of this treatment, lunged at him with his fist clenched, ready to smash him before the guard made a hasty retreat out of the cell slamming the door shut behind him. The Germans realised Frank was a hothead, so they posted extra guards to keep him in check. Frank was continually thinking of how he could escape from the flea and lice- ridden hell hole he was in and the Germans were well aware of this, so kept a watchful eye on him.

In early May, Frank had been in Fresnes Prison for three weeks. He was being moved to another cell when he came across a German officer walking down the hallway. He fronted him with no regard for his safety as he was fed up with his treatment. The officer produced a pistol out of his holster and pointed it at Frank. He told the officer in no uncertain terms he was a downed airman and he should be afforded the rights of the

Geneva Convention and be treated as a POW. He continued by telling the officer that Germany was on the ropes and they were going to lose the war. The guard escorting Frank was about to hit him on the back of the head when the officer stopped him. Frank's conversation had struck a chord with him. The officer put his pistol back inside his holster before informing him in perfect English he would have to look into the matter. He then barked at Frank to fall into line, where he was taken to his new cell.

Although his new cell was no better than the one he had come from, the difference was this one had lighting. Although the lighting was perpetually left on, Frank was glad to be away from the blackened dungeon that had been his home for the last three weeks. He ascertained the Germans had tried to soften him up by keeping him in the dark cell but, not being able to break his spirit, had moved him to a cell with lighting.

Frank had been in his new cell for two weeks when one day he heard the familiar sounds of Morse code being tapped on the water pipe which ran up the inside wall of the cell. From the message, Frank could ascertain that an RAF airman was in a nearby cell. He replied by tapping his spoon on the water pipe. A message soon came through informing him he was among 30 other RAF prisoners in Fresnes. His spirits were lifted as, up until that point, he believed he was the only downed airman in the entire prison, which housed 1200 cells.

Over the next couple of weeks, Frank was able to find out through morse code that more captured airmen were being delivered to the prison, including British, Australian, Canadian and Americans. The downed airmen gathered information from Frenchmen departing the prison each day on working parties by conversing with them through an opening in the heating system which ran up the wall.

Frank had been in Fresnes Prison for almost two months when, in mid-June 1943, Marguerite, Philippe and Raphael made their way down from the Jura Mountains to Besançon. They had received conclusive evidence the traitor in their midst was Gaspard Petit, alias Thiery Bonaparte. Further evidence had revealed that Gaspard was responsible for the betrayal of twenty downed airmen who were now incarcerated in Fresnes Prison and up to thirty members of the Maquis who had been executed by the Nazis. The Maquis had received credible information that Gaspard regularly dined at a popular establishment in Besançon, named Cafe Grainger. It was well known that Gaspard liked to get his fill at the cafe, which was also a popular spot for members of the Waffen SS stationed at the Citadel of Besançon.

With that information, the Maquis decided to launch an operation which they had dubbed *Operation attrape - rats Operation ratcatcher* to exterminate the double agent. Although Marguerite had never met Gaspard, she had seen a number of photographs of him, so she was given the operation to eliminate the traitor. Marguerite was bitter about Father Fournier's execution and wanted to seek revenge on the man who had betrayed both him and Frank. Marguerite gathered Philippe and Raphael to carry out the operation, and made their way from the Jura Mountains to Besançon.

The Maquis learned that Gaspard would be at the Cafe Grainger at noon, where an agent of the GFP would pay him his reward. It would be 8,000 French francs for each airman he handed over to the Germans. Gaspard had been making a very lucrative reward from his dealings with the GFP and he chose his favourite cafe on a sunny but fresh day to receive his payment. Marguerite had packed an assortment of weapons inside her coat to make sure Gaspard departed this earth as quickly as possible. Approaching the crowded Cafe Grainger before noon, Philippe and Raphael sat down at a table while Marguerite positioned herself down the street and out of sight. Gaspard was nowhere to be seen and Raphael and Philippe were wary as, seated on the far side of the cafe, were two Waffen SS officers. The Frenchmen did not notice the two men aged in their early thirties, sitting three tables from them, immaculately dressed in tailor-made dark suits. They were members of the GFP.

Philippe and Raphael had been seated for approximately five minutes. They were quietly sipping on their coffee, engaging in limited conversation when a fat, short, sandy-haired, pasty individual entered the cafe and sat down half a dozen tables from them. The two men shuffled in their seats and checked their weapons hidden inside their coats. They had never seen Gaspard before, but by the description Marguerite had given them, they were certain this was their man. They made limited eye contact with him as they ordered more coffee. Gaspard ordered a coffee followed by an entrée of basil salmon terrine. He was sipping on his coffee when one of the suited men approached his table and discreetly placed an unmarked sealed white envelope in his lap before returning to his seat. Gaspard barely noticed the envelope before carefully placing it inside his coat pocket. Philippe and Raphael witnessed this and were certain this was their man.

Gaspard was looking at the menu when his entrée arrived. He ordered his favourite dish, pork braised in burgundy with steamed potatoes and vegetables, served with a glass of Beaujolais.

"*Merci Madame*," Gaspard said.

The waitress nodded and Gaspard wasted no time in starting on the salmon.

He was into his third mouthful when Marguerite quietly slipped into the cafe, discreetly sat down opposite Gaspard and greeted him by his alias, Thiery. He was surprised by the sudden appearance of the red- haired beauty, who he had never seen before. His expression soon turned to one of delight. Marguerite wasted no time in coming to the point. In a whisper, she told Gaspard she had heard he was the man to see about helping downed airmen, in which he nodded discreetly. Marguerite continued by informing him she had a downed airman she was hiding and could he be of assistance?

Gaspard looked around cautiously before turning to Marguerite and whispering, *"S'il vous plait madame, nous devons etre discrets dans un tel environnement."* Please, Madame, we have to be discreet in such an environment.

Marguerite was aware of the two Waffen SS officers. She had also noticed the two suited gentlemen seated nearby glancing across at their table. Marguerite realised she only had a narrow window of opportunity to get her man. Gaspard indicated the matter would be better discussed somewhere else, to which she agreed. Marguerite produced from her coat pocket a box of the finest French cigars. Gaspard was suitably impressed and discreetly placed them into his coat pocket. Marguerite sensed now was a perfect time, and after quickly glancing across to Philippe and Raphael, she stood up, startling Gaspard. She walked around the table to where he was sitting. He gave her a look of angst before placing his fork on the table. She stared him in the eye and said, *"Et c'est aussi pour toi, Gaspard Petit, gros cochon traître!"* And this is also for you, Gaspard Petit, you treacherous fat pig!

Gaspard's eyes widened with alarm at the disclosure of his real name. With that, Marguerite pulled out a twelve- inch butcher's knife from inside her coat and plunged it into his stomach before pulling it upwards with both hands towards his rib cage, where it remained.

"Ahhhh!"Gaspard screamed as Marguerite wiped the blood off her hand and onto his coat.

The two men in suits jumped up from where they were sitting. Knocking down their table and brandishing pistols, they fired at Marguerite. She avoided being hit by darting to one side where she produced two pistols, and with one in either hand, she fired, missing both of them. Meanwhile, Philippe disclosed a pistol from inside his coat, but it jammed when he tried to fire. Raphael was also brandishing a pistol, which he fired at one of the agents, managing to hit him in the shoulder. The injured agent fired at Philippe, who was trying to get his gun to work, and hit him in the heart, dropping him to the ground. The two Waffen - SS officers had retrieved their pistols from their holsters and were firing wildly from the other side of the cafe while people hid under tables. Marguerite had retrieved the gun from Philippe and fired a burst at the agent, who had shot him, managing to hit him in the chest, killing him instantly. She then fired toward the two SS officers, but they avoided being hit by ducking for cover under a table.

Meanwhile, Raphael had hit the other GFP agent in the side of the head, killing him instantly. While hiding under the table, a bullet from one of the SS officers had grazed the inside of Marguerite's calf, managing to open up a nasty wound. The cafe was full of smoke and the two SS offices were barking orders in French for Marguerite and Raphael to put down their weapons, to which they responded with more gunfire. Marguerite was crawling on her knees, darting from table to table where patrons were madly scrambling out of her way. From the cover of an upturned table, she spotted the uniform of one of the SS officers and with a burst of fire; she hit him in the upper thigh. He rolled over in pain, dropping his weapon before Marguerite lined him up and finished him off with a bullet to the head. The other SS officer, who had managed to avoid being hit, kept firing before Raphael hit him with a single shot, which penetrated his lower lip and came out through his cheek. While incapacitated, Raphael calmly walked up to him and shot him at point- blank range in the forehead.

The cafe was a mess with tables and chairs upturned while bullets had hit windows and doors, leaving smashed glass and bullet holes everywhere. Philippe was lying dead underneath a table, along with the two agents and officers. Gaspard was dead, slumped over his entrée with the knife protruding from his stomach and blood trickling down the tablecloth.

Raphael made his way over to Marguerite, who was groaning from the bullet wound to her leg and, with no time to spare, helped her out of the café. They ran down a side street, where they found a back door open to a hotel that led to the laundry. Raphael then tore a sheet to pieces and made a makeshift bandage, which he wrapped around Marguerite's injury. They hid under a pile of dirty linen, where they stayed well into the night. Outside, they could hear the voices of German soldiers frantically searching the streets for the two of them.

It was in the early morning hours and under cover of darkness, Marguerite and Raphael made their way to a member of the Maquis who lived outside of Besançon, where she had her injury further attended to. They spent several days there waiting for the situation to cool down before making their way back to the Jura Mountains.

Meanwhile, time ticked away slowly for Frank as he languished in Fresnes Prison, not knowing what fate awaited him.

Chapter 18

Sunday, September 3rd 1944. Fresnes Prison, Paris.

IT WAS THE morning of Sunday, 3rd September, 1944, and Frank had been in Fresnes Prison for seventeen months. With the uprising of the French forces of the Interior, which was the military structure of the French Resistance and the approach of American military units after the D-Day landings, the Germans were feeling the pressure, so they decided to evacuate Fresnes prison.

After surviving the bitter cold and stifling hot summer of Paris, it was a humid autumn morning as the sun belted down on the prison. Frank was sitting in his cell in isolation when suddenly there was shouting from a guard as he opened the door.

"Out of your cell on *zer* double," the German guard said.

"What's happening?" Frank said.

"To *zer* courtyard for you. *Schnell!*" the guard yelled.

Although the humidity was stifling, Frank was glad to be out of his cramped cell. Three guards led him down to the courtyard where, to his surprise, there was an ever-increasing group of allied airmen who were not dressed in uniform. Frank immediately recognised many of the airmen, including an English wireless operator named Max Clayton, a member of his squadron. It was a multinational group consisting of Brits, Australians, Americans, Canadians and New Zealanders. There was much shouting and cheers as fellow airmen who had not seen each other for a considerable amount of time recognised each other. The group consisted of 147 allied airmen and speculation grew that maybe they were being transported to a POW camp.

A German officer soon brought the jovial ensemble to attention and told them they were to be taken across to the other side of Paris, where they were to board a train.

Frank turned to Max and said in a laconic tone, "You little beauty, another chance to have a look at the sights of Paris."

A German guard, who was one of 50 escorting the airmen, overheard Frank's remark and in English exclaimed, "*Zis* will be no sightseeing tour *terrorflieger.* Anybody who tries to escape will be shot!"

His sinister comment was an indication of what was coming.

After a breakfast consisting of lukewarm porridge, they were bundled onto buses and driven to the *Gare de L'Est* station. Waiting was a steam locomotive pulling 25 cattle trucks. The airmen were among a group of over 2,300 prisoners consisting of men and women. They were soon bundled into the waiting cattle cars with just under 100 to a wagon. The guards were ruthless in their treatment of the prisoners, with many lashing out with the butts of their rifles and kicking people with their boots. One lunatic guard had a tree branch in his hand, hitting people with demon- like fury as they ran past him while barking orders in German. It was here Frank noticed for the first time the New Zealand officer, who was to become the leader of the allied airmen. The airmen were soon to learn the New Zealander was one tough bastard, and with his rugged features, he didn't take shit from anybody, especially the SS guards. From where Frank stood close to the cattle car, he observed the gutsy New Zealand officer take umbrage with the way the German guard was lashing out at people.

"How about you lay off?" the officer said to the brutal, branch-carrying guard.

His response was to smash him over the side of the head with the branch, which sent him flying backwards and opened up the side of his face. He picked himself up and, after steadying himself, said to the brute, "You must feel like a hero belting defenceless people."

The guard pointed his sub-machine gun at the officer and said in broken English. "Get *zer* hell out of here, *terrorflieger* or I'll shoot you dead like *za* dog."

Knowing the guard was trigger-happy, the officer decided not to test him any longer, so after glaring at the brute, he turned and walked away.

Frank didn't know who this man was or what rank he held, but he was suitably impressed by the sheer guts of the New Zealander. As he walked on, Frank gave him a nod in acknowledgement of his courage and received a nod back.

Soon after, Frank and Max boarded a wagon together and inside, the conditions were appalling. With so many people jammed inside each wagon, breathing in the stifling heat was difficult. The only ventilation provided was a small slit covered with barbed wire at the top of the wagon. Frank took the lead and organised the prisoners to rotate their positions, so everyone had a chance to catch some fresh air near the ventilation slot. Each wagon was allocated a 20- litre container filled with water and a similar container to be used as a latrine. They were given bread and a box of horse meat, which was to be shared between seven of them and meant to last for a week.

There they stayed all day in the oppressive heat, sweating and gasping for air, until around 10.00 pm that night when the train took off very slowly. The movement did offer a little more fresh air to filter into the carriage, but the conditions were still unbearable. As well as the oppressive conditions in each car, many people had dysentery. The smell of them performing their toilet functions and doing so in full view of everyone else was appalling and humiliating.

Overnight, a number of the airmen in another carriage managed to dislodge some of the broken floorboards of the wagon. Around mid- morning of the next day, while the train had stopped, four Americans and several Frenchmen decided to make their escape. They ran towards some trees before a guard noticed them, and with a burst of machine- gun fire aimed above their heads. All escapees were soon rounded up. They were severely beaten before the senior German officer had them lined up at the side of the track. Three machine guns were aimed at them and he ordered them to be executed. There were howls of protest before the officer eventually relented and they were given another beating before all were shoved into the same wagon.

Late the next day, the locomotive broke down and the guards ordered everyone off the train. After everyone embarked and were trudging wearily towards a small French village a few miles away, Frank and Max witnessed the brutality of the German guards. A young Frenchman in his early twenties and obviously at breaking point, decided to make a run for it. He had made it down the side of a ravine when there was much shouting from the German guards. Without hesitation, one of them ran towards the side of the gully and, with his MP 40 submachine gun, shot the young man in the back. Clambering down the small ravine, he finished him off with another burst to the back of his head. A senior guard then ordered a group of French prisoners to bury the man, which they did by using tree branches as makeshift digging tools. After they had finished burying him in a shallow grave, his hand protruded from the ground, creating a macabre sight.

Frank was appalled by what he had witnessed, and had no illusions regarding the true intentions of the German guards. Frank expressed his fears to Max and where they might be going. Max shared his own concerns to Frank by stating he hoped the airmen would be offloaded soon to a Luftwaffe-run POW camp.

The one positive to come out of the episode was, by disembarking from the train, they could get some fresh air and get away, albeit temporarily, from the appalling conditions they had been subjected to.

On reaching the small French village, they were greeted by the local inhabitants who, sympathetic towards the prisoners plight, threw them food, including bread and fruit. Some were even holding Red Cross parcels, which they willingly gave to the prisoners. Others had wine, which they shared with some of them. Still, others were more intent on getting some fresh water into them. The Germans tried to stop the locals from imparting their gifts but to no avail, as many of them shouted to the passing ensemble, *"Vive la France!"* Many of the French replied, *"Merci beaucoup, Vive la France!"*

The Germans were becoming increasingly irritable as the large gathering was disorganised. After leaving the village, they walked for several miles before reaching the awaiting train.

The train made good progress, and after two days, they

crossed over the German border. Tensions eased somewhat, as the German guards were glad to be back on home soil and away from the possible sabotage by the French Resistance. Conditions had become increasingly dire in the cattle trucks, with the heat, dysentery, vomit and overpowering smell, hunger and thirst adding to the dreadful situation. Rumours began to circulate within the airmen that the train was heading towards Frankfurt, where the *Dulag Luft* was situated, which was the Luftwaffe Interrogation Centre. It was here, after interrogation, they would be sent to a POW camp.

The train did not divert to Frankfurt and after five days in their stinking hell hole, it finally stopped. When the wagon doors opened, an English pilot, who spoke German, asked an SS guard for their whereabouts.

"Buchenwald," was his reply.

Frank had never heard of the place, let alone its significance. He was to find out soon.

Chapter 19

Monday, September 11ᵗʰ 1944. Buchenwald Concentration Camp, Weimar, Germany

THERE WERE OMINOUS dark clouds gathering when the train pulled up at Buchenwald Concentration Camp. It shunted before slowly backing up a steep incline past fallow fields, then into a gate with a massive guard tower on either side, before it finally stopped at a platform.

Frank stood on his toes to get a better look out of the ventilation shaft. He could see hundreds of emaciated men and boys with their heads closely shaven shuffling around, going about their work. He noticed they were dressed in what he thought were blue and white striped pyjamas, while some wore a similar type of beret on their heads. They had a deathly stare in their eyes that suggested they had lost all hope. The SS guards barked orders at them while belting them incessantly with their fists or the butts of their rifles. Frank looked long and hard and a shiver went up his spine.

"What can you see?" Max said.

His words broke Frank from his spellbound state. He slowly

turned to Max and, ashen- faced, said, "It looks as though hell has come upon earth!"

Max swallowed hard, then clambered up for a look. After peering at the grim scene, he exclaimed,

"You're not bloody wrong."

Frank's surmise of the situation wasn't far from the truth. He did not know about death camps or the Nazis' 'Final Solution' at that stage. Little did he know the people who ran this camp and others like it were the epitome of evil and their actions would be recorded as one of history's greatest infamies?

Then the doors opened.

"*Raus, raus, schnell, schnell,*" *Out, out quick, quick,* The SS guards screamed.

The SS guards began to drag the prisoners off the train, sometimes by their hair. They kicked and screamed at them in German. All the while, their mouth- frothing Alsatians snapped at them.

Eventually, everyone disembarked from the wagons and chaos ruled as the incessant screaming from the guards and barking dogs led to an atmosphere of confusion. Many of the airmen looked around in bewilderment for someone among them to take charge and lead them. Frank observed the New Zealand officer take control of the situation and exert some semblance of order amongst the mayhem. He quietly asked as many as possible their name and rank. Eventually, he approached Frank and introduced himself.

"Hello, my name is Squadron Leader Dick Lefroy and I am a Lancaster pilot with No. 388 Squadron based at Wickenby."

Frank shook his hand and said, "G'Day, the names Flight

Sergeant Frank Casey and I am a rear gunner in a Lancaster in No. 377 Squadron based at Elsham Wolds."

"Please to meet you, Frank. Good to see an Aussie among us."

Frank smiled. "Where are you from?"

"I am from Wairoa from the Hawke's Bay region on the North Island of New Zealand."

"I am off a farm at Upper Bingara in north western New South Wales."

"Good on you," he said, tapping Frank on the shoulder.

"You're doing a pretty good job trying to put some order into this group," Frank said in a laconic tone while looking around.

Dick nodded. "I can't find anybody who is of more senior rank than me, so it appears I've landed the job."

"I wish you luck, sir, because it looks like a scary place."

Dick nodded in agreement before adding, "I better keep on moving, but we'll catch up later." With that, he moved on.

Frank's short conversation with Dick made him feel at ease. Regardless of the dangerous situation, he felt as though the boss had arrived to take charge.

From the railway platform, the prisoners were walked towards the entrance of the camp, all the while being harassed by the shouting guards and barking dogs. Eventually, they reached a large set of gates. It was here Frank viewed the infamous name of the camp for the first time.

Buchenwald Konzentrationlager

"I am not sure what this place is, Frank, but it sure ain't no POW camp," said Max, pointing to the sign. Frank nodded in agreement before an SS officer approached Max and kicked him in the shins with his jackboot.

"*Zis* is not a sightseeing tour, *Schwein*. Keep moving," he snarled at Max.

Max hobbled on, continually looking back, expecting to be hit again by the snorting officer.

On entering the main campground, an iron gate displayed the nefarious words.

Jedem das was er verdient. To each what he deserves.

Once in the main compound, the prisoners were ordered to attention not far from the commandant's office. Here, Dick Lefroy's assertiveness came to the fore. He instructed all the airmen that although they were POWs, they were to act like a military unit. This included enacting military etiquette at all times.

Frank noticed a tall chimney protruding from a brick building on the other side of the camp. Thick smoke poured from it and Frank gulped hard, as he had heard this was the crematorium. This was especially poignant, as an SS Guard had told one airman on the march from the platform to the camp entrance that the only way out of Buchenwald was through the chimney. A sweet, sickly smell invaded the nostrils and as Frank stood there looking at the black smoke, he muttered to himself, "Perhaps it was good that Jimmy was killed, as he has certainly been spared the atrocities of this place."

Regardless of their situation, after Dick's address, the men's morale lifted somewhat. From then on, they marched in unison wherever they moved. Hence, they at least resembled a military unit. This action upset the SS guards greatly.

They were soon hustled into a room where their pockets were emptied and they were stripped naked. Then several political prisoners, including Poles, Russians, Czechs and French, shaved them of their body hair using old- style clippers. By Frank's account, this was both humiliating and painful, and when finished, he remarked to one of the Czech barbers that he resembled a merino wether that had just come off shears. The Czech shrugged his shoulders as he did not understand a spit of English.

A steaming hot shower followed, which was a relief. Then they were marched naked to a different store and handed their blue and white striped shirt and trousers with a cap but no shoes. The clothes were an assortment of all different sizes and were hand-me-downs from deceased prisoners. Then they were allocated a small tin bowl each.

Shortly after, they were taken to the registry office. The Kapos were prisoners assigned by the SS to supervise forced labour and administrative tasks, and sought to extract personal information from them. But all they got was the name rank and serial number from each airman. This infuriated the senior Kapos and they threatened the airmen, but to no avail, as they were unwavering to their demands.

The Kapos were German communists and serious criminals from other nationalities. The SS guards had given them their role and duties because of their sadistic streak. The Kapos were there to take the pressure off the SS personnel in managing the camps day- to- day running. As a reward for performing their duties, they were given extra food, tobacco, alcohol, or other benefits. If they didn't perform satisfactorily in the eyes of the SS guards, they reverted to ordinary prisoners. It was a dog-eat-dog world which saw prisoners pitted against prisoners. Many of the Kapos were hated by other prisoners for collaborating with the Nazis. After the Americans liberated Buchenwald, many prisoners turned on the Kapos and beat them to death.

Dick Lefroy was pleased by the uniform approach of the airmen and by steadfastly refusing to yield to the Kapos demands, they had seriously disrupted the functions of the Nazi bureaucracy.

It was late in the day when the airmen were moved to a smaller camp on the northern end, which ran adjacent to the main camp. This camp was named Minor Camp and it was separated from the main camp with barbed wire. Minor Camp served as a transition camp before prisoners were moved on to other sub- camps to be used as slave labour for the war effort in the German factories.

The brutality of the SS guards was no less intense when the prisoners were being moved from the main camp to the smaller one. They continuously lashed out at the airmen with wooden clubs while the dogs snapped away at them.

Minor Camp was barren compared to the main camp. There were only a few trees, a number of tents for the very sick and a small stone building which served as the abode for the *Lager Altester Camp Senior.*

The airmen were mixed in with other prisoners from all nationalities. Soon after arriving, the prisoners were issued with a small piece of black bread that, on further inspection, con- sisted of about 30 per cent saw dust. They were also given a tepid soup made up of grass and weevils. For Frank and many of the other airmen, as much as the soup was abhorrent, he was so hungry he consumed it anyway and the weevils served as an additional source of protein. Many of the airmen threw the bread away in disgust and what followed was a mad scramble by other prisoners trying to secure the small portion. Like wild dogs, they fought each other for whatever meagre scraps they could secure, as the Nazis had reduced men to animals. The sole purpose of those sent to Buchenwald was to work as slave labour and if you were not capable of that, you were killed and taken to the crematorium.

The ground at Minor Camp was covered in flat but rough cobblestones and it was here the airmen were marched to and told this was where they would be living. They had to sleep out in the open with only a small issue of blankets to share among the prisoners. Frank managed to get hold of a blanket which he shared with Max, and between them, they settled in for the night as best they could.

Early the next morning, the prisoners were roused for the Appell, or roll call. The men soon learnt it was a tedious affair held twice a day in the morning and evening and could last for hours. The SS Guards would take a head count repeatedly, with prisoners made to stand to attention. Any indiscretion by the prisoners would be dealt with harshly by the Kapos and guards, and many acts of cruelty were perpetrated during the Appell.

This particular morning, the Appell took approximately an hour and a half and afterwards; the prisoners were issued with bitter coffee named ersatz, made from acorns. Frank spit it out after his first mouthful before Dick Lefroy informed him he had better keep it, as food and drink were even scarcer in Minor Camp compared to the main one.

Shortly after this, Dick organised the men into fifteen groups, with an officer in charge of each. All the groups consisted of ten men except the smallest, which was seven. Although Frank was not an officer, Dick had ascertained he was an experienced airman and asked him to take command of the smallest group, as there were no other officers. Frank's group consisted of himself, Max, three other Australians and two Americans. Dick set about organising a structure. Each group was accountable to each officer, who reported to Dick. The men appreciated the structure and they continued to march in unison whenever they were to be moved as a group. Some Americans even sang songs such as "You're a grand Old Flag", which received applause and cheers from some other prisoners. This action annoyed the SS guards, as again it showed that the airmen refused to be treated like the other prisoners.

As the leader of his section of men, Frank followed the directive of Dick Lefroy and made sure they maintained a sem-blance of a military unit at all times, regardless of how much pressure the SS personal and Kapos put on him. This was to bring him into direct conflict with one SS officer in particular. He was a sadistic individual by the name of *Obersturmfuhrer First Lieutenant* Otto Kestelman. He was one of the officers who ran Minor Camp.

It was only days after the airmen had been moved to Minor Camp when Frank had his first encounter with Otto Kestelman. It was the afternoon, Appell and the men had been standing to attention for the best part of two hours. They were tired, weak and agitated as they were standing there for what appeared to be no reason. Regardless of their situation, Dick Lefroy had instructed his men to stand to attention at Appell in the conven-tional Air Force protocol, which included hands tightly clenched and their wrists pointing along the seams of their trousers. The Kapos were standing in front of the men without delivering any instructions. From behind the men walked Kestelman to inspect the large gathering of prisoners.

Martin Otto Kestelman, who went by his middle name

Otto, was a 23-year-old German from Weiden in Bavaria. He stood six feet tall, had dark hair, green eyes and a solid jaw. He was well educated, and he spoke perfect English and French and had picked up a smattering of Russian while at Buchenwald. Otto's devout Catholic mother, Anna, had raised him in an atmosphere of piety and religious fervour. Growing up, he had served as an altar boy at *St Josef* Catholic Church in Weiden. He was an intelligent and courteous boy and, in his early teens, fell in love with a beautiful Jewish girl from Weiden who spurned his advances. Otto was rocked to the core by her rejection and it sowed the seed for his hatred of Jews. His rebuff also coincided with Hitler's rise to power in the early 1930s. Otto embraced the Nazi ideology with a new found fervour. Before the war, he studied law but had deferred his studies to join the SS. His fanaticism for the Nazi ideology was such that he was prepared to die for the Fuhrer.

Otto was one of the most sadistic SS officers in Buchenwald and thought nothing of killing a prisoner if they were not able to work any longer. It was common for him to walk up to a prisoner who was infirm and finish them off by smashing them in the head with a wooden club before they were dragged off to the crematorium.

Frank took particular pride in his section of men. Regardless of the dire situation, he wanted them to feel proud about themselves, so made sure they acted like a military unit while out at Appell. Otto approached the front line where Frank was standing in front of his section of six men. Hank Allman was a twenty-one-year-old from Beaumont, Texas and had served as a bombardier in a B -17 Flying Fortress before being shot down over France. A likeable man, he soon developed a strong bond with the other members of his section, but in particular Frank.

Otto took exception to the way Hank was standing to attention and smashed him over the knuckles with a stick he was carrying. Hank recoiled in pain, to which Frank turned around and confronted Otto.

"What are you doing hitting one of my men?" Frank barked at Otto.

Without hesitating, Otto drew his pistol out of his holster and smashed Frank over the side of the face, managing to draw blood.

"My men are airmen and expect to be treated according to the rules of the Geneva Convention," Frank said while hunched over.

Otto then kicked Frank in the stomach before holding his pistol to the side of his face and saying, "*Zere* is only *vun* set of rules in here, you *terrorflieger Schwein,* and *zey* are our rules," before kicking him in the shins. Without hesitation, Dick walked over and confronted Otto, protesting loudly at the treatment of both Hank and Frank. Otto cocked his pistol and held it up to Dick's face before exclaiming, "Don't test my patience, *Schwein,* or I *vill* shoot you on *za* spot."

With that, he walked away and dismissed the large gathering of prisoners. Frank's introduction to Otto had been a brutal one and it was only a prelude of what was to come.

The airmen settled into their little area in the corner of the camp on top of their rock pile, which they nicknamed Gibraltar. They guarded Gibraltar with great diligence, for among the couple of thousand prisoners in their section of the camp were a group of young Gypsies or Roma who had been thieving food and any other possessions.

They were mixed in with all types of nationalities, including French, Russians, Dutch, Czechs, Poles and Germans, as well as twenty members of the SOE who had told the German's they were airmen. There were German political prisoners, Jews, common criminals, homosexuals, Jehovah's Witnesses and others interned for religious beliefs. Each group wore a distinct colour coded triangle on their clothing to denote which category they belonged to.

Their situation was atrocious. Not only were the food and living conditions appalling, but the hygiene and health of the prisoners were horrendous, with both dysentery and typhoid rife within the camp. The smell of death and the dead waiting to be carted away to the crematorium were everywhere. Then there was the constant reminder of where they were headed if they fell sick with the chimney continuously pouring out pungent-smelling ash. None of the authorities, including the Red Cross, knew of Buchenwald, least of all their families. As far as they knew, the airmen had all been killed because there was no record of them being sent to a Luftwaffe run POW camp.

Through all this, Dick Lefroy was a tower of strength, with his unflinching courage serving as a beacon of hope to the airmen. He stood up to the SS guards and refused to take any crap off them, even though his life was in danger every time he did so.

The situation became even more severe when Dick was informed by Kestelman that the men would be required to work in the armaments factories which were situated nearby. The factories produced everything from aircraft parts and cannons, while another factory produced rifles, pistols and motor vehicles. Dick was in a dilemma, as he did not want his men participating in the production of weapons that would be used against the allies. He was well aware of the repercussions if they refused to obey the orders of the SS command. Dick decided to gather his group leaders and consult with them on the best course of action. They unanimously agreed they would not work in the factories, even though it could lead to their execution. Dick then informed the SS guards on their refusal to work, which was met with a fiery rebuke. One of the guards then marched off, and sometime later, he came back with a fuming Otto Kestelman.

"*Vha*t is *zis* I hear *zat* you and your men are refusing to *vork*?" he screamed at Dick.

"That's correct *Obersturmfuhrer* Kestelman. We are service-men and we are not required to work according to the rules of the Geneva Convention."Dick said calmly, looking him straight in the eye.

"*Ve'll* see about *zat Schwein!*"

With that, Kestelman stormed off.

He returned fifteen minutes later with 10 SS guards, all car-rying rifles.

"Now *ve vill* see if you still refuse to *vork terrorflieger*," he said to Dick.

"*Richten Sie ihn am Geb*äude *aus,*" Line him up against the building. Kestelman barked at his soldiers.

With that, the SS guards lined Dick up against the *Lager Altester's* abode and trained their rifles on him, waiting for the order to fire.

"I am asking you, *vill* you order your men to *vork*? Kestel-man barked.

"No, I won't!" Dick said defiantly.

"*Vhat*?"Kestelman roared.

"As I have repeatedly said, it is against the rules of the Geneva Convention for POWs to work," Dick said.

His defiant stance unhinged Kestelman. He was used to

having prisoners grovel in front of him. His hands were shaking and he was sweating as he walked up to Dick.

"For *za* last time, *vill* you and your men *vork* in *za* factories?"

"No, we won't! We want to be transferred to a Luftwaffe run POW camp. Besides, it would be just plain murder if you shoot me," Dick said assertively while glaring at Kestelman.

"Mord! Warum du verabscheuungswürd iges Schwein." Murder! *Why you despicable pig.* Kestelman screamed.

Dick refused to budge, and like any bully, Kestelman couldn't handle somebody standing up to him, especially a man of Dick's fortitude. Dick continued to stare deep into Kestelman's eyes until the officer turned to his guards and ordered them to ground arms. He then about-faced and ordered his men to march away. Only when Kestelman was out of sight did Dick let out a sigh of relief. He turned to Frank, who was standing nearby, and said, "That was close. I nearly shit myself."

Shortly after this incident, there was the bombing of several nearby armaments works by two large formations of US flying Fortress Bombers. As a result of this action, a small ray of hope shone onto the men.

It was midmorning in late September 1944 and Dick was talking to a French prisoner he had got to know, named Pierre Galliott. Before the war, Pierre had been a *cordon bleu* chef in a high class *Parisian* restaurant. When war broke out, he joined the French resistance and was captured by the Germans in late 1942. After he was tortured in Fresnes Prison, he was due to be executed, but when some of the senior Gestapo officers found out about his culinary skills, they spared his life and sent him to Buchenwald. The SS officers subsequently allowed him to become their cook, while he lived in the quarters with them. Galliott had told the SS officers he could not understand German, but in fact he could speak the language fluently as he had dealt with many Germans in the Paris restaurant before the war.

Unbeknownst to the Germans, Galliott was privy to many of the conversations between the officers and had become a vital intelligence source to a number of other prisoners, including Dick. These prisoners, including several Russians, had told Galliott they had planned an uprising and would kill the SS guards and complicit Kapos when the allies were close to liberating the camp. Dick was aware of this information, as he was well respected by most of the prisoners for standing up to the Germans. Dick had told Galliott he would lead the airmen in a revolt against the Germans if the camp's liberation was imminent. This link with Galliott and the other prisoners had become a vital lifeline for Dick and his airmen and would prove to be their saving grace.

While Dick was talking to Galliott, they heard a rumbling sound. When they looked up, they saw a formation of 200 bombers approaching. As the noise became louder, a number of the Americans noticed they were B17s and had dropped white flares. Hank Allman, who was standing not far from Dick, and being a bombardier, said, "They are target markers. They're going to bomb nearby."

Airmen ran for cover while Frank yelled out to many Frenchmen they were about to be bombed. With a whistling sound, the bombs descended before hitting the ground with a thunderous explosion, rattling the earth like a thousand freight trains passing by. Frank's teeth rattled inside his mouth as he hid in a shallow hole with hands over his head.

"So this is what it's like to be on the receiving end of a bombing," he said to Max, crouched nearby.

"Bleeding hell, we are going to cop it," said Max.

The bombers hit their mark, taking out several factories and the barracks of the German soldiers. Several buildings within the camp were taken out, with prison casualties. After the B17s had dropped their payload, they dispersed with thousands of leaflets. On the leaflets were photos of German POWs dressed in their uniforms with the words underneath in bold print:

Diese Männer sind deutsche Kriegsgefangene in England und werden nach den Regeln der Genfer Konvention behandelt.

These men are German prisoners of war in England, and they are treated according to the rules of the Geneva Convention.

Other leaflets showed a silhouette of a B29 over a B17, warning the Germans there were even bigger bombs coming their way if they didn't surrender. The prisoners collected the leaflets before scores of SS guards stormed the area shouting for them not to pick them up. This did not deter the airmen as they stuffed the leaflets inside their shirts.

Chaos ruled as the SS guards ordered the airmen to report to an area close to the crematorium.

"We are in for it now. This will be payback time, I betcha," Frank said to Dick, who was reading one of the leaflets.

Dick gave Frank a serious look before gathering his men together and marching them to the crematorium.

Dick was ready to give the Krauts a mouthful if they decided to shoot any of his men. It was an ominous scene when they reached the crematorium, as the Germans had placed a machine gun close to the chimney. This was only a scare tactic, as what they wanted them to do was put out the fires which were burning throughout the camp.

Dick refused to allow his men to comply, although he told one guard he would allow them to pull out prisoners caught in the burning rubble. Kestelman approached Dick and demanded he and his men do as commanded. Once again, Dick refused. Kestelman then pulled out his Luger pistol and repeated his demand.

"No, I won't, as it is against the rules of the Geneva Convention," said Dick.

Kestelman cocked his pistol and put it up to the side of Dick's head.

"If you shoot me, the allies will have you tried for murder when they eventually liberate this camp," Dick said to him.

"*Za* allies' *vill* never liberate *zis* camp," he snarled.

"It's only a matter of time before they overrun this camp and my men will be witness to my murder."

Kestelman, alarmed by what Dick had said, withdrew his pistol and put it back into his holster before storming off. This was another example of how Dick stood up to his violent oppressors on numerous occasions and put his life on the line.

With no shoes, the airmen pulled the wounded from the burning debris. They incurred burns and painful blisters on their feet and bodies. They used makeshift stretchers consisting of doors and planks of timber to pull out the wounded and dead.

Frank had his section of men pulling out the wounded when he was confronted by Kestelman.

"You and your men are to fight *za* fires," he barked at Frank.

"We won't be fighting any fires," Frank said to him.

Kestelman pulled out his pistol once again and pointed it at his head.

"You *vill* obey my orders," he said to Frank.

"If you shoot me, you are just a common murderer."

Frank continued to pull bodies from the debris, expecting to receive a bullet, but instead, Kestelman turned and walked away.

"Phew, that was close," Frank said.

The bombers had dropped hundreds of 1000 and 500-pound bombs, as well as incendiaries on the factories and camp. The result was hundreds of dead and wounded Germans as well as many hundreds of prisoners were killed and thousands injured.

The one positive that came out of the incident was one of the senior SS officers commended the airmen on their preparedness to help. The commandant had informed Dick their situation was under review.

The weather began to change in the following days and the rain came. After a couple of days living out in the driving rain, the commandant decided to repay the airmen for their actions pulling the wounded out of the burning rubble. His reward was to relocate them to timber barracks in the adjacent compound in the Minor Camp. The Germans felt no compassion for the prisoners the airmen had pulled from the fires. However, they had saved the lives of valuable slave labour.

Block 81 consisted of fewer than one thousand Jews, French and Poles; all crammed in like a can of sardines. Each barrack consisted of three tiers of timber shelves divided into compartments. Men were crammed on top of each other in the bunks and blankets were scarce. Even though the beds were lice and flea infested, it was a luxury compared to camping on top of Gibraltar.

Dick's persistence, not allowing his men to work, had finally paid off. While the other prisoners went off to work in the factories every day, the airmen stayed back in the barracks. Other than reporting for morning and evening Appell, they were left to their own devices. Many of the men dreamt about their future and some even learnt the language from prisoners of other nationalities.

While the airmen were established in Block 81, they were to bear witness too many SS atrocities at Buchenwald. One day, Frank was asked to go to the crematorium to pass on a message to the head Kapo. What Frank saw would stay with him for the rest of his life. Two young Gypsy boys had been looped together with a piece of piano wire around their throats. They were hanging dead from a meat hook secured on the wall. The two of them had been engaged in their final death throes only five minutes earlier. Now their bodies waited for a fiery appointment with the furnace. Two SS guards were laughing as they had placed bets on which of the boys would die first. Frank was a tough man and had experienced a lot, but nothing could have prepared him for such a sight. He went pale and his predominant thought was how low the human race had stooped to have perpetrated such acts of evil.

"*Vhat's* wrong *terrorflieger*, don't you realise *zat zis* is life in Buchenwald?" one of them said to Frank before laughing.

Frank was still shaking when he returned to Block 81. The memory would never be erased from his mind.

Everywhere you looked, there was death and disease. Dead bodies were piled on top of each other, waiting to be carted off to the crematorium. A multitude of rats could be seen crawling over them. With the rats came the threat of a typhus epidemic and with the shortage of coal towards the end of the war, the SS high command gave the order for mass burials.

As well as death and disease, the Nazis performed diabolical experiments on prisoners. The airmen were told of these gruesome experiments by some of the other prisoners and witnessed the disfigured bodies while going to the crematorium. Many of these experiments were performed on prisoners to simulate what would happen with a war wound on German servicemen. It was indeed the most deviant, evil and twisted mentality of the Nazis.

Not long after the bombing of the factories, an English airman by the name of Squadron Leader Arthur Edwards entered the camp. The other airmen didn't know Edwards was an SOE agent whose real name was Lawrence Bourne-Exley. Bourne-Exley went under the code name of the 'Wise Owl' and he proved to be an essential link in releasing the allied airmen from Buchenwald into a Luftwaffe run camp.

Bourne-Exley soon made Dick's acquaintance and wasted no time in making himself known to some of the other senior prisoners, including Pierre Galliott. The Wise Owl was a man of much ingenuity and courage, and as well as being fluent in both German and French, he could collaborate with the other prisoners. After meeting Galliott and several Russian prisoners, he joined their insurgency to rise up against their Nazi oppressors when the liberation of the camp was imminent.

A number of the prisoners had managed to smuggle small arms, including sub-machine guns, rifles and pistols, into the camp and hidden them. Bourne–Exley became a willing participant in the plan to take over Buchenwald if the SS decided to raze the camp and exterminate the prisoners.

Then, an incident shook all the airmen to the core, but none more so than Bourne – Exley. The twenty SOE operatives disguised as airmen had their cover blown and were executed by placing piano wire around their necks and hanging them off meat hooks. It was a slow, painful way to die and Bourne – Exley knew if the SS found out his true identity, then that would be his fate. The Wise Owl realised he had to act swiftly before his cover was blown.

Then the airmen's fate and their uprising were thwarted by an event in mid- October 1944. Galliott had been privy to a conversation between the camp commandant and a number of his senior SS officers. Over supper, the commandant had received news from Berlin that the allied airmen were to be executed to erase any trace of them ever being in Buchenwald. Galliott had overheard the conversation while preparing the evening meal and observed they were as casual as if they were discussing the weather.

Galliott soon informed both Dick and Bourne - Exley of the devastating news the airmen were to be executed within the week. Dick kept the information to himself and worked tirelessly to try to find a solution to the disastrous news. Providence was on the airmen's side, though, for within days of the order being issued, a Luftwaffe officer made a surprise inspection of the bombed factories which ultimately saved their lives.

No one was certain how *Oberstleutnant Wing Commander* Friedrich von Einsiedel found out there was a large group of allied airmen imprisoned in Buchenwald. Some believe Pierre Galliott had smuggled a letter through to the administration area of Buchenwald addressed to the Luftwaffe high command, alerting them to the plight of the airmen. Others believed the British government had been alerted to the airmen's imprisonment and made it clear to Berlin they knew where the airmen were. If anything happened to them, there would be serious repercussions. Whatever the case may be, Galliott never let on to anybody that it was him, because if the SS ever found out, he would have ended up garrotted on one of the meat hooks near the crematorium.

Friedrich von Einsiedel was a 27-year-old Luftwaffe fighter ace of proud Prussian heritage. He had risen to the rank of *Oberstleutnant* in a short period after forging a distinguished reputation for flying Messerschmitt Bf109s in the German conquests over France and Western Europe. He despised the SS and saw them as barbaric and inferior to everything his proud ancestry represented. On the pretence of investigating the bombed factories and camp, von Einsiedel made a surprise inspection in mid-October 1944. Bourne – Exley and Dick were walking near the camp perimeter when they noticed von Einsiedel inspecting the outside area. The two of them made their way over to the perimeter fence, where Bourne – Exley managed to get the attention of the Luftwaffe officer. Saluting von Einsiedel, he explained in fluent German the plight of the allied airmen and begged for his intervention, as he believed their execution was imminent. Bourne – Exley was still explaining the plight of the airmen when two SS guards noticed them and, with guns drawn and shouting, approached. The SS guards were about to accost the two airmen when Friedrich von Einsiedel gave them a look of disdain, brushing their protestations away like a headmaster dismissing a bunch of disobedient school children. The guards warned von Einsiedel they would return with an officer, to which he again gave them a sharp rebuke. After the guards left, he listened intently to Bourne – Exley's story, informing him if the airmen could prove their validity, then he would do everything in his power to have them transferred to a Luftwaffe run POW camp.

Bourne – Exley was still explaining the airmen's plight when Kestelman approached with the two guards following closely.

Kestelman spat a vile tirade to von Einsiedel, warning him there would be severe retribution if he interfered with any of the camp's prisoners.

Von Einsiedel, being of higher rank, walked closer to the perimeter fence until he was only inches from Kestelman's face. *"Unterwegs prügelst du pratt!" On your way, you thuggish pratt!* He roared at Kestelman, his eyes bulging.

Kestelman was taken aback by the Luftwaffe officer's reprimand and warned von Einsiedel he would report him to the camp commandant for interfering with the prisoners. Von Einsiedel roared at Kestelman to mind his own business and to get back to his vile duties within the horror camp. Kestelman stood there ashen- faced, for he had not expected such a harsh rebuke from the Luftwaffe officer. He continued to stare at von Einsiedel before the Luftwaffe officer dismissed him. Kestelman attempted to about face without saluting before von Einsiedel again gave him a sharp reproach and ordered him to salute. On saluting the flying ace, Kestelman about faced then marched off, his pride severely dented.

As Kestelman was walking away, von Einsiedel said loudly, *"Schwein!"*

In the days following the inspection of the bombed-out ruins by Friedrich von Einsiedel, the airmen were filled with a nervous excitement that they would eventually be transferred to a Luftwaffe run camp.

Then, three days before the airmen were due to be executed, they were ordered to assemble in the main camp around midmorning. It was well after the morning Appell and they were filled with apprehension, as this was a diversion from their routine. As they marched around to the main camp, a buzz ran through the ranks to their possible fate. After they were led into a room, they were met by six Luftwaffe officers. Leading the officers was von Einsiedel. It was his adjutant who addressed the men in English. He informed them they were to fill out a collection of Red Cross forms vital for their transfer to a Luftwaffe run camp. There were rumblings and derision among the men as they had been told by intelligence staff back in England that if captured, they should only give their name, rank and serial number. The adjutant held up his hand, and after clearing his throat, he continued. He informed the airmen that failure to complete all the forms would result in them remaining behind at Buchenwald as political prisoners. With a look of contempt, he reminded them their fate would be sealed at the hands of the SS. The Red Cross forms contained detailed questions relating to their squadron, where they had flown their operations from and with what type of aircraft. It also asked personal questions. Answering them was against everything both intelligence and Dick had advised on what not to divulge to the Germans.

Howls of protest went up through the room before the adjutant again raised his hand and reminded them of their obligations in a more terse tone.

"You are in no position to argue *wiz* me. I suggest *zat* you follow *za* Luftwaffe's directions for your *vell-* being," he said.

The men were then stood down by von Einsiedel, where they gathered around Dick and the officers in charge of each unit. While trying to ascertain which path they should follow, Dick made it clear to the men their situation was dire and failure to comply with the Luftwaffe's request could result in their continued incarceration and certain execution. He informed the men he would be giving his name, rank and serial number, and the rest of the questions he would fill with fraudulent information. He suggested the men should do likewise, but it was up to each individual to follow their conscience on what to divulge. Frank agreed with Dick and instructed his men that was the path he would take. A minor revolt ensued, with a hard core consisting of about twenty men, including Max Clayton, who would only supply their name rank and serial number. They felt they would be tried for treason after the war if they divulged any further information.

The Luftwaffe officers were enraged and immediately separated the dissenters from the rest of the men and marched them back to Block 81. Frank watched Max walk away, and he wondered if he would ever see his mate again. That night he slept a fitful sleep, worrying about the fate of the men who had been marched back to the hellhole of Gibraltar.

The airmen spent the next two days anxious about what their fate would be. Frank thought the Luftwaffe might stop the transportation as retribution for the renegades refusing to fill out the Red Cross forms.

Then, just after midday, the airmen were ordered to gather for Appell, where they were met by SS guards. A murmur went through the gathered airmen. They thought the Luftwaffe had changed their minds and left them to the fate of the SS. Then, to their surprise, the twenty dissenters appeared out of nowhere and were ordered to line up with the rest of the airmen. The SS ordered the men to strip naked, and they were led into the building, where they had initially discarded their clothes when arriving at Buchenwald. There they were given back their old civilian clothes, and after they dressed, they looked like a bunch of scarecrows; the threads hanging off their cadaverous bodies.

The SS guards stood them out in the pouring rain to take a final head count. It was Frank who first realised one man was missing. Bourne – Exley was nowhere to be seen and as the guards shouted and recounted the numbers, they were none the wiser on the whereabouts of the Wise Owl. He had covertly flown the coup and disappeared into thin air. A guard then notified Kestelman and shortly after, he appeared in a rage.

"*Vhere* is *za* missing man?" Kestelman bellowed.

The airmen looked straight ahead and said nothing.

"I can assure you *zat* if *zis* missing *terrorflieger* is not found shortly, you *vill* not leave *zis* camp," Kestelman bellowed.

A shiver went up the spine of every airman.

Kestelman held the men there for the next fifteen minutes, screaming at them about their knowledge of Bourne-Exley's whereabouts.

In his tirade, Kestelman walked up to Frank and stood directly in front of him and screamed, "*Vhere* is *za* missing *terrorflieger*?"

Frank said nothing and stood to attention, looking straight ahead.

Kestelman took his pistol out of his holster and was about to hit Frank when suddenly the gates of Buchenwald were flung open, and the men were greeted by the sight of a Luftwaffe *Hauptmann Flight Lieutenant*. Kestelman lowered his pistol, and after the Luftwaffe officer stared daggers at him, the SS thug retreated. Frank looked at Kestelman, who gave him a vile look before gathering his guards and walking out of the compound. It was the last Frank was to see of Kestelman in Buchenwald.

After the Luftwaffe officer reasonably addressed the airmen, he informed them Red Cross parcels and better living conditions would soon be available. Shortly after this, they walked to the platform where the train was waiting to transport them to a Luftwaffe camp.

When they arrived at the platform, the men were anxious they would be met with the same wagons that had brought them to Buchenwald. The Luftwaffe officers thought the airmen might try to escape and, told Dick that if they did, they would be shot. The men were too weak to contemplate any such thing. It was only after Dick guaranteed the Luftwaffe officers they would not try to escape that the Germans relented from their threat. After they climbed on board and were met with the sight of fresh straw on the floor and a stove in the middle of the wagon, the men finally relaxed.

As the train departed, the men's thoughts turned to the five airmen who had died in Buchenwald due to ill health and the ten who still remained in the hospital. Fortunately, they were taken out of that hellhole, which was anything but a hospital, and taken to a proper infirmary where, after recovering, they eventually joined the rest of the men in late November 1944.

They weren't certain where they were headed, but as the train gathered speed for the three-day journey, the men relaxed the further they travelled from Buchenwald. They began to unwind even further after they were given sausage and bread to eat and ersatz coffee to drink. After a while, Max pulled out his harmonica, which he had managed to hide, and quietly played some tunes while the gentle click- clack of the wheels of the wagon sent the men to sleep. The guards even gave them cigarettes, and after three days on the train, they eventually pulled up at a railway platform in the early morning. When the doors opened and they stretched their weary limbs, they were greeted with the sight of a pine forest that overlooked a huge airforce camp.

Chapter 20

Late October, 1944. Stalag Luft III Sagan Germany

STALAG LUFT III was in the German province of Lower Silesia near the town of Sagan, which is now part of modern-day Poland. The camp was situated on 60 acres (24 hectares) and housed around 11,000 POWs, including RAF officers, NCOs and US Army Air Force personnel. There were also around 900 officers from other Allied Airforces.

After departing the train, the airmen were marched up the hill by Luftwaffe guards to the camp, which was carved out of the pine forest.

On entering the camp, the Luftwaffe personnel were shocked at the men's condition. Many of them commented to the airmen about the disgust they felt for the SS and their treatment. The men were then photographed and registered and, to their surprise, given a hot shower before each being issued with an airman's uniform.

After that, they were taken to their compound and issued with a bunk, each with clean sheets and blankets. Each compound consisted of fifteen single story huts, which slept fifteen men in five triple- deck bunks. They were then issued with Red Cross parcels, which were comprised of an assortment of food such as extra large prunes, biscuits, spam, sardines, and ascorbic acid (vitamin C). Frank went to his top bunk and, without much thought, devoured the prunes, spam and sardines until he was full. Shortly after, he became violently ill, as did many of the airmen, as his body could not handle such rich food after the atrocious diet they had been on at Buchenwald.

It took Frank days before he recovered from his gastronomic ordeal, but when he did, he sat on his bunk in silent contemplation, grateful he had survived the horror of Buchenwald. His biggest thrill, though, was the ability to write a Red Cross letter home to both his family and Geraldine, letting them know he was safe and well.

Frank soon settled into a routine at Stalag Luft lll, but it was not easy to erase the memories, including the routine of Buchenwald. On the initial parade and subsequent head count, many men balked when walking past a Luftwaffe NCO as they expected to be smacked in the back of the head or whacked over the body with a lump of timber.

Days after Frank had recovered from his overindulgence; he sat down to his first real meal, which consisted of a bowl of soup followed by hot potatoes, meat and prunes for dessert. The men from Buchenwald were on double rations for some time, as they were seriously malnourished. Although the German food supply was limited, the prisoners were lucky to have a collection of Red Cross parcels, which supplemented their diet. They included cheese, powdered milk, chocolate bars and cigarettes. As well as this, the POWs had their vegetable gardens with seeds supplied by the Red Cross. Despite their incarceration, the prisoners were engaged in many activities: basketball, soccer, theatre productions, education, libraries and church services.

The Germans, as a rule, did not pester the prisoners. Their presence was always felt as they were often seen crawling under huts and creeping around in the night with a torch, attempting to foil any prisoners who were trying to escape. Fresh in everyone's minds was the escape and subsequent capture of many prisoners from the camp early that year and the execution of many officers on the orders of Adolf Hitler. This had created a lot of tension within the camp, and the atmosphere was a powder keg that could have exploded at any time. The senior allied officers of the camp were mindful of the Buchenwald men's plight and asked them not to talk about it, as it may create a situation that could boil over. Many of the POWs found the airmen's story incredulous, and one RAF NCO stared at Frank in disbelief when one day he enquired how many POWs were getting the chop each week. He found it hard to believe when Frank explained the amount of death at Buchenwald.

Time moved on, and with it, the cold and snow arrived, and by Christmas, the prisoners were lucky to be able to share in thousands of American Christmas parcels. Frank wrote to his family to tell them he was well, considering his circumstances.

By late January 1945, the Red Army's offensive against the Germans was in full swing, as the men could hear the pounding of Russian guns in the distance. Hopes were high that liberation was near, but any chance of their imminent release was dashed as the Germans prepared to march the men away from the approaching Red Army as they came from the east.

The men from Buchenwald had been at Stalag Luft lll for three months and regained their strength through a combination of a better diet and living conditions. Several POWs had made clandestine radios and received regular BBC broadcasts of the allied advance. They were following reports of the Battle of the Bulge in the densely forested Ardennes region in eastern Belgium, northeast France and Luxembourg. Both the allies and the Red Army were approaching on two separate fronts and putting the squeeze on the Germans. The men were hopeful they would soon be liberated. Instead, the Germans ordered them to move out in a westerly direction.

The winter of 1945 was one of the worst on record, and it was in this freezing landscape the POWs were told they were to be marched to their next destination. On Friday, 26 January 1945, at approximately 9.30 pm, the order came through to move out. The men weren't too pleased, as the snow was falling and the temperature was below zero. Like many of the prisoners, Frank had converted his kitbag into a haversack, with food, clothing and cigarettes being of optimum importance. He had made a sled out of discarded Red Cross boxes to load as many provisions as he could handle onto it.

Frank's barracks were the last to be evacuated, and at 6.00 am, they walked into the Red Cross store to stock up with supplies. There were 10,000 of them on the move, and the column stretched back over 7 miles (12 kilometres). Elderly guards lined the snow and ice- ridden road, holding machine guns every 300 feet (100 metres). The guards who were outnumbered by the prisoners 50: 1.They held dogs on leads and gave the POWs menacing stares. Although Dick was no longer the senior allied commander of the POWs, he had given his Buchenwald men explicit orders there were to be no escapes, as the 'Great Escape' memories were still fresh in the minds of the Germans.

Frank was disappointed to be leaving Stalag Luft lll as he had regained his strength there, and the thought of trudging out into the bitterly cold winter brought back memories of Buchenwald. He resented leaving so many Red Cross parcels behind after being starved in Buchenwald.

On that first day, the men walked for an hour and a half before they stopped for a 10 - minute break. On they trudged through the blizzard - like conditions until they stopped for lunch on top of a hill just after midday. The wind was howling and the snow was coming in horizontally as they ate bully beef, biscuits and chocolate.

After lunch, the men trudged on, and so miserable were the conditions that even the guards sought protection from the weather within the ranks of the prisoners.

By mid-afternoon, they stumbled into a small village where Frank managed to exchange some bars of chocolate for half a loaf of rye bread. He was also able to secure some schnapps off one of the villagers after exchanging cigarettes with him. After waiting in the snow for a couple of hours, they were eventually hustled into the local church. The men were packed in like sardines, and although they had tramped the ice and mud into the church, it was at least warm. After tucking into his bread and a can of bully beef, Frank went to sleep on the steps leading up to the altar.

The men stayed in the church the next day, only moving outside to perform their toiletry functions. After a day's rest, the men were up and walking again by 5.00 am. Men were collapsing around him and dying through exhaustion and exposure. Many of the men discarded food and unwanted items, including diaries, as the weight became too much to cart through such atrocious conditions. Frank took the photo of Geraldine and himself out of his pocket, only to have the howling wind snatch it out of his fingers and carry it through the air. He attempted to regather it only to be told by a guard with a gun and dog in tow to fall back into line. Frank felt deflated, but it was an omen, as he was unaware of what had happened to Geraldine.

As they trudged through knee - high snow, older guards felt the effects of such an arduous walk. They could not keep up with the prisoners, so were told by Dick to fall in at the rear of the column, even handing over their rifles to the prisoners. Frank took the rifle off the guard who had told him to fall back into line and ordered him in no uncertain terms to make his way to the rear.

After trudging into a small village, they were met by the burgermeister, who informed the German officer in charge they would have to stay in a fenced - off area for the night. They would be exposed to the elements, and there was no doubt that men would freeze to death in such atrocious conditions. Dick decided to take matters into his own hands and, after approaching the burgermeister, told him very clearly, if he didn't find some covered conditions, then the men would ransack the town and burn it to the ground. Frank was extremely irritable after losing his photo of Geraldine. After he hobbled up to the burgermeister, brandishing his rifle, he said, "Get cracking, kraut and find us some decent digs, or I'll shoot yer arse clean off."

The burgermeister had no clue what Frank was saying, but got the general idea of what he was alluding to. Dick diffused the situation by lowering Frank's rifle and gently persuading him to step back. The burgermeister, without any further delay, led the men into the village, where they found lodgings for the night in churches, schools and halls.

After four days on the road and after walking 60 miles (100

kilometres), the exhausted men eventually arrived at the rail yard at Spremburg. They were split into two groups with many taken to POW camps in Nuremburg and Bremen and the rest, including Frank, Dick and Max, taken to Stalag lll A in Luckenwalde, located 50 km south of Berlin.

After another sleepless night in cramped conditions, the prisoners endured a 60 mile (100km) train journey, where they eventually arrived at Luckenwalde.

Chapter 21

Thursday, February 1ˢᵗ 1945. Stalag lll A Luckenwalde, Germany

LUCKENWALDE WAS APPROXIMATELY 32 miles (52) kilometres south of Berlin and was a transit camp for POWs. It contained British, American, French, Russian, Poles, Serbs and Italians.

It was severely run down with a lack of food and coal for heating. The prisoners were deloused and waited for an eternity for a hot shower before moving them to their barracks. The living conditions were atrocious, with bare boards for beds and filthy lavatories overflowing with excrement.

Unbeknownst to Frank, on the same day they entered Stalag lll A at Luckenwalde, his father Hugh had died of pneumonia, aged 47. With four of her boys away at the war, Margaret needed the assistance of 17- year-old Noel to run Banyula until, hopefully, the others boys returned home in one piece.

It was more than a coincidence that Frank was at his lowest ebb after his father's death. As he slumped onto his bed minus a mattress, he despaired at his situation and hoped they would be liberated. He remained depressed through the night when Max noticed a red robin perched on the windowsill of their barracks early the next morning.

"Look Frank, there is life yet," Max said with a smile, pointing at the feathered guest.

Frank lifted his head from the boards and looked at the bird.

"Don't you worry, mate, we will be free, like that bird, shortly," said Max with a grin.

Max's enthusiasm suddenly lifted Frank from his depression, and after raising himself on his elbow, he looked at his friend and quoted, "*Hope springs eternal in the human breast. Man never is, but always to be blest.*"

"So you are familiar with Alexander Pope, are you Frank?"

"I read *An Essay on Man* at school,"

"Well, you keep your chin up, because we will be liberated from this hell hole soon enough."

The appearance of the red robin and Max's upbeat manner had worked wonders for Frank and regardless of their dire situation; he saw things in a different light.

The weeks moved on and the coal eventually ran out, so the men tore up the bed boards and burnt them while sacks of straw were used for sleeping on. Red Cross parcels soon arrived, which supplemented their meagre diet.

By late March 1945, winter had lifted and the worst of the cold was over. The sun was shining, which prompted some men to sunbake while sporting activities were organised. There was a positive feeling that the end was near and liberation was imminent.

As April progressed, the German's had become more affable, even providing daily briefings on the allied advance. Hot showers and clean clothes were provided.

Then, in mid – April, the prisoners were told they were to be moved to another POW camp at Moosburg in southern Bavaria. Headcounts were taken and they were piled onto a cattle wagon. They spent two nights on the train where they could hear American bombers above on their way to Berlin. As a result, the Germans decided to return the prisoners to Luckenwalde, where the Red Army was fast approaching.

It was just before midnight on April 20th when Frank was woken by a low rumbling sound in the distance.

"Max, do you hear that?" Frank said, turning on his side.

"Sure do, Frank. Liberation is not far away."

"The big question is, will it be the Russians or the Yanks?" Frank said.

The sounds became louder as the night wore on and the distinct boom of artillery and tank fire could be heard.

Two days earlier, the Germans had withdrawn from the camp and left the prisoners to their own devices. The next day, the sounds of battle became louder and there was an air of expectation among the POWs that their release was imminent.

Then at 5.00 pm on April 21st, Frank was walking around the grounds when he spotted a Soviet T34 tank approaching.

"Max, Dick, look what's coming our way?" he said in an excited tone.

The three approached the tank, where a Red Army officer stepped out of the gun turret and addressed them in Russian. Neither of them understood what he had said, but the smile on his face and the waving of his hands indicated he was friend, not foe. Frank turned to Dick and Max and said to them, grinning like a Cheshire cat, "It's bloody well over. Do you believe it?"

Dick replied, "We made it, fellas. We are going home."

Dick was correct, as the Soviet, British, American and Canadian forces had overwhelmed the Germans and thousands of POWs were finally liberated.

The airmen thought their liberation was imminent, but things didn't go according to plan. As more Soviet forces arrived, they took control of the camp.

For the next two days, the POWs were allowed out of the camp to forage for food. On the third day, a convoy of Red Army trucks arrived with food, clothing and medical supplies. The POWs were expecting to be liberated very soon, but shortly after, the Soviets unexpectantly locked the gates and would not let the prisoners out. Confusion reigned as the men had no idea why the Soviets had done this. None of the senior officers would divulge why they had done this to the senior British Officer.

After a couple of days, several American trucks arrived and the Soviets allowed them to take away the sick, but no one else was permitted to leave. The Americans returned the next day to take more prisoners away, but the Soviets refused to let them in.

Dick ferreted out some information from a Red Army officer who spoke English. He informed him Luckenwalde was now under Soviet control and that was why no prisoners were permitted to leave. On further investigation, Dick was able to find out from the officer the real reason was over a diplomatic stoush between the Soviets and the Allies. The officer informed him the Allies had detained Russians they captured at Normandy, who had been fighting for the Germans and this was their payback.

Frank and Max had been under house arrest at the hands of the Soviets for two weeks. Having had enough of being incarcerated, they decided to escape one night. They told Dick about their plans, but he chose to stay with his men and wait for liberation.

It was well after midnight and, using some pliers they had found, they cut a hole in the wire fence and made a run for it without being noticed by any Soviet soldiers. They escaped into the surrounding forest, and then walked for the rest of the night until they rested early the following day under the cover of the trees.

By mid-afternoon, they were up again when they found a couple of bicycles in the bush. They cycled for the rest of the day, evading any approaching Red Army vehicles by hiding in the bushes. At dusk, they crossed paths with an American truck. After informing the American driver who they were, he gave them cigarettes and, with a smile, told them to jump into the back of the truck. For Frank and Max, the war was over.

After Frank's escape, and his return to Brussels, the relevant allied authorities contacted his mother notifying her of his release from captivity and his subsequent return to Elsham in the near future.

Frank and Max arrived back at Elsham Wolds in early May 1945, where many of the faces were new to them. There were some old, familiar ones who gave them a grand welcome home. They had given them up for dead and couldn't believe they had survived.

Shortly after arriving at Elsham, a letter from his mother was waiting, informing Frank his father had passed away. For all their differences, Hugh's death shook Frank and his main concern was for his mother and how she would carry on. He was grateful they had patched up their differences and that Hugh had given him his watch as a parting gift prior to him leaving for the war. He was full of mixed emotions as his release had filled him with joy, only to be taken down with the news of Hugh's death. Frank's primary concern, other than writing to his mother, was to contact Geraldine, as she was no longer on the base. The letters he had written to her at Elsham while in Stalag Luft lll had gone unanswered and he was concerned that she hadn't received them.

The day after returning to Elsham, Frank was summoned to Wing Commander Jackson's office for a thorough debriefing on the operation over Sochaux. Frank was in the Wingco's office for three hours, explaining in detail everything that had happened to him after the crash. He sat in disbelief as Frank explained how he was rescued by the Maquis after the crash, his betrayal and subsequent capture.

On leaving the Wingco's office, Frank was met by Jack Walsh, heading for the mess. After completing his 30 operations, Jack had been transferred to a Heavy Conversion Unit based at Elsham as a gunnery instructor. It was here he had remained for the duration of the war. On arriving at the mess, Jack told him quietly about Geraldine. He told Frank, six months after the operation to Sochaux an English Squadron Leader had been posted to Elsham. He continued,

"Nothing was heard of your crew after the op to Sochaux and Geraldine, like the rest of us, thought you had been killed."

"Go on," Frank said, looking directly into Jack's eyes.

"She hoped and prayed and was heartbroken when you did not return, but after not hearing anything about the crew, she…."

"I know what you are going to say."

Jack shrugged his shoulders and tapped his fingers on the table.

"You know how it is. Geraldine was devastated and the Squadron Leader gave her solace in her time of need," said Jack.

"Yep, I know how it is, Jack, but that doesn't make it any easier."

"I am sorry, Frank, but that's just how it is."

Frank continued to stare into thin air, trying to comprehend this piece of news.

"You know how things are. One thing led to another and they got married."

"When did they tie the knot?"

"In March last year!"

"What's his name?"

"Does it really matter, Frank?"

"I suppose not, but where is she now?"

"He got posted to RAF Wickenby and she got a transfer shortly after."

Frank looked at Jack long and hard before shaking his head.

"I can't believe it. After everything I've been through and to lose Geraldine. This is the final blow!"

"I know, it's tough, mate, but what can I say? All is fair in love and war."

Frank looked up to the ceiling and shook his head.

"I suppose you're right, but I should still go and see her."

"Frank, it may be best if you just let things lie, as it could get a bit messy if you know what I mean."

"I suppose you're right. But this news has knocked me for a six."

Jack's presence and mateship were to lighten the load after the news. After the death of Jimmy, his crew, his father and now Geraldine's marriage, it was a bitter final twist to his liberation. As much as losing Geraldine was painful, he knew it was best that he let her go and move on. Geraldine never did make contact with Frank as it would have been too awkward and as a consequence he never saw her again.

While Frank was adjusting to life as a free man at Elsham Wolds and comprehending the loss of Geraldine, back in Buchenwald, things had taken a sinister twist. When Frank had been evacuated from the concentration camp, he had a burning hatred of the Nazis but none more than Otto Kestelman. Frank vowed that if the opportunity ever arose, he would kill Kestelman with his bare hands, if that's what it took.

In early April 1945, as US forces approached, the Germans began to evacuate 28,000 prisoners from Buchenwald main camp and several thousand from the subcamps. About a third of the prisoners died of exhaustion en route or were shot by the SS. When liberation was imminent, the starved and emaciated prisoners stormed the watchtowers, killing many of the remaining guards and Kapos. That afternoon, the US forces entered Buchenwald and liberated the camp.

When the Germans were evacuating the prisoners days before liberation, Otto Kestelman had slipped away and disappeared into the lines of the retreating Wehrmacht. Taking on the identity of Klaus Bauer, he disguised himself as a *Gefreiter/ private* in the Wehrmacht.

After Germany's surrender in May 1945, Otto was able to pass himself off under his new identity, where he found work in a labour camp.

While Otto Kestelman was busy hiding from the authorities as a wanted war criminal, Frank was trying to adjust to life in post - war England.

In early September 1945, Frank's fortunes changed after he was informed he had been chosen to play in a number of selection trials for a 21 – game tour by a Combined Dominions rugby team as part of the VE (Victory in Europe) celebrations.

Frank's physical condition was poor when he returned to England, but with a better diet and exercise, he soon gained weight and improved considerably. Frank was keen to get back on the rugby paddock and erase the pain of losing Geraldine. After flying to Cardiff for the trials; his abilities were soon noticed by the selectors.

Frank slotted into five – eight and it he could not help but feel melancholic that Jimmy was not playing at scrum - half. During the tour, Frank played on famous rugby grounds such as Twickenham, Cardiff Arms Park and Murrayfield, which he had always dreamed of as a student at Joeys.

Many of the rugby players he played alongside were to have illustrious international rugby and rugby league careers for Australia, New Zealand and South Africa. Along with playing several matches, Frank met many dignitaries, and wherever they went, huge crowds turned up to watch as Britain had been starved of rugby during the war years. They were met with warmth and enthusiasm as they fostered the spirit of rugby and friendship for a people who had been devastated by the war.

Of all the matches Frank played, there was one that was to have special significance. It was played at *Parc des Princes* in Paris in January 1946 against a French selection playing under the banner of the Free French. The French played in a red and blue jersey with the emblem of The Cross of Lorraine. As Frank lined up against his opponents, his thoughts turned to all those members of the French Resistance who had risked their lives to try and help him to freedom. Frank thought of Marguerite and Philippe and Raphael, but he thought mostly of Fr Fournier, who had given his life for him.

That night, when they sat down for their post match dinner in Paris, Air Vice - Marshal Somersby RAF, who had been the driving force behind the series of matches, paid special tribute to the fallen.

When I look around this room tonight, I cannot help but be touched with emotion by the memory of all those brave men from the dominions who gave their lives to defend the British Commonwealth. In particular, we should never forget those of Bomber Command, where 55,000 gave their lives and just fewer than 10,000 were taken prisoners of war. They were the flower of a generation taken before their time. As well as this, we cannot help but pay special thanks to those of the French Resistance who risked their lives in trying to help our downed airmen back to England. We owe an outstanding debt to you and you will never be forgotten.

For those here tonight who have survived this great calamity, seize the opportunity and make your life one of greatness, so the memory of the fallen will not be in vain. In the words of Plato, "The greatest wealth is to live content with little."

Vive la France.

Frank listened carefully to the words of the Air Vice-Marshal and they affected him deeply.

Frank's rugby prowess excelled and he was one of the standout players on tour. Many who saw him play on that tour believed he was bound for greatness and that a Wallaby jumper would one day be his. Fate was to deal a different hand of cards in his case and Plato's words were to be prophetic. Unbeknownst to Frank, his appearance on this tour was to be the pinnacle of his rugby career. As much as he had loved being part of the tour, Frank received some exciting news when in late April 1946; he was told he would be going home.

Chapter 22

Wednesday, May 22nd 1946. Woolloomooloo, Sydney

ON FRIDAY, 26TH of April 1946, Frank set sail on the troopship Galbraith from Liverpool, England, bound for Sydney via Panama. He had been away from home for just over five years and much had changed in him. He longed to see his mother Margaret and the pain she must be feeling after losing her husband and seeing four of her sons go away to war. Fortunately, all of them had survived, although, for a long time, the family believed Frank had been killed.

After a trip lasting 26 days, the Galbraith docked at Woolloomooloo in Sydney on Wednesday, May 22nd 1946. Frank spent a couple of nights with his sister Veronica, who lived at Kogarah. Veronica was now 19 years of age and had been in Sydney for three years after securing a job in the Lands Department in Bridge Street as a secretary.

Frank caught the mail train from Sydney to Tamworth late on Friday night, arriving early on Saturday morning. From Tamworth, he hitched a ride home to Banyula, arriving just before midday.

Frank was walking down the gravel driveway of Banyula when his youngest sister, 13 - year - old Frances, spotted him. Her eyes opened as wide as saucers upon seeing him.

"Frank," she yelled out, "you're home."

"G'day, sis," he said as Fran ran into his arms.

They embraced, and Frank picked her up. "Boy, haven't you grown up since I've been away?"

"Frank, it's so good to see you," Fran said as she hugged him.

Frank held her hand as they walked down the driveway. Fran talked incessantly about everything that had happened since he had been away.

Frank walked through the back door where his mother and his 15 - year - old sister Joan were preparing lunch. His mother had aged, and on seeing Frank, Margaret dropped a spoon on the kitchen floor and ran towards him with tears in her eyes.

"Oh Frank, you're home at last," she sobbed while embracing him.

"I am mum," Frank said, holding his mother tightly.

Joan gave Frank a big hug before Kevin and Bob entered the kitchen. There were handshakes and well wishes from everyone, and Frank was glad to see his two brothers, who had recently returned from the war. Other than his sister Veronica, the only other members of the family who were missing were Brian, who was in the army stationed in Rabaul in New Britain, and Vince, who was at boarding school at Joeys.

After much talking and laughter, Frank made his way to the dining table before Margaret turned to him.

"As you're just home from the war, Frank, I think it is more than appropriate that you should lead us in grace."

Frank rested his elbows on the table and looked at his mother and then at the rest of the family, and a fleeting thought flicked across his mind. It seemed like an eternity when he had last thought of this, but its memory burned deeply into his mind. It was the thought from his childhood when his father had laughed at his desire to join the priesthood. Although it seemed so long ago, the memory of his father's rebuke still stung and he turned to his mother and said, "Mum, I think somebody else a little more versed in prayer would be better saying grace."

"Oh Frank, if only for your mother would you please lead the family in grace," she said with emotion.

Frank turned to his mother and shook his head from side to side without uttering a word.

"You disappoint me, Francis Joseph Casey, but I will say grace if that's how you feel," Margaret said in a conciliatory tone. "Bless us, oh Lord, for these thy gifts which we are about to receive through Christ our Lord. Amen."

The rest of the family responded with Amen. All except Frank, whose lips may as well have been glued together. While Fran held her hands together in earnest prayer, she flashed a quick grin to her eldest brother before her mother gave her a withering stare.

"Since you find your brother's actions so amusing, Frances Mary Casey, you will do the washing up after lunch. Is that clear?" Margaret said.

"Yes, mum." Her grin quickly disappeared from her face.

"I'll give you a hand, sis," said Frank, while he flashed a smile at his sister.

That night the family sat in the loungeroom. There was laughter among the grieving of Hugh's death as they reminisced about their past. Frank had mixed feelings about his father's death. Although his relationship with Hugh had been difficult, he had a better understanding of his father's shortcomings after experiencing the horrors of war himself. The joy Frank had felt on his arrival home was short - lived, for the next day, he was to break his mother's heart.

The next day, while the family was busy getting themselves ready to attend Sunday mass in Bingara, Frank dropped the bomb-shell. Margaret noticed Frank had not gotten dressed in his Sunday best and asked why not.

"Mum, I am not going to mass today, tomorrow or any other day," Frank said seriously.

"Oh, why not Frank?" she pleaded.

"Because I have my doubts whether there is a God," he said bluntly.

"And why is that? Margaret pleaded.

"Because I've seen what man can do to man while I was in Buchenwald and I wonder where God was inside that hellhole?"

"Frank, you can't blame God for what happened during the war?"

"Where was God when Jimmy was killed?" Frank said defiantly, with his hands on his hips.

"Surely, Frank, you can't blame God for man's inhumanity to man. God never set the wheels in motion for World War Two or any other war. It was man that created the war."

Suddenly Frank realised Margaret had him stumped. She begged Frank to come to Mass, if only for her sake. Even Frank could not resist that appeal and as he looked into his mother's tear - stained eyes, he relented.

Frank sat next to his mother at St Mary's Catholic Church in Bingara that Sunday morning in May 1946, contemptuous for everything he was hearing. He saved his greatest mockery for the most sacred part of the mass, the Eucharist. Frank folded his arms and looked at the transubstantiation of the body and blood of Christ with silent but scornful ridicule. The war had brutalised Frank and the last thing he wanted in his life was religion.

When it was over, he was relieved after he had left the church. Although there were great well wishes from those of the parish who had not seen him for so long, Frank smiled and laughed with many of them. He was glad to be out of the place and wasn't in any hurry to return. That night, as he lay in bed contemplating the nonsense he had been through that day, he decided to fulfil a promise he had made while he was in Buchenwald. As hard as he knew it would be, that promise was that he would visit the Cruikshanks and pay them his respects at the loss of their son, Jimmy.

The decision to visit Clem and Anne Cruikshank and express his condolences for the death of Jimmy was an extremely difficult one for Frank. His greatest fear was how he would express his condolences appropriately.

He made his way over to Breeza in Hugh's Ford Prefect, the following Saturday. As much as the Cruikshanks were devastated by Jimmy's death, they greeted Frank like a long-lost son and put on a spread to celebrate his safe return home.

Frank spent the day at the Cruikshanks and although it was hard to talk about the incident that led to Jimmy's death, he was able to tell the family they should be proud of their son as he was operating his gun when the fatal blow came. The Cruikshanks realised the war and Jimmy's death had affected Frank greatly. When Clem saw Frank off, he leant inside the car window and gave him some advice.

"When I came back from World War One, I needed time to clear my head after everything I had been through. I hit the road for twelve months and went jackarooing. I suggest you do the same, Frank. Now that Hugh's dead, there's no pressure for you to stay at Banyula."

He gave Frank a tap on the arm and bade him farewell.

Frank did not need any more encouragement than that, and on the drive home to Bingara, he remembered Jack Walsh's offer to join his shearing team at Julia Creek in western Queensland.

Chapter 23

Thursday, June 6ᵗʰ 1946. "Agnes Downs" Julia Creek, North Western Queensland.

WHEN FRANK THREW his swag over his shoulder and walked down the driveway of Banyula with Frances by his side, instinct told him he would never return there to live. What the future held for him; he had no idea. After Frank had told his family of his decision to leave, it was decided his second eldest brother, Kevin, would run Banyula with their brother Bob.

Frank felt a great sense of relief he had finally decided to leave Banyula. He contacted Jack Walsh and told him he would like to join his shearing team. Jack informed Frank he could join his team as a roustabout immediately. Jack and his brother Vic and their two cousins Gerard and Paul Redmund were also shearers and partners in the team.

Jack and Vic Walsh had been brought up on their family's sheep station, Agnes Downs, located 52 miles (83km) northwest of Julia Creek in north-western Queensland. The station was named after their great-grandmother Agnes Walsh, who settled there with her husband Denis and their family in the 1880s.

Jack's parents, Tim and Annie, had seven children. Tim ran Agnes Downs with his two eldest sons, Dan and Pat, and when Jack and Vic weren't on the road shearing, they lived at home on the station.

Frank arrived at Agnes Downs, where he was to live in the jackaroos' quarters when not out shearing. He was immediately struck by the beauty of second eldest daughter Kate who had been convent educated in Brisbane. Her style and grace captivated him immediately. Kate, 24 years of age, was of medium height, had long brown hair and high cheekbones, and spoke with an elegance that suggested she had been well educated without sounding haughty. She was highly intelligent and, in another time with more opportunities, could have studied law at university. Kate also had a strong Catholic faith with a strong sense of morals, and although she realised Frank was a tough knockabout ex flyer, she recognised his sensitivity and genuine good nature. It was apparent from the start Frank and Kate's feelings for each other were mutual, and this was something the family encouraged as their relationship developed. Frank's sadness at losing Geraldine disappeared as he felt he had at long last met his soulmate.

He was definitely suffering from what is now known as post-traumatic stress disorder or PTSD, but what was then described as war neuroses.

It was a hard life on the road as part of the shearing team and the boys worked five days a week working on properties in all parts of western Queensland. Frank had always liked his drink while he was in the airforce, but this was primarily kept in check because of operational duties and his time as a POW. Frank's drinking increased once he started with the shearing team, but it was never an issue and never affected his work or personal life. Shearing teams are notorious for their boozing, and although the Walsh boys and their Redmund cousins liked a drop, it never seemed to affect them. Like most of his generation who had served in World War Two, Frank never spoke much about his experiences. If they did, it was to reminisce about some funny anecdote during their years of service. This was particularly poignant for Frank, considering his incarceration in Buchenwald. On his return to Australia, he had mentioned his time in Buchenwald to several people, only to be met with total disbelief. Some people thought he had lost the plot and was mistaking his time in Buchenwald for being a POW in a Luftwaffe-run camp. He soon learnt to keep quiet about both his Buchenwald experience and what happened to him during the war. It was to be many decades before Frank really opened up about his war-time experiences as he put a padlock on that part of his life.

Over the next twelve months, the shearing team worked in many big woolsheds on vast sheep stations throughout outback Queensland. As well as shearing around Julia Creek, they shore clips at Barcaldine, Longreach, Winton, Richmond, Cloncurry and out as far as Boulia, to name a few. It was an era when Australia still rode on the sheep's back and the country was stocked with huge mobs with shearing teams working all over the country.

After initially being a roustabout, Frank soon progressed to being the team's wool classer. The shearing shed was a tough environment and wasn't for the faint - hearted. The boys drank in plenty of pubs and saw their fair share of fights. It was a time where arguments were sorted out with your fists, and none of the team was exempt from this type of rough house behaviour.

Frank was a bit of an unknown to an unsuspecting assailant. He was like a duck paddling on the water. All calm and unruffled on the surface, but the feet were going ten to the dozen underneath. Under Frank's surface still lay the Wild Colonial Boy. Several blokes who saw him as an easy target got the shock of their lives when, after inviting him out the back of the pub to settle an argument, got their lights punched out. Frank was a natural sportsman and his timing was impeccable, whether it was passing a footy, hitting a golf club or throwing a straight right.

During this period, Frank felt a sense of unease, as if there was some unsolved question about his life that he couldn't quite put his finger on. As much as he loved Kate, alone in his thoughts, he felt there was another calling for him and marriage wasn't part of it. He brushed off the thoughts and continued to work while enjoying the camaraderie he had built up with the shearing team.

When he did make it back to Agnes Downs, there was always the comfort of a lady waiting for him, and once he gazed into Kate's beautiful blue eyes, everything seemed to come into order. As much as Kate loved Frank and she saw her future with him, there was one thing that concerned her before she committed to a marriage. Kate wanted Frank to commit to his Catholic faith, which included attending mass on Sundays. Frank tried to cajole Kate into having an each - way bet by agreeing to have their children brought up in the Catholic faith, but he wanted a type of roving commission to attend the occasional mass when the need arose. Kate was a woman of substantial moral and intellectual fortitude and would not be coerced into such a weak proposition.

By June 1947, Frank was in a real quandary after she had given him an ultimatum. Either he accepted his Catholic faith, or there would be no marriage. Frank loved Kate and wanted to marry her and finally, after much internal debate, he agreed to take up his Catholic faith so they could get married.

Everything was set. Frank and Kate would marry in March 1948. In the meantime, Frank attended regular masses on Sundays with Kate and the Walsh family, even though it was under duress. He wore a sullen look as he sat through the mass.

It was early February 1948 and the team was away shearing. Frank was in a dilemma about his Catholicism. He and Kate were due to be married in three weeks and all the arrangements were in place. Frank's great unanswered question, the thing niggling him for so long, was about to be revealed. As so often is the case in life, fate steps in and dictates a course of action. In Frank's case, it was to step in and determine the path he was to travel for the rest of his life.

The team had just finished shearing a clip on a station 10 miles (16km) south of Hughenden. They had been staying at The Grand Hotel in the small town in a large room on the first floor known as the "Bull Ring". It had been a stinking hot day and the boys were enjoying a session in Hughenden's premier hotel. They were going to stay there on Friday night and make their way back to Agnes Downs early Saturday morning. Frank was going to stay at the Grand Hotel that night, but at the last moment, decided to make tracks the 217 miles (350km) back to Agnes Downs. He wanted to sort out the "Catholic problem" once and for all with Kate, and time could not wait. After much soul searching, Frank had concluded he could not accept his Catholic faith. He believed he would be a hypocrite if he went into a marriage under the pretence of being a practising Catholic when he didn't believe any of it. Frank had concluded the marriage would be a sham and he would inform Kate it was off. As much as Frank was devastated by this outcome, his conscience dictated it was the only action he could take. The boys had tried to persuade Frank to stay at the hotel with them that night, and it was too late to be travelling back to Agnes Downs. Frank kept his true motives of why he wanted to get back to Julia Creek to himself and instead gave them the excuse he needed to make some wedding arrangements with Kate.

"Wedding arrangements be buggered, Frank. They can wait," said Vic in an exasperated tone.

"It's important that Kate and I talk about the wedding arrangements, Vic."

"Ya bloody mad driving back to Agnes Downs, Frank. There are 'roos and stock all over the place. You're bound to clean something up. Why don't you spend the night here and we can all go back in the morning?" Jack said.

Frank was adamant he was going to travel back to Agnes Downs that night and nothing the boys said could persuade him otherwise.

As Frank had his car, a 1940 Chevrolet Sloper, it was agreed the other boys would get a lift back to Agnes Downs in Vic's vehicle the next day.

The 168 miles (270km) from Hughenden back to Julia Creek on the Flinders Highway was a dirt road, corrugated and strewn with potholes.

Frank left at 7pm, on the lookout for anything he may hit. No sooner was he on the road then he was overcome with great unease, as it reminded him of an operation over enemy territory. Frank's palms and neck became sweaty. He was filled with anxiety at what awaited him as he travelled across the desolate stretch of outback highway. Where it was once night fighters and flak he was on the lookout for, this evening it was 'roos and stock. It made no difference to him, as he was overcome with the same sense of dread he used to feel when flying towards a target. He clutched the steering wheel tightly and his eyes darted around continuously on the lookout for an animal that might suddenly appear in front of him.

As Frank drove along, it became apparent to him that this was more than just a road trip, but the start of a journey where he questioned his destiny and what he was to do with the rest of his life. His thoughts returned to the operations he flew over occupied Europe and the mates he had lost. He thought about Buchenwald and Otto Kestelman and the atrocities he had witnessed there. He thought about whether there was a God. After much thought, he finally admitted there was a higher deity and it had saved his life on countless occasions while on operations and in captivity. Fitting God into the dogma of Catholicism filled him with contempt, however, and he recoiled from the idea.

He let out a huge sigh of relief when he reached Richmond, a small outback town 76 miles (122km) from Hughenden. He felt the same relief when returning to England after completing an operation.

He travelled on, willing himself home. Frank was 45 miles (72km) out of Richmond when he received the shock of his life. Out of the darkness staggered an old Aboriginal man brandishing a flagon of port. Frank hit the brakes, narrowly avoiding hitting the man before screeching to a halt. The man waved his hands in the air and bellowed some abuse.

"Bloody hell, that was close. What the bloody hell is he doing here out in the middle of nowhere?" Frank said out loud.

He drove on be before concluding that the encounter with the Aboriginal man was too close for comfort.

"Bugger it; I'll camp up at the pub in Julia Creek for the night before making my way back to Agnes Downs in the morning," he said to himself.

By this stage, Frank's anxiety was at a fever pitch, so after wiping his brow with his handkerchief, he continued on his way. He was only 10 miles (16km) from Julia Creek and had allowed himself to believe he might make it back to town without hitting anything. Suddenly, from the left shoulder of the road bounded a huge red kangaroo towards the middle of the road. Frank was travelling at high speed when he caught a glimpse of the 'roo. He turned the vehicle sharply to the right, trying to avoid it, but hit the animal on the left side of the car. The impact smashed the left headlight and the car lurched out of control towards the table drain situated on the right side of the road. Once hitting the table drain, the car rolled seven times, and with no seat belt in the car, Frank was tossed around like a rag doll. Finally, the car came to rest on its roof beside the roadway. Two of its wheels still spinning, and one headlight eerily glowing in the dark. Frank was knocked unconscious, and he lay there motionless.

Frank lay there unconscious for half an hour before he came too. He was in a lot of pain and felt as though he had broken every bone in his body. He was lying on his back on the ceiling and managed to lift his hand up to the middle of his forehead, where he felt a huge gash just below his hairline. He wiped his hand on the cut and it was covered in blood. He moaned as he tried to lift his head to survey the damage, but he was in excruciating pain, so quickly lowered it and rested while his breathing was heavy. While lying there trapped, Frank could have turned his thoughts to any number of people: Kate; the boys back in Hughenden; the Walshes or his family. It was none of these who entered his mind. Instead, it was the thought of

Father Jean Baptist Fournier. Frank felt his eyes become moist as he was overcome with emotion. He remembered the incredible kindness Father Fournier had shown him. Frank lay there deep in thought, recounting the many charitable acts the priest had shown toward him.

A good hour passed and there was no sign of help coming. Frank was starting to get desperate as he lapsed in and out of consciousness when a thought came to him.

"If you get me out of this mess, Father Fournier, I will honour your memory forever."

Sometime later, he was awoken by the sounds of rifle shots nearby. The next thing Frank saw were two headlights shining in the cabin of his upturned vehicle.

It was 11.30 pm, and Nick Britton, a professional kangaroo shooter from Julia Creek, had been out shooting in his 1945 Ford Blitz. Usually, he would venture out further, but he decided to stay a bit closer to Julia Creek, as he wanted to get home earlier. Nick was in his mid - fifties and a World War One veteran. He had been a professional 'roo shooter for over twenty years, but like most blokes from the outback, had tried his hand at a number of things, including station work, droving and mining. It was pure chance that he happened to see the dimming headlight of Frank's car in the distance when he was lining up for a shot on a big red buck from the cabin of his vehicle.

"Are you okay, mate?" He said in a gruff voice as he approached Frank's car.

"Ahhhh," Frank groaned after Nick crawled inside the upturned vehicle.

"Don't you worry, mate, I'll get you out of this mess," he said to Frank.

Frank was very weak and could barely talk and soon passed

out again. Nick could smell fuel leaking from the car and hastily pulled him from the vehicle while being careful of his injuries. He laid Frank on his back on the tray of his truck, surrounded by the carcasses of kangaroos. From there, Nick drove to a station a few miles down the road owned by people he knew. Frank was attended to by the elderly wife of the station owner, who happened to be a retired nursing sister. Luck was running Frank's way, and she put him to bed before she could stem the bleeding, which was coming from a deep gash in his head and his leg. Her attention to detail and administration of morphine to Frank saved his life, as he was severely injured.

Early the next day, an aircraft flew from the Royal Flying Doctor Service base at Cloncurry and landed on a long stretch of gravel road not far from the homestead. Frank was loaded onto a stretcher, and flown to Cloncurry, and taken to the hospital, where a doctor performed lifesaving surgery on his ruptured bladder. Frank's injuries were extensive, for not only did he have a ruptured bladder, a severe gash in his head and leg, but several broken ribs, a broken foot and bruising.

Frank's life hung in the balance for several days as he lay unconscious in bed and he was visited by Kate and members of the Walsh family. It was the evening of the third day after being admitted to the hospital and Frank was in a semi - conscious state. He felt the life ebbing from him and he was overcome with a tremendous sense of peace, the like he had never experienced before.

"So, this is what dying feels like?" He thought to himself.

While Frank's life was fading, outside his room, two nurses were giggling. It was the younger one's 21st birthday, and they were laughing at a card she had received from her boyfriend.

In Frank's moribund state, he became conscious of the women giggling.

The sister on duty was attending a patient further down the ward when she heard the noise the nurses were making. Making her way hastily to where they were standing, the sister ticked them off.

"Don't you nurses realise a young man is dying in this room? Please keep your noise down!"

The sister's harsh words broke Frank from his ethereal state and he was brought back to reality. Suddenly he realised he had been dying and the thought came to him, *if this was dying, then I have nothing to fear from death.*

But I am not ready to die. I have too much to live for, he kept thinking.

Then Frank had a profound thought. He knew some great power had been looking after him during those tumultuous war years. He made a decision if he got out of this mess, he would dedicate his life to helping others.

What better way to serve people than to become a priest.

Frank recoiled at becoming a priest, but the more he thought about it, the more peaceful he felt. Then suddenly, he awoke from his semi - conscious state. He opened his eyes and gazed at the ceiling.

"So this is what I have been running away from. I have finally realised the priesthood is my destiny," he murmured.

Everyone was overcome with joy when Frank awoke from his unconscious state, but none more so than Kate.

Frank spent the next day trying to determine how he would break the news to Kate about the decision he had made. He didn't know if he had been hallucinating, but one thing was for sure: the more he thought about becoming a priest, the more comfortable he felt about the decision.

It was just after breakfast the next day and Kate was by Frank's bedside when he broke the news to her.

"I've decided I want to join the priesthood, Kate!" he said to her directly.

Kate laughed and stroked his head before she said, "Oh, Frank, my dear man, that blow to your head really did knock you silly."

Frank looked directly into Kate's eyes and she knew he wasn't kidding.

"I am serious, Kate. I almost died and while I was lying in this bed unconscious, I had a revelation."

"So you are serious."

"Yes, I am Kate. I've been running away from my vocation for years and it has just dawned on me that this is what I am supposed to do with my life. As much as you are a fine lady and I have no doubts you would have made a beautiful wife and mother, I believe I have a higher calling and I must follow it."

Kate gazed at Frank solemnly and said nothing for an eternity, before saying,

"If that is what you believe God wants you to do with your life, you must do it. But rest assured, Frank Casey, if the priesthood does not work out, then don't ever come back to me because there is no way I would ever want to be married to an ex - priest."

With that, Kate about - faced and walked out of his ward. It was the last time he would ever lay eyes on her.

Although he realised Kate must have been devastated by his decision, he knew he had made the correct one and he felt comfortable within himself. The Walshes were incensed at Frank's decision to break off his engagement with Kate and study for the priesthood, so they cut all ties with him. They were embarrassed as the wedding was to be one of the biggest events on the social calendar in Julia Creek that year. They had future plans for setting Frank and Kate up on a property of their own and this ended abruptly. Only Jack, who accepted his decision, was to remain a lifelong friend of Frank's.

On receiving news of the accident, Margaret and Kevin drove up to Cloncurry. As soon as they arrived at the hospital, Frank wasted no time in telling them of his decision.

"You're pulling my leg, Frank," Kevin said through muffled laughter.

"No, I am not, Kevin. I have decided to become a priest."

"Crikey, you sure did get a fair whack to the head to come out with such an idea," Kevin said.

"I am serious. Something powerful happened to me shortly after they brought me in here. I was dying and I realised God had spared my life on countless occasions during the war. Then it just hit me! I want to serve people and being a priest is the best way I can do that."

Kevin looked at Frank for some time while Margaret, who had been sitting in silence in a chair next to his bed, spoke.

"Well, Frank, I must say it comes as a complete surprise, but people do have massive shifts in their thinking and it's obvious that it has happened to you. If you truly believe that's what God wants you to do, you must follow your conscience."

"Yes, it is mum."

Margaret then hugged Frank.

Frank explained he had always believed running Banyula was not his destiny and it would be left to his younger brother.

"I have always known you would tread a different path to the rest of my children," said Margaret.

Frank spent the best part of a month in hospital recovering from his injuries with his mother by his side while Kevin drove back to Banyula to run the property.

It was early March 1948 when Frank was released from Cloncurry Hospital. Kevin drove back to Cloncurry to pick Margaret and Frank up and take them back to Banyula.

After farewelling all the hospital staff who had cared for him so well during his stay, they spent three days getting back to Banyula. Frank had prepared himself for the reaction his family would have at his momentous decision.

The three of them arrived home at Banyula on Thursday, March 11th 1948. Kevin had informed the family of Frank's decision when he had initially returned from Cloncurry. The family were perplexed as to what Frank would be like now he had made such a momentous decision. Some thought he may have become very holy and pious, but on arriving he was the same as he had always been, albeit with a new found purpose.

"Is it true you want to study for the priesthood?" exclaimed Bob.

"Yes, you heard it right. I am going to give it a go, as I believe that's the best way I can help people."

There was stunned silence from the family before Joan broke out giggling. This was the signal for the rest of Frank's siblings to let loose with howls of laughter.

"Did he say what I think he said?" Brian said through shrieks of laughter from the family.

"Yes, he did, Brian. Can you believe it, Frank, of all people? The one who wouldn't have a bar of religion," said Veronica, who was home.

"People do change Veronica!" Kevin snapped.

"Yes, but do you honestly believe that Frank is cut out to be a priest? He's a firebrand if ever there was one!" Veronica said.

There was more laughter before Margaret intervened and yelled in an uncustomary fashion.

"Be quiet! Frank has thought long and hard about this and has not made this decision lightly."

Everyone settled down after Margaret's rebuke.

"Don't worry, regardless of my decision to join the priesthood, I am still the fiery bugger I've always been," Frank said with a wink.

Everyone laughed and Frank reiterated what Kevin had told them that he had not lost his mind and his decision had been a result of his near - death experience. Frank further explained he would work at Banyula for the rest of 1948 and apply for acceptance into the seminary for the following year.

It took most of the family some time to accept Frank's decision. It was only after talking to him about his momentous shift in thinking after the accident that they fully accepted that this was the path he wanted to travel.

Meanwhile, after a series of interviews, he was granted admission to St Columba's Catholic Seminary at Springwood in the Blue Mountains in 1949.

In June 1948, as Frank prepared to enter the Catholic seminary the following year, unbeknownst to him on the other side of the world, the authorities had finally caught up with his old nemesis, Otto Kestelman. Kestelman was on the list of the Americans' most wanted Nazi war criminals. A former German prisoner of Buchenwald had tipped them off to his whereabouts. Otto, who was still going under the alias of Klaus Bauer, had been working as a foreman on a farm in Bavaria.

The previous month, Otto had made contact with an organisation named "Ratlines", which were helping known Nazi war criminals escape from Germany through two main routes. One was from Germany to Spain, and the other was from Germany to Rome. From there, they escaped to Nazi havens in South America, such as Argentina, Paraguay, Colombia, Brazil and Uruguay.

Some members of the Catholic Church supported the Ratlines and some even claimed the Vatican was involved in aiding many of these Nazis to escape. One of the most prominent Ratline members was the pro - Nazi German Catholic priest named Monsignor Rudolf Becher. Becher was unashamedly pro - Nazi and believed National Socialism was a right and just ideology to combat the godless forces of bolshevism during the war. He had actively aided a number of wanted Nazi war criminals to escape from Germany by providing passports and visas to Argentina.

Kestelman had contacted Becher and the priest was aiding him to escape from Germany via Spain and then on to Argentina. Becher had provided Kestelman with a forged passport and an Argentinean visa. He was making his way through Germany via the Ratline when he was identified by a former prisoner of Buchenwald and arrested by the Americans.

Kestelman was put on trial for crimes against allied nationals and they were held within the walls of the former Dachau Concentration Camp in Germany. The Dachau trials were held for all war criminals caught in the United States zones in Germany and Austria. They were conducted by American military personnel.

The Dachau trials, numbering in their hundreds, included charges of main camp offence, subsidiary camp offences and atrocities against downed fliers. The trials were for crimes committed not only in Dachau but Flossenbürg, Mauthausen – Gusen, Nordhausen, Mühldorf and Buchenwald concentration camps.

From the onset, Kestelman displayed belligerent arrogance towards the American military prosecutors. He vehemently denied any wrongdoing and stated he was merely following orders. He continued by reinforcing his beliefs that the prisoners in Buchenwald were sworn enemies of Nazi Germany and he was within his rights to administer the punishment that he did.

Kestelman's trial was short, and he was charged with all three offences, including main camp offence, subsidiary camp offense and atrocities against downed fliers. For these offences, he was sentenced to death by hanging and sent to Landsberg Prison in the southwest German state of Bavaria. Landsberg Prison, which was named War Criminal Prison Number 1 by the US Forces occupying Germany, was the prison used for holding Nazi war criminals.

It was expected that Kestelman's execution would be swift, but it was delayed. While he was incarcerated, he heard both the gangplank drop and the sound of shots fired as numerous Nazi war criminals were executed. Kestelman remained steadfast to his Nazi ideology and never shifted his dedication to Hitler's fascist ideals, regularly greeting his American guards with the Nazi salute followed by the customary *"Heil Hitler."*

Towards the end of 1948, with the foundations of the Federal Republic of Germany (West Germany) in place, politicians, the clergy, industrialists and artists had petitioned to abolish the death penalty. With growing protest rallies outside of Landsberg Prison, Otto Kestelman's death sentence was commuted to life imprisonment. Time was on Kestelman's side, as he would have certainly been executed if he had been captured a year earlier.

With life imprisonment in solitary confinement hanging over his head, Otto had plenty of time to contemplate the atrocities he had perpetrated during the war.

Chapter 24

Monday, February 14th 1949. St Columba's Catholic seminary, Springwood NSW

IF THERE WAS ever an individual who came to the Catholic priesthood through the 'back door', it was Frank Casey. It wasn't Frank's age, or that he was a returned serviceman, for others were in a similar position. Frank had not been guided to the priesthood through a religious brother at school or a priest from the parish, as was common. Frank's vocation had come through a traumatic event cumulating in a spiritual awakening. His revelation had come after the trauma he had endured during the war rather than a naïve, albeit honest and fervent, vision of an ecclesiastical vocation. It was this that set Frank apart from many of his fellow students.

St Columba's was known as the minor seminary, where it was divided into senior and junior students. The first group of the senior section included students who were in first and second - year philosophy who studied other subjects like Greek, Latin, Hebrew, Ancient History and Logic. The second group of senior students was trying to understand the intricacies of Latin in which the Mass was still spoken.

The juniors were much younger students, some as young as 12. They were completing five years of secondary education at the hands of the Marist Brothers in preparation for the public Leaving Certificate. They dressed in black cassocks like the older students. On completion of their secondary schooling, they became senior students.

The philosophy behind admitting boys as young as 12 was so the seminary could indoctrinate them before the 'evils' of the world could stain their souls. Frank had no problems with that happening to him. He had already had a head - on collision with the world's evils and they had left a massive impact on him. Springwood was where men started their training for the Catholic priesthood for all dioceses in New South Wales.

After three years of study at Springwood, the senior students were then sent to St Patricks College Manly in Sydney, which was the major seminary, to complete four more years of training. Subjects included theology, morality, dogmatic theology, sacramental theology, ethics, Christology and martyrology. After seven years of training, a student was ordained into the Catholic priesthood.

As Frank lay in his bed in St John Bosco dormitory that first night, tossing and turning in the oppressive heat, he reflected on his arrival at the seminary earlier that evening. He had caught the 4.00 pm Blue Mountains service from the country platform at Central Railway Station in Sydney, bound for Springwood. Frank had stamped out the butt of a Craven A cigarette under his foot before boarding the train. The 140 students who had boarded the train ranged from 12 to his age of 28. There was incessant chatter and laughter as they discussed how they had spent their Christmas school holidays.

Frank kept to himself and said nothing. Instead, he tried to make himself comfortable on the tough leather seats and found solace as suburbia disappeared to make way for the bush.

The steam engine laboured up the mountain, taking two hours to complete its journey. On arrival, the students were ushered onto a fleet of old buses where they were taken to St Columba's Seminary. On entering the front gates, a hush enveloped the students. The older students understood the drill. The bus drove up a mile - long gravel driveway where it swung around a grassed circle in front of the college. On departing the bus, Frank was met with the sight of a large honey combed sandstone structure with large windows running down the side. Students jostled as they dragged their luggage from the bus and through the dimly lit entrance.

On dropping off his bag in the senior dormitory, which consisted of 30 beds, he got dressed in the supplied black soutane and collar. It was a hot evening, exacerbated by the unfamiliar clerical attire.

The students were soon ushered into the refectory, where a priest said grace in Latin before they were served a very plain meal of bread, butter and jam. Frank spoke to nobody but sat in silence and contemplated the ordinary fare they were served. It was the start of many such meals. It was after the meal that the 'great silence' began. This meant no talking was allowed until after breakfast the next morning.

The students were then led into a room for meditation. It was there for the first time Frank laid eyes on the rector of the college: Monsignor Dermot O'Slattery. Dermo, as some of the students covertly referred to him, was an imposing figure. Aged in his early sixties, he stood six feet four inches tall, of heavy build, with white hair, a flushed face and he wore black - rimmed spectacles. Instinct told Frank the Monsignor was one he should be wary of. He spoke in a nasally, gruff, authoritarian tone, and after a fleeting welcome, he gave the students a brief talk about the rules of the college. The new students remained for a more thorough drill on the college rules, which the Monsignor laid down in no uncertain terms. There was to be absolute silence in the chapel. No talking, coughing, nose - blowing, sniffling, laughing, hands in pockets or rumbustious behaviour. Monsignor O'Slattery had laid the rules out clear and simple. After prayers, it was into bed at 9.15 pm and then lights out.

Frank lay in his hard, narrow bed with its accompanying stiff mattress wearing his new starched pyjamas. It was stifling hot, made even more so by the grey woollen blankets. There was a deathly silence in the dormitory, albeit the sounds of snoring or the occasional release of foul air, punctuated the quiet from time to time. Everyone seemed to be asleep, except Frank. He was hot and irritable and everyone seemed to have their blankets over them as though it was not permissible to have them off. Finally, after half an hour of tossing and turning, Frank sat up in bed and said quietly.

"Crikey, I've had enough of these blankets."

With that, he threw the blankets off and it was only then did he find some relief and went to sleep.

At 6.00 am the following day, Frank was awoken by a student walking through the dormitory ringing a bell. It was to become a familiar sound to Frank, as the seminary was a highly disciplined place where everything ran to the sound of a bell. Sleeping in the bed beside Frank was 19 - year - old Tony Casaceli. Tony, whose

Italian parents had migrated to Australia in 1930 to escape the impending Second World War, had worked hard to set up a fruit shop in Marrickville in Sydney. The student rang his bell beside his ear incessantly before the slumbering Tony was woken.

Frank got dressed, forgetting that modesty was paramount in the seminary. He had spent too many years in the airforce to be worrying about such prudish things. As Tony rolled out of bed, he caught an eye full of Frank's private parts, as did the bell ringer. Frank continued to dress casually, unaware of the silent commotion he had caused. They both stared in disbelief at Frank before the bell ringer scurried off, flushed with embarrassment, while Tony hastily donned his attire, shocked into submission. Frank didn't know it yet, but he had already broken two cardinal rules in the short time he had been at the seminary.

Frank's day was up and running. A day in the seminary was always full as the powers that be believed idle hands were the devil's workshop. Morning prayer in the chapel consisted of rapid - fire decades of the rosary, followed by communal prayer. Then it was Mass at 7.30 am, then a very ordinary breakfast at 8.00 am. Morning lectures went from 9.00 am to midday, followed by lunch from noon to 1.00 pm. Sport, which was an important part of college life, went from 1.00 pm to 3.00 pm, followed by two more hours of study. At 5.30 pm, the students were summoned to prayer until 6.00 pm, where tea ran from 6.00 pm till 7.00 pm. It was a highly regimented day devoid of any external influences such as radio, newspapers or magazines and it went on like this daily.

At 7.00 pm, Frank's ordered day came to a grinding halt. Instead of engaging in two hours of study, one of his dormitory prefects named Peter English summoned him to a meeting with the head man himself, Monsignor O'Slattery. Dermo's dishevelled room was cluttered with books and papers lying on the ground. The Monsignor motioned Frank to sit down, and as he made his way through the mess to his seat, Dermo took a cigarette from his packet of Peter Jacksons. Frank could not help noticing that his fingers were nicotine - stained as the Monsignor patted the filter of the cigarette into the palm of his left hand. He lit the cigarette, took a deep drawback and exhaled, blowing smoke in Frank's direction.

"Mr Casey," he said, raising his left finger as his elbow rested on his desk, "there are rules in this college that are put in place for a specific reason. It has come to my attention that you have broken two very serious ones in the short time you have been here."

"What may that be, Monsignor?"

"I'll ask the questions here, Mr Casey!" Dermo said gruffly.

Frank felt resentful about being ticked off.

"As an older seminarian, you may think you are a man of the world and have experienced many of the unsavoury things that life dishes up. Let me assure you that you are one among many at this seminary, and you will be expected to obey the rules set down for all the students."

The Monsignor's cold demeanour brought back memories of Otto Kestelman to Frank.

Dermo cleared his throat and continued.

"When we say there is to be no noise from the end of the evening meal to breakfast the following day, we specifically mean that."

Frank wracked his brain trying to remember what he had said during that time, but for the life of him could not remember.

"You were heard muttering obscenities about being too hot in bed last night. That pales into insignificance compared to the unconscionable act you performed in front of two of your fellow students this morning."

Frank stared at the Monsignor with bewilderment etched on his face.

"Do I have to remind you that you undressed in front of two of your fellow seminarians, exposing yourself to them and, by doing so, giving them a reason for thoughts of sin?"

"But Monsignor......." Frank said forcibly.

The Monsignor raised his finger and said, "Don't test my patience, Mr Casey. You are skating on thin ice as it is. I thought about expelling you from this seminary, but after consulting with the Dean of Discipline, Father McCarthy, I have decided to give you one last chance. He brought to my attention that you held a position in Bomber Command during the war and had worked with rough shearing teams. This has obviously left you with many crude habits, and I am prepared to cut you some slack because of this. Let this be a final warning, Mr Casey, that your unruly behaviour will not be tolerated, and the next time a foul indiscretion as the one you have performed takes place, it will be the end of the road for you. We are training men to be holy and pious ecclesiastics here at the seminary, and any crude distractions cast in the direction of impressionable minds can bring on appalling behaviour. Is that clear? "

Frank looked at Dermo long and hard before replying coldly, "Yes, Monsignor."

"Now go," the Monsignor said with a wave of his hand.

Frank walked to the study, flummoxed by what he had just heard. As he sat at his desk in the study in deep contemplation, he thought about running.

"But where do I run to?" he thought to himself.

"There is nothing left for me out there. This is where I believe I am meant to be," he concluded.

Frank sat in silence and thought long and hard about what he had just witnessed. He had figured out there were snitches among the students who would think nothing of giving someone up. He had seen it at school and in the air force. He realised while most seminarians were dedicated to their vocation, some would give you up if it meant currying favour with the powers that be, so they could climb the ladder of promotion. The seminary was no exception to that rule. History was repeating itself. Frank realised he had no ambition to hold a high office in the realm of the Catholic Church. If he was to stick the distance and be ordained, he would be most effective as a humble parish priest.

Shortly after his meeting with Dermo, Frank learnt that Peter English had dobbed him in. English, who came from Turramurra on the leafy North Shore of Sydney, had come to St Columba's as a 12 - year - old and been at the seminary for six years. He had grovelled his way through his schooling to receive favours from the priests. His reward was the position of a prefect. Many prefects were dobbers, but English was of the highest order. He would think nothing of putting a student into one of the priests for some minor misdemeanour to earn extra brownie points. Frank took a mental note to keep an eye on English.

At 28, Frank was the oldest student at Springwood. There were other late vocations, including those who had seen service during the war and others who had professions. Among them was Bill Doherty, who had been a sergeant stationed in Darwin during the war with a Heavy Anti - Aircraft Battery. Brian Cruden had fought in the Middle East and PNG with an AIF battalion. Anthony Ryan had been a medical doctor and Joe Cleary had been a surveyor and would later become a bishop. Richard Stenning was ordained, but he left the priesthood after ten years and became a schoolteacher. He was so disillusioned with the Catholic Church he stopped practising his faith. A number of these late vocations were to hold positions as senior prefects while at Springwood. All except Frank! From the beginning, the powers that be saw Frank as a rebel.

Dermot O'Slattery had quickly concluded Frank was an agitator and there was no place for people like him in the seminary. As a result of their initial meeting, he had Frank firmly set in his sights. He believed Frank's days were numbered at Springwood and it would only be a matter of time before he left. Dermo, who loved a punt on the horses, proposed a wager with Father McCarthy that Frank wouldn't last six months. As a gambling man, he wanted to retrieve his kitty, and besides, it would have been too easy to have expelled Frank for some indiscretion.

"Give him enough rope and he will hang himself," he was reputed to have said to Father McCarthy.

Frank thought long and hard after his initial run - in with Dermo. He soon learned Dermo wanted him out of the seminary, but was determined to last the distance no matter the pressure. The anvil of experience had given him a steely resolve never to give up. He would always have a penchant for being anti - establishment.

Frank largely stuck to himself in those early days while he got attuned to seminary life. There was much to learn about this new way of life. There was daily prayer and the Mass, which was said in Latin. There was the rosary and the Stations of the Cross. Many Catholic rituals went back centuries and Gregorian chants sung by priests filled Frank with a great solace. The philosophy of St Columba's was to break the man down into an individual, so he was reliant on no-one. He was meant to form no close attachments, especially with his family. He was meant to be remote, aloof, cold, puritanical, and to be seen as a type of demigod. When the Bishop moved him to another parish, he could do so without the hindrance of not having formed any close attachments. One of the rules of the college stated:

All excessive familiarity and friendships are dangerous and contrary to charity.

From the outset, Frank rebelled against this. He had known what it was like to be part of a team on the sporting field and as part of a bomber crew. Each crew member relied on the other as if his life depended on it. He knew the importance of being a team player and being on common ground with his other crew members. He was aware he had many character defects and he viewed the priesthood as his way of doing God's will rather than imposing his superiority over others. His life experiences enabled him to sort out the wheat from the chaff and figure out what he needed to do to keep his serenity. His thinking was ahead of its time and something that allowed him to keep his sanity.

He did form a friendship with Tony Casaceli, who worked in his parent's fruit shop after completing his Leaving Certificate. Frank saw in Tony, a man with a warm personality who possessed a beaming smile. He was naïve to many of the ways of the world growing up in a large, tight - knit Catholic Italian family. Frank took him under his wing and discreetly tutored him on many of the realities of the world.

Frank was a mystery to many of his fellow seminarians and they knew he was a tough man with a bit of a temper who called a spade a spade. Although most of them knew he had served in WWII, none of them, including Tony Casaceli, had any idea what he had been through. He discussed that part of his life with no one. Although many tough men dominated the Catholic priesthood of the 1940s/50s, many of the students thought he didn't fit the image of a priest and he wouldn't last the distance. Many failed to see Frank had a tremendous spiritual capacity and a great compassion for the underdog and those who had been forgotten by society. These qualities were to be the foundation of his life as a priest. During the significant changes that took place within the Catholic Church after Vatican II in the 1960s, many men left the priesthood. Although many challenges came his way, Frank stayed faithful to his vocation by helping those who had fallen through the cracks.

Some of the professors, as the priests were called, did have a great influence on Frank and impressed him greatly. They were liberal thinkers who challenged the students to think more broadly. The times were such that they were ensconced in an archaic system rigidly stuck within dogmatic confines and they were limited in how much they could stretch the boundaries.

Frank had been at St Columba's for three months and became well acquainted with the food, both plain and scarce. He had starved in Buchenwald and had a nagging fear of never having enough. Along with most of the other students, they had stomachs that ached with hunger pangs. As a result, Frank would never miss an opportunity to grab a spare morsel of food to satisfy his appetite.

At the back of the refectory was the kitchen, where the nuns worked tirelessly, cooking in anonymity. Nobody seemed to notice the work they did, but their role was crucial in the seminary's day to day running. Like most women in society back then, they were seen but not heard. The seminary was a man's domain!

Breakfast consisted of Weet-Bix or Cornflakes. Canned spaghetti that had been re-cooked a number of times was never quite al dente enough for Frank. Stale bread was bountiful. When the occasion did arise, and they were provided with freshly baked loaves, Frank would always manage to scrape up some extras. He had learned how to covertly grab any spare morsel of food and hide it from his days of incarceration. Old habits die hard and it wasn't uncommon for Frank to have a stash of bread hidden under his cassock to be consumed in secret later on.

Lunch, which was the day's main meal, was not much better. It consisted of a bowl of soup, a couple of sausages and maybe some rissoles. Occasionally, they would be served a shoulder of hogget that had to feed eleven people seated at the table. The meat dish came with mashed potatoes or mashed pumpkin, carrots and maybe turnips or parsnips. Dessert consisted of pudding, spread with Golden Syrup, or a bowl of creamed rice.

Dinner was a very meagre affair and in the dead of winter, when the nights were freezing, what was served was very inadequate. A slice of stale bread with devon and tomato served with half a fruit bun. Everything had to be shared. There never seemed to be one of anything for an individual. This included the butter, where a quarter of a pound had to be shared between eleven people.

There was no talking in the refectory. All that could be heard was the ceaseless din of knives, forks and cutlery while each student tried to secretly stuff as much into their mouths as possible. Monsignor O'Slattery would look over his black spectacles in disdain at the students, simmering like a volcano while his face became red. He believed the meal should be eaten in total silence, and there was no need for the crashing of plates and cutlery. Dermo was always on the lookout for some minor misdemeanour at the dinner table and had his prefects out as spies. Peter English was always ready to report a student breaking a rule. The seminarians were being trained to have all the etiquette of a gentleman from the Victorian era. Food was never to be consumed with the mouth open and bread was to be cut into small portions with a knife and fork before being eaten. Elbows were not too wide at the table, and cutlery was to be used appropriately. When Dermo had had enough, he would ring a little table bell where the noise would stop. With his right - hand finger, he would indicate a culprit to be disciplined, and if the offence occurred twice, then the inevitable meeting in the rector's office would happen. When the noise had settled down, there were wags like Frank who would set the cat among pigeons. From where he was seated at the back of the refectory, he would discreetly drop a spoon on the floor on purpose to annoy the powers that be. There would be calls for the perpetrator to own up, which they never did and the student body would never give one of their own up. Prefects like English were always looking for a culprit, but most times, Frank stayed one step ahead of him.

There were nights when a student had broken a rule and went without their evening meal, sitting among the assembled with an aching stomach. Frank received this punishment several times, but always managed to have some food stowed away in a covert area where prying eyes would not notice.

There was public speaking during the evening meal, where a student would read from a book the priests had chosen. *The Imitation of Christ* by Thomas à Kempis or *The Cattle King* by Ion Idriess was some of the literature that would be read. There was never anything too liberal in its thinking and especially not risqué. The literature was meant to keep the student's mind in a tight niche.

After dinner, one of the priests would ring a small bell and announce *'benedicamus domino'*, to which the students would reply *'Deo gratias'*, which was the sign to talk.

"It is August Monsignor O'Slattery and I notice that Mr Casey has not left us?" Father McCarthy said with a wry smile.

Dermo looked at the Dean of Discipline with disdain, huffing and snorting as he laid the wager on his office desk.

Father McCarthy was about to pick up the money when Dermo put his hand on top of his and said, "I propose double or nothing, Fr. McCarthy?"

"What is your wager, Monsignor?"

"That Mr Casey will be gone by Christmas."

"What makes you so sure he will be gone by Christmas if he has stuck it out for six months, Monsignor?"

"Because it's the Rugby League season, and Mr Casey is the winning side's captain. There is no way he will want to quit until the season is finished."

"Consider it done," said Father McCarthy.

The two clerics shook hands and the deal was set.

Sport and work were compulsory and no excuse was tolerated not to participate. Handball, shuttlecock, tennis, cricket, boxing, Australian Rules Football, hockey, athletics, basketball and Rugby League were the sports at the seminary. It was an important avenue for young men with the vitality of youth and raging hormones to allow their fierce competitive spirit out in a constructive manner. Many of the seminarians would have had stellar sporting careers, but for the priesthood. Sporting fixtures were played with a fierce competitiveness, with nobody giving any quarter.

Alongside sport, work was seen as equally important. Every student was required to swing an axe, uproot a tree, or clear a patch of land, even though it appeared to serve no purpose. Here, Frank found the perfect release for the frustrations he felt about living under such an antiquated, archaic and oppressive system.

Every afternoon after the midday meal, a crowd of students would rush out into any number of sporting facilities to unchain their energies and feel human once again. Woe betide any student found loitering in some covert corner of the college and not seen playing sport. The powers that be would come crashing down upon him.

Frank participated in many sports, including cricket, athletics, boxing and tennis. But it was Rugby League where he really shone, and when he was on the footy paddock, he felt the wrath of Dermo was off him, albeit for only a short period of time.

Although the car accident had reduced some of his pace, he still possessed the silky skills that had made him such an incredible player in his youth.

The Marist Brothers would referee the Rugby League matches and many of them were not much older than the students. In Frank's case, he was older than a number of them.

The Rugby League games were sometimes rough affairs, with players receiving broken noses, black eyes and split lips. Dermo would always be prowling around at the back of the spectators, hoping Frank received a king hit from an opponent that would put him out of action. Frank gave as good as he got and never took a backward step and was able to avoid any serious injury.

Frank's Rugby League prowess allowed him to get one back on Dermo as all of his opponents respected him.

The evening of the day the students had left the college for the Christmas break was when Dermo received a knock at his office door.

"Come in," he said gruffly.

Father McCarthy walked in, trying to conceal his smile. Dermo looked up and gave him a look of disdain.

"What are you so jovial about?"

"Don't you remember Monsignor, but we had a little wager on whether or not Mr Casey would last the distance? It appears he has, and that being the case, I believe you owe me."

Dermo gave him a look of contempt before rummaging around in the bottom drawer of his desk, where he produced a small brown paper bag and slammed it on the desk.

"There it is," he hissed.

"Thank you. I presume the case is closed?" Father McCarthy said with a wry smile.

"The case will only be closed when Mr Casey leaves this college for good."

"Why then don't you expel him if you believe he is not suitable for seminary life?"

"Because I am going to let the rogue hang himself!" Dermo said, slamming his fist on the desk.

"I think you seriously underestimate the resolve of Mr Casey. He is a man of considerable fortitude and I think he will be a hard nut to crack."

"You wait and see what the New Year brings. I can assure you that life will be very tough for him." Dermo said.

Chapter 25

Thursday, July 20th 1950. The Piggery St Columba's Seminary, Springwood NSW

ST COLUMBA'S WAS not for the faint - hearted. The summers were stinking hot and the winters bitterly cold. The biting cold exacerbated the lack of food and the hunger pangs that went with it at the seminary. In particular, the cold southwest winds would cut right through you in the winter months. There was no heating on site, which made for very tough living conditions.

By mid – 1950, Frank had got himself a position running the piggery at the college. This had nothing to do with him earning favour with the priests but rather more to do with having a good knowledge of pig husbandry as he was off the land.

Although he was still on Dermo's radar and the Monsignor had prefects on the lookout in case he should trip up, Frank was always able to stay one step ahead.

Mother Mary Phillip was the head nun who ran the kitchen. Dangling alongside her rosary beads on a black leather belt were the keys to the refrigerator's locks, where all the perishable food was kept. She was always vigilant about padlocking the refrigerators, but occasionally she would forget and it was then that Frank would strike. He would raid the refrigerators in the dead of night and secure a collection of tasty morsels where he would hide them under his black cassock. On entering his dormitory, Frank hid his booty in the bottom draw of his lowboy (dresser) without being noticed. The first time he did it, he realised he had a small problem. What would he do with the half - cooked chook he had secured? He solved the problem by hiding it in the toilet's cistern before attending morning prayers. Returning from breakfast via the toilets, he was able to devour the chicken and managed to flush the broken frame down the bowl. Dermo erupted like a volcano when he found out the chicken had been stolen, but no one had any idea who the perpetrator was, so the act went unpunished.

Frank had managed to secure a position for Tony Casaceli in the piggery, although he knew nothing about pigs. One afternoon in late July 1950, Frank convinced Tony to make a trip into Springwood and stock up on some food. Tony was petrified at being caught, but after some serious cajoling by Frank, he agreed to go. Frank had been left some money by his sister Veronica after a college family day the previous Sunday. Dressed in their tatty work clothes, the two aspiring ecclesiastics escaped under the barbed wire fence of the piggery, through the bush and walked down the road to the shop. Once they had stocked up, Frank suggested a refreshing ale at the pub would top their visit off. Tony was even more petrified about being caught visiting the pub. It was only after Frank informed him he would have to go back to the college alone if he didn't come to the pub, did Tony reluctantly agree to go.

As the two seminarians were dressed in their work attire, no one was the wiser about who they were. They were finishing off their second schooner of beer when who should come walking down the street but Peter English. Alongside him were another prefect and a junior from the college.

"Shit," Frank said, almost choking on his beer, "it's English. Quick Tony turnaround before he sees us." They turned around on their stools while English strode past, casually looking into the pub. English and the other prefect were accompanying the junior student to the doctor in Springwood. From the mirror on the inside wall of the hotel, the two boys could see English stop and give an over - inquisitive look at the backs of the two patrons sitting on the stools. He looked long and hard for what seemed like an eternity before the three of them strolled off. They made sure he was out of sight before they polished off the remainder of their beers and got out of the pub quick smart.

When they got back to the college, Frank took Tony up to where the beehives were beside the orchard. He had an empty beehive kept aside where they could hide their assortment of confectionary. The two men had been lucky, as if Peter English had spotted them; they would have both been expelled.

Frank had become mates with an old roustabout who worked at the college, named Billy Kirkland. Billy was an old bushy who had knocked around with the toughest of them but possessed a lot of wisdom. He had worked as a drover, shearer and fencer, among his many jobs. He was employed by the college to trap foxes, stoke the boilers and be the maintenance man. He struck up a firm friendship with Frank, as they were both from the country and had common ground. Billy spoke a lot of common sense and it was an important relationship to Frank, as it kept him grounded from becoming institutionalised. Billy was the one bloke Frank could share what was on his mind.

One day, they were deep in conversation when Billy gave Frank some advice.

"If you become a priest, Frank, don't ever forget that you are no better than anybody. Remember that you are there to serve the people and by doing so, you will earn their respect."

Frank nodded in agreement.

"I've knocked around a lot Frank and I might not have a great education, but I've seen a lot of life, and those who go about their work quietly without drawing attention to themselves have the most effect. I figure you're not the type of man who will be trying to gain promotion and accolades. Your role will be best served as a priest for the people."

It was sage advice from the barely literate old bushy and Frank was to carry that counsel with him throughout his life. Regardless of the trials and tribulations that were to beset him in the future, he stayed true to that vision for his entire priesthood. Billy's conversation with Frank that day was to sow the seeds for an entirely different type of religious vocation for the seminarian. It invigorated Frank with a vision for the future that was to cause him to lock horns with many of the Catholic hierarchy in Sydney in the years to come.

Friendships were frowned upon in the seminary. What was known as 'particular friendships' were prohibited by the rule book, and strict control was administered by teachers, prefects and the student body. Juniors were separated from seniors and prefects appeared in pairs when mixing with them.

The system was structured to protect the vulnerable juniors from maturing seniors who were on the cusp of puberty. With raging hormones and the normal desires and drives of maturing young men, they had been starved of the company of females and there was fear they would be attracted to their gender. Young men's powerful drives were being stifled, and in its place, a rigid set of rules were established to repress all those natural urges.

The seniors were not permitted to speak, eat, pray, play sport or sleep with the juniors as young pubescent boys can seem attractive and feminine. The seminaries and monasteries were no different to gaols, the army, the airforce or the navy. When heterosexual men with natural impulses are grouped together without female company, urges can become distorted. Effeminate men can become strangely attractive to other men and a crush may form. For this reason, the seminary endeavoured to prohibit any personal friendships forming.

Avoiding personal friendships were also put in place so no one would feel rejected. The students had to learn to be sociable and make conversation with people they would not usually mix with. It was seen as an act of charity where the philosophy was to be 'all things to all men'.

Frank was fortunately long past his pubescent stage and, as a young man, had sown his wild oats. It would be wrong to suggest he didn't have all the natural urges a male had, but he was better able to cope with them as he had matured.

Regardless of the college's official rule, friendships naturally occurred. Frank's circle was small and he mainly mixed with the seniors who were late vocations. Bill Doherty and Brian Cruden who, like Frank, were returned servicemen, and were two he related to. He mixed with Tony Casaceli. Although he was naïve, Frank liked his honest approach to life.

Even though the seniors were not permitted to mix with the juniors, Frank observed those around him. He had always been a good pick of people's personalities and among the juniors, he saw those younger students who were doing it tough.

Terry Norton was a country boy from Grenfell in central NSW who had arrived at St Columba's in 1950 as a 12 - year - old. Frank saw he was suffering from homesickness and had been ostracised by many of his peers. Frank identified because of what he had been through when first attending Joeys. Even though Frank could not fraternise with him, he kept a close eye, so if the occasion arose, he could step in if the lad was being bullied too much. He observed that Peter English had taken a liking to the lad, but for entirely different reasons. Frank observed that English would give the boy a suggestive glance or smile and he took note.

In the early 1950s, paedophile wasn't a word used much in society, let alone associated with the Catholic clergy. The Catholic Church would have denied it, as no one in their right mind would have believed the accusations of a child over a member of the clergy. Frank kept a close eye on English when he was around Terry. Although he was in no position to confront him, as English was a prefect, he made a mental note to look after the boy. For the first time in his life, Frank observed behaviour that was to be exposed within the Catholic Church in decades to come. Instinct told him this was not right, and in the years ahead, he was to speak out against it, to his detriment.

Throughout 1950, Frank was taught subjects including ancient history philosophy, and philosophers like St Thomas Aquinas, Aristotle, Plato and Socrates, which enthralled him.

Other subjects were Logic, Italian, Greek, Latin and a rudimentary type of psychology taught by Father McCarthy. His attempts to explain the mechanics of sexual behaviour left most of the students dumfounded. Many of the students blindly wrote down the notes without considering if they were correct or not.

McCarthy gave no hint that love and intimacy might enter the process of sexual intercourse. Instead, he was more interested in reminding the students that certain filthy words used to describe intercourse were not to be used on any occasion. Frank had to bury his shaking head in his hands when McCarthy talked on this subject, for fear of bursting out into laughter.

"Is there something you find terribly funny, Mr Casey?" Father McCarthy would say on such occasions.

"No, Father. I just thought of something amusing from my school days." Frank would reply.

"Please share it with us, Mr Casey, if it is so amusing. Otherwise, please wipe the smile off your face!"

Some subjects Frank struggled with, but Tony Casaceli was a bright boy who was always on hand to help. Frank always rewarded Tony with some tasty piece of confectionary he would miraculously provide.

There was no access to outside media such as newspapers, journals or radio at Springwood. Everything was highly censored, even the films they were allowed to watch occasionally. There were no bedroom or beach scenes, too much of a woman's leg and definitely no cleavage shown. It was a sanitised form of entertainment.

Despite himself, Frank had become attuned to the ebb of clerical life and for the most part enjoyed it. What had seemed foreign to him at the beginning had become natural. The mass, benediction, the rosary, the Stations of the Cross, prayer and meditation had become a part of his day-to-day life. Frank had always been a free thinker and, in that regard, was among a minority in the student body as well as Catholic society in general. Because of his maverick tendencies, he was able to separate the wheat from the chaff regarding what he believed was the truth. He kept his mind like a locked vault, so very few knew what he was thinking while all the time forming his specific philosophy on life. In some areas of Catholic theology, he was very conservative but, in other ways, very liberal.

Time flew and he had completed his second year and 1950 was boxed and buried before he knew it.

Chapter 26

Thursday, August 16ᵗʰ 1951. "Manly Rugby League Day". St Columba's Seminary Springwood.

IF THERE WAS a highlight on St Columba's calendar, it was "Manly Day."

Manly Day was the annual Rugby League game between St Columba's seminary, Springwood and St Patrick's seminary, Manly. It was an intense affair where clergy from all over NSW would travel to St Columba's to watch the two seminaries belt the living daylights out of each other. The clergy travelled from Sydney, Balranald, Albury, Coonamble, Hay, Bourke, Wilcannia and many other regions dressed in their clerical gear. There was no love lost between the aspiring ecclesiastics on that one Thursday of August every year when they fought for the title of champion seminary.

Manly seminary travelled on a bus while those aboard were dressed in black suits with black ties, white shirt and black hats. They would arrive with all the cordiality expected of aspiring priests and be suitably greeted by the Springwood seminarians. Once the Manly team were dressed in their red and Springwood in the blue jerseys, all affectionate gestures between the budding men of the cloth was soon forgotten.

Manly, with their older seminarians, were rarely beaten and in the two years Frank had been at St Columba's, they had never won. Frank was captain this day and playing in his customary five-eighth position. Springwood had trained hard in the weeks leading up to the game. Old Father Hayes had been given the job of refereeing the game. He was in his early sixties, but looked like he was about eighty. His hair was white and he possessed a pair of spindly legs that looked as though they could have snapped at any moment. He lectured at Manly on a number of subjects, including morality, and was a prickly character that did everything by the rule book. Father Hayes was a connoisseur of the mediaeval church and was highly conservative in an already orthodox Catholic Church.

Father Hayes blew the whistle and Springwood kicked off with the Manly tight head prop Bernie Manning, a brute of a man, catching the ball. He took the ball up hard before receiving the mandatory softening up from Tim O'Neil, his opposite number. This included wrestling him to the ground before rubbing his head into the turf with his elbow.

"How's that for an entrée?" Tim said.

"You haven't seen the last of me today, mate," said Bernie with a mouthful of dirt.

For the remainder of the game, Bernie chased Tim all around the oval, trying to knock his block off. Rugby League was the working man's game and Tim's actions were seen as quite acceptable. Bernie and Tim were to become respective parish priests of Manly and Lewisham and remain lifelong friends.

The game went on with neither side giving an inch while the Catholic clergy on the sideline yelled themselves hoarse barracking for their respective sides. Just before half-time Frank had the ball and was running it back from the opposition's try line when the Manly lock forward Pat O'Connor came for him, hell - bent on knocking his chops off. Frank told him to piss off before giving him a stiff arm, managing to break his nose. Father Hayes was incensed, not by Frank breaking Pat's nose, but by his swearing. After berating Frank for a number of minutes about his language and informing him that he would be reporting him to Springwood's Dean of Discipline, he gave Manly a penalty right in front of the posts. Manly easily converted the try before going into the halftime break with a 2- 0 lead.

The second half was an equally gruelling affair with neither side giving an inch. Hay makers and rabbit killers were being thrown with wild abandon. Halfway through the second half, the sprightly Manly winger Noel O'Malley, who had played 3rd grade for the Canterbury – Bankstown "Berries" before entering the seminary, received the ball. He sprinted down the oval with lightning - quick speed and scored near the right-hand corner post. The conversion was missed and Manly led 5- 0.

Springwood was on the attack with ten minutes to go when Frank saw an opening. He threw a dummy and then put Tony Casaceli, playing at outside centre, through a gap. After dodging and weaving, Tony pinned his ears back and scored in the left - hand corner. Frank narrowly missed the conversion and Manly led 5- 3. Manly sensed they were going to lose and piled on some really dirty play, to which Springwood responded with equal measure.

There were only minutes to go and Frank had the ball on the halfway line. Using all of his brilliance, he sensed a gap in the Manly defence. He sidestepped through the opening with speed and beat the wall of defenders. Frank dodged and weaved before putting a chip kick up on the 25 - yard line. He regathered the ball in one hand and ran like his life depended on it, managing to score under the goalposts. He converted his own try and Springwood were the victors, 8- 5. There were weary and busted up players everywhere as they trudged from the field. For the rest of his life, Frank was to remark that the only other game of Rugby League that came close to the brutality of that one was the 1973 Grand final between Cronulla and Manly.

The remarkable juxtaposition of the day was that afterwards everyone assembled in the chapel for a solemn benediction where the Manly choir sang Gregorian chants to perfection. Many players were carrying black eyes and swollen lips, but this did nothing to diminish the solemnity and ethereal nature of the occasion.

On leaving the chapel, everybody squeezed into the refectory, where a roast was served. The clergy drank and cajoled with each other after being let off the leash for the day. Manly day was a great opportunity for old friends to catch up. When it was all over and Frank was leaving the refectory, he received a tap on his shoulder. He looked around to see Peter English sporting a smug face.

"You're to report to Father McCarthy in his office right away."

"What for?" Frank said tersely.

"I am not sure, but I believe it is for some type of offence you committed during the game today."

"Hmph," Frank said.

Regardless of Frank winning the game for Springwood, he was found guilty of swearing on the field and went without any movies for the next month. Frank walked from McCarthy's office, shaking his head at the absurdity of it all.

It was a couple of weeks after Manly Day in late August 1951 and all the students were busy with their evening studies. Fresh in Frank's mind was his punishment for swearing during the Manly Day Rugby League game. Peter English was one of two prefects in charge of a room full of juniors, including Terry Norton. Around 8.00 pm, Terry asked English if he could be excused so as he could go to the toilet. After giving him permission, Terry made his way from the study hall through the darkness and cold of the winter's night. He was a nervous boy at the best of times, particularly in such dark surroundings. Walking towards the toilets near the recreation hall, he was startled by even the slightest of shadows dancing in the night. He walked along the dark covered quadrangle pathway up the external staircase, eventually reaching the toilet block. He was alone and just as he reached up for the light switch, a black cassocked figure lunged from behind and pinned him against the lavatory wall. He started rubbing himself up against Terry with his hardened member. Terry was so petrified he couldn't speak.

"Now be quiet and everything will be okay," said the mature male voice.

Terry could not see the perpetrator, as his face was up to the wall, but was well aware of his voice. On the cassocked figure went, inflicting his perverted and heinous act on the poor boy. He was still rubbing himself against Terry when a hand appeared from out of the darkness and grabbed English around the throat.

"What the fuck are you doing, English?" said the new arrival.

Peter English stood terrified, still leaning on Terry.

"What are you doing here, Casey?"

"I was in the study hall beside yours when I saw you follow Terry down the hallway."

"I was going to the toilet, and besides, I don't have to answer to you as I am a prefect."

"I think you had something else in mind other than just going to the dunny," Frank said with an icy glare.

"Don't you forget that I am a prefect Casey and I could report you for this incident."

"I don't care what you are, because there is one thing for certain and that's you're a pervert."

Frank pulled English away from the boy and said. "Are you okay, Terry?"

Terry was too much in shock, but nodded his head to acknowledge he was alright.

"You better get back to the study hall while I deal with this creep, Terry. I'll check to see you are okay later on," said Frank.

Terry made a hasty retreat before Frank tightened his grip on English's throat and pinned him against the wall.

"You're the epitome of evil, English. I've seen the worst of the worst in my life, but you are the scum of the earth."

"I'll have you reported to the rector, Casey!"

"And what will he say if he knows what you've been up to in the toilet block?"

"He wouldn't believe you, Casey. He knows what an incorrigible individual you are."

Frank lifted English six inches off the ground while looking him in the eyes and said, "I guarantee you English that if I ever see you near Terry Norton again, they will cart you out of this place in the back of an ambulance."

"Oh, your history now, Casey. Wait till both the rector and the Dean of Discipline hear you have been making violent threats against me. You've been skating on thin ice ever since you arrived at the college and you've just sealed your expulsion from this seminary."

"I guarantee, English, I will tell every student in this college what you've been up to."

"Oh, you are gone now, Casey, with a threat like that."

Frank gave English a short, sharp jab in the stomach, to which the pervert keeled over in agony before slumping on the ground.

"I hope you never get ordained as a priest, you piece of filth," Frank growled through gritted teeth.

He then walked away into the darkness, leaving English lying on the floor of the toilet block.

The next day, Frank sought out Terry and discreetly enquired about his well - being. Terry informed him he was okay, but Frank could see he was far from alright from his body language.

"If that English ever approaches you again, you make sure you tell me, ok?"

Terry nodded his head and Frank could see the boy was traumatised.

After the events of that night, two things happened. Frank never heard a word from the powers that be about the incident, and within a month, Terry had left the seminary, never to return. Frank learned Terry studied accountancy after he finished his schooling and walked away from the Catholic Church for the rest of his life. He was one among many who had been abused by a system supposed to look after the vulnerable. Although Frank witnessed several other abuse victims at the hands of the Catholic Church, the memory of Terry Norton was to stay with him for the rest of his life.

As 1951 ended, so did Frank's time at Springwood. To the surprise of many, Frank had lasted the distance. Monsignor O'Slattery could hardly hide his contempt for Frank and the fact he had stayed the three years. He growled silently whenever he saw Frank, but could not bring himself to expel him. Although he would never have openly admitted it in the confines of his own mind, he knew he had met his match in Frank Casey. He realised Frank had experienced things in his life that he could never have imagined in his wildest dreams. Dermo and the professors knew Frank was a tough individual, and if the truth be known, they were petrified of him. He just didn't fit the mould of your average priest at that time in Australia and they didn't know how to handle him. Instead, they let him be and hoped he would leave the seminary in time. Frank's memory of Father Fournier was one of the key elements that kept him going. His maturity enabled him to see some of the subject matter they were taught was illogical and that it didn't really align itself to the true Christian message.

The next four years were spent at St Patrick's College, Manly. During that period, Frank was to study in even more depth subjects like theology, morality, dogmatic theology and ethics. As he got closer to the business end of being ordained a priest, he realised the seriousness and the solemnity of the vocation he had entered.

Meanwhile, Peter English, as one of Dermo's 'special ones' had been one of three students chosen to study at Propaganda College in Rome. This was a stepping stone to becoming a bishop after they had been indoctrinated in the ways of the Vatican. They were the very antithesis of Frank, where they showed a blind obedience to dogma while he was a true individual with flair and enterprise coupled with a rebellious streak. After seven years of study, Frank was ordained a priest. His first parish as a curate was at St Brigid's at Quirindi in northwest NSW, where it was under the control of the Irish parish priest, Father Thomas

McGinity. Frank's introduction into the life of a country priest was the very opposite of the two seminaries he had just come from.

Chapter 27

Monday, January 30th 1956. St. Brigid's Catholic Parish, Quirindi NSW

WHEN FRANK LEFT to study for the priesthood in 1949, his family was lured into the false belief he was set for life. They believed his spiritual condition and eternal salvation were guaranteed because he had decided to study for the priesthood. Nothing could have been further from the truth.

Lurking in the background of his life was a sleeping giant that was to rear its ugly head in the years to come. It ultimately led Frank to the gates of insanity and hell before redemption finally stepped in to save him.

Frank had always enjoyed a drink and loved the joy and companionship alcohol brought to him. He had loved a drink while in the airforce and never suffered from any serious side effects other than the customary hangover to be expected after tying a big one on. He had always managed to pick himself back up and get on with the job. When Frank was posted to his first parish at St Brigid's in Quirindi as a curate, he was to step over a line he was never to return from. The catalyst for that was the parish priest, Father McGinity. What made matters worse was he had been ordained in an age where the clergy were seen as above the rest of society and beyond reproach. For a priest to admit he had a problem with alcohol during that period in Australia would have been inconceivable.

When 34 - year - old newly ordained priest Father Frank Casey stepped off the Northern Mail at Quirindi railway station on that stinking, hot Monday afternoon in late January, 1956, he could never have imagined what he was entering into. He had been sent to St Brigid's as he was from Bingara, and like Quirindi, it was located in the Diocese of Armidale.

As he trudged up Thomas Street towards the Catholic Church with his small suitcase, dressed in his black soutane, his only desire was for a cool glass of water on arrival. On knocking on the front door of the presbytery, he was met by the housemaid Miss O'Riordan, a dour spinster in her early sixties. Miss O'Riordan had been born and bred in the area to a wealthy pastoralist family at Wallabadah, north of Quirindi. In her mid - twenties, her fiancé jilted her at the altar for another woman and it became the scandal of the town. She left her secure job in her brother's stock and station agent business and retreated into the bosom of the Catholic Church, where she had been the housemaid at St Brigid's for many years.

"How do you? I am Father Casey, the new curate for the parish."

"I am Miss O'Riordan. Father McGinity has been expecting you, Father Casey," she said in a sour tone.

"Please to meet you, Miss O'Riordan," Frank said with a smile.

She nodded without showing any expression. She led Frank to his small and austere bedroom, where she gave him a brief rundown on the schedule of the presbytery. She then informed him Father McGinity would meet with him in the loungeroom in one hour, where he had something extremely important to discuss with him.

As Frank unpacked his suitcase with his meagre belongings, he wracked his brain about what Father McGinity wanted to discuss with him. Being fresh from the seminary with high ideals of applying his vocation best, he thought deeply on the importance of what Father McGinity's message might be.

"Perhaps he might want to emphasise the importance of teaching a good catechism to the school students at the local convent, or maybe giving a solemn homily from the pulpit at Sunday Mass," he thought to himself.

Frank continued to unpack his bag, hoping he could live up to Father McGinity's high expectations.

A dozen thoughts raced through his mind.

"Maybe he wants to discuss the infallibility of the Pope or the sanctity of marriage or of hearing a good confession or making sure I administer the sacraments in a holy and sanctimonious manner," he thought to himself.

When Miss O'Riordan knocked on his bedroom door to summon Frank to the meeting, she led him into the lounge room, where he sat down on a single lounge seat. She quickly departed the room, and while he waited for the grand entrance of the PP (parish priest), he surveyed his surroundings. There was an old three - piece lounge with two single chairs to accompany it and several other pieces of furniture. Perched on a small mahogany table was an HMV radio. After perusing the carpet and the wallpaper, Frank could not help but notice near the doorway a large glass cabinet. Inside was a selection of liquor. His eyes zeroed in on the impressive array of alcoholic beverages, including scotch whiskey, bourbon, port, sherry and brandy. Frank was suitably impressed by what was on offer as he looked over the splendid selection of drinks. *A stiff drink wouldn't go astray,* he thought to himself.

Frank forced himself to look at a picture of the Blessed Virgin Mary hanging on the wall to bring his mind back to more ethereal things. He was busy studying the picture when unannounced; Father McGinity entered the room wearing a black suit with a Roman collar. Father Thomas McGinity was aged in his early 60s of solid build, standing 6'4"tall with a neck like a gorilla and a head that resembled a robber's dog. His puffed up cheeks were flushed red, his teeth were stained yellow, and Frank could not help noticing his nicotine - stained fingers. Father McGinity's introduction to his newly arrived curate was both brief and anything but congenial. There was no pleasant introduction to St Brigid's Parish and a rundown on the presbytery and the Church. Not at all! Instead, Father McGinity rummaged around in his inside coat pocket, where he produced a packet of Ardath 20s. He slipped a cigarette into his mouth and lit it with a match. He drew back heavily and, after looking at Frank sternly, he stood to the left of the drinks cabinet. With his cigarette in his left hand and his right - hand fingers dancing on the top of the drinks cabinet, he said,

"I've summoned you here, as I have something vitally important to say, Father Casey."

"Yes, Father."

"Do you see this drinks cabinet that my fingers are so merrily dancing away on Father Casey?"

"Yes, I do, Father McGinity," Frank said seriously.

"Under no circumstances," he said, pointing his left hand at Frank, "is this liquor cabinet to run dry?"

Frank looked at Father McGinity and back at the drinks cabinet a number of times, making sure he heard him correctly.

"Is that clear, Father Casey?" he said in a gruff tone.

"Perfectly clear, Father," Frank said.

"It will be your job to make sure that this drinks cabinet is well stocked. We have accounts at all the hotels in town and it will be your job to purchase the liquor discreetly," he said with narrowed eyes.

"Yes, Father McGinity, I understand," Frank said with a big gulp.

"Never are you to walk into the bottle shop announced, but you are to ring first to say you are coming down to the hotel to pick up an order. Is that clear, Father?" He said, pointing his finger at Frank.

"I understand perfectly,"

The conversation was so intense that Frank felt he was at a war trial.

Father McGinity took a big draw from his cigarette, looked Frank squarely in the eyes, and said, "There is a card game this Friday night in this loungeroom with another three parish priests and it will be your responsibility to make sure we are all adequately served."

"I understand totally, Father," Frank said.

Father McGinity was about to leave the room when he turned to Frank and said, "And by the way, you will be holding Benediction this Wednesday night."

"Yes, Father.

When he left the room, Frank took a deep breath before sitting back down in his seat, totally bemused by what he had just heard. Everything he had learned over the last seven years seemed to go out the window.

"If this is my introduction to St Brigid's, I must be in for a colourful ride," he thought to himself.

Father Thomas McGinity was born in Ballinrobe County, Mayo, Ireland, in 1894. After completing his education, he entered the College of Mount Melleray, a Cistercian seminary where he was ordained a Catholic priest in 1920.

He arrived in Australia in 1933, where he was appointed to several parishes in the Catholic Diocese of Armidale. He was eventually appointed Parish Priest of St Brigid's in Quirindi in 1940.

Father McGinity was known for his fire and brimstone sermons from the pulpit, but had an excellent relationship with his parishioners outside the church. He had a Dr Jekyll and Mr Hyde personality when preaching and thought nothing of abusing a parishioner if he thought they were out of line. One of his legendary outbursts concerned Mrs O'Leary, a stalwart of the parish who had a propensity for being late for Mass on Sundays. This was due to her having to attend to her bedridden husband Denis before attending.

"And you can take back that Christmas cake you baked for me if you're late for Mass once again, Mrs O'Leary," he barked during one of his homilies one Sunday morning.

When Mass was finished, he walked out of the church and greeted the parishioners with a smile, including Mrs O'Leary, like nothing had happened.

It was well known that "Old Tom", as his parishioners called him behind his back, had a liking for liquor. His once a month Friday night card game with the parish priests from neighbouring towns was the stuff of legend. The booze ran freely and the stakes were high as they played the card game 500.

A shrewd businessman he had a great social agenda, including very successful Housie nights where cash prizes were won with proceeds going to the parish.

Old Tom was also a passionate supporter of his beloved St George Dragons Rugby League side. Saturday afternoons were spent listening to the ABC broadcast on the radio in the loungeroom. He also loved Rugby Union and if there was a rugby test being played in Sydney, he would make special arrangements to make sure he was at the Sydney Cricket Ground for the 3.00 pm Saturday kick- off.

Although there was a clear social divide between a parish priest and his curate during this period, Old Tom took a liking to Frank. He liked the fact that Frank was a knockabout bloke who liked his footy and boxing, and it was a perfect place where Frank could hide his own drinking. Although they were on good terms, Frank always referred to his parish priest as Father McGinity and vice-a-versa, so the lines of over familiarity were never crossed.

During that first week, Frank familiarised himself with the inner workings of the parish. He managed to get through his first Benediction on Wednesday night without too many problems and introduced himself to the children at the local convent school.

By 6.00 pm on the Friday, the three neighbouring parish priests arrived at the presbytery. They were Father Fahey of Werris Creek, Father Boyle of Gunnedah and Monsignor Hughes of Tamworth. As the curate of the parish, Frank was not invited to participate in the card game as he was on a lower social scale than the other men. The Catholic Church is structured so there is a pecking order from the Pope down to a seminarian.

After dinner, the four priests adjourned to the loungeroom and prepared themselves for a serious game of cards. Frank was kept busy all night tending to the needs of the priests, making sure they were well served with refreshments in the smoke - filled room. There was a lot of laughter between the priests, and their ability as raconteurs was second to none. Among the conversation were subjects such as who was missing their Sunday masses, who was taking the plate up on Sunday and if there was a scandal in the parish. It was always a time for them to let their hair down. While keeping his talk to a minimum other than to make sure the four of them were adequately served, Frank kept his ear close to the ground and took in everything they were saying.

Around midnight, Old Tom suggested they give Father Joe Driscoll, the parish priest of Scone, a call on the telephone. They had him on by telling him they were in town and would be paying him a visit shortly. He didn't buy any of their shenanigans, laughing loudly before telling them to get to bed.

There were some heavy heads when they finally wound the card game up at 1.00 am. After falling off his seat and picking himself up, Father McGinity bade the other priest's farewell as they made their way to their separate bedrooms.

By Sunday, Frank was ready to say his first mass at 8.00 am in the neighbouring town of Willow Tree. Many of his family and relatives had come down from Bingara and the Cruikshanks travelled from nearby Breeza. Frank made a good account of himself impressing the congregation with his homily, which was a mixture of anecdotes from his rural upbringing and some humour.

A month after Frank arrived in Quirindi; he purchased a little 1946 Standard Eight 2-door motor car from Tamworth. This car enabled him to traverse around the country so he could meet his parishioners. Frank worked tirelessly for the parish over the next two years, serving the parish and getting to know many people. He socialised with many families and was invited to their homes for dinner. There was usually alcohol served while visiting families and Frank always enjoyed a drink with them.

Bill McGuire was a local parishioner and the station master at Quirindi, and he lived in the house adjacent to the railway station. Along with his wife, Anne, they had six children. He was a dyed–in–the–wool Australian Labor Party man and he and his family soon became good friends with Frank. Bill loved to talk about sport, politics and religion with the priest. After dinner, they would adjourn to the loungeroom, where they would engage in rigorous debate aided by an adequate supply of liquor.

"Father Casey, how best do we combat the communist element in the ALP?" he would say as he poured a tipple of scotch into Frank's glass.

"Well, Bill, it's the duty of every decent Catholic in the Labor Party to oppose the communist influences," Frank would say passionately.

The nights were usually long affairs, sometimes lasting into the early hours of the morning. Whether discussing politics or both men's beloved South Sydney Rabbitohs or religion, there was always an ample supply of scotch whiskey to aid the men's conversation. He still enjoyed the booze and, being only a short walk from Bill's residence to the presbytery, he could make his way home without too much care.

One night in March, 1959, Frank had been out to dinner at a parishioner's house at Wallabadah, 9 miles (15km) north of Quirindi. He had consumed a reasonable amount of alcohol when he drove back to Quirindi around 9.00 pm. Approaching the outskirts of the town, he hit a tree and damaged the bonnet. After being alerted by a passing motorist, the local police sergeant Ray Dwyer, a parishioner at St Brigid's, was soon on the scene. This was long before the days of Random Breath Testing and Ray dealt with the incident discreetly by maintaining Frank's anonymity. He gave Frank a lift back to the presbytery while he organised for a tow truck to take the vehicle to the local mechanics for repairs the next day.

Father McGinity heard about the accident but made little of it other than a passing remark, to be a little more careful next time and to make a good confession. He merely saw it as a minor setback, and other than Frank's pride being dented, nothing more came out of the incident.

Old Tom's remarks that Frank's accident was a minor setback couldn't have been further from the truth. It was to be the start of a downhill slide, and over the next two years, Frank's drinking was to increase involving him in some embarrassing incidents.

Frank become sneaky with his drinking and started taking a morning drink to settle the shakes from the night before. He would drink on the quiet during the monthly card nights while serving up drinks to the priests. He spilled a glass of port on Monsignor Hughes' lap one particular evening, which earned Frank a stern rebuke from both the clergyman and Old Tom.

On one occasion, he was drunk while addressing the school students at the convent, while another time; he celebrated a wedding under the influence. He heard the bride whisper to the groom that he was drunk. Frank was most embarrassed by her comment, but it wasn't enough for him to confront his problem.

For all her harsh demeanour, Miss O'Riordan was sympathetic to Frank's predicament. After a night on the drink, when he had the shakes at the breakfast table, she would discreetly pour a nip of brandy into his cup of tea. Frank's eyes would light up when the brandy hit the spot, and although nothing was ever said between the two of them, Frank would silently thank her. Old Tom seemed to be oblivious to Frank's condition because he was pretty well inebriated most of the time himself. Frank was a protected species living in a presbytery where the parish priest was a drinker.

Frank's condition steadily worsened. The drinking affected him physically, mentally and emotionally. He forgot things and bad memories from the war began to surface. These were things that he had buried deep inside himself and had not dared to mention to anybody. Memories of Buchenwald and the treatment by the SS, particularly from Otto Kestelman, he recounted with frightening regularity. Frank would wake up in the middle of the night and sit straight up in bed in a lather of sweat. He would have images of ovens and prisoners being tortured and beaten to death. He woke up screaming several times, remembering when Otto Kestelman had held a gun to his head, threatening to shoot him. Frank would put his head back on his pillow and think about Kestelman's plight and whether he was still alive. Little did he know Kestelman was in Landsberg prison in Germany, serving a life sentence.

Late one afternoon in October 1960, Frank visited a sick, elderly lady at her property in Willow Tree, 9 miles (15km) south of Quirindi. She was a parishioner and had been laid up in bed for weeks, so Frank was taking her Holy Communion. Frank had been drinking before his visit and it was dark when he left the property, situated on the road to Merriwa. On the way back to Quirindi, he stopped his vehicle on the side of the road and took a big swig from a port bottle he had hidden under the driver's seat. Wiping his lips, he continued on his way, stopping the vehicle at least half a dozen times and performing the same ritual. He was only a couple of miles out of Quirindi when he ran off the road and hit a telegraph pole. This time, Frank's luck ran out. A couple of miles behind him was old Charles Ainsworth, a farmer and grazier at Blackville, 25 miles (40km) southwest of Quirindi. Charles was a one - eyed protestant and a stalwart of the Anglican Church and thought nothing of putting the boot into the 'Tykes' if the opportunity arose. The sectarian divide between Catholics and Protestants was well and truly alive during this time. After coming across Frank's predicament, he checked his wellbeing and told him he would contact the police. Charles bade Frank goodbye with a smirk on his face and drove away. In the meantime, Frank polished off the remainder of the bottle of port before Ray Dwyer arrived on the scene about half an hour later in his police car.

"It's not the accident that I am concerned about Father Casey, but the fact that Charles Ainsworth has witnessed it."

"Oh, and why is that, Ray?" Frank said, slurring his words.

"To be perfectly honest with you, Father Casey, Charles is an old bigoted bastard and news of this accident will spread around the district like wildfire."

"Bloody hell we need that like we need a hole in the head," Frank said with a frown.

With that, Ray helped Frank out of his vehicle and into the police car, where he took him straight back to the presbytery.

When Ray told Father McGinity what had happened the next day, his reaction was typically subdued. He was happy Ray had been able to cover up the accident and not too many people knew about it. It wasn't until the following day, while he was pruning his roses; Old Tom blew his stack after Miss O'Riordan informed him that Charles Ainsworth had been a witness to the accident. She had a cousin who lived on a property not far from the accident site who had been a witness. He summoned Frank to a meeting in the loungeroom that afternoon and, dressed in old work clothes, explained the dire repercussions of the accident.

"It's not that you were as drunk as a parrot when you had the accident that worries me, Father Casey," he said with a trembling hand.

"It's not, Father?"

"No, that's the least of my concerns. What worries me is that protestant heathen Charles Ainsworth will use this as an opportunity to slander the name of the holy Catholic Church, and heaven forbid it will get back to the Bishop of Armidale," he said with his fingers to his lips.

"Bloody hell!" Frank said.

"That's putting it lightly. If that happens, we will have the powers that be, down here snooping around the parish like a hound after a fox."

"I need that like I need a hole in the head." Frank said.

"I want you to stay real low, for the time being, until this whole incident blows over. Is that clear?"

"Yes, Father McGinity."

He dismissed Frank and went back outside, where he continued to tend to his roses.

As much as they tried to hush the incident up, it turned into a local scandal after the news reached the Bishop of Armidale. Consequently, a few days after the accident, the Bishop sent his

Vicar General, Monsignor Carroll, to Quirindi to investigate the accident.

Old Tom greeted the Monsignor with open arms, treating him with all the cordiality and warmth that one in his position could expect. Before the visit, Old Tom had informed his good friend and card playing mate, Monsignor Hughes of Tamworth, of the incident and in turn, he had spoken to Monsignor Carroll.

Father McGinity and the Monsignor paid a visit to the convent school and then spent a considerable amount of time in the garden in animated discussion inspecting Old Tom's roses. Monsignor Carroll had a problem with powdery mildew on his own roses. As Old Tom was widely known as an authority on growing roses, he was very interested in his advice on how to rectify the problem.

While they were in deep discussion, Frank was in the loungeroom peering through the curtains at the two of them, wondering when his appointment with destiny was going to arrive.

They were still discussing the roses as they made their way to the presbytery for lunch, when Monsignor Carroll remembered why he had come to Quirindi in the first place.

He briefly addressed Frank; paying scant attention to the details of the accident other than they didn't want that sort of information getting into the hands of their opponents again. He then heard Frank's confession in private in the loungeroom before giving him ten Our Fathers and ten Hail Mary's to say as penance. Frank was full of contrition and thanked the Vicar General for his understanding and compassion. He then blessed Frank before he and Old Tom adjourned to the dining room, where Miss O'Riordan served a sumptuous lunch and they continued their discussion on roses. Everything was swept under the carpet and the 'Catholic Mafia' had once again sorted the problem out.

After the accident, Old Tom suggested Frank take it easy behind the wheel of his car. Frank tried his best and abstained from alcohol over the next six months, but he inevitably broke out and he soon found himself drunk while driving again. When the following accident happened, drastic measures were taken this time.

It was early May 1961, and Frank had been at Tamworth for the day. Around 9.00 pm, he decided to call into Bill McGuire's house for an evening nip. Bill was one of the few parishioners still inviting over, as he had worn out his welcome at most people's places. The curate who had been so popular when he first arrived in the parish was now out of favour with most people. When Frank left Bill's home at midnight, it was raining, and in his inebriated state, he completely lost his bearings. As a result, he crashed his car through the front fence of a house just up the road from the railway station. As a result of the rain, his car got bogged, and in his efforts to try to reverse the car back out, he ended up destroying the front lawn.

As a result of Frank's accident, the Bishop of Armidale had him transferred from Quirindi to St Andrew's parish at Wee Waa. By sending Frank to an outpost of the Armidale diocese, he had hoped to sweep the incident and Frank under the carpet. It did anything but! Frank's drinking became a whole lot worse before a miracle happened.

Chapter 28

Thursday, May 11th 1961. St Andrew's Catholic Parish Wee Waa NSW

WHEN FRANK ARRIVED at St Andrew's he was a shadow of his former self. Fortunately, the parish priest of St Andrew's, Father Dominic Cooper, was the very antithesis of Old Tom. He was a man in his mid - fifties and a person of great compassion and understanding. He wasn't interested in sport, didn't play cards and didn't drink. Instead, he enjoyed a game of chess and reading the classics while listening to Beethoven and Mozart. He was not the type of man Frank would have been drawn towards in ordinary circumstances, but these were unordinary times and Father Cooper was the right man for Frank.

Father Cooper had been sent to Wee Waa two years earlier. He had endeared himself to his parishioners for his honesty and compassion. He knew Frank had been sent to him as his alcoholism would be less conspicuous in the far western NSW town. It was typical of how the Catholic Church operated at the time. Instead of addressing an issue, they tried to cover it up. Moving a problem priest to another parish was their modus operandi.

From the beginning, Father Cooper, unlike many of his contemporaries, realised Frank was not a bad man but a sick man. Although he was unaware of the true nature of alcoholism, let alone the treatment, he understood Frank was suffering from an illness, not a moral weakness. He didn't fall for the trap so many other ecclesiastics believed that a priest was above reproach and could never succumb to the bottle. He endeavoured to help Frank as much as possible, even if that meant doing the only thing he knew, praying for him.

Father Cooper would get up from the dinner table and Frank would ask him where he was going.

"I am going to the church to pray for you, Father Casey, and don't worry, I will dehydrate you through prayer," he would say.

Often when Frank had the shakes, he would throw him the keys to the drinks cabinet and say,

"There you go. Fix yourself up with a drink, Frank!"

Frank would invariably fix himself up with a bottle of whisky.

All the enjoyment had gone out drinking for Frank, and life was a frightful proposition by this stage. He was perplexed as to what he should do to save himself from his hideous predicament.

Frank attempted to make a fresh start at St Andrew's. He endeavoured to keep himself dry through his own means, but he would inevitably break out 'on the scoot'. The parishioners soon learned that the newly arrived curate was a bona fide piss head. As a result, they secretly gave him the nickname 'Firewater Frank'. Frank heard one of the altar boys whispering the nickname to a mate one Sunday after Mass and he flew off the handle, chastising the boy. Frank's behaviour didn't endear himself to the parishioners, either. Frank was seen as an outcast, unlike his early days at Quirindi, where he cemented many friendships. This only drove him further inside himself, where he would break out again and hit the bottle.

On Anzac Day 1962, Frank attended the dawn service, followed by the march in Wee Waa. Afterwards, he visited a local pub where he drank while a game of Two - Up was being played. He had consumed a lot of alcohol when, that afternoon, he visited an elderly parishioner at Pilliga, 37 miles (60km) west of Wee Waa. Being Anzac Day, Frank had been contemplating the loss of Jimmy Cruikshank and was overcome with an incredible feeling of melancholy. It was dark when he began his drive back to Wee Waa. He was 20 miles (32km) from town and dodging 'roos left, right and centre. He stopped to take a swig out of a flagon of sherry he had behind the driver's seat. He sat on the side of the road in the dark drinking to his great mate and wondered what Jimmy would have thought about his predicament.

"Here's to you, Jimmy," he said before raising the flagon to his lips.

He had resumed his trip and only travelled a few miles down the road when a big grey 'roo came bounding out onto the shoulder of the road. Frank pulled the car sharply over to the right, but to no avail. He collected the giant marsupial on the front left - hand side of the car. The result was that it knocked out the left headlight and damaged the exterior panels. Frank managed to limp back to Wee Waa with no further damage, but was shaken by his ordeal.

While Frank was slipping into the depths of alcoholism, Father Cooper had been endeavouring to find a solution to his problem.

In late May 1962, he read an article in the *Sydney Morning Herald* concerning a Sydney psychiatrist by the name of Dr Thomas Croak, who was having success treating alcoholism. Dr Croak ran a private hospital in Strathfield in Sydney to treat alcoholics.

Father Cooper's find coincided with Frank making a fool of himself while celebrating Sunday Mass about a week later. While ripped to the eyeballs on whisky, it was during the most sacred part of the Mass, the consecration of the Eucharist, that Frank fell over at the altar. Even though he growled at them to leave him alone, a couple of altar boys helped him to his feet. He brushed himself down in a dazed state before continuing to muddle up his Latin in the process. It was the most embarrassing act of his priesthood and something that would take him years to forget.

By now, news of Frank's forgettable episode had reached the upper echelons of the Sydney diocese. As a result, the Archbishop of Sydney had instructed Frank to have an indefinite stay at Banyula, where it was hoped he could sort out his predicament. Everyone was at their wits' end with what to do with the out-of-control priest. If they thought they had seen the worst, they hadn't, for Frank would spiral further out of control, shortly.

In late May 1962, Frank arrived at Banyula after another big bender. His brother Kevin met him with trepidation, as he wasn't sure what he might do.

While Kevin was living in the homestead with his wife, Eunice, and their six children, their mother Margaret was living in a small cottage, within walking distance from the homestead.

Frank was in a very sordid state. He had lost weight and his skin was yellow, coupled with dark rings around his eyes. Frank was a priest only in name by this stage, as he had lost any semblance of spirituality and belief. His family was shocked at his appearance and put him to bed in his old room at the back of the homestead. They hid all the booze and no one was permitted to drink while Frank was staying at Banyula.

Frank stayed in bed for a week while he detoxed. Even after

a week, Frank was still shaky and it was a further few days before he was able to get out of bed and sit in a chair in his bedroom. Frank's last bender at Wee Waa had been a big one and he was not fit to say Mass, let alone administer any of the sacraments.

He sat in the chair like a dummy for days on end, barely speaking to anybody and only consuming chicken and vegetable soup that his mother had prepared. Not only was his mother devastated at what had become of Frank, but totally lost as to how he was going to overcome his predicament.

It was only after a couple of weeks that he could get up and walk around. He would sit with his back to the homestead, protected from the biting south west wind while he enjoyed the winter sun. Nobody in the family thought he would want to drink again, but Frank was far from finished. After three weeks, he had recovered enough to get up and walk around, travelling down the paddock in the ute with Kevin and his eldest son Tony, who was fourteen.

Shortly after this, Frank got tight and craved a drink. Full of rat cunning, he waited till the family had gone to Mass on Sunday before going on a mission to find the hidden booze. His endeavours came to fruition when he eventually found a padlocked cupboard inside the butcher's room. He had a hunch the booze may be hidden there, and after gently rocking the cupboard back and forth and hearing the tinkling of bottles, he knew he was on the money. He found a set of bolt cutters in the machinery shed, and although jittery, he managed to cut the padlock. His face lit up with delight when he found a substantial collection of alcoholic beverages stored away in the cupboard. When the family arrived home mid - afternoon home from Mass and visiting relatives, Frank was nowhere to be seen. A frantic search began where they eventually found him in the woolshed sprawled out on a couple of wool bales containing skirtings. Frank was yelling out while having flashbacks of being in a burning aircraft. There was nothing anybody could do as he lashed out if anybody came close to him. They left him in the woolshed while he drank the booze. Frank truly went into the horrors this time as he hallucinated about seeing burning aircraft falling from the sky and guards in Buchenwald beating inmates senseless.

He drank through Sunday night, finally running out of grog in the early hours of Monday morning. It was late Monday afternoon when the noise from the shearing shed stopped, and the family realised Frank must have either died or passed out. Kevin opened the door to the shearing shed with great angst and nervously approached Frank, lying flat out on the wool bales. After checking his pulse, he was relieved to find him still alive. With the help of Tony, they managed to pick him up and take him up to the homestead, where they placed him in bed. Frank stayed in bed for a week while recovering from this latest ordeal.

Frank took over a week to recuperate from his latest ordeal. Nobody in the family thought he was capable of a repeat performance after what he had just been through. However, he had one last trick up his sleeve. While the last performance had only embarrassed his family, the next time around, Frank put on a public display that was to be the talk of the town for years to come.

It was a Saturday, a couple of weeks after Frank's last bender, when he got customarily tight. With no booze in sight, and even the bottles of methylated spirits tipped down the sink, the Casey household was as dry as the Simpson Desert.

Frank had the family fooled, as they believed he was spending most of his time in bed, still very sick. They were right that he was ill, but Frank was determined to feed his insatiable desire for a drink, and nothing would stop him, even if it meant hitching a ride the 19 miles (30km) into Bingara.

Frank found it hard to walk with acute peripheral neuritis, but even that did not stop him from attempting to get into Bingara. Covertly, he got out of bed, got dressed and clambered out the bedroom window before making his way through the paddocks that led to the gravel road to Bingara.

Frank picked up a lift from a man in his early fifties who was a drilling contractor from out of the area. Frank did not know the man and hid the fact he was a priest. Frank said very little to him other than he was going to town to get some supplies.

When dropped off at Bingara, Frank headed straight for the Imperial Hotel and with meagre money; he tried to purchase a flagon of sherry. The publican, who had known Frank for years, was aghast when he saw him and was reluctant to sell him any liquor. After Frank put a real turn on inside the hotel, where he thumped his fists on the counter and reminded the publican that he was a priest, did he finally relent. Frank then headed down to the Gwydir River, where he sat under a gum tree and consumed the flagon.

After a couple of hours down by the river bank, Frank became very drunk and staggered up to Finch Street. He put on a big performance, yelling and screaming. Several men tried to settle Frank down, but to no avail. A couple of men then went to the police station only to find the sergeant was playing tennis. Frank continued to rant and rave before making his way back down to the river bank where he sat on a fallen tree and consumed his flagon. Frank was stark raving mad as he hurled abuse into the thin air. He finished the flagon and lay on the ground wriggling around like a worm while in the horrors.

Meanwhile, a couple of the local men had made their way to the tennis courts to alert the sergeant of Frank's predicament. By the time the police officer reached Frank, he was in a state of wild intoxication. Frank was hooting and hollering like a Tasmanian devil. It took the police officer, aided by a couple of men, to subdue Frank so as he could put a set of handcuffs on him.

"I am sorry, Father. I hate to do this, but it's for the safety of the community," the officer said.

"You will pay for this; you bunch of pagan heathens. This is abhorrent behaviour to be subjecting a Catholic priest to this type of treatment," Frank yelled.

"I am sorry, Father, but you're out of control, and it's the only course of action I can take," said the police officer.

"You reckon I am out of control? Why you faithless brutes, I hope you rot in hell," Frank screamed.

The sergeant, aided by the other two men, then picked up Frank and carried him to the police car while he struggled and heaped abuse on them. The sergeant then took Frank to the Bingara District Hospital.

Chapter 29

Saturday, June 9th 1962. Bingara District Hospital.

MOUNT KAPUTAR IS located 70 kilometres to the west of Bingara and just east of Narrabri. It has an elevation of 1457 metres and can receive a dusting of snow in the cold of winter. That wild and woolly weekend of mid - June 1962 was one of those times when snow fell at its peak.

On arriving at Bingara District Hospital on that freezing day, Frank was hastily taken inside and strapped to a bed while still in handcuffs. In colloquial terms, Frank was in the 'Horrors'. His final performance on the drink had been *a grand finale* and one he and others would never forget.

Frank's withdrawal from that final bender was a horrendous ordeal that drove him to the gates of insanity. Two days after his last drink, he suffered from delirium tremens or DTs, which lasted three days. While suffering from the DTs, Frank had hallucinations which included rats crawling out of the walls of the hospital and giant snakes biting him through his mattress. He sweated profusely and shook uncontrollably while hearing voices from long-lost relatives. It was lucky he was strapped to the bed otherwise; he would have fallen on the floor. The sister in charge administered small amounts of brandy to bring him down off the DTs. The following Thursday, Frank took his last drop of alcohol and he finally came out of his trip to hell.

It was Friday 15th when Frank awoke around mid-morning. Standing at the end of his bed was a man in his mid - sixties. His hair was grey, as was his moustache, and he was wearing a tweed coat and tie. Frank was still very hazy and tried his best to identify the unfamiliar figure, but to no avail.

"I heard you've been tying a big one on Father?" the man said.

"Who might you be?" Frank said groggily.

"My name is Dr Tom Croak, and I am a psychiatrist."

"What brings you here?" Frank said.

"Your parish priest, Father Cooper, contacted me after he read an article in the Sydney Morning Herald I had published about alcoholism."

Frank stared at the doctor intensely.

"And what have you come here to tell me, doctor?"

"I have come here to tell you, Father Casey, that you are an alcoholic and you cannot drink."

"An alcoholic?" Frank said with a raised voice, "why, that's an absurd allegation, Doctor! Don't you realise I am a Catholic priest?" Frank said, full of pride.

"This has nothing to do with your religion, Father. Alcoholism is a disease and can affect anybody regardless of class, colour, creed or status."

"I couldn't in conscience say I am an alcoholic, so please don't waste my time with your ludicrous nonsense," Frank growled.

"Let me remind you, Father that you were close to death's door, and another episode like the one you just pulled off may be your final curtain call!"

"I know I've gone over the top a bit lately, but it's inconceivable that I, a Catholic priest, could be an alcoholic!"

"The fact that you're a priest won't stop you from being an alcoholic, Father. I am both a Catholic and an alcoholic. It has nothing to do with religion. Alcoholism is a disease," said the doctor.

"A disease! How preposterous!" Frank said with conceit.

Frank stared at the doctor for what seemed like an eternity, his contempt for him palpable.

"It appears that your pride may be hindering you from accepting your condition, Father."

"My pride?" Frank growled.

"You're an alcoholic, and AA has your answer. Get it!" The doctor said bluntly.

"AA, you'd have to be joking. I wouldn't be seen dead in the doors of that outfit," Frank said with disdain.

"With all due respect, Father, you're not in the position to argue with me. You're an extremely ill man on the edge of death's door."

Frank swallowed hard as the doctor's words hit him like a sledgehammer.

"I work in a private hospital to treat alcoholics in Strathfield, Sydney, named Amaroo House. I will be admitting you there to treat your alcoholism," with that, Dr Croak about - faced and walked from the room.

The doctor's words hit Frank hard. Even though Frank was in denial about his alcoholism, he instinctively knew he was telling him the truth.

Even though Frank was over the worst of his DTs, he still spent a sleepless night tossing and turning, contemplating what the doctor had said. Even though he was extremely sick, common sense had prevailed the following day. Frank realised he had no other choice than to take the doctor's advice and be admitted into Amaroo House.

The next day, Frank was taken by ambulance to an airstrip located on a local property where a Royal Flying Doctor Service aircraft was waiting. He was then flown to Sydney, the one concession being his handcuffs had been removed, although he was still strapped to the bed.

During the flight, Frank sunk into a deep depression as the thought of never being able to drink again terrified him. He believed he had come to the end of the road and life would not be worth living. As the aircraft approached Sydney, it banked sharply to the left and Frank looked across to see the magnificent sight of the Sydney Harbour Bridge and the glistening blue water of the harbour below. A smile came across his face and he was filled with an incredible feeling of serenity. It was the first positive thing that had happened to him for a long while. Little did Frank know that it was the beginning of a new way of life.

Chapter 30

Saturday, June 16th 1962. Amaroo House Strathfield Sydney.

AMAROO IS AN Aboriginal word meaning "a beautiful place." The hospital was a Victorian-style double storey red brick building built in the 1880s. It had a wide entrance leading to the front door with a gable roof. On the first floor, it had two verandas on either side of the dwelling. It had been the home of a wealthy businessman and his family who owned a flour mill and bred racehorses.

On first appearance, it did not seem anything special. What made it unique was it was a place of new beginnings for alcoholics who had thrashed themselves close to the gates of insanity and death. In the early 1960s, most people who came to Amaroo House were alcoholics at the very bottom. There were very few high bottom drunks that graced its doors. As a broken - down priest, Frank was right at home in Amaroo House.

A couple of days after arriving at the hospital, Frank first set eyes on Stan Hitchcock. Stan was a tall, thickset Londoner aged in his late thirties. Stan had been part of the British Airborne Division at the Normandy landings on the 6th of June 1944. He had seen plenty of action, including the Battle of the Bulge in Belgium and Luxembourg.

Stan had immigrated to Australia in the early 1950s, eventually taking up an oyster lease on the Hawkesbury River north of Sydney. Although his wife and family lived in a comfortable home in the Sutherland Shire, Stan spent most of his time in his shed on the oyster lease. He drank copious amounts of booze with his oyster farming cronies and, in the ensuing years, picked up the taste for overproof rum. The end result of all that rum drinking was it sent him crazy and he found himself admitted to Amaroo House entirely around the twist.

Frank was dozing in his bed when he was woken by one hell of a commotion coming from the room next door. Among the yelling and screaming, he could hear what he thought was furniture being thrown about. Little he did he know, Stan was having a meltdown. Like himself in Bingara District Hospital, Stan had also been strapped to his bed. He was a huge man weighing over 18 stone (114kg) and as a result, his feet hung out over the end of the bed. Stan was in an alcoholic rage. He had managed to tip the bed up, so his feet were on the ground and was walking around the room with the bed strapped to his back. Frank was looking out his bedroom door into the hallway when he saw this huge man lumbering around with the bed still attached to his back. He was thrashing about like a gorilla while yelling out expletives in a cockney accent. Following him up the hallway, trying to subdue him, was Matron Sally Conway. Sally Conway was an ex WW ll army nurse who ran the hospital. She was as tough as nails and she had to be, considering the calibre of patients who graced the doors of Amaroo House. Stan looked into Frank's room with wild eyes and inquired who the man was lying in bed.

"He is a Catholic priest, and he is very ill, and most importantly, he does not wish to be disturbed," she said.

"A Catholic priest?" Stan yelled out, "well blimey Charlie padre, I feel sorry for you. It must be terrible to find yourself in such a shocking state!"

"Have you seen yourself in a mirror lately?" said Frank laconically.

With that, two male orderlies crash tackled Stan into the entrance of Frank's bedroom, and he ended up on his side with the bed still strapped to his back.

"Will you say a prayer for me, Father, so I get out of this rather unfortunate predicament," said Stan.

"I would if I could remember any," quipped Frank.

"God bless you, Father. May all your sons grow up to be bishops," said Stan.

It was a bumpy start in what was to become a lifelong friendship between the priest and the oyster farmer.

Amaroo House was the start of Frank's recovery and he learned more about himself in the five weeks he was there than he had his entire life.

Dr Croak explained to him the nature of the illness he was suffering from and that he would never be able to drink again. Frank accepted that and, by doing so, realised it was the biggest step he was ever to make. He also realised that being a priest was no exemption from him being an alcoholic and it was his foolish pride that had blinded him from this fact. Dr Croak also introduced him to AA and Frank willingly accepted that this was the path to his recovery. Frank listened intently to Dr Croak and learnt much from the wise doctor and they later on became very good friends.

Matron Conway and the staff were very kind to Frank, and

as the weeks went by, he slowly regained his strength. Frank spent a lot of time with Stan, who was also on the road to recovery. The two men talked about their war experiences. They also spoke about what had happened for them both to end up in such a predicament. They laughed a lot at what had happened to them, but ultimately; they identified with each other. It was this identification that was the beginning of both men's healing. It may have seemed like a strange friendship to the outsider, the priest and the rough oyster farmer. They soon learnt they had much in common. For Frank, it was his friendship with Stan that made him feel like a human being again and life was worthy living.

By the time Frank was ready to be discharged, the Catholic Archdiocese of Sydney had made plans to send Frank to a parish in the metropolitan area. This was because they wanted to keep an eye on the wayward priest to make sure he wouldn't trip up again.

Chapter 31

Monday, July 23rd 1962. St Michaels Parish Hurstville, Sydney

AFTER LEAVING AMAROO House, Frank's first parish was at St Michael's, Hurstville in Sydney, where Father Edward Moran was the parish priest. St Michael's had been deliberately chosen as Father Moran, who was in his early sixties, was extremely conservative and known to be close with the upper echelon of the Sydney Archdiocese. If Frank committed any indiscretions, it would quickly get back to the hierarchy. He took a relatively hard line towards his recently arrived curate and their relationship was icy at the best of times.

Frank's new found sobriety was an enigma to the powers that be as they had no experience in dealing with priests like him. Some viewed his sobriety with scepticism and thought it would not last.

Frank was more concerned about finding his feet. His sobriety was as much a quest from abstinence from alcohol as it was for him finding his faith again. In those early days, Frank felt uncomfortable from the pulpit as he preached a Catholic doctrine he was unsure about. He felt awkward in his own skin. He grieved the loss of his good friend booze, who had supplied him with so much joy in the early days, only to deceive him in the end.

His gradual spiritual awakening came through sharing with those recovering from alcoholism and in particular, Stan Hitchcock. His introduction to those recovering from alcoholism was the real catalyst for finding his Catholic faith again. Frank realised that helping those people who were the last, the lost and the least were the essence of Christianity. It was there he believed his true life's work lay. In time, his faith grew, at times slowly, but ultimately, he became stronger than before. Like a piece of steel that has been broken and welded again, only to be made tougher, Frank became a stronger man by what he had experienced.

The 1960s was a time of great change in society, and Frank's sobriety also coincided with a major event within the Catholic Church, namely the Second Vatican Council. The Second Vatican Council or Vatican ll addressed relations between the Catholic Church and the modern world. It was held in Saint Peter's Basilica in Rome, where it was opened by Pope John XXIII in October 1962 and closed by Pope Paul VI in December 1965. Some of the changes that occurred due to the council, included the use of vernacular languages instead of Latin, the disuse of clerical regalia, and to celebrate the Mass with the officiate facing the congregation. Some within the council resisted the changes, but most were sympathetic to the instigated reforms. Frank was by nature conservative and would dress in clerical attire for the remainder of his life. In other areas, he was very progressive. For example, the council instigated change from biblical literalism to modern human experiences into church principles. This suited Frank, as he liked to be at the coalface helping people rather than be seen as a remote cleric who preached from the pulpit with no real relationship with his congregation.

All this coincided with Frank's new found life. As time progressed, he found he was no longer a second class citizen, but he had an important contribution to make both to his vocation and society.

Over time, Frank applied himself to his duties with great enthusiasm. In particular, he payed special attention to those in the parish who were struggling financially and he rendered assistance as much as he could. He was on the side of those on the fringe, like single mothers and divorced Catholics. He was sowing the seeds for what was to become his life's work.

During his time at St Michael's, Frank developed his own style with regards to his sermons. They were a reflection of him. They were down to earth, with relevant anecdotes about his life and with plenty of humour thrown in. They were always short and to the point, as Frank believed brevity is the soul of all wit.

In October 1963, Frank was reading The Sydney Morning Herald one morning when a heading took his attention:

NAZI WAR CRIMINAL INCARCERATED IN LANDSBERG PRISON

On reading the article, Frank realised that it concerned Otto Kestelman. It listed the atrocities he had committed while an officer in Buchenwald and his arrest and subsequent incarceration in Landsberg Prison in Germany. The hairs stood up on the back of Frank's neck as all the memories came flooding back to him. He spent the remainder of the day filled with disdain for the man who had perpetrated so many heinous acts.

He spent a few sleepless nights recounting the evil acts Kestelman had done and was filled with revulsion for the Nazi. Then, after another night of fitful sleep, he realised it was his duty as a priest to try and save the man's soul. Frank knew resentment was a cancer and, first and foremost, he was to forgive the man before he had any chance of helping him, regardless of the crimes he had perpetrated.

It was the early hours of the morning when he went to his office and penned a letter to Kestelman. Frank reminded him of who he was and that he was now a Catholic priest. He then listed the many things that he had been witness to while in Buchenwald, reminding Kestelman that he had threatened to shoot him. He said the allied airmen should not have been taken to Buchenwald but a Luftwaffe run POW camp. He told him the Nazi ideology was evil and the atrocities it had performed would be judged for all time. It was only after completing the letter was Frank able to go to sleep.

After editing the letter the next day, he went to the local post office to find the address for Landsberg prison before posting it. He thought there was little chance Kestelman would respond but was glad he had sent it, as it had been a cathartic experience.

To Frank's surprise, he received a letter back from Kestelman only days after the assassination of President John F Kennedy on November 22nd 1963.

In the letter Kestelman said he felt no guilt about the plight of the airmen, as he was only following orders. Kestelman also said he still believed in the Nazi ideology. Regardless of his radical attitudes towards Nazism Frank sensed Kestelman was troubled and, his incarceration in Landsberg had left him a broken man.

Kestelman and he wrote to each other a number of times over the next four months. In the ensuing correspondence, Kestelman expressed his desire to meet face to face with Frank if the opportunity ever arose.

As a result, Frank asked the Sydney Archdiocese for leave and he was granted 10 weeks. He planned a trip to Europe, including a visit to Landsberg Prison. Frank asked Stan Hitchcock if he would like to accompany him, which he gladly agreed. The trip was a chance to see some of the places he had been stationed at during the war in England, including visiting the gravesite of Jimmy Cruikshank. It was also an opportunity to visit Marguerite and Raphael in France, who were now married, and to pay his respects to them for all they had done for him. Ultimately, it was a chance for him to come face to face with Otto Kestelman.

Chapter 32

Thursday, June 11th 1964. Kingsford Smith Airport Sydney.

IT WAS MID - morning in June 1964 when Frank and Stan prepared for takeoff to London in the Qantas Boeing 707 they were to travel on. Among those to see them off was Father Tony Casaceli who had recently been appointed parish priest of St Christopher's at Panania in Sydney. Frank had kept close ties with Tony after they had been ordained and he had been a great source of strength as Frank battled his demons.

The weather was cold and rainy, and from his seat, Frank noticed a huge commotion near the terminal as thousands of people gathered for the arrival of The Beatles. Frank peered out of the aircraft window into the pouring rain and noticed the four mop tops being driven around on the back of an open - back truck.

"I think the Beatles have been a relief valve for the trauma England suffered during World War II," he said to Stan.

It was a pretty progressive thought from a member of the older generation who viewed The Beatles with suspicion.

"They are certainly turning the world upside down. There music sends my eldest daughter crazy!" Stan said with a laugh.

Frank continued to survey the scene before him and contemplated the impact these four lads from Liverpool were having on the world.

He was broken from his reverie on the members of the world's most popular band from Liverpool when the aircraft began its taxi out to the runway. His thoughts turned to the trip ahead. He was enthusiastic about what lay ahead but had a sense of apprehension about the memories it would bring back.

As they took off, the roar of the jet motors brought back memories of his flying days during the war and the countless close scrapes he had endured until that fateful night over Sochaux. It still sent a shiver up his spine, thinking about that last operation he flew.

After being in the air for a short period, a sumptuous meal was served, including lobster and carved beef. It made the meals of modern - day flying look positively ordinary. When he was finished, Frank fell into a deep sleep. He had always been able to sleep on a bed of rusty nails. Lucky for him, there wasn't much else to do except eat, drink, read and breathe in the cigarette smoke on the long flight to London.

After they arrived at Heathrow Airport, Frank spent a couple of days with Stan's brother in London. He then caught up with some of his English airforce mates including Max Clayton who owned hardware shop in Bradford in West Yorkshire. Together, they toured their old RAF stations, Marham and Elsham Wolds. Many of his old aircrew including George Marsden who was a farmer in the Yorkshire Dales were still perplexed that the tough rear gunner they once knew had decided to become a Catholic priest and was no longer a drinker. This did not diminish their affection for the man they respected and regarded as a good bloke. Little did they know of the internal revolution he had been through to get to his current station in life.

By the time Frank departed England for France, he felt good he had been able to pay his respects to Jimmy Cruikshank and the many he had served with and who had paid the ultimate sacrifice.

Stan remained behind in London to spend more time with his family while Frank flew to France. On arriving in Paris, he set about experiencing the sights he had only glanced from the back of a prison truck before being taken to Fresnes Prison. The Arc de Triomphe, the Eiffel Tower, and the magnificent Cathedrale de Notre –Dame were included.

As much as Frank enjoyed visiting Paris, it was Marguerite and Raphael he had come to see, and he made his way to the city of Montbeliard, where they lived with their four children. Montbeliard is situated 2miles (3.2km) west of Sochaux, where Raphael held a senior position with the Peugeot Motor Works.

Much joy was expressed and tears were shed when Marguerite and Raphael greeted Frank on his arrival by bus to Montbeliard early Friday evening. Although it was twenty - one years since Frank had last seen the two of them, Marguerite was still beautiful, and Raphael had greyed a little. Marguerite had not lost any of the sharpness that made her such a deadly fighter during the war.

After introducing Frank to their family, which included three sons and their red - headed daughter named Sylvie, Marguerite pulled him aside and spoke to him.

"*Franc*, Raphael and I '*ave* mentioned very little about what *'appened* during the war to our children. The details of what we went through are too shocking for their young ears to *'ear*. We never talk about the war around them, *oui*."

"I understand Marguerite because I have tried to block out many of the things I experienced during those days."

Marguerite smiled and then shrugged her shoulders.

"And now you are a priest. Now who would have believed that?" she said, smiling.

"Who has known the ways of the Lord, Marguerite? He had other plans for my life that I was unaware of during the war," he said with a smile.

"Come, *Pere Franc,* you must say grace before we sit down to a sumptuous dinner."

After Frank said grace, they sat down to a five - course meal which included hors d'oeuvres of soup and vegetables. This was followed by the main dish of meat and salad followed by cheese. A rich dessert followed: sweet crepe and coffee to finish the meal.

The children were all teenagers, and the youngest, Sylvie, with striking red hair like her mother, was of equally sharp intelligence. The children were fascinated by Frank's presence from a country they had only read about and seen in film. They were captivated by his description of being shot down during the war and heard snippets of their parent's involvement in Frank's rescue for the briefest moments. They engaged Frank in animated discussion in English, which they spoke very well. Finally, Marguerite felt that too much information was being divulged about the war, upon which she told them it was time for bed.

"*Doit-on aller se coucher maman?*" *Do we have to go to bed, mum?* said the eldest boy, Jules.

"*Oui. Maintenant rapidement!*" *Yes, now quickly!* Said Marguerite with a stern look.

"*Mais nous apprécions les histoires du pére Franc, maman!*" *But we are enjoying Pere Frank's stories, mum!* Olivier, the second eldest boy, said.

"*Au lit maintenant ou tu sentiras le dos de ma main,*" *To bed now or you will feel the back of my hand*, said Marguerite sharply.

"*Bonne nuit, maman et papa,*" *Good night, mum and dad*, said the youngest boy, Andre.

"*Goot* night *Pere* Casey, "said Sylvie.

"Good night children," said Frank

With that, the three children departed for bed.

After the children had left, the three adults engaged in a serious discussion about what they had experienced during the war. They whispered, so the children could not hear about things they had not discussed in years. Frank told them about the private insurrection he had experienced in his life and the events that led to him joining the priesthood. He told them how the booze had brought him to the gates of hell and how he had put the bottle down. They drank copious amounts of coffee and ate macaroons from Marguerite's favourite patisserie until the early hours of the morning.

The night was long when Raphael turned to Frank and said, "*Franc,* tomorrow Marguerite and I will take you to the Peugeot Motor Works in Sochaux and then onto Besancon. There we will show you the Citadel and the Cathedral."

"That is something I have been looking forward to," said Frank.

"There will be a few surprises waiting for you, *Franc*," said Marguerite.

Despite the late night, everyone was up early for breakfast. Being a Saturday, the children did not have to attend school, so they were going to entertain themselves for the day.

After breakfast, Raphael, Marguerite and Frank travelled to Sochaux in the family sedan, a Peugeot 404. After Raphael gave Frank a tour of the Peugeot Motor Works, highlighting what parts were blown up by Cicero and his operatives, they travelled to Besancon and then to the Citadel. Here, Frank was taken to the spot where Father Fournier was executed by the Nazis. Frank knelt and prayed for the brave young priest who had given up his life for him.

From the Citadel, they travelled to Saint John's Cathedral at Besancon, where Frank was taken to the Cavern. Once there, they showed him a plaque dedicated to Father Fournier. Raphael and Marguerite left Frank by himself. He sat in silence and contemplated while continuing to pray for Father Fournier and all those who had suffered at the hands of the Nazis.

Frank eventually exited the cavern, deep in thought, when Marguerite and Raphael introduced him to the Archbishop of Besancon, Cardinal Louis de Vienne. The Cardinal greeted Frank warmly like a long - lost friend.

"Come, I will show you the glory of our ancient cathedral, *Pere* Casey," he said with open arms.

"Merci, votre Eminence," said Frank.

"I know all about your story, *Pere* Casey, as do many people of Besancon. We honour the memory of *Pere* Fournier and all those who fought so bravely against the tyranny of the Nazi invaders."

Cardinal de Vienne spent a couple of hours showing Frank, Marguerite and Raphael the cathedral before inviting them for refreshments.

When they were finished, Marguerite and Raphael showed Frank the sights of Besancon. The sun was setting when Raphael suggested they go to a restaurant for dinner. It had been both a long and emotional day recalling places Frank had been and they all looked forward to sitting down to some fine food.

Raphael had chosen the Cafe Grainger for them to dine at. There, sitting at a table, were a couple aged in their early fifties. Frank did not recognise them at first until Raphael introduced them to him.

"Do you remember these two people, *Franc?*" he asked. "Jacques and Marion Deneuve worked for the Comet Line during the war. They were going to escort you to safety before Gaspard Petit, under the alias of Thiery Bonaparte, betrayed you."

They greeted Frank and warmly embraced him.

"Thank you so much, Jacques and Marion. To both of you, I owe a great debt of gratitude."

"It was the least we could do, considering the bravery of people like yourself in trying to rid our country of the Nazi invaders," Jacques said.

"If my memory serves me correctly I think I got my French a bit muddled up after our initial introduction," Frank said.

"Please *Franc,* it was an honest mistake and we have long forgotten about it," Marion said slightly embarrassed.

Sitting at a table only a short distance away were two men in their mid - twenties. One had a deep scar on his chin, while the other had a black patch over his left eye. They spoke in German and were intoxicated, with their booming voices overriding the restaurant's din.

After being served their aperitifs, Marguerite gave the Germans a look of contempt. She cleared her throat, leaned forward in her seat, and looked Frank in the eyes.

"We 'av brought you to this cafe tonight, *Franc,* as it *as* special significance with regards to Gaspard Petit," she said quietly.

"Is that so?" Frank said, surprised, while he edged forward in his seat.

"It does indeed," said Raphael.

"*Franc,* this is the cafe Gaspard Petit used to frequent to receive '*is* reward for those he had betrayed to the Germans," said Marguerite.

Frank looked at Marguerite, intensely sensing what she would say next.

"It was '*ere* that Gaspard and several Germans met their grisly end all those years ago."

Frank nodded, but said nothing.

"It was Philippe. God rest '*is* soul," she said, blessing herself, "and Raphael and I who came '*ere* all those years ago to dispose of that treacherous pig Gaspard. Unfortunately, we met resistance in the form of two Waffen SS officers and members of the Geheime Feldpolizei."

"Go on, Marguerite," Frank said, shuffling in his seat.

"A shoot - out ensued and as a result, Philippe was killed," she said with emotion.

"He was a fine man," Frank said, lowering his head.

"But Gaspard and all the Germans were killed," said Raphael with a steely look in his eye.

Frank looked long and hard at them and was about to speak when he was interrupted by a commotion from the Germans. They had tipped a bottle of wine on their table and were speaking loudly while displaying boorish behaviour. Frank looked across in their direction with disdain, which caught the eye of the one with the patch over his eye. Recognising Frank was dressed in his clerical attire; he made the sign of the cross then gave Frank the thumbs down. Frank continued to stare at the German as bitter memories of his incarceration in Buchenwald came flooding back. Eye patch staggered towards Frank while the other egged him on with loud and aggressive language. He spoke to Frank in German. Frank responded by telling him he spoke English.

"So you only understand English, do you, priest? *Zen* I will tell you what I really *sink* of you. I think *zat* you and *everysing* you represent is all bullshit!"

"So if what I represent is all bullshit, what is your philosophy for life?" Frank said, staring at him intensely.

The German raised his eyebrows, not expecting to hear a profanity coming from a priest. He could see he did not perturb Frank, so he edged closer to him and said,

"What is my philosophy, you ask, priest? *Zer* Fuehrer had *zer* answer. He had no time for *zer* carpenter from *zer* plains of Galilee, who he viewed as a fool. Adolf Hitler believed *zer* Aryan race is *zer* master race, which is also my philosophy," he said with a wry smile.

"It's bad luck he is no longer here to promote his philosophy as he took the coward's way out and committed suicide."

The German glared at Frank and shouted, with his face only inches from his.

"Watch it, priest!"

Frank crossed his arms and said.

"You are an empty shell following a hollow philosophy."

Marguerite, quietly simmering away, sat motionless before the German grabbed Frank by his coat lapel.

"I'll break your nose, priest," he said with a raised fist.

"You wouldn't be the first German who has threatened me with that," said Frank.

That was more than Marguerite could tolerate and she rose from the table and confronted the man.

"*Vhat* are you going to do about it, you slut?" he said to her.

As quick as a flash, Marguerite grabbed him by the balls with her left hand and squeezed them tight. He immediately let go of Frank's coat while giving out an almighty roar as he shrieked in agony. The other German rushed from his table and, seething with rage, was preparing to hit Marguerite before she said,

"Lay a '*and* on me and I guarantee I will crush your friend's balls in my '*and, oui?*"

He stopped in his tracks, angry that Marguerite had total control over his friend.

Raphael, Jacques and Marion sat there shocked into silence.

"You '*ave* the '*ide* to display such vulgar behaviour after all the misery your country inflicted upon ours during the war. As well as that, you insult a Catholic priest who '*as* given' *is* life to '*elping* others," she said, squeezing his balls a little tighter.

The German let out a scream before his companion once again threatened to hit Marguerite. She picked up a steak knife from the table and held it up in front of her.

"If you touch me, I will cut off your friend's balls before I cut off yours," she said with venom to the man with a scar.

He looked at Marguerite with alarm while the whole restaurant was shocked into silence. She had been transported back to the war and all her memories had surfaced.

"I killed my fair share of Nazi pigs during the war and I wouldn't '*esitate* finishing you scum off if I '*ad* to," she said with viciousness to Scar Face.

His look had changed from rage to terror as he had become convinced that the red - headed woman brandishing the knife could do what she threatened to do.

"Don't you cut off my friend's balls," he said with panic in his voice.

"Then I suggest you and your thuggish friend leave this cafe and never return *oui*!"

He nodded his head in agreement.

"Before you leave, you must first apologise to the priest," she said to Scar Face.

He gave Marguerite a look of contempt.

"Apologise now, or I WILL cut off your friend's balls," she said with clenched teeth.

"My apologies, Father, for my behaviour," said Scar Face.

"Now you apologise," she said to Eye Patch.

"I apologise to you, Father, for insulting you," he said.

With that, Marguerite marched the German out into the street with her hand still tightly secured on his scrotum while the other followed, being careful to keep his distance from the enraged woman. Marguerite held the knife up and slashed the cheek of the man she had by the testicles, leaving him with a deep cut. She thrust him out into the street before he let out one last agonising scream.

"Get out of '*ere* and don't ever return," Marguerite screamed at them.

The Germans walked away, totally shocked by what they had experienced. Shortly after, the manager of the cafe ran down the street screaming on top note, demanding they pay for the meal. After paying him cash they made a swift retreat. When they were out of sight, the cafe erupted into a spontaneous applause, with calls of *Vive la* France. Marguerite sat back down at the table, embarrassed at all the attention she was receiving.

With a sheepish smile, Raphael put his hand on Marguerite's shoulder, turned to Frank and said,

"That's my lady *Franc*. She '*as* always got you by the balls in one way or another, *oui*?"

Frank put his hand up to his mouth and tried to silence his laughter. It was to no avail, as he broke out into a loud chortling.

Frank spent the next week with Raphael, Marguerite and their family. Nothing was mentioned of Marguerite's confrontation with the Germans in front of the children, but it wasn't long before the community became aware of what she had done. Marguerite had lost none of her fire and underneath there still burnt the heart of a warrior.

After the café confrontation, the couple were perplexed why Frank wanted to visit Otto Kestelman. Frank explained although Kestelman was a convicted war criminal, it was his duty as a priest to render assistance. Regardless of what he had done, Frank saw it as his mission to help a man who was still in denial of his actions during the war. Although they understood Frank had his priestly duties to carry out, they were in two minds with the value of his mission to save Kestelman.

After Frank left Marguerite and Raphael, he travelled through France, on to Spain and then eventually to Rome. As much as he appreciated the magnificence of the Vatican and its structures and was overwhelmed by the Sistine Chapel and the frescos painted by Michelangelo, something did not sit right with him. The juxtaposition of the incredible wealth of the Vatican and Christ's own humble life left him in conflict. He pondered that it must be the rebellious Irish in him that had always seen him in conflict with the establishment. It reinforced his life's work in helping the underprivileged. Regardless of his conflicts, visiting Rome and seeing its history for the first time had been an ethereal experience for him. Now it was onto Germany and his appointment with Otto Kestelman.

Chapter 33

Monday, August 17th 1964. Landsberg Prison Bavaria, Germany

AS FRANK TRAVELLED by bus the 40 miles (64km) from Munich to Landsberg Prison, he contemplated where he had been since first arriving in Germany in early August. As well as visiting Buchenwald concentration camp, Frank had been able to experience some of the beauty of Germany, especially in the state of Bavaria, located in the southeast of Germany.

He had visited castles, the Bavarian Alps, Konigssee Lake, Bamberg Cathedral, as well as many other spectacular sites. By doing so, he could see another side of Germany he had never experienced before. It had enabled him to restore his faith in the German people. Before his arrival, his only experience of Germany had been of his incarceration and the brutality of the Nazis. Now he was travelling to Landsberg Prison to come face to face with a man who symbolised the very brutality of that regime.

Landsberg was best known as the prison Adolf Hitler was held in after the failed Beer Hall Putsch in 1924.It was here he dictated his memoirs, *Mein Kampf.* After World War ll, the US Army designated the prison as War Criminal Prison No. 1 to hold convicted Nazi war criminals. Over 250 of them were executed at Landsberg over five years, and many were handed life sentences. By 1958, the US Army had relinquished control of Landsberg Prison and released all remaining prisoners except Otto Kestelman. Kestelman had been handed a life sentence and it was at Landsberg he was to spend the rest of his days.

From the beginning of his life sentence, Kestelman showed no remorse for the crimes he had committed and he held steadfast to the Nazi ideology. Sixteen years had passed since Kestelman had been sentenced, and although his incarceration had broken him, he still held onto his Nazi beliefs.

Before leaving Australia, Frank had applied to the Bavarian Ministry of Justice for a meeting with Kestelman. On arrival at Landsberg Prison, and going through the necessary security checks, Frank was met by the German prison chaplain, Father Franz Schmitt, aged in his early sixties. Father Schmitt was of medium height and build, had a head of snowy white hair and spoke haltingly in English. He greeted Frank warmly and wasted no time informing him that Kestelman was still in denial of his actions during the war.

Frank was dressed in his clerical attire when he was led toward a small room by a prison officer carrying a Walther MPK submachine gun. The officer was dressed in a green tunic and tie offset by a yellow shirt and brown trousers. On the right - hand chest of his tunic was a badge with the words:

Bayerisches Justizministereium Bavarian Ministry of Justice

Upon entering the room, the officer asked Frank to sit down behind a small timber table. On the other side of the table was positioned another chair. The officer soon left and Frank surveyed the room. The walls and ceiling were painted white and there was a small window in the middle of the wall, which had steel bars covering it. The floor was covered with black linoleum and the room was austere in its presentation.

After a few minutes, the officer returned with Kestelman walking in front of him. Kestelman was handcuffed, wearing a long - sleeve green shirt and matching green trousers. He walked through the door and the officer ordered him to sit down. He then about - faced and walked back to the door entrance, where he stood with his submachine gun.

Kestelman was aged in his mid – forties, his hair had streaks of grey through it and he had lost weight from the days he was at Buchenwald.

"Good morning Otto," Frank said without a hint of emotion.

"I *sink* it is only right *zat* I address you as *Farzer* Casey," Otto said with an air of formality.

"It is indeed Otto," Frank said bluntly.

"I appreciate you taking time out to pay me a visit, *Farzer* Casey."

"As a priest, it is my duty to help any individual regardless of who they are and what they have done in the past."

"I do not receive any visitors and I am grateful *zat* you have travelled so far to meet with me."

"What do want to talk to me about, Otto?"

Kestelman looked at Frank for what seemed an eternity before he spoke.

"I would like you to know *zat* I was only doing my job at Buchenwald and held no grievances towards you."

"You could have fooled me, Otto, considering you kicked me in the stomach and held a pistol to the side of my head before threatening to shoot me."

"You have to understand *zat* I was under a lot of pressure and I had many prisoners to guard over."

"Did doing your job include the systematic murder of thousands of prisoners in Buchenwald?"

"*Zey* were prisoners who were too weak to continue and *zer* most humane *sing* to do was finish them off," Kestelman said bluntly.

"They were too weak to continue because of the brutality inflicted by the SS and acts of barbaric torture that cost thousands of lives."

"We had to be brutal; *ozawise*, we would have lost control of *za* camp."

"Your brutality also extended to the torture and murder of a Catholic priest!"

Kestelman glared at Frank before answering with a raised voice, "He disobeyed an order. *Zat* is why he was treated so harshly!"

"*Sprich nicht so laut!*" *Keep your voice down!* The prison officer barked from where he was standing by the doorway.

Otto looked over his shoulder and gave the officer a look of disdain before slowly turning back towards Frank.

Frank looked at the officer and then back towards Kestelman.

"He heard the man's confession. That is why you tied him to a pole out in the snow before throwing buckets of water over him and letting him freeze to death."

"As I said, he disobeyed an order. *Zat* is why he was treated so harshly."

"So hearing a man's confession warranted him being brutally murdered."

"I have nothing more to say about *zer* matter!" Kestelman said bluntly.

Stony silence between the two men lasted for some time before Frank spoke.

"They are all dead, Otto!"

"Who are all dead?" Kestelman growled.

"Hitler, Himmler, Goebbels, Göring and scores of other Nazi henchmen. They all committed suicide. Your heroes of The Third Reich all died by their own hands and you are clinging onto their memory."

Kestelman leaned forward in his seat, stared at Frank and whispered, *"Heil Hitler!"*

"Hitler won't save you or his memory, Otto," Frank said.

Otto stood up and glared at Frank before he shouted, "How dare you talk about *zer* Führer like *zat*!"

"Sich hinsetzen!" Sit down! The prison officer shouted as he approached Otto with his submachine gun raised.

Otto sat back down and continued to glare at Frank.

Frank leaned forward and folded his hands on the table, and said, "I am talking to a pitiful little man who is still living in the illusion that he belongs to the master race."

"How dare you insult *za* memory of all *zoze* great men and woman who fought and died for *za Zird* Reich?" Kestelman said with spite.

"So you are showing your true colours, Otto? You have no guilt for the crimes that you perpetrated. You are a lonely man devoid of any friends and that is why you have asked me here today."

Kestelman smashed his hands down on the table and yelled, "How dare you talk to me like *zis*, priest!"

"Ich warne Sie, Kestelman!" I am warning you, Kestelman! said the prison officer raising his sub-machine gun.

Kestelman looked at the officer contritely. He knew he was

skating on thin ice and any further indiscretions on his account would see him forfeit any further privileges.

"Remember Otto; the truth will set you free," Frank said.

Otto stood up and turned to the prison officer and said, *"Hol mich hier raus!" Get me out of here!*

"What's wrong Otto? Is the truth too hard to handle?" Frank said.

"Genugend!" Enough! Kestelman yelled before the prison officer led him away to his cell.

Frank sat back in his seat, satisfied he had won the first round. He knew it was a long fight ahead to save Kestelman if he could be saved. Frank was up for the challenge and committed himself to the task, whatever it would take. He also knew that time was a great healer and Kestelman's isolation could work in his favour, for it was the one thing that could break down his denial.

After he rendezvoused with Stan in London, Frank returned from Europe and settled back into parish life at St Michael's, Hurstville. He was active in all aspects of the parish, including sport, and he continued to pay special attention to those who were disadvantaged.

Never far from his mind, though, was Otto Kestelman. Shortly after arriving home from Europe, he wrote to the German prisoner. In his letter, Frank told Kestelman to own up to the heinous crimes he had perpetrated and that his ideology was a complete lie.

Over the next six years, he wrote to Kestelman every month, urging him to see the fragility of his ideology and to own up to his crimes. In his correspondence, Frank told many parables illustrating a moral or spiritual lesson that was the very antithesis of the Nazi ideology that he clung to. Kestelman never responded. This did not deter Frank from continuing his correspondence, for he believed in the old analogy that persistence leads to resistance.

Chapter 34

Friday, March 20th 1970. St Patrick's Catholic Church Sutherland, Sydney

AS 1970 APPROACHED, Frank began wondering whether he would ever get his own parish or remain a curate forever. This did not perturb him, as he was content to fulfil his priestly duties in whatever capacity. It just so happened the powers in the Sydney Archdiocese felt Frank had served his time as a curate and his unbroken sobriety was enough to warrant a promotion to parish priest. In March 1970, they gave him the fledgling parish of Sutherland in the southern suburbs of Sydney.

Within months of arriving at St Patrick's at Sutherland as the new parish priest, Frank realised there was the need for a new church. He set about organising a committee to raise funds for its design and building. At the head of the committee was a parishioner and local builder named Pim Janssen. Pim was from Holland and had immigrated to Australia in the early 1950s, where he had settled in Gymea. Along with his younger brother, who had come to Australia a year earlier, they started a building business together.

The curate at St Patrick's was a young Irishman in his mid - twenties named Father Vincent Mulcahy. Father Mulcahy had only been in Australia for six months, and St Patrick's had been his first appointment. Before Frank's arrival, he had heard stories about the rebellious and fiery Father Frank Casey and his first reaction on hearing of his appointment to St Patrick's was one of trepidation.

"I suppose you've heard stories about my irascible nature?" Frank said to Father Mulcahy on first meeting him.

"I have Father Casey, and to be perfectly honest with you, I feel rather apprehensive as to how things are going to work out between us."

"You need not worry," Frank said, putting his arm around the timorous young man's shoulder. "Everything you have heard about me is absolutely correct." He wore a big grin.

Contrary to what Father Mulcahy had thought about Frank, it was to be the start of a very solid friendship, as the two priests had much in common, including their passion for rugby and boxing. Between the two of them, they were to achieve a lot together. Included was the planning for what was to be a very unique church built into the side of a hill.

Frank had been at St Patrick's for over a year when he ventured overseas to Europe once again. After stopping in London and France to visit Marguerite, Raphael and their family in Besancon, he made his way to Germany and Landsberg Prison.

Otto Kestelman was still in solitary confinement in the same cell he had been in when Frank had visited him in 1964 and had not received any visitors other than the prison chaplain. Kestelman was led to the same room Frank had met him seven years earlier. Frank noticed he was still underweight and his hair was completely grey.

"Have you received the letters I have been writing to you, Otto?" Frank said.

"Yes I have *zay* are piled up in *zer* corner of my cell," Kestelman said with a nod.

"Has any of what I have said resonated with you, Otto?"

Kestelman shrugged his shoulders and said, "*Nein!*"

"When will you admit your guilt for the crimes you perpetrated Otto?"

"I was simply carrying out my orders," said Kestelman.

"Do you think torturing and killing civilians, not to forget the execution of a Catholic priest, was carrying out orders?"

"I was an SS officer and I was under *zer* direct command of my superiors."

"Surely your conscience must have told you what you were doing was not only a crime but also morally wrong?" Frank said.

"Morally wrong, you say, *Farzer* Casey? How can you say it was morally wrong when all I was doing was merely punishing *zer* opponents of *za Zird* Reich?"

"You and all your Nazi cronies were just a bunch of thugs murdering anybody who stood in your way. How can you justify your actions?" Frank said sternly.

"You and *your terrorflieger* comrades were our enemies and *zer* punishment you received was justified."

"What a load of bullshit!" Frank growled.

"Please mind your language, *Farzer* Casey. After all, you are a priest," Kestelman said with a devilish grin.

Frank looked at Kestelman steely - eyed and pointing his finger at him, said, "Firstly, we were prisoners of war and should have been given all the rights of the Geneva Convention. We should have been taken to a Luftwaffe - run POW camp, not to a concentration camp. The allies never treated downed German airmen in the same way. Your deceit and arrogance are unbeliev-able and I believe there is no hope for you unless you face up to your past." Frank stood up and walked towards the doorway.

"Wait!" Kestelman said.

The prison officer standing at the door holding his sub -machine gun gave Kestelman a steely look.

"*Zere* is something you can do for me before you leave *Farzer* Casey," he said, lowering his voice.

"What is that?" Frank said abruptly.

"I have found out *zer* whereabouts of my son and have been writing to him for *zer* last twelve months, but I have received no reply from him."

"And what do you want me to do?" Frank said tersely.

"I have *zis* letter and I would like you to deliver it to him personally."

"After the way you have treated me, you would have to be joking?" Frank said.

"He lives in *München* and I have his address, and if you are *zer* man you say you are, then as a priest, you could not turn down *zer* request of a desperate man."

Frank walked back to the table and looked Kestelman in the eye.

"After all the crimes you committed, and without any sign of contrition, you expect me to fulfil your request and hand -deliver your letter?"

"As a priest, aren't you obligated to help *zose* who are in need?" Kestelman said while he held the letter in his hand.

"You give no thought to those you murdered in Buchen-wald, but you want me to hand deliver a letter to your son?"

"He might not want to listen to me, but perhaps he will listen to a priest?" Kestelman said with a look of contrition.

"And what is in the contents of the letter?" Frank asked.

Kestelman looked long and hard at Frank and gulped before saying, "I have asked for his forgiveness for all *zer* grief I have caused him."

Frank looked at Kestelman for some time before stepping forward and taking the envelope from his hands.

"Your deceit and arrogance are breathtaking, Kestelman, but since you have asked forgiveness from your son, there may be a glimmer of hope for you," said Frank as he took the letter.

With that, Frank walked out of the room.

"*Sank* you." Frank could hear Kestelman say as he walked down the corridor.

Frank left Landsberg Prison shortly after and caught a bus for the hour - long trip to Munich. On arrival, he took the envelope from his Qantas travel bag and looked at the address. It read:

Herr. Hans Kestelman

Karisfelder Strabe 72

8095 München, Deutschland.

He had not a clue where Hans Kestelman lived. So made his way to the closest *Deutsch Post* branch, where he enquired about Hans' residence. His first attempt fell on deaf ears as the middle - aged woman behind the counter could not speak English. She then called a colleague over to the counter, a man in his mid - twenties who spoke perfect English. He informed Frank his residence was on the northern side of Munich and he could catch a bus there.

Frank walked to the closest bus stop and approached a middle-aged man waiting there. After showing him the address on the envelope, he asked if the bus pulling up would take him to Hans Kestelman's residence.

"*Nein!*" was his gruff reply before turning his back on Frank.

A shiver ran up Frank's spine. The man's response reminding him of the SS guards from Buchenwald. He was becoming increasingly irritable about his predicament before a petite - looking brunette woman in her early twenties walked up to the bus stop. Frank enquired from her which bus he should take. She very kindly informed him in perfect English the next bus would take him to a bus stop within walking distance from Hans' residence.

"*Danke sehr,*" Frank said.

"*Ihr Willkommen,*" she responded.

Shortly after, a bus pulled up, which Frank caught and he found Hans' residence within five minutes of arriving. The house was single storey and situated not far from a leafy park. He checked the number on the envelope and knocked on the front door. As he waited, he could hear music playing on a stereo from inside the house. Unbeknownst to Frank, the song playing was *Almost Cut My Hair* from Crosby, Stills, Nash & Young. Frank was soon met at the door by a man in his late twenties. He had long brown hair and a moustache with a headband and beads around his neck. He was of medium build and was dressed in colourful hippie attire.

"*Ja?*" he said.

"My German is very poor, but is this Hans Kestelman's residence?" Frank asked.

"Yes, it is," he said in very good English.

"My name is Father Frank Casey and I have come to talk to him."

He looked Frank up and down carefully.

"Wait here a minute," he said.

He went back inside and turned the music off before walking back to the front door.

"I am Hans Kestelman. How can I help you?"

"I am an Australian. I have visited your father Otto in Landsberg Prison and he asked me to deliver this letter to you," Frank said, showing him the envelope.

Hans stood there motionless, looking at Frank's outstretched hand without taking the envelope.

"How did *zat* monster find out where I live?" he said sternly.

"I am not sure, Hans," Frank said with the envelope still in front of him.

"What does *zat* beast want from me?" he said.

"I believe he wants to ask for your forgiveness for the grief he has caused you."

"Forgiveness, you say? That evil man would not know what *zer* word meant," he said bitterly.

"I can understand you not wanting to read this letter, but I gave your father my word that I would deliver it," Frank said with his hand still outstretched.

After an eternity, Hans then stepped forward and took the letter from Frank's hands. "What is an Australian priest doing helping my *farzer?*" Hans said.

"During the war, I was a rear gunner in a Lancaster bomber shot down over France. After I was captured, I was sent to Buchenwald Concentration camp, where I was exposed to the full horror of what the Nazis did there."

"And it was there *zat* you met my *farzer?*" Hans said.

Frank nodded.

"God help you!" Hans said.

"I am sure He did. That's why I am standing here today," Frank said.

Hans looked at Frank long and hard before he invited him into the house and led him into the loungeroom, where he invited him to sit down on a plush sofa. The interior was dimly lit. The walls were decorated with a number of Andy Warhol paintings and blown - up photos of Janis Joplin, Jim Morrison and Jimi Hendrix as well as numerous psychedelic images. Incense and candles were burning, and Frank could sniff marijuana. Hans pulled out Joni Mitchell's recently released LP *Blue* from its album sleeve and played it on the stereo at low volume. Then he made his way into the kitchen, where he prepared some afternoon tea. While he was there, Frank surveyed his surroundings. He had never experienced anything like it before, and he felt like he had been transported into another world while Joni sang the title track *Blue* with exquisite mastery.

The floors were covered with bright coloured rugs, numerous pot plants growing, and an acoustic guitar leant up against a wall. Frank felt overwhelmed. It was alien to his austere and conservative tastes.

After ten minutes, Hans entered the loungeroom holding a serving tray with coffee and cake. He poured Frank a cup of coffee and offered him some cake before sitting down in a cane chair, which had the hippie peace sign as its cover.

"Tell me about yourself, *Farzer* Casey," he said.

Over the next half hour, Frank recalled what had happened to him during the war and how he had been trying to help Kestelman over the last seven years. When he was finished, he said to Hans, "What of your mother, Hans? Where is she?"

Hans looked into his mug of coffee, a sombre expression on his face before answering. "She died when I was ten years of age."

"I am sorry to hear that."

"*Zank* you. If the truth be known, I think she died of shame."

"Go on," Frank said.

"During *zer* war, she thought Buchenwald was a prisoner of war camp and had no idea, like most Germans, of *zer* atrocities taking place there and in other such concentration camps. After my *farzer* was caught and tried for his heinous crimes, my mother was so appalled with what he had done *zat* I believe she just gave up," said Hans.

"You mean she lost the will to live?" Frank said.

"Yes," said Hans, nodding his head, "I think she was so ashamed of being married to such an evil monster *zat* she lost *zer* will to live."

"What happened to you, then?"

"I lived with my maternal grandparents till I was eighteen. *Zay* were good people who gave me a stable upbringing and a good education."

Frank nodded his head.

"Your father is in total denial of the crimes he perpetrated."

"They should have hung my *farzer* for what he did at *zat* ghastly place," said Hans.

"It was only luck that prevented him from being executed," said Frank.

"I am very grateful for you trying to help my *farzer*, but unfortunately, he is too indoctrinated in *zer* filthy ideals of *zer* Nazis, and I feel *zere* is no hope for him," said Hans.

"You must never forget, Hans, that where there is life, there is hope, and every human being has the chance for redemption, no matter how far down the ladder they have gone," Frank said.

Hans looked at Frank sympathetically.

"That is on the condition they are prepared to face their past," Frank added.

"You are a very kind and decent man, *Farzer,* and I appreciate all *zat* you have done in helping my *farzer.* It would help if you remembered, though, many people in *zis* country are in denial of *zer* atrocities Germany committed during *zer* war," said Hans.

Frank looked at him thoughtfully and mused on the predicament Hans found himself in.

"And what do you do with yourself, Hans?" Frank asked.

"I have a law degree, but I am working with Amnesty International as a volunteer promoting human rights."

Frank looked at him carefully and thought that Hans was the most way - out lawyer he had ever laid his eyes on. "I know what you are thinking, but I lived through *zer* sixties and learnt the only way forward is through love and peace. Let me assure you I will do *everyzhing* I can to guarantee *zat* what happened to our country during *zer* war never happens again."

Frank nodded in agreement.

"And that men like my *farzer* can never promulgate their evil agenda ever again."

"I would like to agree with you, Hans, but I am afraid that man will always be capable of evil acts. It is the way of the human race.

Frank looked at his watch. "The time is getting on, and I must be off," he said.

"Thank you so much, *Farzer* and please keep in touch," said Hans with a smile.

"I will, and thankyou so much for your hospitality, Hans."

Frank made his way from the house towards the bus stop, where he travelled back to Munich.

Frank arrived home from Germany perplexed about what he should do regarding Otto Kestelman. Part of him felt like letting Kestelman go, as he thought he was beyond help. His conscience told him to keep going and that Kestelman was worth fighting for. Frank knew as a priest, he must try to help Kestelman, even if it was only for his own sake. As a result, he continued his letter writing in the hope something might change in him. Unbeknownst to Frank, events far out of his control were to serve as a catalyst for the seismic shift that was to take place in Otto Kestelman's psyche.

In late August 1972, a new inmate came to Landsberg prison named Max Swart. Swart was a Dutch Jew aged in his mid – thirties with black hair, of solid build and standing six feet two inches. He was an intelligent man with a quick wit and cheeky disposition. After breaking into a wealthy Munich socialite's residence, he had been sentenced to two years. Swart had done a number of minor sentences before his current one. He was seen as a petty criminal and was kept in the minimum security section of the gaol.

Many of Max Swart's relatives had been exterminated in the concentration camps during the war. His father had been liberated from Majdanek concentration camp in Poland, by the advancing Red Army. In contrast, his mother was released from Bergen-Belsen concentration camp in Germany by a British armoured division in April 1945. It must have broken their hearts to find their only son had turned to a life of crime after all they had been through during the war.

Max Swart's life of crime may not have been in vain, for it was to bring him in direct contact with Otto Kestelman and ultimately alter the course of both their lives. As well as being a good safecracker, Max was handy with his fists, where he had briefly fought in the ring as a light heavyweight.

In 1959, he was looking for excitement. Consequently, he moved to the major port city of Hamburg in northern Germany and spent much of his twenties working around the bars and clubs in the red-light district known as the Reeperbahn. The area was known for its prostitutes, transvestites and gangsters and one notable club named the Kaiserkeller, where he worked as a doorman. As a boxer, Max sorted out many an unruly patron in the Kaiserkeller before tossing them out on the street. While working there in 1960, he encountered a young English band fresh off the boat from Liverpool named The Beatles. Max was drawn to both their music and irreverent antics and wit.

Max was well aware that one of Landsberg Prison's most notorious inmates was Otto Kestelman, and as a Jew, he would have given anything to sort out the Nazi thug. The events that were to unfold shortly after Max's arrival in Landsberg were to accentuate his confrontation with Kestelman.

The 1972 Summer Olympics were held in Munich from 26 August to 11 September. They have been largely overshadowed by the Munich Massacre, which took place in the pre - dawn of 5th of September. Members of the Palestinian terrorist organisation, Black September, broke into the Olympic Village and took eleven Israeli athletes, coaches and officials hostage. The result was all the Israelis were killed.

When news reached Max, he was incensed and determined to seek revenge. Max's thoughts soon turned to Kestelman and he wanted retribution on the Nazi, who he despised as much as those who had perpetrated the heinous act in Munich.

Max's small window of opportunity came in the form of a small exercise yard Kestelman could access for an hour every day. With the help of a nail file and a piece of wire he had acquired, Max shaped a tension wrench and a pick. With both small tools,

Max was able to pick the lock into the secured area where he confronted Kestelman. He told the Nazi who he was, and Kestelman addressed him with customary belligerence. That's all Max needed to act. He grabbed Kestelman around the throat and picked him up, so his feet were six inches off the ground. He then beat the living daylights out of him, starting at his head and working down to his torso before two prison officers got to Max and dragged him off. In only a few minutes, Max had inflicted grievous bodily harm to the Nazi. Kestelman may have avoided the hangman's noose after the Dachau Trials, but that day, Max Swart beat him to an inch of his life. It may have been only a small measure compared to what he had dished out in Buchenwald, and it wasn't going to bring back the Israelis, but in Max's mind, it went a small way to exacting revenge for what had happened. As a result, Kestelman spent six weeks in the prison hospital while Max was handed another two years on top of his existing sentence. Max never reoffended and turned his life around, completing his trade as a locksmith and moving to Australia, where he started a successful business.

On the other side of the world, Frank was oblivious to what had happened at Landsberg. Although he was busy with his parish duties, always at the back of his mind was Kestelman. More pressing issues on the political home front also had his attention. As 1972 drew towards its end, there was a shift about to take place on the Australian political front that was to change the social landscape of Australia forever.

Chapter 35

Saturday, December 2nd 1972. St Patricks Catholic Church
Sutherland, Sydney

IT WAS 6.00 PM on Saturday, 2nd December, 1972, and Frank had rushed back from the church to the presbytery after hearing confessions that afternoon. He hastily switched on his Pye black and white television to watch the federal election results from the newly opened National Tally Room in Canberra.

The Australian Labor Party, under opposition leader Gough Whitlam, had run a very successful campaign with the slogan "Its Time" as its catchphrase. As the evening wore on, it was obvious Prime Minister Billy McMahon's Liberal/ Country coalition was going to be defeated. After 23 years of Liberal / Coalition rule, the ALP was about to be handed the reins of government.

Frank, being of Irish Catholic descent, had always supported the ALP. That was, until the split that took place in 1955 within the party over its position on communism. Many members of the ALP, particularly Catholics, were alarmed at the growing influence of communism within the trade union movement.

As a result, they split from the ALP and formed the Australian Labor Party (Anti-Communist,) later renamed the Democratic Labor Party or DLP.

Frank had long opposed the growing influence of communism within the ALP, and as he could not bring himself to support the Liberal /Country coalition, his allegiance swung towards the DLP.

Now Gough Whitlam was about to be sworn in as Prime Minister of Australia after a wave of popularity at his social reform agenda. With Lance Barnard as deputy prime minister, the two formed a diarchy for the first two weeks before a full cabinet could be formed. Whitlam wasted no time implementing many of these reforms and set about fulfilling many of his campaign promises. They included ordering negotiations to establish full relations with the People's Republic of China and ordering back home all remaining Australian troops from Vietnam, though most had been withdrawn by McMahon.

Frank viewed Whitlam's early days of government with circumspection. He fully comprehended his huge popularity and the changes he intended to carry out to make Australia an equal place to live in, but was weary of his agnostic views and authoritarian - type leadership. Frank knew change took time, and Whitlam's crash - through mentality could spell disaster in the end. How right he was. Frank also realised it took all the crew, not just the pilot, to pull off a successful bombing mission. With the cabinet elected, Whitlam set about on a set of reforms with breathtaking speed. Among those reforms were abolishing the death penalty for federal crimes, establishing legal aid with offices in each state capital and abolishing university fees. Other reforms included indigenous rights, which Frank supported and changing the national anthem to 'Advance Australia Fair'.

Frank realised that among his parishioners, there was support for both sides of the political spectrum, so never spoke directly about politics from the pulpit. If it concerned an issue of morality, he would make his voice be heard in no uncertain terms.

On one occasion in 1973, while giving his sermon at mass on Sunday, he spoke forcibly about a particular issue irritating him. It concerned what he called 'the ridiculous decision' of the Australian National Gallery under Whitlam's permission to purchase the painting *Blue Poles* by the American artist Jackson Pollock for A$1.3 million. A staggering amount at the time!

"I've been told the cost of this piece of so - called art is a third of the annual budget. Is this the type of reckless spending we can expect from the current government?" With a sly grin, Frank continued, "On viewing *Blue Poles* for the first time, I contemplated whether Jackson Pollock had made a decision to strap himself to the bed and come down from whatever drugs he was on after he painted this piece of work." The congregation broke out into howls of laughter, and it was a considerable time before Frank could continue his sermon.

In the conservative climate of the time, the purchase of *Blue Poles* had created a political and media scandal, but Frank's indignation was curbed when he received a letter in the mail the following day.

The letter was short but to the point. In part, it read:

Dear Father Casey,

I do not know if you are aware, but I received some rough treatment from a fellow inmate back in late September last year. He is a Dutch Jew named Max Swart. He took great exception to the Munich Massacre and took his revenge out on me. Swart beat me to an inch of my life and I spent six weeks in the gaol hospital recovering from my injuries. I was in a coma for a week, and it took me weeks before I recovered from my physical injuries.

I had been in the hospital for about a month and was lying in bed one night when I dreamt of my mother. My mother died before the war and had been a devout Catholic all her life. She brought my two brothers and me up in the Catholic faith, and I followed my faith right up until the time my mother died when I was fourteen years of age. I blamed God for her death when she died and walked away from the Catholic Church forever. In the dream, my mother spoke to me by calling me by my birth name, Martin.

"Martin," she said, "what have you done with your life?"

"What have you done with your life Martin?" she kept saying

I awoke from the dream in a lather of sweat and was very disturbed and her words have been etched on my mind. Something has shifted in my conscience from that moment on, and I have been different ever since.

What can I say other than I would like to talk to you?

PS: Thank you for sending my letter to my son Hans.

Yours sincerely

Otto Kestelman

Frank sat for a long while, deep in thought, contemplating the contents of the letter, and he knew that Kestelman had had an enormous shift in his thinking.

"I might just win a race with this bastard after all," he said before a smile came across his face.

It was a grey day on Saturday 15th September, 1973, for the New South Wales Rugby League Grand Final being played at the Sydney Cricket Ground that afternoon. The match was between the Cronulla - Sutherland Sharks and the Manly- Warringah Sea Eagles. Frank had been given tickets to the game by his good mate, Father Bernie Manning. Bernie was a passionate Manly Warringah supporter and Frank had adopted Cronulla Sutherland as his side since he had been parish priest of Sutherland.

The two priests had good seats in the Bradman Stand and were preparing for the 3.00 pm kick – off. Seated directly in front of them was a drunken man in his mid thirties wearing a Manly - Warringah football jersey. He was frantically waving around a homemade Manly - Warringah banner and hitting surrounding spectators, including a man in his early twenties decked out in Cronulla attire sitting beside him.

"Keep waving that shit Manly banner around dickhead and I'll end up shoving it right up ya fucking arse!" The Cronulla fan screamed.

"Just try it dickhead and I'll knock ya teeth out!" he responded.

"I'd love nothing more than to knock out your lights ya silvertail cocksucker!" the Cronulla fan said.

"Righto, that's it, you're on," the Manly supporter said.

He threw his banner on the ground before a fight ensued. They were going hammer and tongs at each other with the Cronulla supporter giving the Manly fan a pasting when two burly police officers arrived. They had witnessed the obnoxious behaviour of the Manly supporter before the lead up to the fight.

They broke up the fight before dragging the Manly hooligan down the stairs to the cheers of the crowd. He was eventually placed in a paddy wagon which was parked to the side of the Sheridan Stand.

After things had settled down Frank turned to Bernie and mentioned the letter he had received from Otto Kestelman the previous week. In all his correspondence with Kestelman, Frank had never spoken about religion other than to highlight a spiritual axiom to show the German how much his Nazi ideology was fallacious.

Kestelman first brought the subject of religion up in the letter Frank received from him. In the letter, the German said he doubted the existence of God but enquired of Frank, "What was the one thing that could prove He existed?"

A boy was selling ice creams and nuts when Frank turned to Bernie and told him the question Kestelman had posed, just as Father Manning was lighting up a cigarette. Bernie was about to respond to Frank's enquiry when the band struck up God Save the Queen, and the two men, alongside the other 52,000 spectators, stood up to sing. With the national anthem finished, referee Keith Page blew his whistle to indicate the start of the game.

"Okay, Frank, it's on," said Bernie, clapping his hands together.

"May the best side south of Sydney Harbour win," Frank said with a grin.

"Ha ha, nice touch," Bernie laughed, "I'll get to the question that Kestelman asked in a minute Frank."

Bernie didn't get a chance to respond to Frank because shortly after the start of the game, the Cronulla hooker Ron Turner hit the Manly lock Malcolm Reilly with a ferocious tackle. The Englishman was left writhing in agony as he lay on his back on the ground after Turner's devastating blow.

"That was uncalled for!" Bernie said, turning to Frank.

"That tackle reminded me of some of the Manly v Springwood matches back in our seminarian days," said Frank.

Bernie grinned and nodded his head in agreement.

While Reilly was taken from the field for pain - killing injections, the two sides belted into each other. Reilly returned later in the first half and created havoc as he tried to belt as many Cronulla players into submission. He eventually succumbed to his injury and was forced to leave the field. The game would become known as one of the toughest and dirtiest grand finals in Rugby League history.

As the game continued, several fights broke out in the first half, and referee Keith Page called all 26 players in. He warned them the next time a scuffle broke out, he would give the player or players concerned an early shower. This did not deter any of the players and the rough house tactics continued without Page ever sending anybody from the field.

It was halftime before the two priests could discuss Kestelman's question.

Bernie poured Frank and himself a coffee out of the glass thermos he had brought to the match. Lighting up a cigarette and drawing back, he prepared himself for a discussion on the existence of God.

"Kestelman's question indicates he is at least prepared to ponder on a key philosophical point," Bernie said.

"Kestelman has yet to come to the conclusion that reason and faith, as proposed by Thomas Aquinas, is the key element to prove the existence of God," Frank said.

"I agree. Regardless of Kestelman's present belief, it looks as though all the hard work you have put in over the years might be coming to fruition."

"It appears that way," said Frank.

"Kestelman is having a crisis of faith and is finally seeing the error of his ways and his mortality," Bernie said, drawing back on his cigarette.

"And he is finally searching for the true meaning of his life, and what his path may be," said Frank.

Frank and Bernie continued their philosophical discussion during the halftime break, and as the players returned to the field for the second half, Bernie turned to Frank and said, "Keep plugging away with him, Frank and your man might just come home before it's too late. Now let's prepare ourselves for this second half." He puffed away on his cigarette. "I think Bob Fulton could be the difference for Manly in this second half," Bernie continued.

Bernie's comment was prophetic. In the 58th minute, the Manly centre, Bob Fulton, scored a try in the Brewongle Stand corner that sealed the game for them 10- 7 and earnt him the man of the match award.

Chapter 36

Monday, September 24ᵗʰ 1973.St Patricks Catholic Church Sutherland, Sydney

SHORTLY AFTER THE 1973 Rugby League Grand Final, Father Vincent Mulcahy was given his own parish after spending the last four years with Frank. Frank was disappointed to see the young Irish curate leave his parish as they had become good friends and achieved a lot together concerning pastoral activities.

Frank's new curate was Father Gerard Venables, who had served in one other parish before coming to St Patrick's. A trendy, well - tanned Australian 28 year-old, Father Venables wore his blonde hair collar length and was a very athletic individual who did a lot of bushwalking, swimming and abseiling, among other activities. He enjoyed bands like Led Zeppelin, Deep Purple and Jethro Tull and was seen as hip and "with it" by the younger set in the parish. The parish enthusiastically welcomed him, and he set about organising outdoor activities, including days out in the Royal National Park for the younger parishioners.

Frank welcomed his new curate with his customary courtesy, but instinct told him something was not quite right with

Father Venables. Being a conservative priest, Frank was initially taken aback by his 'groovy blonde hair', as he used to call it. His taste in music was totally foreign to Frank and may as well have come from planet Pluto for all he related to it.

The juxtaposition of the two priests' personalities was evident from the start. As many of the parish was overcome with a wave of enthusiasm for the new arrival, Frank's popularity, not that he nurtured it, was put on the back burner.

At first, everything seemed normal enough as Father Venables went about his pastoral duties. His popularity only seemed to grow as he spoke the language of the younger set and he was given rock star status. He was a vocal advocate of Gough Whitlam's government, particularly his social reform agenda. He favoured Whitlam's pledge to help the disadvantaged, particularly supporting local government in providing infrastructure like roads and sewerage to many of the western suburbs of Sydney, which successive conservative governments had forgotten. Who could disagree with that as the least, the lost and the forgotten were finally being heard?

What alarmed Frank were the young priest's subtle digs at established Catholic practices such as praying the rosary and the Stations of the Cross from the pulpit during his Sunday sermon.

"These archaic medieval practices belong in the dustbin and have no place in the modern church which is trying to align itself with the 20th century," Father Venables was heard to say at Mass one Sunday.

As a conservative priest, Frank was opposed to such views and told the young priest, in no uncertain manner, what he thought of his beliefs.

"Let me remind you, Father Venables that is not for you to make up the rules as you go along. The church is very clear on its doctrine and it is up to us as members of the clergy to uphold those teachings," Frank said to the young priest in the presbytery one day.

"But Father Casey, it is a modern world we live in and the Catholic Church must adapt itself to an ever-changing and progressive social environment," Father Venables said enthusiastically.

"Some things will never change in my parish. Is that clear?" Frank said forcibly.

Father Venables gave Frank a look of disdain before reluctantly agreeing.

As a result of their discussion, the young curate begun a campaign of 'white anting' Frank's reputation. He surreptitiously told the younger set Frank wasn't open to change and he wasn't prepared to move with the times. Within a short period, the attitude of many of the younger members of the parish had turned against Frank.

Father Venables cemented his reputation as the 'good guy' by inviting several of his favourite altar boys on weekend camping trips to places like the Royal National Park, just south of Sydney. These were fun - filled weekends with swimming, barbeques and evening stories around the campfire.

One of these camping weekends was up to Blackheath in the Blue Mountains west of Sydney on the Australia Day weekend in January 1974. On Saturday, 26th January, Father Venables and his six altar boys aged ten to twelve crammed into his 1967 Volkswagen Kombi Camper van and took off for Blackheath for two nights camping. It was a hot summer morning when they traversed a rough bush track, down the valley leading to a tranquil river. Once at the bottom of the valley, they set up their tents on a flat grassed area not far from the river. It was a sweltering summer's day, so they wasted no time in heading for the river, where they enjoyed a swim and the thrill of tumbling down the rapids.

That night, after a cooked barbeque, they sat around the campfire where Father Venables insisted they tell the spookiest stories they could imagine. It was just after ten - year - old Troy Ashburn, who he particularly liked, had told a ghost story, that the young curate most endeared himself to the group. He permitted them to call him Gerard and not Father Venables while they were away on these camping weekends.

"Can you imagine crusty old Father Casey giving you all permission to call him Frank?" Gerard said with a snigger while drinking a hot chocolate around the campfire.

All the boys, except Jim Whelan, laughed at the young priest's jibe at Frank. Jim Whelan was a tough twelve - year - old who played front row for the school rugby league team. He was to go on and play Under 23s for Cronulla Sutherland rugby League in his early twenties. Jim was wary of the 'rock star' priest, as he didn't like his propensity to touch many of the younger parishioners. Venables had tried to prod Jim in the stomach several times, but the young boy disliked the priest's behaviour, and he shrugged it off. Regardless of Jim's attitude towards Father Venables, the bricks that held the wall of respect between the priest and the boys slowly dismantled piece by piece. If you would have mentioned the word grooming to somebody in 1974, they probably would have thought you were talking about preparing a dog for the Sydney Royal Easter Show. In his own cunning, deceitful and evil way, that is precisely what Father Venables was doing. By allowing the boys to become over familiar with him, he was preparing himself for the moment when he could pounce like a dingo on a stray lamb.

The next day, Father Venables' over familiarity came crashing down when Jim Whelan took great exception to his beach towel being burnt. Before going for a swim with the other boys, Jim had asked Gerard to keep an eye on his beach towel beside the fireplace.

When Jim returned from his refreshing dip, his towel had fallen into the fire and was smouldering.

"You fucking dickhead, Gerard! Why did you let my fucking towel fall in the fire, you knob?" Jim screamed at Father Venables.

"Now look here Whelan, that's no way to talk to a priest," Father Venables said, pointing his finger.

"Well, you should have been on the ball and not let my towel burn you dick brain, Gerard!" Jim said.

"I am warning you, Whelan, if you keep this sort of language up, I'll tell your father about it."

"Yeah, and I'll tell the old man that you get your cheap thrills by touching up young boys."

With that, Father Venables lunged for Jim, grabbed him tightly around his arm, and said, with fire in his eyes, "You do that and I'll make your life hell."

"Let me go, you weirdo," Jim said with clenched teeth.

"I'll let you go when I am ready, you little smartarse," said Father Venables angrily.

"This is one arse you won't be getting smart with, Gerard, ya fucking perverted wanker," Jim managed to break free from his grip, where he made a hasty exit back to the river.

Jim Whelan's father, Laurie, was not only a local parishioner but a detective sergeant in the No. 21 Division. The No. 21 Division was set up by the NSW Police Force as a flying squad for areas requiring attention within NSW. It also had a reputation for being very tough and taking no prisoners.

Father Venables' wings had been clipped somewhat by Jim Whelan's reaction, but it was only a temporary setback for his evil desires. Nothing more was said of the incident during the trip and Father Venables swept it under the carpet as though nothing had happened.

After they returned from the camping trip, everything went along as per usual until after Easter Sunday Mass in 1974.

The 8.00 am Mass on Easter Sunday in 1974 was no different to any other except afterwards, Father Venables was to show his evil hand. Four altar boys served that morning, including Jim Whelan and Troy Ashburn. As Frank was to celebrate the 10.00 am Mass, Father Venables had been given the duties for the earlier service.

After Mass, the altar boys busied themselves packing everything up, and when completed, they all left the sacristy. Everyone except Troy Ashburn, who Father Venables asked to stay behind to supposedly talk to him about serving benediction the following Wednesday night. Jim Whelan and the other altar boys had walked behind the church where their pushbikes were parked. The three altar boys spent the next ten minutes talking before they mounted their pushbikes to ride home. Jim was sitting on his pushbike when he suddenly realised he had left his new white linen surplice behind. He had ordered a new one through the church because his current one was a bit old and shabby, and it had been brought to the sacristy by one of the ladies who arranged the flowers. After dismounting his push bike, Jim made his way back to the sacristy, where, as quiet as a mouse, he entered through the back door. The sight that greeted him shocked him to the core. Jim saw Father Venables had pulled

Troy's trousers down and was interfering with his private parts. The images of the priest perpetrating a sexual act could not have prepared Jim for the real thing. Jim stood there with his mouth open, unable to speak, a tingle running up his spine.

"What are you doing here, Whelan?" Father Venables screamed.

Jim tried to respond, but the words would not come from his mouth, and he noted Troy's look of terror in his eyes. Jim stood there motionless, his mind racing with a multitude of thoughts, while his heart pounded.

"Get the hell out of here, Ashburn. I'll deal with you later!" Father Venables screamed.

With that, Troy hastily tidied himself before grabbing his bag full of altar serving attire, where he made a hasty retreat out the back door of the sacristy. Jim stood there, shocked into submission, when Father Venables approached and grabbed him by the shirt collar. He pinned Jim to the wall, his face only inches away.

"Let me make this very clear, Whelan, that if a word of this ever gets out, then your life will be absolute hell. Is that understood?" he said with rage in his eyes.

Jim was speechless and petrified of the figure of Father Venables towering over him.

"I said, is that understood, Whelan?" he said with a maniac look in his eyes.

"What are you up to, Gerard?"

"It's Father Venables to you, Whelan. Is that understood?" he continued to scream at Jim.

Jim opened his mouth, and all that came out was a short yelp similar to what a dog would make. All the pluckiness that had seen him give Father Venables a 'hot serve' on the camping trip to Blackheath the previous summer was gone. In short, Jim Whelan was petrified. Not only of the imposing figure breathing fire down his throat, but also of the repercussions that would come his way if he ever mentioned a word of this to anybody.

"You make sure you tell that little turd Ashburn if he ever mentions a word of what happened here today, then his life won't be worth living. Is that clear, Whelan?"

Jim nodded in agreement.

"No one would ever believe you if you told them anyway, Whelan," he said with an evil snigger. "After all, who would believe the evidence of an altar boy over a Catholic priest?"

With that, he released his hold on Jim.

"Now get your scrawny little arse out of here, quick smart Whelan, and tell Ashburn I'll be having a quiet word with him the next time we meet."

As Jim tucked his shirt into his shorts, he noticed the plastic bag with his new surplice sitting on a table. He grabbed it and, without looking back, made a swift retreat from the confines of the sacristy.

Jim stayed silent about the incident and told nobody what had happened.

It was the following day at school when Jim approached Troy. He could see his friend was visibly shaken about his ordeal and consoled him as much as he could. He told him in no uncertain terms that what he had been through was shocking. He told Troy he could never mention it to anybody as they would not believe him, to which he agreed.

The following Sunday after Mass, when all the altar boys had gone, Father Venables ordered Troy to stay behind. He gave Troy the message he had told Jim the previous week: that if word ever got out what had happened between the two of them, then his life would be hell. Troy agreed, fearful of the repercussions if he should mention anything.

As a result, the sexual assaults continued. Not only was Troy assaulted, but three other altar boys also. Father Venables kept his assaults to his close - knit circle of altar boys to keep a tight rein over his evil deeds. As much as he desired some of the other schoolboys, he didn't want to spread his wings too far lest his actions drew attention. There was one altar boy he wouldn't touch: Jim. Although he had given

Jim the ultimatum not to mention the incident between Troy and himself, he also knew he was the type of kid with the guts to disclose his actions.

While Father Venables continued on his abominable path of assaults, Otto Kestelman continued with his correspondence to Frank. Otto liked Frank's worldliness and the wisdom he imparted to him. He realised Frank was not only a man of faith, but a person who had experienced a lot in life. As a result, Frank earnt Kestelman's respect and in time this turned into a friendship.

By this stage, Frank didn't trust his curate, as the mood of some of his altar boys had changed. Instinct told him he was up to no good, but he couldn't find any evidence to accuse him of anything untoward. Frank questioned his curate on his activities, but Father Venables was a cunning fiend who covered his tracks very well. He had the altar boys he was assaulting sworn to secrecy and they were petrified of mentioning anything lest they incur the wrath of the evil priest.

As 1974 turned into 1975, the assaults continued. Frank was busy with his campaign of raising funds for the new church and his monthly correspondence with Otto Kestelman, whose attitudes had changed decidedly for the better. Otto Kestelman had seen his past deeds as evil. Frank was in the unenviable position of dealing with an ex - Nazi who was coming to terms with his evil past and a priest who was perpetrating evil in the present.

Frank had always liked Jim Whelan. In particular, he enjoyed his honest approach to life and the no – nonsense way he played rugby league. Jim was a product of his upbringing. The middle boy in a family of eight children, his father Laurie, before joining the police force, had served in an infantry battalion in World War ll.

Laurie had seen heavy action against the Japanese in the Ramu Valley- Finisterre Range battles in Papua New Guinea and then on the Buin Road in Southern Bougainville in 1945. Laurie had joined the NSW Police Force in 1952 and, after three years in uniform, had transferred to the No.21 Division, where he had eventually achieved the rank of detective sergeant. A no - nonsense character with high morals and principles, Laurie and his wife Eileen had brought their children up to be honest in all their dealings. Frank was a great observer, and he could see the attitudes of some of his altar boys had changed, not least Troy Ashburn. It was just after they came back from the August school holidays in 1975 that Frank approached Jim. He had noticed Troy had lost some of his spark and asked Jim if he knew what might be bothering him.

"Troy seems a bit down on his uppers, Jim. Is everything okay?" Frank said.

"Everything is just fine with Troy, Father Casey," he responded.

"Is there anything wrong at school or on the home front with Troy that you know about?" Frank said.

"Everything is okay as far as I know, Father," Jim said.

"Is everything okay serving on the altar and with Father Venables?" Frank said with piercing eyes.

Jim glanced away and gulped before answering.

"Everything is just fine with Father Venables," said Jim.

Frank knew from Jim's response everything was not okay with Father Venables, but no manner of prodding by Frank could get Jim to divulge any further information. Frank walked away from their meeting convinced Father Venables was up to no good, but had no proof of it. In the following months, the sexual assaults on the altar boys continued. Eventually, it all came to a head simultaneously with one of the greatest constitutional crises in Australia's history.

Frank had always taken the altar boys for their annual picnic on the Saturday before Remembrance Day, which was on 11th November. On Saturday, November 8th 1975, Frank took them to Warragamba Dam, situated on the southwest outskirts of Sydney. Once there, Frank had issued the fourteen altar boys under his care, each with a $1.00 note, which they were free to spend however they liked. One of the dads worked for a confectionary company and brought boxes of chocolate bars, which the boys consumed with ravenous delight. Frank and some of the boy's fathers then sat down to a picnic lunch.

Meanwhile, the altar boys divided themselves into two groups of seven and engaged in a full - scale war against each other in the surrounding bush. Sticks, rocks and branches of trees were the weapons of choice in a conflict that saw prisoners taken and threatened with 'thirty days in the cooler', a 'dead leg' to the thigh or thrown into the dam if the captured individual didn't divulge 'vital' information. It was all done with great hilarity and enthusiasm, with Laurie Whelan in the rear of the two armies, giving essential tips on military tactics. One of the altar boys was even bold enough to ask Laurie Whelan a question concerning his war experiences.

"Hey Mr. Whelan, how many Japs did you kill during the war?"

"The war is long over and I don't talk about those sorts of things," said Laurie ashen faced.

After lunch, Frank walked down one of the many tracks that traversed around the bush adjacent to the dam. He came around a bend to find Troy Ashburn alone on the track and crying.

"What's the matter, Troy?" Frank exclaimed.

"Nothing's the matter, Father," said Troy, startled.

"Have you hurt yourself?"

"No, Father."

"Did one of the older boys bully you?"

"No, Father."

Just then, Jim Whelan walked into view from around the bend and noticed Troy hunched over, crying.

"Quick, Troy, let's get out of sight before we get captured by the enemy," Jim said, looking at Frank nervously.

"Wait a minute Jim. Do you know why Troy is crying?" Frank said.

"I think Troy hurt himself, Father Casey."

"He appears to be okay, Jim. Is there something else you boys aren't telling me? Frank enquired.

"No, Father," Jim said.

"Are you sure, Jim? Is there something going on within you altar boys that you are keeping secret?" Frank said with a steely gaze.

"No, Father, everything is just fine within us altar boys."

Frank walked closer to the boys, only a couple of feet away, and said with piercing eyes. "Is Father Venables treating you boys okay?"

Both boys stared at Frank with wide - open eyes, ashen - faced, but said nothing.

"If Father Venables is mistreating you in any shape or form, you would tell me about it, wouldn't you, boys?"

Still, the boys said nothing.

"You seem to be both lost for words, boys? Are you certain Father Venables is not mistreating you? Are you certain he is not interfering with you?" Frank said, his gaze peering down on the boys.

"Quick, Troy, let's get back into the game before it's all over," Jim said, grabbing Troy by the arm before sprinting down the track and out of sight.

"Hey boys, I am not finished," Frank yelled.

Frank stood there with his hands on his hips; convinced Father Venables was up to no good but troubled because he had no evidence of what he was up to.

"I'll nail you if it's the last thing I do, you bastard," Frank said to himself.

The following Tuesday, 11th November 1975, Frank was to find out the truth about Father Venables. As the country's constitutional crisis was coming to a head, so did the despicable actions of the curate.

Chapter 37

Tuesday, November 11th 1975. St Patricks Catholic Church, Sutherland

REMEMBRANCE DAY ON Tuesday, 11th November 1975, started like any other for Frank. At 7.00 am he celebrated morning Mass, and then went back to the presbytery for breakfast. Frank was seated in the dining room while Father Venables was having his breakfast at the kitchen table, as was the usual practice. As it was Frank's modus operandi at that time of the morning, he was tuned into the ABC radio program AM. Frank's thoughts were preoccupied with the busy day ahead and he gave scant attention to the program. What caught his attention was when the ABC presenter referred to it as Remembrance Day, the 10th anniversary of UDI (Rhodesia's Unilateral Declaration of Independence), and the possibility of there being an end to Australia's constitutional deadlock. Frank looked up at the radio and was deep in thought at the presenter's final comment.

"Could this be the day when Gough meets his Waterloo?" he said to himself.

Little did he know how prophetic his comment would prove to be.

Frank finished his breakfast and prepared himself for the hectic day ahead. Not least was his meeting that morning with Auxiliary Bishop John Powell, who was paying a visit to the students at the parish schools.

As Frank prepared himself for his busy schedule, in Canberra Governor – General Sir John Kerr was preparing himself for Remembrance Day commemorations. Unbeknownst to the nation, Kerr had already decided Whitlam's fate and the dramatic events that unfolded later that day were to leave an indelible mark on the country.

After the Whitlam Government had been elected in 1972, they had introduced a range of new policies. After their re-election in 1974, they had been embroiled in a number of political miscalculations, economic mismanagement and scandals, not least the Junie Morosi and loans affairs.

In October 1975, the opposition used its control of the Senate to block the passage of appropriate supply bills needed to finance government expenditure, which the House of Representative had already passed. The opposition stated they would continue to block supply unless Whitlam called an election for the House of Representatives. With that demand, the opposition leader Malcolm Fraser advised the Governor - General there was no other avenue than to dismiss Whitlam, which was in his powers if he didn't adhere to their demands. Whitlam refused to call an early election, as Kerr had not given any indication he would dismiss him if he refused to do so.

That afternoon, Whitlam went to see Sir John Kerr with the intention of calling a half - Senate election in an attempt to break the deadlock. Instead, Kerr dismissed Whitlam as Prime

Minister and installed liberal opposition leader Malcolm Fraser as caretaker Prime Minister shortly after.

When Auxiliary Bishop Powell arrived at St Patrick's that morning, he was more interested in talking to Frank about the upcoming West Indies test series against Australia that summer. Bishop Powell, a cricket tragic, was aged in his early seventies, and was an arch – conservative, reluctant to any type of change.

At 11.00 am, the school paused for Remembrance Day commemorations before the bishop resumed with his official duties. When they finished, Frank and the bishop adjourned for lunch. He engaged Frank in a vigorous discussion about the Australian side's team selections for the cricket series.

After lunch, Frank saw the bishop off before he made his way to the church, where he had a meeting with his builder, Pim Janssen, concerning some new windows that needed to be installed. It was just after 1.00 pm, and the two men were oblivious to what was happening in Canberra.

Frank and Pim spent the best part of two hours together discussing, among other matters, the new church's design. When they had finished, Frank went back to the presbytery. Once there, he informed his elderly housemaid, Mrs. Hanrahan, he was going to his office to attend to some urgent matters and did not want to be disturbed.

Frank spent the best part of the afternoon in his office and was oblivious of the time when he heard a knock on his office door.

"Yes?" he said in a terse tone.

"I know you said you didn't want to be disturbed, Father Casey, but there is an important matter that I think you should know about," came the housekeeper's voice.

Frank got up from where he was seated and opened the door to an ashen - faced Mrs Hanrahan.

"What is the problem, Mrs. Hanrahan?" Frank said, annoyed.

"I am so sorry to disturb you, Father, but I thought you should know Mr. Whitlam has been sacked."

"What?" Frank said incredulously.

"It's true, Father the Governor – General Sir John Kerr has dismissed Mr. Whitlam, and it's all over the news.

"Thank you, Mrs Hanrahan," Frank said seriously.

Frank made his way to the loungeroom and switched on his recently acquired colour television, where the live footage was coming from the steps of Parliament House. He was greeted by the sight of Australian comedian Norman Gunston addressing a large crowd gathered at the steps of Parliament House.

"What I want to know is this an affront to the constitution of this country? Or was it just a stroke of good luck for Mr Fraser? ……… *Thanks very much."* Norman said to the cheers of the crowd.

Frank stood there with his hand covering his mouth, sniggering to himself before turning to Mrs. Hanrahan and saying through muffled laughter, "He's very good that Norman Gunston, isn't he, Mrs Hanrahan?"

"If you say so, Father Casey," Mrs. Hanrahan said before slipping out the door.

Frank then sat down to watch the TV. After a short while, the governor- general's official secretary David Smith read the proclamation to dissolve parliament from the front steps of Parliament House. As David Smith continued to read, Gough Whitlam strode out from inside the building, where he positioned himself directly behind the governor – general's representative. When David Smith was finished, Gough addressed the crowd.

"Well may we say God Save the Queen? Because nothing will save the Governor – General………… The proclamation which you have

just heard read by the governor – general's official secretary was countersigned - Malcolm Fraser.......... Who will undoubtedly go down in Australian history from Remembrance Day 1975 as Kerr's cur?"

"Well, Gough, you've certainly got yourself into a bloody big mess this time!" Frank said to himself.

Frank sat there glued to the television, stunned by the events unfolding before his eyes. He had been there for some time when Mrs Hanrahan approached the loungeroom.

"Excuse me, Father Casey, but there is a boy waiting at the front door to see you," she said.

"Oh, can't it wait, Mrs Hanrahan? These events unfolding in Canberra are extremely important," Frank said, exasperated.

"I realise that, Father Casey, but he seems a bit uptight."

"Oh, what seems to be the problem?" Frank said bluntly.

"He didn't say Father, but he is one of your altar boys."

"Which altar boy is it, Mrs Hanrahan?"

"It's that young Jim Whelan, I believe, Father."

Frank stared wide eyed at Mrs Hanrahan. He went to the front door where Jim Whelan was standing with his hands in his pockets.

"What's' the problem, Jim?"

"I need to talk to you urgently, Father Casey. It's about Father Venables."

"Certainly, Jim. Come into my office."

Frank then led Jim into his office, where he shut the door. From inside the office, he could still hear the events from Canberra playing on the television, so he stuck his head outside the door.

"Mrs Hanrahan, could you please turn the television off?" Frank said, calling up the hallway.

"Now, Jim, what do you want tell me about Father Venables?"

"He has been interfering with some of the altar boys."

"Interfering?" Frank said with narrowed eyes.

"Yes, ya know what I mean, Father. Fiddling with them and doing all sorts of dirty acts with them."

"Which altar boys, Jim?"

"There are four of them, including Troy Ashburn."

"What about you, Jim? Has he touched you?"

"No, Father, he hasn't landed a hand on me!"

"I knew it," Frank said, leaning back in his chair with his hand on his chin.

Over the next half hour, Jim explained how his conscience had gotten the better of him. He said Father Venables had interfered with one of the altar boys once again and he felt compelled to come and see Frank. He told Frank, in detail, all he knew about the assaults and how long they had been happening. Frank sat there with his hand on his chin, listening intently to what Jim told him. When he was finished, he leaned across, put his hand on Jim's shoulder, and assured him he should not worry about Father Venables any longer, as he would deal with the situation immediately.

When Jim left, Frank sat there perplexed. He had no precedent in a situation like this. He wanted to seek advice on the best way to handle the situation before confronting Father Venables. He thought long and hard about who he could see.

Suddenly he thought of Laurie Whelan.

"As a detective, surely Laurie will see Father Venables' actions as not only morally wrong but also a crime," he said to himself.

Frank contacted Laurie Whelan shortly after and arranged to meet him the next day.

Just after 9.00 am the next day, Laurie met Frank in the presbytery office. Over the next half hour, Frank told Laurie the extent of his Jim's allegations. When Frank was finished, Laurie leaned forward in his chair, looked at Frank before speaking with gritted teeth.

"A man ought to finish the bastard off?"

"I can understand how you feel, Laurie," Frank said in a conciliatory tone.

"It's just lucky he didn't fiddle with Jim; otherwise, I'd kill him," Laurie said with an icy glare.

"What I want to know is if Father Venables could be prosecuted for such acts of indecency?"

Laurie sat back in his chair and paused for some time before leaning forward with his fingers together.

"I've gotta be honest with you, in all the years I've been in the police force, I've never busted a member of the Catholic Church before. It's a bit of a hot potato."

"So you don't think there is any way Father Venables could be prosecuted for these acts?" Frank said, leaning forward in his chair.

"With all due respects, Father, the church has always been seen as off - limits by the cops," Laurie said, leaning back in his chair.

"Mmm, I thought that may be the case," Frank said.

"In theory, Father Venables could be charged with sexual assault, but the problem lies with, who is going to believe the evidence of an altar boy over a priest?" Laurie said.

"I realise that is a big problem," Frank said with a sigh.

"If he can't be prosecuted, can he be defrocked or at the least thrown out of the parish?" Laurie said.

Frank gave Laurie a serious look before looking away, deep in thought.

"Father Venables being defrocked could be easier said than

done. After all, once you are ordained, then you are a priest for life."

Laurie shook his head before continuing.

"If what he has done is true and I have no doubts Jim is telling the truth, then I can't understand how he can stay a priest," Laurie said.

"Unfortunately, that is just the way it is, Laurie."

"What about you approach the bishop and see if he could do anything about it?" Laurie said.

"That was my next step, Laurie, but I first wanted to find out whether or not Father Venables could be prosecuted."

"I think that is the best way to handle the situation, but in the meantime, I will not let Jim serve on the altar and I will be informing the other parents until this creep is out of our parish."

"I appreciate your help Laurie. I appreciate it very much. I will follow this up with the Bishop," Frank said before standing up and shaking his hand.

Late that afternoon, Mrs. Hanrahan approached Father Venables and informed him Father Casey would like to see him in his office at 7.30 pm as he had an important issue to discuss.

That night, Frank sat at the dining table eating his dinner in solitude. The Whitlam government's dismissal paled into insignificance compared to the problem he now had on his hands with regards to Father Venables. He realised the chances of Father Venables being prosecuted were minimal and the prospect of him being relinquished from his Holy Orders was next to none. At best, he could only hope he would be transferred to another parish, although he knew this would not solve the problem. Frank also realised if he went to the bishop, he would be stirring up a hornet's nest. In doing so, his actions would be seen as inflammatory and mount more evidence against him as being an agitator. Regardless, he believed it was imperative he confronted Father Venables about Jim's allegations and at least have him temporarily removed from the parish until the matter was resolved.

After dinner, Frank adjourned to the loungeroom and switched on his television to be greeted by blanket coverage of the Whitlam dismissal on the ABC news. It was 7.25 pm when Frank went to his office. At 7.30 pm sharp, there was a knock on his door.

"Come in," Frank said.

Father Venables entered and Frank asked him to shut the door and take a seat.

Frank wasted no time in asking his curate about the accusations.

"Father Venables, there have been allegations brought forward to me that you have been engaging in inappropriate behaviour with a number of the altar boys?"

"Altar boys? Which altar boys are you referring to, Father?" he said, sounding agitated.

"That is not important, as the maintenance of their anonymity is imperative. What is important is what you have to say about such allegations?"

"What did they allege I have done?"

"Fiddling, groping and......even worse," Frank said, swallowing hard, "fornication!"

"That is an absolute lie. Do you actually believe that I, as a Catholic priest, would engage in such lewd and despicable acts against adolescent boys?"

"I certainly hope not, Father Venables. But I am not sure as I have had my doubts about your behaviour for some time."

"What do you find about my behaviour which is so offensive?"

"When you first came to the parish, you took the altar boys away for camping weekends. I notice that has stopped recently."

"And that is grounds for suspecting that I have been engaging in inappropriate behaviour?"

"No, but it seems peculiar that none of the altar boys are prepared to go away with you anymore."

"Perhaps they have other activities like footy and cricket that take up their time these days."

"Perhaps, but it seems strange that a number of my older altar boys have recently decided to retire from their duties. On top of that, many of them are reluctant to discuss with me your treatment towards them."

"I treat them with the utmost respect!"

"I have heard rumours they are permitted to address you by your first name while away on these camping weekends?"

"How is that supposed to implicate me in the allegations you are levelling against me?"

"Doing so breeds over - familiarity and a lack of respect, and that may be grounds for you taking advantage of them."

"As Bob Dylan wrote, the times they are a changing and the formalities that were expected with your generation are disappearing."

Frank gave him a steely look before continuing.

"That brings me to another matter. I don't like your attitude towards some of the more traditional rites of passage within the church."

"Many of them are past their used by date and have no place in the modern church."

"I disagree! They are the foundation of our faith and you trash them because they don't align themselves with your trendy ideals."

"Once again, I fail to see the connection between that and what I am being accused of."

"I believe they may contribute to the case against you," Frank said.

"Here we are in the depths of the greatest constitutional crisis our country has ever seen, and you pick me to pieces about a bunch of trivial issues. On top of that, you accuse me of the most abhorrent acts of indecency."

"I haven't accused you of anything. I am simply asking for your response on such allegations."

"I categorically refute these allegations and am deeply offended that you would even remotely suggest I have been involved in such debauched acts of indecency."

Frank leaned forward in his chair, rested his hands on the desk, and looked long and hard at his curate.

"I certainly hope these allegations are incorrect, Father Venables. I can assure you if it is proven you have been involved in such depraved acts, then Gough Whitlam won't be the only one dismissed."

The curate looked at Frank anxiously before swallowing hard.

"You know very little about my past," Frank said, looking at him intensely. "I rarely discuss my wartime exploits. I've seen a lot of this world, and nothing surprises me about the depths of depravity the human race can plunge to. You may know that during WWII, I was a rear gunner in a Lancaster bomber shot down over occupied France."

"I am aware of that, Father Casey."

Frank cast his thoughts back to the distant past and continued to stare intensely at his curate.

"You have probably not heard that after I parachuted out of

the Lancaster, I was rescued by the French Resistance. I was then put in the care of a young French priest named Father Jean Baptist Fournier, a member of the Maquis. He was a one of the most remarkable and decent men I have ever met, and his example of love and compassion convinced me to become a priest. While I was in the care of Father Fournier, I was betrayed by a French double agent and handed over to the Germans. I was taken to Buchenwald Concentration camp, which was run by the SS. Father Fournier was subsequently executed by the Nazis for his involvement in my rescue," said Frank seriously.

"I was not aware of that," Father Venables said, ashen-faced.

"Father Fournier was a real man. A priest dedicated to his vocation. He was a man who would never have violated a child in any way," Frank said.

"Let me assure you, Father Venables, that inside of Buchenwald, I was witness to the worst of human depravity. I rarely speak about it, for I saw the worst of man's humanity against man. It was as though hell had come upon earth."

Frank stood up, faced the office window and stared out into the evening twilight before continuing "Although the actions of the Nazis inside Buchenwald were abhorrent, there is something that I regard as being more depraved and immoral than what I witnessed in that concentration camp," Frank said, staring at Father Venables.

"What is that, Father Casey?" Father Venables said, swallowing hard.

"Paedophilia!" Frank shouted through gritted teeth before smashing his fist down on the desk.

With that, Father Venables lifted from his seat before coming back down in an undignified position.

"And there is only one thing I find worse than a paedophile, and that's a member of the clergy who is a paedophile," Frank said, leaning across the table and peering into the younger man's eyes with an icy glare.

Father Venables was visibly shaken by Frank's outburst.

"And let me assure you, Father Venables, that I believe a paedophile priest is the very epitome of evil! A wolf dressed up in sheep's clothes! The scum of the earth! The lowest of the low! A mockery of his vocation! Is that understood?"

Father Venables shook his head in agreement without saying a word. The fear in his eyes was palpable.

"If it is proven that you have engaged in such deprived not to mention evil acts, then my earnest wish is that they throw the full weight of the law at you, although I doubt if that will ever happen. In the meantime, I am giving you a month's leave effective immediately. I do not want you to come near this parish while I endeavour to get to the bottom of this. Is that clear, Father Venables?"

"Yes, Father Casey."

"That is all," Frank said sternly.

With that, Father Venables stood and trudged out of the office while Frank sat back down in his chair.

"Can you believe it? I've witnessed two dismissals in two days!" Frank said as he slumped back into his office chair, emotionally drained.

He sat there for some time when the thought of Norman Gunston addressing the crowd on the steps of Parliament House came into his mind.

"This could only happen in Australia!" he said, laughing out loud.

It seemed to lighten what had been a very trying couple of days.

Over the next two days, Frank met with all of his altar boys, past and present, and told them of his meeting with Father Venables and the accusations levelled against him. Only then did they decide to open up and tell the truth about Father Venables' assaults. Of the twelve altar boys Frank spoke to, all of them were unanimous in their allegations against him. Troy Ashburn was distraught as he recalled his ordeal at the hands of Father Venables. Frank asked him why he did not tell either his parents or himself about his ordeal, and he stated he did not think anyone would believe him. Frank expressed his sadness but realised this was the awful truth and some clergy were a rule unto themselves and thought they could act with impunity.

It was Friday when Frank contacted Bishop Powell's office and made an appointment with him at 9.00 am on Monday.

When Frank entered his office, the bishop addressed him. "Good morning Father Casey. How are you today?"

"Very well, thank you, Bishop," Frank said, bowing at the waist.

The bishop then invited him to sit down, where he was more interested in continuing his discussion on the upcoming cricket series with the West Indies.

"I'd like your ideas on who should be our openers in the first test at Brisbane Father Casey?"

"I am leaning towards Redpath and Rick McCosker to open our batting, Bishop."

"Mmm, interesting," the bishop said with his hand on his chin. "I like the left - hander Alan Turner. He's had some good seasons playing Sheffield Shield for New South Wales and I particularly liked the 100 he hit before lunch against Sri Lanka in the World Cup in England this year," the bishop quipped.

They continued to talk cricket for the next fifteen minutes

before Frank brought to the bishop's attention why he was really there. After Frank explained in detail, the allegations levelled against his curate, Bishop Powell was shocked and could barely believe what he was hearing.

"Are you sure your altar boys aren't just making this all up, as they have had a disagreement with Father Venables?" the bishop said.

"I am pretty sure Father Venables has been up to no good, bishop, as I have noted the change in attitude towards him by a number of my altar boys."

"Well, that is outrageous," the bishop said. "What do you think we should do, Father Casey?"

"I would like to see him charged as it is both immoral and criminal what he has been doing."

"Charged?" The bishop said incredulously before coughing into his hand. "We couldn't do that! Could you imagine the scandal the church would be embroiled in if we took that path of action?"

"Then I fail to see why he should remain a priest if these allegations against him are proven to be correct!" Frank said forcibly.

"Oh please, Father Casey, that is far too excessive! As you know, once a priest is ordained, then he remains a priest for life," the bishop said before raising his hand. "No, we need to be subtle and, dare I say, surreptitious in the way we handle this situation."

"But Bishop, we need to address this issue head – on otherwise, it will get swept under the carpet."

The bishop raised his hand before getting up from his chair and approaching the drinks cabinet.

"Would you like a drink, Father Casey?"

Frank gave him a look of dismay before the bishop responded.

"Oh, please forgive me, Father Casey, for my memory lapse. I clean forgot that you are a man of sober habits these days. How long has it been since your last drink?"

"Thirteen years, Bishop."

"You are to be commended,"

"I have maintained my sobriety through my rigorous attendance at AA meetings."

"You are a shining example to those caught in the grip of alcoholism, Father Casey."

"I try my best, Bishop."

The bishop picked up his telephone and contacted his secretary to organise for some tea to be brought in.

While waiting for tea to be delivered, the bishop reassured Frank he would deal with the situation swiftly.

When the tea came, the bishop resumed his conversation regarding the upcoming summer's cricket. In among his discussion, he promised Frank a ticket to the Members Stand at the Sydney Cricket Ground for a day's play at the Sydney test in early January 1976. Nothing more was mentioned of the Father Venables issue and Frank departed after spending another 30 minutes with the bishop.

Frank drove back to his presbytery, frustrated at the lack of interest shown by the bishop. He knew the whole case would be swept under the carpet and Father Venables would most probably be transferred to another parish. He had seen his alcoholism treated in exactly the same way when he had been sent to Wee Waa. He shook his head in dismay at the lack of action taken in such cases by the powers that be, but did not know any course of action he could have taken.

Frank carried on with his parish duties, and it was two weeks after meeting the bishop the Sydney archdiocese informed him he was to receive a new curate at St. Patricks.

Father Terry Lennon was 26 and fresh out of the seminary

and Frank liked him from the start. His enthusiastic approach to his pastoral duties and fund-raising efforts to build the new church endeared him to Frank.

Just before Christmas 1975, Frank received a phone call from Father Tony Casaceli just after dinner one Monday night. He had rung Frank to inform him Father Venables had been transferred out of Sydney to the parish of Gerringong on the south coast in the Illawarra region of New South Wales.

Just as Frank had expected, the whole incident had been swept under the carpet. Frank expressed his displeasure to Tony about how the issue had been handled. He was annoyed that a paedophile priest had been let loose in another parish. It was still years before the scope of sexual abuse within the Catholic Church would come to the public's attention. The issue with Father Venables was over, but it would never leave Frank.

After the Father Venables affair, Frank reflected on what had been a tumultuous time in Australian political history. The dismissal of the Whitlam Government left a divided Australia, and for those who lived through that period, emotions still ran high surrounding the events that took place. As a result of the Whitlam years, Australia was a very different place. There had been reform in areas such as health care, education, indigenous Australia and multiculturalism. It was a more ostentatious and flamboyant Australia, and many of the more conservative elements had been left behind.

Frank could barely recognise Australia from the one he had been brought up in. In the years that followed the dismissal, his political loyalty was divided as he grappled with a post - Whitlam Labor party he could hardly recognise. He swayed back and forth between the Labor party and the coalition, supporting Malcolm Fraser but swinging back towards both Hawke and

Keating. He despised communism and the radical left, and in later years when the Greens started to take a foothold in Australian politics was heard to say openly, "that those mob of greenie radicals should all be potted."

Frank played golf regularly and off a single figure. When his good mate Stan Hitchcock was home in the Sutherland Shire from his oyster lease on the Hawkesbury River, they would have a hit of golf. Though from very different backgrounds, Frank and Stan's friendship had remained rock solid from when they had first met in Amaroo House. Like Frank, Stan had remained sober and helped many who were having a battle with the bottle.

At the dawn of the 1980s, the project Frank had worked so hard to achieve was in sight. The building of the new church was ready to commence.

Chapter 38

Monday, February 11th 1980. St Patricks Catholic Church Sutherland, Sydney

ON MONDAY, 11TH February, 1980, with a shovel in his hand, Frank symbolically turned the first sod of soil on the new church. In charge of the project was his builder, Pim Janssen. Pim had employed a local earthmoving contractor named Bob Rowe, or Rowy as everyone called him, to look after all the civil works on the project. Rowy, a Vietnam veteran, was originally off a big property at Coolabah in western New South Wales. After arriving home from Vietnam, he had started his civil contracting business with a single backhoe in the early 1970s while based in the Sutherland Shire.

Frank was lucky he had such a good man on the job as Pim, as it took a lot of the pressure off him with his responsibilities of running the parish. Frank was never far from the project. Along with many of his parishioners, he regularly rolled up his sleeves and helped with the building of the church.

The building was only in its infancy when Frank's passion for his new project was tempered somewhat. On 3rd March

1980, he received news that his mother Margaret had passed away, aged 90. Although Margaret's life had been a good one dedicated to her Catholic faith and family, Frank was deeply saddened at the death of the lady who had been his rock, supporting him through all the fluctuating fortunes of his own life.

Frank celebrated the requiem mass for his mother at the Catholic Church in Bingara, which was attended by a large congregation. Margaret Casey had been a prominent citizen of the district and had lived all her married life on the family farm at Banyula. In the weeks following Margaret's funeral, Frank reflected on his mother's life and drew great strength from the wise counsel she had imparted to him throughout his life.

With the building of the new church in full swing and Frank mourning his mother's death, he received a letter from Otto Kestelman in early May 1980. Frank was still writing to Kestelman every month, and they had developed a strong friendship by this stage. Otto had come to value Frank's wise counsel and wit. In Otto's corresponding letters with Frank, he would discuss topics such as literature, music, sport and religion to which Frank would respond with his thoughts.

In this particular letter, Otto asked Frank to hear his confession if he visited Landsberg Prison in the future. He wanted Frank to listen to it, as he owed the greatest act of contrition and debt for all the priest had done for him. Frank wrote to Otto immediately and told him he had planned a trip to Europe in July 1980 and would gladly hear his confession. With his airfare booked, Frank wrote several letters to Otto in the months leading up to his meeting and prepared him for his confession.

It had been nine years since Frank had last seen Otto and, although he had aged, what struck Frank was that Kestelman had a look of serenity about him. Kestelman's peace of mind resulted from finally acknowledging the great deceit of the Nazi ideology he had embraced. Now he was to sit before the man he had hated so much and confess to him the evil acts he had perpetrated as a result of living that lie. It was the ultimate act of humility.

After Frank entered Kestelman's cell, he asked the prison officer to shut the door, and the two men sat opposite each other. Frank greeted Kestelman with warmth and humour and commented to his former adversary on their mutual love of both Beethoven and Mozart. In his correspondence, Frank had instructed Otto on how to make a good confession, as it had been many years since he had made his last one. Just as Frank was preparing to hear Kestelman's confession, the prison officer looked through the bullet proof glass slit in the door to make sure everything was okay between the priest and the former Nazi. He saw Otto Kestelman fall to his knees in front of Frank Casey in an act of contrition. Frank had not instructed him to do this. Instead, it was Kestelman's compulsion to do so as a sign of revulsion for the evil acts he had performed. Only Father Frank Casey would know what Otto Kestelman confessed to him that day, as he was bound by the seal of confession. One can only guess what Otto Kestelman revealed through his labyrinth of filth and deceit and all he had done in the name of The Third Reich. As the prison officer spied through the glass slit, he could not hear anything the priest and Kestelman were saying, but what he witnessed was Otto Kestelman howl tears of bitterness. When it was over, Frank absolved Otto from his sins and, placing his hand on the German's shoulder, asked him to rise and take a seat.

When Otto resumed his seat, Frank smiled at him. "I bet you feel better for getting that off your chest."

"I do, *Farzer* Casey. It certainly is a load off my mind," responded Otto, wiping his eyes and blowing his nose with his handkerchief.

They spent the next hour talking about a range of subjects, and there was much laughter between them when the prison officer indicated that Frank's time was up. Otto shook Frank's hand, and just as he was leaving, he said to him. "I might be incarcerated here for *zer* rest of my life, but it is only through you, *Farzer* Casey, that I have been truly liberated."

"It was through your confession today, Otto, that you have been released from your past," Frank said.

"I will be forever in your debt."

With that, Frank smiled and walked out of his cell. It was the last time he would ever see Otto Kestelman.

After leaving Landsberg Prison, Frank contacted Hans Kestelman and organised to meet him at his home in Munich. Hans lived at the same address since Frank's last visit in 1971.

Gone was the hippy attire from his first visit in 1971. Hans' clothes were more conservative, although the walls of his loungeroom were still adorned with remnants from his more liberal lifestyle, including a number of his Andy Warhol paintings.

Frank was also pleasantly surprised to find Hans had married. His wife Claudia was a striking looking German, slim and blonde and of medium height. At thirty years of age, she was seven years younger than Hans. She worked as a fashion designer and had recently gone out on her own designing women's clothing. Hans was now working in his law firm, specialising in criminal law. They had two children, a boy and a girl aged six and three respectively, who were with Claudia's parents that day.

Frank could not help but notice Hans seemed calmer than the first time they had met. He said his marriage had given him much happiness.

After they adjourned to the loungeroom and Claudia served coffee and cake, Frank explained to them how he had heard Otto's confession. Although Hans appreciated Frank for hearing his father's confession, he expressed no interest in seeing Otto.

"I think you will find he is a changed man, and after confessing to the evil acts of his past and asking forgiveness, a lot of weight came off his shoulders," said Frank.

"That sounds very nice, *Farzer* Casey, but I have doubts about whether my *farzer* has really changed," Hans said.

"I can understand your scepticism, but I believe your father has finally owned up to his horrendous past."

They continued to talk about Otto, and Frank sensed it was dredging up many unpleasant memories for Hans, and the atmosphere had become heavy. Claudia could see this and decided to break the ice.

"Perhaps you would like another slice of my homemade German Marble cake, *Farzer?*" she said before bounding to her feet.

"That would be very nice. Thank you, Claudia," Frank said.

After more coffee and cake, they talked about everything from Claudia's fashion business, the children's interests and the incredible sights of Germany.

On leaving, Hans again thanked Frank for helping his father, but reiterated he did not want to visit him. Turning to both Hans and Claudia, Frank said, "Time is a great healer. Perhaps in time, you will see fit to forgive your father for his past transgressions." With that, Frank bade farewell to them both.

On leaving Germany, Frank flew to London, where he caught up with several friends from his squadron including Max Clayton before flying to Paris and visiting Marguerite and Raphael.

They wondered why Frank had spent so much time with a person they believed was the epitome of everything they despised in the Nazi regime.

After arriving in France and making his way to Montbeliard where they still lived, Frank was greeted with the customary tears and hugs from the entire family. They sat there in amazement while Frank told them of Otto Kestelman's conversion and subsequent confession. They were astounded by Frank's persistence and the fact a man of Kestelman's evil past could own up to the crimes he had perpetrated.

Frank spent four days with the family before flying back to Australia, where he was eager to see the progress of the new church.

From 1980, Stan had been frequenting the AA meetings held at Long Bay Gaol in Malabar, Sydney every Sunday at 8.00 pm. It was early February 1981 when Stan asked Frank if he would like to come to the AA meeting at Long Bay Jail with him and speak. He agreed, and on Sunday 22nd February 1981, Frank attended his first AA meeting in Long Bay Gaol with Stan.

After going through all the necessary security checks to get access into the gaol, Stan, Frank and an old Aboriginal man named Jack entered the meeting room. Gathered inside the room were twelve inmates of various ages and nationalities. They were a rough-looking lot, and before the meeting began, they were milling around, smoking and drinking cups of tea as they spoke in low tones. Jack was the chairperson and called Stan as the first speaker. Stan recalled how a week after the D -Day landings in Normandy on 6th June 1944, he got his hands on a bottle of Cabernet Sauvignon and got well and truly pissed.

Next cab off the rank was a wiry bloke in his mid-twenties, named Skinny Lambert, who was doing a stretch for armed robbery. Skinny was a dour, humourless type of individual who wasn't the sharpest tool in the shed. He spoke in a depressive monotone, and his spiel got the ire of a thick - set inmate nicknamed Dingbat, seated at the back of the room. He told Skinny, in no uncertain terms, what he thought about his story.

"Ya talking shit as per usual, Skinny, so why don't ya sit down and shut the fuck up?"

The inmates laughed. When Skinny was finished Jack turned to Frank.

"Can we hear from you, please, Father Frank?"

Frank was dressed in black trousers and a white shirt with two gold crosses on the collar. There was murmuring from some of the inmates concerning the presence of a priest in their midst. They were worried Frank had come to convert them. Little did they know he was there for the same reason they were. Frank approached the front of the meeting and was preparing to introduce himself when an inmate named Billy said from the front row.

"Get a load of this bloke. He looks like a bloody ring in?"

Quick as a flash, Frank looked at Billy and addressed his opening comments to him.

"My name's Frank and I am an alcoholic, and you're absolutely right. I was brought into AA so full of booze they had to ring it out of me."

There were howls of laughter from the audience and Dingbat had some choice words he directed at Billy.

"Cop that, Billy, ya fucking dopey bastard."

"Who are you calling a dopey fucking bastard Dingbat?" Billy said.

"You ya dick brain," Dingbat said.

This brought more laughter.

Once the hilarity had died down, Frank continued.

"Looks like Billy is a bit of a joker, but let's face it, there is one in every pack."

"On ya, padre, don't listen to a word the dopey bastard says. He's full of shit," Dingbat said.

Frank told them how his drinking started when he was in the airforce and that he had been shot down over France. He said he could identify with them being locked up as he had been taken to Buchenwald concentration camp. There were murmurings and rumblings as Frank continued his story. He told them about his numerous car accidents and how he ended up with the DTs before being taken to a hospital in a little country town strapped to a stretcher. He said that by the time he was admitted to Amaroo House, he had lost his faith and was a disgrace to the priesthood. When he finished his share, he went to sit down, and as he passed Billy, he tapped Frank on the arm.

"Nice one, padre. Why don't you pull the other leg?"

The meeting finished and Frank was talking to Jack when a thick set Maori aged in his earlier thirties and weighing 16 stone (101kg) approached them. He was a mean - looking character whose body was adorned with numerous tattoos.

"Hello, Father, my name is Rangi," he said to Frank quietly.

"G'day, Rangi. I'm Frank," he said, shaking his hand.

"Don't worry about what these clowns are saying, Father. Some of them are only here for some free smokes and a cup of tea."

"Thanks for that, Rangi, and you can call me Frank."

Rangi nodded his head in agreement before continuing.

"I really enjoyed what you had to say. I related to it a lot."

"Thank you very much. I appreciate that."

"My father was in Bomber Command during WWII, and like you, he was a rear gunner in a Lancaster."

"Is that so?"

"I know from the little he told us as kids that it was pretty tough on those raids over Germany."

"I was scared out of my wits on many occasions," Frank said.

"That was interesting what you were saying about being taken to Buchenwald concentration camp. I've never heard about that before."

Frank spent the next fifteen minutes explaining to Rangi what happened after being shot down over France. While Frank shared his experiences, Rangi listened intently to what he had to say, nodding his head in agreement until he had finished.

"That's an amazing story. You certainly leave a lot of our stories for dead!" Rangi said.

"You keep coming to these meetings, and your life will get better," Frank said.

"I can't see it getting better. I'm serving a life sentence after I murdered a bloke in a blackout. There isn't much chance of me leaving this place anytime soon," Rangi said, casting his eyes around the room.

"Regardless of how bad your situation is, life can get better if you get honest with yourself."

Frank proceeded to tell Rangi about Otto Kestelman. He said the Nazi was the worst of the worst, and he had murdered many innocent people.

"Compared to this lot," Frank said, glancing over his shoulder, "Kestelman's actions would make some of these blokes look like saints."

Rangi nodded his head in agreement.

"Eventually, Kestelman got honest with himself, saw the evil of his ways and repented for what he had done. So Rangi, no matter how far you have gone down, there is always hope," Frank said.

Rangi shook Frank's hand and once again thanked him for his share.

"I hope you return, Frank, if not for them but for me," Rangi said, glancing over his shoulder.

"I will indeed," said Frank.

It started Frank's long association with the AA meeting at Long Bay Gaol. A few of the men present that first night who initially viewed Frank with scepticism, in time, changed their attitude towards him. Most of them realised he had a powerful message and it was the first bit of hope they had received in a long time. They could see there was a way out of their dire predicament. Frank left an indelible mark on many he met within the walls of that gaol, and regardless of him being a priest, they realised that, like them, he too was an alcoholic.

The early 1980s were a busy time for Frank. Foremost was the opening of the new church, which had been a long time coming. Its inception had been not long after Frank had become parish priest in 1970. It had not been without its challenges and it had been built by teams of volunteer parishioners, with both Pim and Frank at the helm. It had been an - all - hands - on - deck approach with even Frank rolling up his sleeves and getting dirty.

In November 1982, the church was complete and Frank was pleased with the result. The underground church blended into the surrounding country and gave it a feeling of being far away from the surrounding suburbia. In December 1982, the church was opened by the archbishop of Sydney.

With the completion of the new church, Frank took a well - deserved rest. It had been a big project to which he had devoted much of his time and energy. Although he had a full-time maintenance man to look after the grounds, it was nothing for him to put on an old set of work clothes and prune some bushes or water the gardens. Being off the land, Frank had always been a practical man, and he felt comfortable in pottering around the grounds doing some gardening. It was one of the ways he used to find solace and reflect. Many a stranger did not realise who he was when first meeting him. Frank never gave any ostentatious display and would often have them on by telling them he was the gardener, before letting on he was the parish priest.

It was dusk one Monday afternoon in March 1983, when Frank was doing some gardening, when a chance meeting took place that was to change his life.

It had been a busy day, and Frank was a bit irritable. He decided to don his work clothes and do some gardening to relieve some of his stress. He was pruning some large bushes at the back of the church when something caught his eye. Inside the dense thicket of bushes up against the church wall, he noticed an object. He parted the branches and walked in a little further to get a better look. What he saw was an old foam mattress and a blanket. While crawling on his hands and knees, Frank made his way up to the mattress.

"Someone sleeping rough in here," he said.

Suddenly, he heard a rustle in the bushes about five metres to his left. Upon further inspection, he could see a man crawling on his hands and knees at breakneck speed away from him.

"Hey, what are you doing?" Frank yelled out.

There was no response as he made a mad scramble for the edge of the bushes and to safety.

"Hey, what do you think you're up to?" Frank yelled out.

There was still no response, so Frank turned on his hands and knees and made a mad dash to the garden's edge. Although aged in his early sixties, Frank was still fit, and he covered the ground in quick time. Once out of the garden, he chased after the man, who was now making a beeline for the street.

"Hey, you stop where you are!" Frank shouted.

Frank continued to chase the man while he had his secateurs gripped in his right hand. Frank eventually caught up with him down the road on President Avenue, where he grabbed hold of his arm. Frank could see the man was aged in his mid - twenties with long brown hair and a slim build. He had a dishevelled look; his long - sleeve flannelette shirt and jeans were old and tattered and he wore no shoes.

"What are you up to?" Frank demanded, while panting heavily.

"Don't call the cops, will ya?" the man pleaded.

"I won't call the cops if you tell me what you're up to," Frank said, agitated.

"I've got nowhere to live and the garden at the back of the church was the best place I could find without being detected."

Frank looked him up and down long and hard, and he cooled down.

"Why are you out on the street?"

"I haven't got a job, and I can't afford anywhere to live," he said despondently.

Frank could see the dire predicament the man was in and,

despite the man's unkempt appearance, Frank noticed he was well - spoken.

"I am sorry if I was a bit heavy - handed, but the church has only been recently completed, and I don't want anybody breaking in," said Frank.

"I wasn't going to break into it. I just wanted somewhere to sleep."

Frank looked at the young man and could not help seeing himself all those years ago when lonely and desperate he found himself in the care of Father Jean Baptist Fournier.

"Are you hungry?" Frank said.

"I am," the man said, nodding his head.

"You better come over to the presbytery, and I'll fix you something to eat. Do you like lamb chops and vegies?"

The man nodded his head.

"Are you the gardener at this church?" he asked Frank.

"No, I am the parish priest," Frank said with a whimsical look.

"Oh, I am so sorry, Father, I didn't realise."

"That's okay. You weren't to know, especially the way I am dressed," Frank said, pointing to his attire. "Come on over to the presbytery. I am about to cook dinner."

"Thank you, Father. I really appreciate that."

"My name is Father Frank Casey," he said, putting out his hand.

"How do you do? My name is Wayne Vella," he said, shaking Frank's hand.

They made their way to the presbytery, where Frank showed Wayne to the bathroom.

"Take a shower and clean up, and in the meantime, I have some old clothes in here that will fit you."

Frank went into the kitchen and prepared dinner. When Wayne came out of the bathroom, cleaned up and shaven, he looked like a new man. Frank made him a cup of tea and asked Wayne about himself. He proceeded to tell his tale of misfortune. He had been brought up around Campbelltown in southwest Sydney, left school at the end of fourth form and had mainly worked in the building industry as a labourer.

He said that a set of circumstances happened quickly that saw his life spiral out of control. First his father, with whom he was very close, died. Then he lost his job as a builder's labourer when the company he worked for went into liquidation. Then the straw that broke the camel's back happened when he parted with his long - term girlfriend. All this had occurred within six months. As a result, he went into a deep depression and suffered a mental breakdown. Frank could see he was a good man. He realised these three calamities in his life had seen him fall through the cracks. Wayne ended up living on the streets, along with a stint in the Mathew Talbot Hostel for homeless men in Woolloomooloo in the inner city. Frank asked him if he had a problem with drink and drugs. He said he didn't take drugs and drank occasionally. He told Frank he was of Maltese background and had been brought up and educated at Catholic schools around Campbelltown.

They sat down at the dining table and Frank could tell by the way Wayne devoured his meal he hadn't eaten well for some time. Frank prepared him some dessert, and when he was fin-ished, he made another pot of tea, and they sat down in the loungeroom and watched an episode of *Porridge* on the ABC.

"Tomorrow, I will take you to our St Vincent de Paul branch here at Sutherland and get you some clothes to wear."

Wayne nodded in a show of appreciation.

"In the meantime, you better bunk up here for the night. It looks like it's going to rain tonight and we can't have you sleeping in the garden."

The next day, Frank organised some clothes for Wayne through the local branch of the St. Vincent de Paul Society. After they arrived home, Frank told Wayne he could stay at the presbytery until he was on his feet again.

Wayne stayed in the presbytery for the next three weeks. With a combination of decent food, a good bed and plenty of conversation with both Frank and Father Lennon, he was able to get himself out of the dark hole he was in.

Around this time, Frank was thinking long and hard about Wayne's predicament and how he could best help him. He contemplated the many people doing it tough and what more he could do to alleviate their problems. Suddenly, the thought of Bob Rowe popped into his head. Rowy had done all the earthmoving on the new church and Frank had struck up a good rapport with him. Rowy liked Frank, and they often discussed, among other things, rugby league, boxing and rural issues. Frank wondered if Rowy would give Wayne a start in his business. After all, Wayne had worked in the building industry as a labourer. Perhaps Rowy could show Wayne the ropes as he earned an income while adding stability to his life.

The next morning Frank celebrated mass, and when he arrived back at the presbytery, Wayne was having breakfast with Father Lennon. Frank asked Wayne if he would be interested in working in the earthmoving industry. He indicated he would.

That night, Frank contacted Rowy on the telephone and explained the situation concerning Wayne. Rowy agreed to give him a start. The next day, Frank drove Wayne to Bando Road,

Cronulla, where Rowy was doing a bulk excavation on a block of home units. After introducing Wayne to Rowy, he briefly explained the nature of the work and that he could start the next day as a labourer. The next morning, Wayne caught the train from Sutherland to Cronulla, where Rowy was waiting at the railway station in his work ute at 6.45 am.

Rowy was a straight shooter who called a spade a spade and made it clear to Wayne from the start his conditions.

"I realise you have been doing it tough and I am prepared to give you a start, but any fuck arsen around and I'll give you the punt. Is that clear?"Rowy said.

"I appreciate you giving me a start and I'll make sure I do the right thing by you Rowy," said Wayne.

"Good now jump in the ute and I'll give you the run down on what we do.

From the outset, Wayne proved to be a good worker and keen to learn, and he was always on site at 6.45 am. Slowly, his life started to take shape. He stayed at the presbytery for another two weeks until Frank helped him find a one - bedroom unit in Clyde Avenue, South Cronulla.

Rowy's company Rowe Civil Contracting employed seven people. Wayne worked as a labourer for Rowy on various projects for the next six months until he taught him how to operate a backhoe, excavator and in time other equipment. He proved to be one of Rowy's most valuable employees eventually gaining the position as a foreman for him.

Frank never intended to start Break through the Barriers, but as fate should have it, meeting Wayne Vella was the catalyst that started the ball rolling. It just so happened shortly after Frank helped Wayne, he met another man in his early twenties named Bart in the rooms of AA whose life had spiralled out of control. Once again, Frank helped him get back on his feet before helping him to secure a job as a storeman/forklift driver in a major pharmaceutical company in Caringbah.

In those early days, there was no formal structure as Frank tried to find work for those who had fallen on hard times. Instead, he saw it as just part of his duties as a priest. It was in May 1983 that Frank formally started Break through the Barriers after a conversation he had with a young Indigenous man he was helping.

Dave Hudson was in his early twenties and was from La Perouse. He was coming to the end of a two - year stretch inside Long Bay for stealing several cars around the Eastern Suburbs. Dave had been a troublemaker during his time inside Long Bay. He had earnt the ire of a number of the *screws* with his bad attitude. With only a couple of months left on his sentence, Dave had been drinking *boob booze* when he was involved in an altercation with another prisoner, which saw him badly beaten up. Boob booze was a filthy concoction of fermenting vegetable and fruit scraps mixed with yeast and hops. It tasted awful but was guaranteed to knock your head off. After that incident, Mal, an Aboriginal elder inside Long Bay, pulled Dave aside. He told him a few home truths about what was coming his way if he continued on his path. Mal was doing a life sentence for murder, and he suggested to Dave he should get himself along to the AA meeting inside the gaol on a Sunday night, as it might just turn his life around.

"A Catholic priest named Father Frank goes to the meeting. You would be well advised to listen to him, as he has a good story and a lot of wisdom," said Mal.

"What's a priest doing at an AA meeting?" Dave said.

"He's an *Alkie,* and believe me, he's been around the traps!"

After the meeting, Mal introduced Dave to Frank. From

the start, Frank liked the plucky young man he could see had a lot of spirit.

"I want to '*elp* my indigenous brothers," Dave kept saying to Frank.

"You're not much help to your people if you're still drinking grog and smoking dope!" Frank said in response.

"But I want to '*elp* my people desperately. They need my '*elp,* and I want to '*elp* them to see the error of their ways on the drink," he kept repeating to Frank.

"You concentrate on helping your bloody well self before you try to help anybody else!" Frank said.

Dave looked at Frank with narrowed eyes, obviously taken aback by Frank's rebuke.

"First thing you have to do when you get out of *The Nick* is to stay off the drink and drugs and find a job," Frank said.

Dave nodded his head in agreement and contemplated what Frank had said.

"It sure is tough turning my life around, but if I put my mind to it, I reckon I can break through the barriers," Dave said, punching the air with his fist.

A smile came over Frank's face. "That's the spirit, Dave. If you break through the barriers, you can accomplish anything."

Dave gave Frank a toothy grin before talking incessantly for the next fifteen minutes about how he wanted to turn his life around once he had finished his sentence.

"You don't need to finish your sentence before you turn your life around, Dave. You can start right now. It's a matter of changing your attitudes of mind," Frank said.

Dave nodded his head in agreement.

"Remember the attitude is the father to the action. How we think is how we act," Frank said.

"Mmm that certainly is some food for thought Frank."

When Frank was driving back home from Long Bay Gaol that night, he contemplated Dave's words and how he wanted to turn his life around. The more he thought about it, the more he warmed to the idea. By the time he arrived back at the presbytery, a seed had been sown in his mind of how he could further his ability to help the disadvantaged get back on their feet and get a job. Frank was a great advocate for work and believed a job was a positive way to put stability and discipline into a life.

In early June 1983, Dave was released from Long Bay Gaol and Frank helped him to get a position on Randwick Council as a labourer. Dave was lucky because it was there he met an indigenous man named Tommy Atkinson. Tommy had played 1st grade for the South Sydney Rabbitohs rugby league side in the mid - 1970s. As a kid growing up in La Perouse, Dave remembered Tommy from his playing days and considered him a hero. Dave, like a lot of indigenous people, was an ardent Rabbitohs supporter and was chuffed to not only meet Tommy, but work with him. Tommy was a very stable influence on Dave and became a father figure to him and would set him straight if his young charge looked like playing up at all.

After Dave's release from Long Bay Gaol, Frank set up Break through the Barriers with the valuable assistance of Father Lennon and Father Tony Casaceli who was still the Parish Priest of Panania. Frank believed in men helping men and women helping women. When he saw women doing it tough, he would pass them onto a nun he knew named Sister Carmel Evans who was already helping disadvantaged women.

It was from these humble beginnings Frank continued his work by quietly helping those who were disadvantaged, to get their lives back in order.

Chapter 39

Friday, July 8th 1983. Landsberg Prison Bavaria Germany

OTTO KESTELMAN HAD never fully recovered from the thrashing Max Swart administered to him in 1972. The German felt the effects of migraine headaches and the sight in his right eye had been reduced. As a result of his migraines, Otto stopped smoking cigarettes in 1977.

In early July 1983, Otto slipped while taking a shower and split his forehead. As a result of his slip, his migraines increased and he felt nausea regularly. Shortly after, he was diagnosed with a secondary tumour in his brain. A neurosurgeon operated on him in Munich soon after his diagnosis. It was the first time he had been out of Landsberg Prison since he had been incarcerated there in June 1948.

The operation had been a difficult one, but the team of surgeons had successfully removed the entire brain tumour. The problem for the head surgeon treating him was that he knew there was a primary tumour, but was unsure where it was.

Otto wrote to Frank shortly after his operation and expressed his concerns for his well - being. In the letter, he stated he was unsure about his future, as the surgeon was perplexed about the source of his primary tumour. He continued by saying he had become more philosophical about his life. Regardless of his conversion, Otto expressed his fear about his past. He was worried about how his maker would deal with him when his time came to leave this earth. Frank reassured him that because he had come to terms with the crimes of his past, he would be able to meet his maker fair and square with a clean conscience. Frank's words put Otto's mind at rest and he was able to find peace within himself.

Otto continued to write to his son, but Hans never replied. Shortly after his operation, he wrote to Hans again and told him about his tumour. He expressed his concerns about the future and that he did not expect to survive. Once again, Otto asked his son to forgive him for his past crimes, and if he could find it in his heart, he would appreciate it if he would visit him. Again, Hans never replied.

After Otto had been diagnosed with a secondary tumour to the brain, he received both chemotherapy and radiotherapy. In early October 1984, Otto was diagnosed with a primary tumour in his lungs. Although it had been seven years since his last cigarette, the damage had been done. The fall in the shower had been the catalyst for the brain tumour, but fifteen months later, the primary tumour had revealed itself.

At 8.00 pm on Sunday, October 14th 1984, Otto Kestelman died in a hospital in Munich, aged 67. Two days before, Otto had been rushed to hospital after collapsing in his cell, where he never regained consciousness.

Otto had written to Frank a couple of weeks before he had died. In the letter, he thanked Frank for everything he had done for him. He expressed his gratitude for leading him out of the darkness and for helping him find his faith. Otto noted that although he had long reconciled with his past and was ready to meet his maker, he knew the world would remember him as nothing but a Nazi war criminal. Otto further noted that although he did not like this, he accepted that would be how he would be remembered by many.

Three days after his death, Otto received a Catholic burial performed by the prison chaplain at Landsberg, where he was buried in an unknown grave. No one else was in attendance other than the chaplain and a prison official.

In the weeks that followed Otto's death, Frank mourned his old adversary and he reflected on how their lives had been intertwined over the last forty years. Frank was satisfied he had been able to help Otto find his faith, but a great feeling of melancholy still hung over him.

Frank's melancholy might have stayed with him, but for a chance meeting, he had at Long Bay Gaol one Sunday night. It was November 11th 1984, Remembrance Day. Frank travelled to the meeting alone, as Stan was sick in bed. When he got to the meeting, there was the usual assortment of people there, including Jack the old Aboriginal, Skinny Lambert, Dingbat, Billy and Rangi.

Eventually, Frank was called to speak, and he noticed a prisoner sitting at the back of the room, who had not attended before. The man was familiar and over the next week, Frank wracked his brain trying to remember who he was, but still, it wouldn't come to him.

Frank did not always attend the Sunday evening AA meeting, as he often had to say Mass, but it just so happened that he was in attendance the following week. Once again, he was called to share, and when the meeting was finished, he was talking to Skinny Lambert when the prisoner he could not identify approached him.

"How do you do, Father? My name's Ed."

"G'day Ed, you can call me Frank," he said casually.

"I related to what you've said the both times I've heard you, Frank," Ed said to him.

Frank smiled. "Well, thank you. This gift of sobriety is open to anybody who is willing to accept their alcoholism."

Ed said he was in denial of his alcoholism for many years. He had been wary of approaching Frank, as his brother was a Catholic priest, and he did not get on with him. He did not tell Frank that due to his strict Catholic upbringing, he had an aversion to the faith of his childhood, and it had taken a lot of courage to approach him.

"What's your brother's name?" Frank said, narrowing his eyes.

"John Costigan."

Suddenly, the pieces of the jigsaw puzzle came together and he remembered who Ed was.

Frank smiled. "Well, I'll be buggered. You're John's brother. How is he, anyway?" Frank said.

Ed explained he didn't talk to his brother as they did not get along. Frank urged Ed not to be too hard on his brother, for although he could be pedantic at times, he had helped many people.

Then Frank placed his hand on Ed's shoulder. "I know who you are, Ed?"

"You do?"

Frank explained he was there the night Ed beat Vince Cosoleto at the Hordern Pavilion for the Australian middle-weight boxing title in December 1970.

"You were?" Ed said, surprised.

"I certainly was. In fact, I followed your boxing career closely," Frank said.

Ed said his glory days of boxing seemed liked a distant memory, to which Frank replied that it was one of the best fights he had ever seen. Frank continued by saying he knew about his family and that his grandfather, Jack Costigan, had won the VC in World War I.

"You know about my family?" Ed said, surprised.

"Yes, I do. I know what happened for you to end up in here, Ed," said Frank.

"Then you know I killed a young girl in a truck accident when I was drunk," Ed said, closing his hands into fists.

Frank nodded his head. "I know all about it. I read it in the newspaper. It was a great tragedy."

Ed told Frank that he was full of guilt for what had happened. He continued by saying he was a shadow of himself and found it hard to look in the mirror.

Frank reassured him that there was an answer to his problem and Ed found comfort in this. His eyes filled with tears as he related his sad tale of alcohol abuse where he ended up in gaol. Frank placed his hand on Ed's shoulder and told him everybody has a redeeming side, no matter how far they have gone down. Ed wiped the tears from his face. As a Vietnam veteran, truck driver and boxer, Ed felt uncomfortable about breaking down in front of another man. He told Frank that killing a young girl was the unforgivable sin, to which Frank replied no sin was unforgivable. As Frank looked at Ed, he was absorbed in his thoughts, and he could not help but draw a similar parallel between Ed and Otto Kestelman. Both men had come to terms with one of life's paradoxes, that being, you have to give in to win.

Ed took a deep breath and thanked Frank for his kindness and reassuring words. He felt as though a great weight had been lifted from his shoulders.

Frank and Ed continued to speak for another fifteen minutes before the prison officer indicated it was time for Ed to return to his cell.

For Frank Casey, meeting Ed seemed to fill a void after the death of Otto Kestelman had left. From the outside, it appeared both men were polar opposites but little did they know how much they actually had in common. Their first meeting was the start of a lifelong friendship for the two of them.

About a week after Frank had met Ed, he had the plumber around to replace a section of sewer pipe broken in the presbytery yard. The plumber had called in Rowy to dig a trench with his backhoe.

After Rowy had finished, he was having a cup of tea with Frank at the presbytery, where they were engaged in a conversation about Break through the Barriers. Frank mentioned he had been to Long Bay Gaol to help some prisoners get their lives back in order. Rowy casually said he had a good mate who he was with in Vietnam with doing a stretch inside Long Bay. He told Frank he had been involved in a fatality while driving a truck. Frank's ears pricked up at the mention of this, and after he enquired, further realised Rowy was talking about Ed Costigan.

"Ed and I have been best mates since we first met at Kapooka at Wagga while we were doing our basic training," Rowy said.

"I met Ed while visiting the gaol," said Frank.

"You don't say Father? Ed has had a big problem with booze

for some time and has really hit the skids. His life is a far cry from the days he was a champion boxer," Rowy said.

Frank and Rowy's connection was vital to Ed's recovery when he was released from gaol, as the two men worked tirelessly to get him back on his feet.

Chapter 40

**Monday, June 17ᵗʰ 1985. St Patrick's Catholic Church
Sutherland, Sydney.**

IN MID - May 1985, a month before Ed Costigan was due to
be released from Long Bay Gaol, Frank asked him if he would
like to come and live at the presbytery until he got back on his
feet.

Ed had been sentenced in August 1982 after he was involved
in a fatality in Dubbo while drunk behind the wheel of a Ken-
worth truck. After returning from Vietnam in April 1969, he
won the Australian middle-weight boxing title in December
1970. During the bout, he broke his wrist, and his boxing career
came to an abrupt finish. In January 1971, he moved up to
Dunbogan on the mid - north coast, where he drove trucks for
a living. Soon after, he met his first wife, Kim Rooney, and in
June 1973, they had their only child, Michelle.

By this stage, Ed's drinking was causing many problems in
their marriage, so he proposed they move out to Dubbo, where
they could make a fresh start. Kim was reluctant to go out there
as her family was from the mid - north coast. Ed eventually

bought his own rig, and his drinking spiralled out of control as he drove road trains from Dubbo to Darwin and throughout the outback.

After a particular incident in 1982, when Ed went berserk on the drink, Kim had had enough, and she packed Michelle and herself into the car, took off and never returned. Shortly after this, in mid - June of the same year, Ed was involved in the accident that was to change his life.

When Frank first met Ed in Long Bay, he thought he was one of the most shattered human beings he had ever met. Ed felt his life was a waste and he had come to the end of the road. Frank was the catalyst Ed needed to ignite his life and lift him out of the mire.

Frank gave Ed a sense of his own worth and something worth living for. They soon found out that they had much in common. Both men were off the land, with Ed brought up on a farm at Eumungerie in central west New South Wales. They loved sport, including both rugby codes, boxing and cricket. They were knockabout men who had both been to war, and from the outset, Frank could sense Ed would understand what he had been through in his own life. Ed was one of the few people Frank could talk openly about his experiences during the war and particularly, what had happened to him in Buchenwald.

As a mechanic by trade, Ed was a practical person. No sooner had he moved into the presbytery, he took it on himself to become the handyman around the parish. If a tap needed fixing or there was some gardening to be done, Ed was onto it. It started so small, but it became an important part of his recovery.

Rowy took Ed out fishing on the Port Hacking River in his tinnie and simple pleasures like this helped him reconnect with the human race.

One Sunday morning, a month after leaving gaol, Frank took Ed to the AA meeting at the Mathew Talbot hostel. It was a real eye - opener for Ed, as it was a place where skid row alcoholics lived. This meeting was to become an integral part of these men's lives for many years. Frank taught Ed about service and helping others, and slowly, he regained a sense of his own dignity and worth.

Although Ed was making progress, he hit a dark spot in his life when the realisation of his predicament hit him hard. He was 39 years of age. He didn't have a job, a home, or a woman in his life. He fell into such a deep depression he seriously contemplated getting back on the drink. Once again, Frank saved him from his dire predicament.

One Friday night, he stood across the road from a bottle shop in Sutherland, contemplating going in and buying a drink. Fortunately, he was able to drag himself away from the civil war that was raging inside his head and back to the safety of the presbytery.

The next morning, Ed was walking around near the garage at the presbytery, very despondent. He heard Frank whistling, so stuck his head inside the garage to see what he was up to. He noticed. Frank was placing his golf clubs into the boot of the car. In the ensuing conversation, Ed said his ex - wife Kim had been a great golfer. He said they had played regularly when they were first married. Frank told Ed he played with a social group every Saturday morning at Woolooware Golf Course and he was most welcome to join them. Ed was initially hesitant, but after some prodding from Frank and deliberations about his self – worth, he eventually accepted the offer. Soon after, Ed started playing regularly with both the social group and Rowy. As his life took on a whole new meaning, he never thought about drinking again.

Ed stayed at the presbytery for the rest of 1985 and through most of 1986. His life slowly started to take order, so much so that in November 1986, Rowy asked Ed if he would like to live with his family in their home overlooking Yowie Bay. The Rowes lived on a waterfront, and down below from their house on the water's edge was a dilapidated two - bedroom dwelling named Shiloh. Rowy had done a deal with Ed that if he helped the builder refurbish Shiloh, he could live there when completed and pay rent to the Rowes. So ended Ed's time living at the presbytery, and it was just another example of one of the many people whose life Frank touched.

Over the next two years, Frank continued with Break through the Barriers, managing to help many young men get back up on their feet and find work.

Frank had seen several assistant priests come and go, and in August 1988, a Vietnamese priest named Father Thomas Long Van Nguyen came to the parish. Father Tom, as the parishioners called him, was a refugee who had escaped Vietnam in 1975 as an 18 - year - old with his parents and four siblings in a rickety old boat. After spending two years in a refugee camp in Thailand, they were eventually accepted as immigrants to Australia. The family moved to Cabramatta in Sydney's western suburbs, which had a strong Vietnamese community and his father Trung worked as a baker. Before entering the priesthood, Father Tom had been a motor mechanic.

Although from vastly different cultural backgrounds, Frank liked Father Tom. He liked him for both his sincerity and humility as he had come from a war - torn country and seen the worst of human depravity. Father Tom had a great sense of humour and was a hard worker and he soon endeared himself to many of the parishioners.

Not long after Father Tom arrived at St. Patrick's, Frank

received news that Father Gerard Venables had left the priesthood. Frank had followed Father Venable's path since leaving St. Patrick's in 1975. He had been transferred to several parishes, and anecdotal evidence suggested his paedophile activities had been the reason behind all these moves.

During this time, Father Tony Casaceli informed Frank that Venables had taken up residence in Ballina in the Northern Rivers of NSW. It was here Venables continued his grooming of adolescent males, managing to keep under the radar of the authorities.

Venables' paedophile activities while a priest weren't the only ones Frank was aware of. He had received anecdotal stories that other members of the clergy were involved in such actions, but they were all kept hidden and moved on.

He spoke out on several occasions, but was rebuked by the hierarchy. Prudence told him to be quiet and get on with his own work. It was something he would regret for the rest of his life.

Meanwhile, Venables had taken up a position as a salesman with a local real estate agent in Ballina. As a charismatic and quick - talking man, real estate was an ideal place for Venables to both compromise his morals while he went about his paedophile activities. Although he had left the priesthood, Venables was still a practising Catholic and attended mass regularly in Ballina, where he was active in church activities, particularly those involving the younger set.

Meanwhile, Frank followed Ed Costigan's progress over the last couple of years. Not only had he landed on his feet, gaining employment with Rowy as a mechanic, but he had fallen in love with a local girl and they had decided to get married.

Ed Costigan had met Karen Monaghan a year earlier on the October long weekend of 1987. Karen was 31 and a local girl from Caringbah, where she worked as a palliative care nurse at St Vincent's Hospital in Sydney. Ed was smitten with the dark - haired beauty at first sight and a relationship soon formed. Their budding romance did hit an early hiccup when Ed disclosed his past. Karen knew Ed had been a drinker, but had no idea of the destruction it had caused. She was naturally devastated and needed time to process Ed's horrific past before she committed herself to a lasting relationship. In the meantime, Ed sought Frank's counsel. Frank told Ed to live and let live. If was meant to work out between the two of them, then it would. Frank reminded Ed it was his honesty leaving no stone unturned and telling Karen the truth about his past that would ultimately be in his favour.

"It is by being honest with Karen that you hold the trump card in your hand," Frank said to Ed one day.

After Karen had time to process Ed's past, she realised she was on a good thing and had met the right man. Soon after this realisation, she contacted him.

Their relationship was built on mutual trust and respect, one of the major factors that persuaded them to marry. Frank and Ed's older brother John celebrated the nuptial mass of Ed and Karen on what was a very happy occasion. Ed and Karen often sought Frank's counsel as they went through life's highs and lows. As with Ed and Karen, countless others sought Frank's advice and counsel over the years.

One notable person who crossed paths with Frank was Barry Kilgannon. Frank first met Barry in AA in mid - 1989 after his life had spiralled out of control on the booze.

In his early 40s, Barry came to Sydney from Warialda in North West NSW in the early 1970s to play hooker for the Balmain Tigers rugby league side. A tough nuggetty individual, it was through a member of the Balmain club that he found work as a builder's labourer on a high rise development in the inner city. He soon joined the Builders Labourers Federation (BLF), a powerful left - wing union group dedicated to giving basic rights to workers. Barry rose through the ranks of the BLF and eventually gained a position as a union organiser. He was a thug who was also a member of the Communist Party of Australia (CPA).

Barry loved the BLF mantra: 'There are only two things that'll stop a concrete pour on a building site, and they are the rain and the BLF.'

Whenever he said this, Barry would break out into fits of laughter, exposing a mouth minus a lower tooth which had been knocked out in a game against the Parramatta Eels.

The BLF fought hard for the rights and conditions of labourers who were at the bottom of the heap in the construction industry at the time. They were poorly paid, worked under very unsafe conditions and were treated with contempt by many employers. As the BLF directly confronted construction bosses over better conditions, they also demanded they have a say on what was built in the interests of working - class people and the oppressed. This was most famously expressed in the form of the 'Green Bans', which shut down a massive amount of environmentally destructive projects. At its high point in the early 1970s, the NSW BLF was easily the most militant, radical union in Australia. For all the good they did, they were also involved in many corrupt dealings. After a Royal Commission, they were disbanded in 1986.

In late 1987, Barry Kilgannon was asked by a couple of the BLF heavyweights to look after the union's funds until things cooled down. As a result, he found himself in possession of a large amount of cash which he stashed in the ceiling of his home in Balmain. Barry had a twelve - gauge shotgun hidden under his mattress, and the only other person who knew about the stash was his wife, Norma.

Barry had always been a heavy drinker, but the stress of having the BLF disbanded and the chance of being caught with the cash weighed heavily on him, and his drinking increased. By March 1989, the authorities were closing in on him. So he made a midnight dash to Condell Park, to the home of one of the ex - heavyweights of the BLF, where he deposited several suit-cases bulging with $50.00 notes. Barry was relieved to have the funds out of his hands, as the temptation to spend the money on his ever - increasing drinking habit had become overbearing. Soon after, Barry's drinking reached a peak. In June 1989, after a three - day bender, which resulted in him trashing his house and giving Norma a severe bashing, Barry found himself at an AA meeting in Balmain one Thursday night.

Barry was relieved to be finally off the drink but wasn't too pleased about all the God stuff hanging off the banners within the rooms. As a communist, he was an atheist, and no amount of AA meetings was going to sway his attitudes in that department.

Imagine his reaction when, in July 1989, he bumped into Frank at an AA meeting in Sutherland one Saturday night. The hairs bristled on the back of his neck when Ronnie Sander-son told him Frank was a Catholic priest. Ronnie, a Balmain supporter and a former underworld figure in Sydney prior to entering the rooms of AA, was just as incensed about Frank shar-ing his message off the floor. Not that Frank ever spoke about religion at an AA meeting.

"There would have to be one of these fucken sky pilots in here," he muttered under his breath to Ronnie.

"Too bloody right. There's nothing worse than a god both-erer shoving religion down your throat," Ronnie replied.

Over the next seven months, Barry kept running into Frank at meetings all over Sydney, and although no words were spoken between the two men, Barry's resentment towards Frank was palpable. Although Barry had never said a word to Frank, he hated his guts for everything he represented.

Finally, one night in January 1990, Barry's resentment against Frank reached a crescendo. When the meeting was fin-ished, Frank was having a cup of tea with Stan Hitchcock when Barry and Ronnie sidled up beside him. Barry saw this as his opportunity to tell Frank what he really thought of him.

"Hey, Frank!" Barry said, talking through the corner of his mouth.

"Yes, Barry," said Frank.

"When you kick the bucket, you're gonna look like a com-plete idiot when you realise that there is no God!" he said bluntly.

Frank looked at Barry for some time and contemplated what he had said before answering.

"You're absolutely right, Barry!" Frank stared into his eyes. "When I come to the end of my life and realise there is no God, I will look like a complete cretin."

Barry turned to Ronnie and gave him a smug look before Frank continued.

"Whereas when you come to the end of your life and realise that there is a God, then you're going to be left up shit creek in a barbed wire boat," Frank said, still staring intensely into Barry's eyes.

Barry's head jerked backwards and his eyes opened to such an extent that they looked like he'd been sniffing lines of speed for a week.

"Oh and by the way, I hope you've stopped giving Norma a bashing now you're a sober man! Frank said.

"Hmph!"Barry snorted.

"Good evening, gentlemen," Frank said before walking away.

Barry was left speechless at the quick jibe directed towards him by the knockabout padre.

"I think Frank snookered you that time, Barry," Ronnie said before breaking out into laughter.

Barry stood there for some time, his eyeballs twirling around inside his head, contemplating Frank's quick barb before making his way from the room alone and in silence.

In the following weeks, Barry thought long and hard about what Frank had said. His pride wouldn't allow him to admit defeat, but Frank's comments had taken the wind out of his sails and left him with some food for thought. Barry had met his match and was reluctant to have a go at Frank again.

It was a Saturday in late March 1990 when Barry and Ronnie travelled out to Penrith Park to watch Balmain take on Penrith in the first grade rugby league match. They eagerly waited for the 3.00 pm kick off, as this was the first round, and they both had high hopes Balmain would perform well during the season.

They were both despondent when Balmain was defeated by Penrith 24 – 10. They were performing a post mortem on their team's performance as they drove home. Barry was behind the wheel of his Holden HQ sedan for the drive back to Leichhardt to drop Ronnie off when things went wrong. They were on the Great Western Highway at Wentworthville when suddenly a dilapidated Datsun 180B came hurtling over the grass medium strip at high speed towards them and smashed into the right - hand side of Barry's car. The huge impact crushed the driver's side of Barry's car from the bonnet back to the front door. Barry screamed in pain as his right leg had taken the full force of the accident. Besides a sore neck, Ronnie had come out of the accident relatively unscathed. Dazed, he looked across to see Barry bleeding profusely from his forehead. He quickly unbuckled his seat belt and leant across to assist Barry.

Behind the wheel of the Datsun was a twenty - year - old man with shoulder - length blonde hair and sporting numerous tattoos on his arms. He was wearing denim jeans and minus a shirt and shoes. He had unsuccessfully tried to make a run for it, but with blood streaming from a bad gash to his forehead and in a drunken state, he tripped over the kerb before landing face - first on the ground. With skin off his forehead and chin, he was soon accosted by a couple of pedestrians who had stopped to help.

"Let me go, ya pricks," he screamed.

"Hell will freeze over before I let you go ya dickhead!" said one of the pedestrians.

With that he, clocked him with a couple of punches to the side of the head which quietened him down while he lay on his stomach.

Meanwhile, Ronnie tried to free Barry from the wreckage but to no avail as his right leg was trapped. Barry screamed in pain as Ronnie did his best to console him. As many people gathered around both cars, the sound of emergency services vehicles could be heard in the distance. The first on the scene was a Police Rescue truck. After quickly surveying the situation, the two officers put the 'Jaws of Life' into action to free Barry from the wreckage. Soon after, several police, ambulance and fire brigade vehicles arrived. One of the paramedics treated Barry with a sedative, which eased his pain. Within fifteen minutes, they had removed him from the wreckage and placed him into an ambulance, where he was driven to nearby Westmead Hospital while sucking on a 'Green Whistle'. Ronny was stretchered to another waiting ambulance, where he also took a ride to Westmead Hospital for assessment.

As Barry and Ronnie were being carted off to the hospital, a third ambulance arrived on the scene to take the blonde man away. By this stage, he had been handcuffed by two police officers before being given a police escort to the same hospital. After being treated at the hospital, he was interviewed by a couple of detectives. He told the detectives a pack of lies before they came down heavy and informed him he was looking at a lengthy stint in gaol if he didn't come clean and tell them what he had been up to. After some serious probing by the detectives, he eventually confessed and told them he was travelling to Mount Druitt to sell some bags of Buddha (marijuana) before returning to his home in Doonside.

Meanwhile, Barry had been taken to the emergency department of Westmead Hospital, where doctors assessed him. They found he had broken the tibia in his lower leg in two places, fractured his right pelvis, broken his nose and received multiple lacerations to his face. In short, Barry wasn't in real good shape. On the other hand, Ronnie had received some whiplash. After spending the night in hospital for observation, where he chatted up the nurses, he was released the next day.

Barry had been in hospital for two weeks, and although most of his facial lacerations were on the mend, his right leg was still in traction. It was mid - afternoon on a Wednesday and Barry was lying on his back, when who should walk into his room but Frank. Barry looked at him like he had just seen a ghost.

"What do want, Frank?" Barry snorted.

"I've come here to see how you're recovering."

"I hope you haven't come here to pray over me."

"You're always in my prayers, Barry," Frank said with a grin.

"Well, you know where you can shove your candle burning God bothering stuff!" Barry snarled.

"Putting the prayers to the side, I thought you may be interested in this," Frank said before placing a copy of Rugby League Week on his bed.

"What's this?" Barry said, fumbling with his hands. "Rugby League Week?"

He picked up the magazine and examined it. On the cover was a photo of Steve Roach, Tina Turner and Martin Bella with the words *SIMPLY THE BEST* written underneath.

"Mmm crikey that Tina Turner sure is a decent bit of crumpet!" Barry said.

"I know it's not the latest copy but it was lying around the presbytery and I thought you might enjoy it while you're recovering from your injuries," said Frank.

"Hmph! Are you trying to butter me up, Frank?"

"Not really. I just thought you might need a bit of cheering up while you're lying in this hospital bed. Besides I thought you would like the photo of Steve Roach dressed in his Balmain jumper."

Barry stared at Frank for some time.

"Well, that's decent of you," Barry said.

"I had a quick glance through it and there are some interesting articles in there," Frank said.

"Do you follow Rugby League?"

"Yes, I do. I come from a family of staunch South Sydney Rabbitohs die hards, but I've had a soft spot for the Cronulla Sharks since I became parish priest of Sutherland."

"Ha. Waiting for those gummy Sharks to win a premiership is like waiting for the next ice age," Barry said.

"They have been close on two occasions in '73 and '78 but got pipped by Manly both times," Frank said.

"Hmph there's nothing worse than being beaten by those Manly silvertails," said Barry.

"I was at the '73 grand final and it was a very tough game," said Frank.

"It sure was!"Barry said before pausing. "Don't hold your breath Frank because I can't see a title coming their way in the near future."

"They'll win the premiership one day," Frank said.

Barry looked at Frank for some time.

"Did you play footy as a young bloke?" Barry asked.

"I played 1st XV rugby for Joeys when I was at school, and after the war, I played in some dominion representative rugby sides throughout the British Isles."

"So you were a Rah Rah?" Barry said as he looked Frank up and down.

"I certainly was. They even touted me as a future Wallaby, but the war happened, and then my life took on a different direction, as you can see," Frank said, pointing to the cross on the collar of his white shirt.

"I appreciate you bringing me in the magazine Frank, but don't think as a payback I'll be coming down to your church on bended knees and praying in front of the altar," Barry said, talking through the corner of his mouth.

"Barry, I don't give a shit what you believe in. I only came in here today to see that you're okay."

Barry looked at Frank long and hard before saying, "Well, I appreciate that."

They continued to talk about all things rugby league for the next fifteen minutes before Frank shook Barry's hand and bade him farewell.

As Frank was leaving the room Barry said to him, "I haven't laid a finger on Norma since I've been sober."

That's good to hear."Frank said.

Barry lay back in his bed and thought about Frank's visit before exclaiming to himself, "For a priest, Frank's not a bad bloke after all!"

Frank visited Barry every Wednesday afternoon over the next four weeks and would always bring in the latest issue of Rugby League Week. Frank would sit on the chair beside Barry's bed and the two men would engage in a spirited conversation about football. In time, Barry began to warm to Frank. He liked his down -to - earth style and his knowledge of rugby league, and slowly a friendship started to form.

On the fourth week, Frank visited Barry on a Wednesday night, but he brought Ed Costigan with him this time.

"I believe you've met Ed before, Barry?" Frank said.

"Yeah, I know you from the rooms, Ed and I saw you box years ago. How's it going, mate?"

"I am good, mate, but you've obviously been in the wars," Ed said.

"Yeah, mate, I've got a bit of bark off me here and there, but I am on the mend. Besides, I am getting out of traction in the next few days, and then I am out of this place."

Just then, Ronnie Sanderson walked into the room and over the next thirty minutes, the four men engaged themselves in some spirited talk about sport and other subjects. There was plenty of laughter between the group before Barry propped himself up on one elbow and said,

"When I get back on my feet, we should all go and watch Balmain play Cronulla one afternoon."

"I suppose I could stoop down that low as a South Sydney Rabbitohs fan," Ed said.

"Ah, you'll keep ya mad bastard," said Barry with a laugh.

"I am keen on the idea," Frank said.

"So am I," said Ronnie.

"Okay, it's a done deal, then. Let me get mobile on my pins again and I'll get it organised," Barry said.

And so it came to pass that on Sunday, 10th June 1990, four of the most unlikely people you could ever have imagined were seated together to watch Cronulla play Balmain at Endeavour Field on their home ground.

To the uninitiated, not in their wildest dreams could have they imagined who was seated next to them. A Catholic priest, an ex gangster, an ex BLF heavyweight and the former middleweight boxing champion of Australia watched the Cronulla Sharks defeat the Balmain Tigers 18- 10. The four recovering *alkies* enjoyed each other's company while they munched on meat pies, followed by drumstick ice creams and bottles of Coca - Cola.

It was the start of an enduring friendship between the four men that was to last the test of time, despite their vastly different backgrounds. The four men were to watch many rugby league games together over the years and regularly play golf on Saturday morning at Woolooware golf course. In time, Barry, Ronnie and Ed became active in Break through the Barriers, helping young blokes get back up on their feet and find a job. Although Barry changed his views from an atheist to an agnostic, he grew to respect Frank and the two men became very good friends.

Chapter 41

**Friday, January 19ᵗʰ 1996. St. Patricks Catholic Church
Sutherland Sydney**

OVER THE NEXT five years, Frank worked tirelessly in the
parish, at AA and with Break through the Barriers. Even though
he was now in his seventies, he still possessed a lot of energy.
He played golf regularly and visited his family at Upper Bingara
several times a year.

On Friday, 19ᵗʰ January 1996, Frank received a letter from
the Sydney Archdiocese asking him to tender his resignation on
his 75ᵗʰ birthday on the 21st March that year. Frank had always
believed the parish was his until well after his official retirement
age, as long as he was still both physically and mentally able to
do his job, which he was. He was not too keen on the idea of
retirement as he felt he still had much more to give to the parish.
He had many plans for the future he wanted to implement and
was looking forward to doing just that.

His vocal protests of the Catholic hierarchy's inaction in
addressing paedophilia within the Catholic clergy earned him
the ire of the establishment and prompted them to ask for his

resignation. Frank had rocked the boat one too many times and this was their way of bringing his time at St. Patricks to an end.

Frank dug his heels in and refused to go. With the support of the majority of the parish, he defied the Sydney Archdiocese hierarchy. Frank argued his case and told them he had built the parish to what it was today and still had much he wanted to achieve.

The establishment wasn't interested and it appeared Frank's fate was sealed when he unexpectedly received support from a most unlikely source. Richard Knox was Sydney's leading commercial radio 'shock jock'. With his silky smooth voice, he had a vast and loyal following of listeners over a period of thirty years. Knox had no great love for the Catholic Church and held them in contempt often criticising them over paedophilia. In fact it was a thinly disguised veil of good old - fashioned 'Catholic Bashing'. Knox heard about Frank's predicament after a parishioner contacted his radio program and explained his position. Knox took up Frank's case and invited him onto his morning radio program to explain the stance he had taken against the issue of paedophilia within the church.

At first, Frank refused to appear on his program on two accounts. Firstly, he had never had much time for Knox because of his over inflated opinion of himself, and secondly, he felt it may be an ostentatious display on his account. Knox urged him to reconsider, as it may help many who had suffered at the hands of clerical paedophiles. After much consideration, Frank agreed to appear on the program, but what he did not know was Knox had done some research and discovered Frank's incredible exploits during World War Two.

When Frank appeared on Richard Knox's radio program in early March 1996, he put the broadcaster in his place from the outset. In his opening comments, Knox referred to Frank by his first name but the padre reminded him in no uncertain terms that it was Father Casey to him. The broadcaster's ego took a hammering and he bristled at being ticked off, but he knew he had met his match. The conversation returned to a more even keel when Frank explained the situation he found himself in, with regards to his retirement. The audience then heard his unbelievable story of what happened to him after he was shot down over France. Knox listened with intense interest. Frank explained how the French Resistance had rescued him, and then Father Fournier had looked after him before being betrayed and sent to Buchenwald Concentration camp.

Such was the interest shown by Knox's audience that he invited Frank back on his program on two other occasions to talk more about his story after being shot down. After the ice thawed between them, Knox became a vocal supporter of Frank's situation, and through his radio program, he pressured the Catholic establishment to reconsider his retirement.

Eventually, the establishment relented and allowed him to remain at St. Patrick's but stipulated that he must retire when he reached the age of 80. Frank felt vindicated by their decision and felt as a great weight had come off his shoulders. As a result of Knox's intervention Frank was grateful towards the broadcaster and wrote to him thanking him for his help.

Over the next five years, Frank took a number of overseas trips, including his final one to Europe in 1997, where he caught up with Raphael, Marguerite, and their family. It was a timely visit, as Raphael passed away a couple of months later, aged 79. Marguerite was heartbroken, losing her husband of so many years. Frank was able to write to her and provide comfort in her time of loss.

On his 80th birthday on, Wednesday, 21st March 2001, Frank officially retired from St. Patrick's Catholic Church Sutherland.

He was given a stirring send - off by the parish, which included a mass followed by supper. The church was packed to the rafters as people from all walks of life gathered to thank him for his years of service at St. Patrick's. A number of the upper echelon of the Sydney Archdiocese were present for his send - off and openly praised him for his efforts. Some of them were glad to see him go, as he had been a thorn in their sides for too long.

Frank settled into a Catholic retirement home on Ewos Parade, South Cronulla, where he lived in a self - contained unit. Although officially retired, Frank was as active as ever, spending much time helping the underprivileged and tending to his rose garden. In time, he grew to like his retirement, as he wasn't shackled to the parish and he could dedicate more time to his other projects.

Over the years, Frank had become very good friends with Ed and Karen Costigan. He was regularly invited for dinner at their home at Shiloh on Yowie Bay. During the Sydney Olympic Games, Frank accompanied Marguerite and her daughter Sylvia, who were visiting Australia, to the games. Along with Ed and Karen, they all attended a number of the events.

Karen soon struck up a firm friendship with Sylvia. Karen was of Italian ancestry on her mother's side and could speak the language fluently and some French. Sylvia could also speak Italian and the two of them were often engrossed in conversation about a range of mutual interests, particularly on Europe and its history.

When the Olympics were over, Ed and Karen took the two French ladies out to Eumungerie in the central west of NSW and showed them the family farm he grew up on named Coorigil. For Marguerite and Sylvia, it was one of the highlights of the trip to visit an Australian farm before continuing on their travels.

For Ed and Karen, it had been a tremendous year, with the Olympic Games being the highlight. Then, in early December 2000, Karen was diagnosed with Inflammatory Breast Cancer, and they felt as though the bottom had fallen out of their world.

When she first received her diagnosis, Karen was initially devastated and feared for the worst. It was Frank that both Ed and Karen came to for support, and he proved to be a tower of strength, giving them both spiritual and practical guidance through their ordeal. Through his guidance, they were both able to front up to the illness inflicted upon Karen and see it for what it was. Frank prepared them both for the worst if it did happen, and with his advice, Karen was able to accept if she was to die from this illness, she would be prepared.

"The attitude is the father to the action," Frank would often say to them.

Despite her fate, Ed and Karen lived their lives to the fullest and as though every day was their last. They travelled during this period, and their love for each other deepened. They also bought a 200 - acre farm named *Goodgidgee,* 30 kilometres from Mittagong on the Wombeyan Caves Road, which became an excellent retreat for them. Frank was invited down to Goodgidgee on several occasions to share a weekend with them and take in the natural beauty of the surrounding area.

They had their days when the reality of Karen's illness would hit them hard. Frank was always there to give them the necessary guidance to face the situation.

By late 2002, it appeared Karen's extensive chemotherapy

may have beaten the cancer and she had gained a new lease on life.

Then, in early 2003, Karen had a bad turn, which resulted in a mastectomy of her right breast as well as lymph node surgery. This was followed by extensive radiation treatment, which made her extremely tired.

In November 2004, Karen was diagnosed with brain metastasis, and by this stage, she knew what her fate was and prepared herself for the end.

On Monday, February 14th 2005, Frank gave Karen the sacrament for the dying. The previous day, Karen had got Ed to send a birthday present and card to one of her nieces, although she was very ill. That was the type of woman she was, always thinking of others. Karen was at home at Shiloh, surrounded by her immediate family, their dog Foo and Bob and Julie Rowe. Around 11.00 pm that night, Karen passed away in her sleep, with Ed by her side. The first person Ed contacted the following day was Frank, who gave his good friend solace after his loss.

After Karen's death, Ed went into a deep depression, so much so he thought he was never going to come out it. He had lost all his zest for living, and it was after he received a letter from Frank in early July 2005 he was to see life in a new light. In short, Frank had told Ed he was made of the right stuff and that Karen had accepted her fate. He told Ed, Karen would have wanted him to get up and live again. For Ed, it was the catalyst for change and it only deepened his friendship with Frank.

Frank's guidance in Ed and Karen's ordeal was only one of many similar incidents during his years as a priest. Frank's kindness and wise counsel touched countless other people during their time of grief, and it was something they never forgot.

Over his many years in the priesthood, Frank crossed paths with people from all walks of life. There were many that he helped, and others who were beyond help. Not everybody he met agreed with his views, but most people respected him as they realised he was a man of principle.

One of the people he helped was Keith, who was a chronic alcoholic aged in his early thirties. When Frank first met Keith in September 1987, he was living in a one - bedroom granny flat in Bexley in the southern suburbs of Sydney. Keith was a printer by trade, but unemployed at the time. He spent most of his day in bed, chain - smoking White Ox rolling tobacco. White Ox was the preferred tobacco of the homeless and those in prison. Before the prison smoking ban in 2015, it was the standard - issue tobacco in NSW prisons, where it was colloquially referred to as 'Boob Shit'. Keith's transistor radio, which sat on his bed-side table, was tuned to the ABC's Triple J, twenty four - hours a day. Triple J was like a security blanket to Keith. With his bottle of Lindeman's Montillo Dry Sherry, which was never far from his side, he had no urge to leave his bed other than to ring a taxi to deliver another supply of sherry to his premises.

When Frank first met Keith, he thought he was one of the worst alcoholics he had ever seen. Frank's initial reaction on seeing Keith, was that he looked like he had stuck his finger into an electric wall socket and received 240 volts. His hair stood on end, he was pale and he looked he had just seen a ghost. Frank introduced Keith to the philosophy of AA and, after spending half an hour inside his smoke filled den, he thought that there wasn't much hope for him. On leaving his flat, Frank glanced behind and honestly thought Keith would end his days in that hellhole.

To Frank's total surprise, Keith took the bait, dragged himself out of bed the next day and caught a bus to an AA meeting in Bexley, dressed in pyjamas and dressing gown. Keith never touched a drop of alcohol from that day onwards. Within twelve months, he had resumed his trade as a printer, and five years later, married and had two children with his wife. Today, Keith runs his own printing business in Kogarah, which employs seven people.

Then there was Andy, who also had a problem with the booze. Andy was in his mid - twenties and when Frank first met him, he was working as a stripper in a gay nightclub on a backstreet of Kings Cross.

On first meeting Frank at an AA meeting, Andy exclaimed to him, "Father Frank, I realise you're a man of the cloth, and I am sorry for being so risqué, but I just love getting my gear off and performing in front of other men!"

Frank looked at him long and hard and while doing his level best to keep a straight face exclaimed, "That's an area that I haven't had a lot of experience in, Andy. Perhaps another member more attuned to that line of activities would be more suitable to talk to."

In time, Andy left his stripping days behind him, and with Frank's assistance remained sober and started a very success-ful business as a travelling salesman selling his brand of honey throughout NSW. When choosing a business name, Andy was influenced by his former life as a stripper and, in an act of irrev-erence, named it *Bee – Hind Honey*.

Some didn't agree with Frank's views and let it be known. Annie was one such case. Annie was a lesbian, aged in her early forties. She was short, plump, had the number one shears over her head, sported piercings above her eyes and had numerous tattoos on her arms. She had recently arrived in the Sutherland

Shire and decided to attend Mass one Sunday morning. In his sermon, Frank expressed his opinion that marriage should only be between a man and a woman. Annie vehemently disagreed with Frank's view and decided to confront him after mass. Dressed in bib and brace overalls and tan Blundstone boots, she approached Frank after he had been talking to some parishioners.

"Hi there, Father Casey. My name's Annie and I think you're way out of line," was her opening remark.

Frank looked at the strange - looking woman he had never laid eyes on before, confused as to what she was talking about.

"You're totally off the mark, Father Casey."Annie repeated.

Frank looked at her, dumfounded before exclaiming, "Who are you, the local plumber?"

"Plumber, you say? Hmph," Annie said with indignation. "I'll have you know you're right out of line with your views regarding same sex – marriage, Father Casey," she said, snorting with contempt.

"Is that so, Annie?" Frank said, staring at her. "I'll have you know that it happens to be God's view and my view that marriage is between a man and a woman. Always was and always will be!" Frank said, continuing to glare at her.

Annie stood there with her hands on her hips, huffing and puffing.

"You are so typical of the draconian views of an outdated Catholic Church, Father Casey. You are just a dinosaur that is past his use - by date. A man who has spent his entire life hidden inside the walls of the Catholic Church," she said with contempt, "and besides, what earth - shattering experiences have you been through in your life that can add something positive to an ever - changing contemporary world?"

Frank glared at Annie with his piercing green eyes for what

seemed like an eternity before he exclaimed, "Annie, if you would have experienced some of the hell holes that I have, you probably wouldn't have lasted one minute."

"What is that supposed to mean?" She said with withering sarcasm.

"What I mean is that you wouldn't have been able to handle the degradation that I was subjected to during the war," Frank said.

"What type of degradation?" She said with contempt.

Frank leaned forward and looked Annie in the eyes before he said, "I was imprisoned in Buchenwald Concentration camp and experienced the brutality of the SS. Don't you ever talk to me about living a sheltered life! I saw the worst of humanity and was lucky to get out alive. I hope you have a nice day, Annie," Frank said before walking away.

Annie stood there in mute stupefaction.

Annie was only one among some who were opposed to Frank's views. He never backed away from his beliefs and those who sought to degrade the Catholic Church. If you wanted to take him on, you could expect a fight, for he wasn't the type of man who backed down.

Frank was a paradox of a man. On the one hand, he was extremely conservative and radical in other areas. He believed in the Catholic Church's traditional aspects, like the adoration of the Virgin Mary, Stations of the Cross and the seal of the confessional. On the other hand, he saw his life as a priest as being at the coalface and helping the underprivileged. He was critical of the lavish opulence of the Catholic Church, as he believed this had nothing to do with Christ's message. He was critical of the Catholic Church for not dealing with paedophiles within their ranks, and this one point, more than any other, saw him clash with the hierarchy. Frank was to live long enough to see some of these clergy brought to justice. One, in particular, was to be of special significance to him.

By April 2011, Frank had turned 90 and long ago handed over the reins of Break through the Barriers. Although he was an old man, he still helped those he could, despite not being as mobile as he once was. During that month, the process was started to have Gerard Venables brought to justice for child sex offences. The investigation began when police from the Richmond Local Area Command received a complaint from a local man in his early thirties. It concerned an alleged assault by Gerard Venables on him when he was an altar boy in Ballina in 1990.

After Venables had moved to Ballina in 1988, he became active in the parish, including taking a number of the altar boys away on camping trips. As the phrase goes, "a leopard never changes his spots", and just like his days at St. Patrick's, Venables was up to his old tricks of molesting altar boys. Shortly after, another man from Lennox Head aged in his late twenties came forward to police concerning a sexual assault by Venables when he was an altar boy in late 1991. After detectives from Ballina Police Station interviewed the man, they made further inquiries and identified another five boys who had been assaulted by Venables around the Ballina Shire. They soon realised that a pattern of historical sexual abuse had been perpetrated by Venables. As a result they called in State Crime Command specialist detectives from Child Abuse and Sex Crimes from Sydney for investigative support. It was they who uncovered another 20 sexual assaults by Venables when he was a priest in the Sydney Archdiocese. Frank was one among many who gave evidence against Venables for his assaults. The officer heading the investigation in the department was none other than Venables' former altar boy, Detective Jim Whelan. Jim, who now stood 6'4", had followed his father Laurie into the NSW Police Force and was now a senior detective in that division.

In December 2011, after further investigation, detectives lead by Jim Whelan arrested the 66 - year - old Venables in his home in East Ballina. Venables got the shock of his life when he realised the arresting officer was none other than Jim Whelan. Venables subsequently soiled himself at the front door of his home after Jim arrested him. As Jim was leading the handcuffed Venables to the paddy wagon he tuned to him and whispered, "The chickens have certainly come home to roost, hey Gerard."

Venables looked at Jim ashen-faced, his top lip quivering and before Jim locked the door of the paddy wagon behind him, the detective added, "And by the way, Gerard you certainly do smell like a barn yard fowl. Still it's to be expected as you have always been a bit of an animal. Enjoy your time locked away in the fowl house!"

Venables was taken to the Ballina Police Station, where he was charged with multiple counts of sexual assault and multiple counts of indecent assault. A magistrate conducted the preliminary procedure in the Ballina Local Court where Venables was remanded in custody to await sentencing by a judge in the District Court.

In March 2012, Venables was sentenced to an aggregate term of imprisonment of 10 years, with parole possible after five years. He was taken to the Mid North Coast Correctional Centre at West Kempsey to serve his sentence.

Frank's only satisfaction over the case was Venables had been taken off the streets, where he could not harm young boys again. He took no superfluous pleasure from Venables' conviction and incarceration. What appalled Frank was he had once dedicated his life to God but had stooped to such evil and degrading acts.

Frank was unaware that while Venables was incarcerated, he had been beaten up by other inmates on several occasions. Paedophiles or 'rock spiders' as they are known in gaol, are seen as the lowest of the low. Right or wrong, they are dealt with harshly by other prisoners. Even if Frank had known about the beatings, he would have not derived any perverse satisfaction from the treatment Venables received. Frank admonished himself for not pursuing Venables' acts with both the church and the law. After all the good work he had done throughout his life as a priest, Frank felt guilty believing he could have done more.

It was some months after Venables had been sentenced that Ed Costigan said something to him that changed his perspective.

"Perhaps you have been a victim of the system yourself, Frank?"

"What do you mean by that, Ed?"

"What I mean is that you are caught up in a system that is sworn to secrecy from top to bottom?"

Frank stared into Ed's eyes while he continued,

"The Catholic Church is sworn to secrecy from the pope to the lowest of its clergy. You are just a single cog in a big machine."

"But the Catholic Church is my life!" Frank said defiantly.

"I realise that, but you have been blinded by the big mechanism that you are a part of. If any one member of the clergy has been an example of the true meaning of what it is to be a priest, then it is you. You have dedicated your life to the least, the lost and the lowest in society, and if that is not Christ's work in action, then I'd like to know what is?"

Frank smiled at Ed and, with a raised finger, said, "Ed Costigan, you are a man of great wisdom. I always knew I would win a race with a bastard like you."

Frank had always been a man of action and didn't indulge in morbid self – interest, but as he was in his autumn years, he allowed himself to reflect on what had been a remarkable life.

He realised his life had been a difficult one, but he accepted this was the cross he had to bear. During his long life, the anvil of experience had knocked him into shape, and by doing so, had humbled him so he could reach out and help the most vulnerable in society. He felt no self - pity for what he had been through, rather a deep satisfaction that the tough times had taught him to think less of himself and more of other people. Through his life experiences, he had learned that real self - fulfilment and happiness comes from commitment to others.

By 2018, the only other members of his family still alive were his two youngest sisters, Joan and Frances, who were aged 87 and 85, respectively. Stan Hitchcock had passed away, including many with whom he had studied for the priesthood, including Father Tony Casaceli. During these final months, he thought about his great mate, Jimmy Cruikshank, and the life he could have had if he had not been killed. He thought about Geraldine Simpson and the love they had once shared.

In July 2018, he took his final trip to Banyula. His nephew Tony, his brother Kevin's eldest son, now ran the property, and he spent five days on the farm. He knew it would be the last time he would ever be there and he reflected on his life growing up in such a special place. He thought about his father, Hugh, and the harsh treatment he had dished out towards him when he was growing up. He had long forgiven his father, for he realised, like him, he was an alcoholic who had never received treatment for his problem.

The Great War had only compounded an existing condition. Like so many of his generation, he had returned to Australia after the conflict, deeply scarred. He thought about his long - suffering mother Margaret and thought of her as nearer to a saint.

Frank returned to Sydney, satisfied that he had seen Banyula for the last time. He realised the end was near and he felt his life's work was complete and was prepared to meet his maker.

In the final week of his life, Frank was visited by several close friends and relatives at his unit in South Cronulla. Barry Kilgannon and Ronnie Sanderson were still actively involved in Break through the Barriers and visited Frank a number of times in the final week of his life. They laughed and recounted stories about many of the people they had helped through AA and Break through the Barriers.

The day before he died, Ed Costigan visited Frank and they spoke at length till the late afternoon, where Ed thanked him for his great friendship and all he had taught him about life. Before he left, Ed shook Frank's hand and said,

"Thank you, Father Casey. I owe my life to you."

When death came to Frank, it came peacefully. Contrary to the violence he had experienced during his war years, which could have seen him killed numerous times, Frank died in his sleep in the early hours of Friday, September 14th 2018. He was 97 years of age.

Chapter 42

Thursday, September 20th 2018. St Patrick's Catholic Church Sutherland Sydney.

BEFORE BISHOP MULCAHY gave his final blessing, he approached the lectern and spoke to the congregation.

Father Frank Casey was a truly unique man of a type that we will possibly never see again. His early life was difficult and he felt out of sorts and lonely. A naturally gifted sportsman, he found his feet on the rugby paddock, where he excelled, and if it wasn't for the war, he could have scaled the heights in that sport. He experienced the horrors of World War Two, losing his best mate, and when he thought it couldn't get any worse, he was shot down over France. It was here he saw both the best and worst of human nature. First, he was rescued by the French resistance and put into the hands of a brave young priest who gave his life for Father Frank. Then, after being betrayed, he was captured and sent to a concentration camp where he experienced the worst of human depravity. This must have been a shocking experience for such a young man, and left a permanent scar on his life. These experiences he went through while in captivity and, in particular, the bravery of Father Jean Baptist Fournier were to leave a lasting impression on him.

His spiritual awakening was slow, but it ultimately led to his decision to become a priest and to be of service to people. From the outside, he must have seemed like a most unlikely candidate for the seminary. As a World War II veteran, he was much older than many other students and must have seemed like a father figure to them. While in the seminary, he often spoke his mind, and he often clashed with the powers that be.

As a priest, he often aggrieved the church's hierarchy, but his rebellious nature was born out of a sense of justice for those with no voice. Many within the establishment saw him as a radical, but no one was more aligned with Christ's work than Father Frank Casey.

He devoted his years as a priest to the destitute, the lonely and the forgotten. He dared to speak up about paedophiles within the church when many were sweeping their despicable actions under the carpet. For this, he received criticism from many within the church because he had rocked the boat.

He was a knockabout priest with a great sense of humour. He loved both codes of rugby, cricket, golf and boxing. He was most at home with common people and his love of the country, its people and the indigenous were to stay with him for the rest of his life. As a young curate recently arrived in Australia from Ireland and sent to this parish he was to leave a lasting impression on my life as he was on countless people he crossed paths with. The people gathered here today is a testimony to that influence.

When he was finished, Bishop Mulcahy gave his final blessings. He invited the congregation to meet at Woronora

Memorial Park at Sutherland for Frank's burial and afterwoods at the presbytery grounds for refreshments.

There were over a hundred people gathered around Frank's gravesite as Bishop Mulcahy and the seven priests, who had concelebrated the Mass, prepared for his burial. Before his coffin was lowered into the ground, Bishop Mulcahy gave his final blessings. Included were readings from scripture, offering comforting words to the bereaved and committing his body back to earth.

After the burial had concluded, those gathered walked away from the gravesite and broke out into spontaneous conversation. Little groups scattered throughout the area, talked, and reminisced about Frank while the priests intermingled in conversation with those gathered around. At the centre of the gathering stood Bishop Mulcahy, engrossed in conversation while other people eagerly waited for their opportunity to talk to him. The crowd stayed steadfast for the next 40 minutes before little groups dispersed with many making their way back to the presbytery for the wake.

Finally, Bishop Mulcahy made his way slowly towards his car which was parked 100 metres from the gravesite with a small entourage of people following, eager for their opportunity to engage him. Following them from a distance was the grey - haired man who had been seated in the front row of the church. With his Tyrolean hat made of green felt secured on his head, he waited for his opportunity to talk to the bishop. By the time he had reached his car 15 minutes later, all of the people had dispersed. The bishop was about to enter his car, which was being driven by the parish priest of Sutherland, when the man with the hat approached him.

"Excuse me, bishop, but could I have a quick word with you?" he said in a German accent.

"Yes, certainly," the bishop said, turning to greet the stranger.

"I would like to *sank* you for a wonderful service," he said to the bishop.

"Thank you very much," Bishop Mulcahy said with a smile, shaking his hand.

"Your homage to *Farzer* Casey was both accurate and very moving. He was a man of exceptional qualities who touched *zer* lives of so many people he met."

"Thank you very much, and may I enquire of your relationship with Father Casey?" the bishop said with a quizzical look.

The man looked long and hard at the bishop and broke into a smile.

"Let's just say *zat* I admired *Farzer* Casey from a distance!" he said.

"I appreciate that, but what is your name?" the bishop enquired.

Once again, the man looked at the bishop for some time before he answered. "My name is Hans Kestelman."

With that, the bishop's jaw dropped and he stood there motionless, like he had just seen a ghost.

Finally after some time the bishop said, "Well, this is a momentous moment!"

"Why is *zat*?" Hans enquired.

"When I was the curate at St. Patrick's many years ago, Father Casey told me what had happened to him in Buchenwald and how he had tried to help your father, Otto."

Hans stepped forward, so he was only inches from the bishop's face.

"Frank did more *zan* help my *farzer*, bishop. He saved his life. It was because of what Frank said, rather than what he was, that convinced my *farzer zer* philosophy he had followed for so long was pure evil. In the end, the example of Frank's life saved my father's soul."

The bishop stood there motionless, nodding his head in agreement.

"Let it be known that *Farzer* Frank Casey was ordained for my *farzer*," Hans said.

"Indeed he was," said the bishop.

"It was through Frank's example *zat* I rediscovered my Catholic faith. I wouldn't say I am a particularly good one, bishop, but if Frank left me with one message, it is this. Christ showed us the way to live our lives, and our Lord forgives all sinners. My father is living proof of that."

The bishop nodded in agreement before taking a deep breath and, after looking at Hans intensely, said,

"Those long trips back from bombing missions in the Ruhr Valley dodging flak and night fighters must have been terrifying for Frank. But those journeys back from enemy territory paled into insignificance compared to the journey he took from his head to his heart. It was that journey that ultimately led him to his life's work. His work here on earth is done. Today, he is with his maker in paradise. Frank Casey's life was indeed a long flight home."

"It has been a pleasure to meet you Vincent," Hans said, shaking his hand.

"As it has been likewise for me, Hans. Now please join me at the presbytery for some refreshments. Frank would have expected nothing less."

About the Author

S.E. Nethery was born in Sydney, the seventh child of a seventh child of a seventh child. He has written numerous newspaper articles on his travel experiences and has a love of war history and rural travel. He's been to many remote destinations including Kokoda, and was in Gallipoli for the 100 year Anzac Day anniversary. His first fiction novel *Heavy Load* was published in 2018 and Long Flight Home is his second work of fiction.

S.E.Nethery lives in the Northern Rivers region of New South Wales, Australia.

Feedback

If you enjoyed Long Flight Home consider leaving a review.

Your support and encouragement is what helps authors to continue creating their art, and gives other readers an idea of what to expect from the story.

Also, feel free to drop me a line or find me on social media.

Facebook: S.E.Nethery – Author
Website: www.senethery.com
Email: stephen.nethery@bigpond.com

Thank you!

Printed in the USA
CPSIA information can be obtained
at www.ICGtesting.com
LVHW051450090324
773913LV00005B/613

9 780648 362630